THE HEALING

THE HEALING

AN AMISH ROMANCE

LINDA BYLER

New York, New York

THE HEALING

All rights reserved. No part of this book may be reproduced in any manner without the express written consent of the publisher, except in the case of brief excerpts in critical reviews or articles. All inquiries should be addressed to Good Books, 307 West 36th Street, 11th Floor, New York, NY 10018.

Good Books books may be purchased in bulk at special discounts for sales promotion, corporate gifts, fund-raising, or educational purposes. Special editions can also be created to specifications. For details, contact the Special Sales Department, Good Books, 307 West 36th Street, 11th Floor, New York, NY 10018 or info@skyhorsepublishing.com.

Good Books is an imprint of Skyhorse Publishing, Inc.®, a Delaware corporation.

Visit our website at www.goodbooks.com.

10 9 8 7 6 5 4 3 2

Library of Congress Cataloging-in-Publication Data is available on file.

ISBN: 978-1-68099-394-3
eBook ISBN: 978-1-68099-402-5

Cover design by Jenny Zemanek

Printed in the United States of America

TABLE OF CONTENTS

CHAPTER 1

THE LATE SUMMER HEAT SHROUDED THE RURAL PENNSYLVANIA VALley, the humidity sapping the enthusiasm of teachers and children alike.

Flies droned through the classroom, distracting the perspiring upper graders who had just come in from a round of baseball. Boys swiped at uncomfortable curtains of hair that hung to their eyes, rolled up sleeves, yanked at collars with forefingers, raised flapping hands to ask to be allowed to go for a drink.

Although every window was open, there was no hope of a breeze, so the boys lifted sweating palms, gripped slippery pens, and set to work on their vocabulary.

The teacher, Anna Beiler, was tall, and of considerable weight, circling the room the way John Stoltzfus imagined a commander of an army managed his troops. There was no getting away with anything, certainly not in this heat. The teacher's face was the color of a Concord grape, more or less.

John settled his thick, wire-framed glasses farther up on his nose and swatted viciously at a fly that had settled on his textbook, resulting in a loud whopping sound that brought the teacher to a standstill.

"John."

His name like a crashing cymbal.

"Explain yourself."

"The fly sat on my vocabulary book."

"The sound you just made was unnecessary."

John sat, eyes downcast, tried to make himself agree, then discarded that idea when he felt her perspiring presence beside him.

"Apologize."

"I'm sorry."

It was spoken through a thick net of rebellion, but still spoken. He held his breath till he sensed her large form moving on, then sighed a long, deep breath and leaned forward with his head bent over his workbook, thinking that was the third apology he had uttered that day, and it was only early afternoon. Likely there would be a few more before the day was over.

His life as one long string of apologies stretched before him, an endless river of failures that cropped up with regularity.

The youngest of a family of ten kids, with six brothers in various stages of single, adolescent, teenaged, or hoping to be married. He also had three sisters who had all found a "chappy" somehow, married, and left the house in the wake of Tupperware and Pampered Chef, quilts and sheet sets and new furniture, wedding gifts packed into sturdy banana boxes, directions scribbled with black Sharpie markers, corners crammed with crumpled newspaper for the trip to Kentucky.

He could hardly believe his good fortune, every one of them moving to Kentucky, marrying Yoder cousins endowed with a pioneering spirit. Good riddance.

John navigated his world of brothers as best he could.

Often teased, and always hovering on the edge of a world inhabited by bigger, smarter, better humans, John felt himself an afterthought. He felt mostly forgotten, easily dismissed by a preoccupied father who had too many cows and was farming too many acres. The boys took no interest in the old ways of driving six mules across the land and tearing up thin strips of soil when the tractor on the neighboring farm hummed effortlessly across fields, drilling corn seeds into the ground using the no-till method.

Why toil endlessly, with ever thinning profits, if there were newer methods of making a living? Wouldn't it be better to go to work and come home at the end of an eight- to ten-hour day and relax with your family? Better, even, to start up your own business, draw blueprints, write estimates, take that chance of making a quick ten thousand?

Or lose a quick ten thousand, the father reminded them.

All this John heard from the outskirts, forming his own opinion, his nose in yet another book, one leg draped over the arm of the recliner.

"You know you'll turn into a marshmallow," Abner muttered, taking his book between thumb and forefinger, flicking it across the room.

"You need to walk behind Dawdy's plow," Amos snickered. "Fat. You're getting fat."

They'd tease and roughhouse him good-naturedly, but John heard the undertones, the things left unsaid, Mam's presence his only guardian.

So he ate shoofly pie in creamy oatmeal loaded with brown sugar and rich milk from the gleaming bulk tank in the milk-house. He ate rounded, crackled molasses cookies rolled in white sugar like diamond crystals; bacon sandwiches, the thick homemade bread toasted in the oven broiler, spread with mayonnaise. He ate chicken potpie with applesauce and rolls with strawberry jam.

He pulled in his stomach, measured the snugness of his trousers by inserting four fingers, yanking on his elastic suspenders. He never wore T-shirts beneath his shirts—why add an extra layer to make his clothes even tighter?

His mother had given up sewing shirts years ago, with seven boys growing like jimsonweed, yelling about hand-me-downs and tight underarms, faded colors and popped buttons. She bought them by the armload, those blue, gray, green, and white button-down cotton shirts from Walmart.

She was as Amish as they come, but she had to cut corners somewhere.

Three times a day, there were meals to prepare. Not just a small amount of food, but large quantities for seven hungry boys. His mother often wondered why God had chosen to give her the three girls first then present her with seven boys in quick succession, sturdy little chaps that arrived into the world red-faced, already hungry and squalling.

Oh, but she loved her boys and suffered right along with them when they were dealt blows, heartaches, longings. Especially during the teenage years. Navigating the world of girls was a rocky journey, like shooting down wild rapids in an untrust-worthy boat.

She prayed, she worried, she placed her trust in God alone, most of the time, although sometimes she sank beneath waves of anxiety. There were whole days smothered in the pressing duties around her, sometimes resulting in short barks of frustra-tion or eruptions of emotion.

She knew Abner longed to be dating at twenty-two years of age. Knew, too, the fair Malinda would not have him, but was holding out instead for his cousin Elvin Fisher. The whole situ-ation wouldn't be so trying if it wasn't her own sister's boy, and her with that calm unruffled exterior, that certain superiority that irked Mary like a pin that jagged from her apron.

And here she had six more boys to go.

The Stoltzfus farm was located in southern Pennsylvania, nestled in the picturesque hills and valleys of Jefferson County, close to the wide and meandering Juniata River, surrounded by the mountains named Tuscarora by the Indians of a bygone era. Folks from Lancaster County became restless from time to time, acknowledging the fact they were being hemmed in by the tour-ist industry, as well as the growth of the many Amish churches called districts, stretching from Ephrata to the Maryland line. So in the '90s the Jefferson County settlement began, started by three pioneering families looking for good soil at a reasonable price.

Pleased with the area, they put down roots, buying farms for less than half of the price of a farm in Lancaster County.

They cleaned, painted, built dairy barns and horse barns, tilled the soil, became acquainted with the *ausry*—the English, as they called them, meaning the non-Amish.

English farmers with thumbs hooked in overalls straps stood for hours with Henry Lapp, Rueben Fisher, and Davey Beiler, sharing local wisdom, took them to town for calf starter, taught them the maps of the towns surrounding them, which feedstores delivered free of charge, which lumber company would present them with the most lucrative deals.

The community flourished as more men came to check out Jefferson County, bringing wives and children with varying levels of compliance.

Homesickness was not uncommon for many, usually assuaged by the hiring of a van and driver to convey them back to Lancaster County to spend time with mothers and sisters. Having been able to hitch a horse to a gray carriage and travel a few miles to see family—even less, in most cases—had been a way of life taken for granted.

Never again. Hearts yearned for *chvischtot*; bonds became stronger, the distance of over a hundred miles between them a buffer for any petty grievances one had toward another.

Over 130 households inhabited the valley from Dexter Falls to Rohrersville, a distance of roughly twenty-five miles. The Amish farms and homes were tucked into wooded nooks, or sprawled along busy Route 365 where the land was mostly level.

The English learned to adjust (with varying amounts of patience and forbearance) to the sign of a slow-moving emblem on the back of the gray buggies with canvas tops, the gleaming black wheels traveling at a pace of ten to fifteen miles an hour. Of course, some folks became openly annoyed and gunned their mufflerless pickups past a doddering horse in hopes of frightening the lazy animal, but that was to be expected.

The hitching posts sprang up at the local Lowe's and Walmart, and the proprietors learned to scoop up horse manure with wide steel shovels.

Retired men recognized the part-time side job, bought fifteen-passenger vans to haul the Amish, making a dollar a mile, or eighty-five cents for a minivan. All through the community, lists of Amish drivers appeared in phone shanties, the small buildings where telephones rested on shelves, a posterboard of phone numbers written with a black marker tacked to the wall. Telephones in the house were verboten, an unnecessary luxury in the opinion of the ministry. The elderly bishops were strong on church history, and liberalism was eyed with suspicion.

A telephone in the house would bring hours of idle gossip, and the women were doing too much of that already. As it was, the ones prone to loneliness spent hours in the cold phone shanty wrapped in heavy fleece comforters, wearing a coat, scarf, and gloves in winter.

In summer, the door was flung open, skirts adjusted, brows mopped as they told their sisters they had no idea what was wrong with the pea crop this year. The well-meaning sister threw caution to the wind and told her outright if she wouldn't be so *dick-keppich* and used lots and lots of granulated lime, she'd have a bumper crop, which resulted in a short goodbye, a clapping of the receiver, a miserable afternoon till a message was left on the well-meaning sister's voice mail, a sort of apology (the kind that justified its actions).

There were those, of course, who had telephones in offices close by, and these days some folks even had mobile phones that were easily hidden, easily procured, and an ongoing, thorny issue that refused to go away.

Since human nature is unavoidable, no matter the religious sect, cell phones were acquired in secret—the guilt-ridden individuals knew they were forbidden, but found too much enjoyment, too much handiness and knowledge at their fingertips.

Among the liberal *rumschpringa*, they quickly became prevalent, bringing contention and judgment from many of the more stalwart church members.

How to cling to the old ways of the forefathers with so strong an adversary in the form of technology? This was the lament of the godly clergy, deciding among themselves how to address the problem.

For one man's conscience is unlike that of another. *Ordnung* were observed stringently by some, and not so much by others. And with wisdom sought, with love and admonishment, the Amish church strove to keep the ways taught to them generation after generation.

Elmer Stoltzfus raised his boys with strict but loving discipline. At twenty-two, Abner had given his life to God, was baptized, and became a member of the Amish church, shunning all technology, as did his brother, Amos. Upright and honest, they drove their high-stepping Friesian-cross horses to the youths' suppers and hymn singings, played volleyball, never made any undue sorrow for their parents.

Marcus and Samuel were different, going away to the Saturday-night volleyball games that invariably turned rowdy, texting their friends on their cell phones, slouching at the breakfast table with red swollen eyes and unhappy expressions every Monday morning. Allen hovered between the two brothers, unsure which path he would go down.

It was a large group of youth and some were conservative and some liberal. When the parents saw a need to separate the two, there was a division, a friendly, amicable split, the *gehorsam* forming one group to socialize with and the more liberal folks another.

And so time moved on in the Jefferson valley. The sun rose and set on the righteous and the unrighteous as it had been since the beginning of time, God presiding over all, the final and ultimate Authority, the beginning and the end of each man's faith.

And so John Stoltzfus scootered home from Hickory Ridge School, one leg up on the iron bar between two bicycle wheels, his sweating hands gripping the handlebars, one leg propelling him forward, his lunchbox just barely fitting in the wire basket attached to the front.

It was so hot. He yanked his straw hat off his head, gave up pedaling, and walked the rest of the way up the steep grade. Below him, a gaggle of children on scooters was an accident waiting to happen, laughing, talking, distracted by each other, oncoming vehicles the least of their concern.

The top of the hill meant a long, cool breezy ride to the bottom, so John pedaled furiously to gain speed for the full benefit of his downhill coast. He hoped he would not have to chop corn when he got home, although he could see no way out of it. His mother planted so much corn she may as well build a silo for it. If he mentioned it, she tsk-tsked the very thought of less corn, saying the vegetable was the boys' staple, their favorite, and if she froze a hundred quarts it was barely enough from year to year.

The boys. He often wondered where he came in regarding the pecking order of the boys in the family. The caboose? The tail end? Barely attached, for sure, more like running on behind, calling out for everyone to wait up. Really, he just wanted to be noticed from time to time. His thoughts were not mired in self-pity—that's just how it was, but he did wonder how many of the boys would be married before he qualified as a real person to his family.

All he ever heard was his nose was like Samuel's, his hair like Abner's, he had Allen's build, long in the torso, long legs, big feet.

He was also a chunk. Decidedly overweight. Heavy. Glasses as thick as welder's safety goggles. Hair that sprang out of his skull with no clear direction, without having the normalcy of curls.

"Wavy," Mam said. "You have wavy hair."

He seemed to have cowlicks all over his scalp, a bunch of hair growing left, another one in the opposite direction, and yet another group growing straight up, not even thinking of being wavy until the very end, where they should have lain flat against his neck. Sometimes when he looked in the mirror he wondered if he was actually born mildly handicapped and everyone was too kind to tell him.

He knew he was odd looking, for sure, with those colorless eyes squinting out from the thick lenses of his wire-framed glasses. As if the glasses were not enough, his teeth protruded in front, much like a rabbit's.

He remembered a picture of the mice in the Cinderella story, those little chaps that wore hats and dresses and sewed the ball gown for her. Their two teeth hanging from their upturned noses always brought a fear of his own growing teeth. What if those two front teeth went right on growing until they hung over his lower lip like that? He used to check their progress, daily, secretly, pulling back his upper lip, knowing with a kind of clammy fear that, yes, in a week's time, his teeth had grown. Until suddenly, they stayed the same and his life took on little moments of gladness in the belief that he was normal after all.

Excluding the hair, of course.

Now that he was in eighth grade, a whole new set of problems reared their frightening heads. Small red pustules appeared beneath his bangs, five or six of them, before being joined by another bunch on his chin.

He envisioned acne, pocked cheeks like a sea sponge, fissured with tough, scarred rivulets that stayed his whole life.

That's what people would remember him by. *Oh, Elmer's John. The one with the abnormal skin. Oh yeah. Him.*

So he squeezed the life out of the intruding monstrosities, which resulted in a dozen more, red and angry looking.

Finally, unable to contain all the misery of the boiling pimples, he asked his mother to buy something next time she went to Walmart. She took his chin in her hand, turned his face right then left, peered through her bifocals, said "Tsk-tsk. *Pucka.*"

She bought him some kind of orange, grainy gel to wash his face, a lotion to put on after, a vile-smelling beige concoction that dried on the surface of his skin like plaster. Before a week had passed, the brothers were ribbing him about wearing makeup, laughing uproariously at their own jokes.

John learned early in life that it was easier to be carried along, mock punching, laughing with them. The tears only surfaced at night, in the privacy of his own bed, until his own humiliation at being a crybaby stopped them.

The Clearasil did help. His face cleared up, more or less, and with Mam being so alert, a new bottle would appear in the upstairs medicine cabinet when the old one ran low.

But then, a whole new disaster struck, in the form of his voice playing mean tricks on him. A lot of throat clearing, gruffness, and sudden unexpected squeaking ensued, causing him to be the subject of his brothers' hilarity. It hardly ever failed— when he wanted to say something of importance, he lost the use of his voice, resulting in a high squeak.

Singing in class was out of the question. He had a choice between a breathless squeak or a way low bass that sounded like a bullfrog, so he gave it up, held the corner of a songbook with Fannie King, hooked his hand in his pocket, and waited it out.

"John."

He knew it was coming, tried to look respectful.

"Why aren't you singing?"

"I can't."

"Certainly you can."

"No. My voice isn't right."

"Oh, that."

The teacher said it with all the distaste of carrying a dead mouse in a trap to dislodge it. As if he was growing an extra ear, or sprouted broccoli from his nose.

"Well, that's no excuse. You can still sing. Reuben does."

Rueben beamed his superiority.

John raised his hand. "Rueben's voice hasn't changed."

Teacher Anna glared at him, mouth compressed. John tried hard not to think how much she looked like a water buffalo. A Mennonite neighbor in the vicinity raised the big creatures, and John never forgot the lowered heads, wide brows, and curved horns, the unabashed belligerence, the pawing at cakes of mud and grass slung up over the shoulders.

"Bad-tempered creatures," he'd warned them. "Stay away from the fence."

He turned into the drive in a wide arc, leaning to the left, a spit of gravel, the crunch of homecoming. The house was off to the left, sitting white and square in the heat, the maple leaves like limp dishrags, covered with dust and summer's end. There were cement steps with a black railing leading up to the porch, and pots of pink geraniums, ivy, and a fig tree beneath the porch roof.

The barn had new red metal applied after the hip-roofed dairy barn had been added. The fields fell away on either side, corn like a small forest of uniform trees marching in rows, sagging with the weight of new ears of corn, two to a stalk. Already the hayfields had produced three cuttings of alfalfa, good timothy, and clover for the Belgians and the six driving horses. Every young man needed his own horse and buggy, even if it was a used one to begin with. At the age of sixteen there was too much craziness going on to afford a new carriage—everyone said it was better to wait till you're older, ready to settle down.

John took to snooping in the buggy shed—a sort of parking garage for buggies—a year or so ago, finding empty cigarette packs and English T-shirts. He was disturbed and told Mam about it in a trembling voice.

"Oh, you know how it goes. They're with the 'youngie.' They'll have some of these things for a while. Did you find anything in Marcus and Samuel's buggies?"

When John nodded soberly, she told him not to worry, she'd tell Dat. *He'll know how to deal with it*, she thought, shooing John out of the way so she could set up the ironing board. He was ushered out of the kitchen with all the aplomb of one of the barn cats, then went to change his clothes and get on with his life.

John threw his scooter in the door, where it fell on one of the fiberglass shafts of a carriage, grabbed his lunch, and went to the house.

The kitchen was empty and there was a table full of folded laundry. He could hear Mam's footsteps upstairs. Quickly, he went to the pantry. Fresh chocolate cake with buttercream icing. He knew it. Exultant, he carried the pan high, plunked it on the counter, and grabbed a knife and cut a huge square. He set it carefully in a cereal dish, added milk till the only visible part of the cake was the icing, then dug in with a spoon.

There was absolutely nothing better. Snug trousers and red pimples were insignificant in the face of chocolate cake. He lowered his head to shovel precariously perched wedges of soggy cake into his mouth, opening wide to insert the wobbling mass safely.

He listened to the footsteps. Mam was still scuttling around.

He cut another square, added more milk, and ate it quickly. He felt better, but now he needed something salty. Back in the pantry he found the Tupperware container of potato chips. Perfect. He took a long drink of water from the pitcher in the refrigerator, shot a guilty look at the basket of oranges and apples on the countertop, and then made his way up the stairs.

Mam was in his room, changing sheets, snapping a fitted one across the top of his mattress.

"Oh, that you, John? How was school?"

"OK."

"That's good. Grab ahold there, would you, John?"

He tugged, adjusted, helped his mother pull the striped blue sheet up over the fitted one, then the thin brown quilt, fluffed the pillow, and returned her smile.

"There we go. Thanks. It's so hot up here, I bet you anything it's ninety-five degrees. How you boys sleep up here is beyond me."

"It's not so bad. We just don't use covers."

Mam nodded. "Well, if it gets too hot, you can always sleep on air mattresses on the porch."

"You know what Abner says. Mosquito city."

Mam laughed, flapping the hem of her apron in front of her face. She looked pretty good for fifty-one years of age, John thought. She was plump, her arms tanned and freckled, her wide face rounded with pink apple cheeks. Her dark brown hair was smoothed on either side of the part in the middle and her white covering was clean and neat. John thought she was one of the prettiest mothers in church. After ten children, tending to all those boys, she still retained a youthful vigor, a zest for life, an eagerness to start up the grill on the back patio, make burgers and hot dogs, invite the neighbors, throw together a bowl of potato salad, make a pitcher of meadow tea.

She carried the clothes basket down the stairs, calling to John to get his clothes changed, there was corn to chop.

He knew it. He just knew it.

He flopped on his bed, turned his head to the side and grimaced. He would never be a farmer, would never make his wife have a garden. They'd live in a double-wide trailer, a nice one, on an acre of ground with trees and shrubs and at least ten bird feeders so when he came home from work he could drink coffee and gaze at the birds.

CHAPTER 2

B UT HE DID CHOP THE CORN, ONE MORE TASK ON THE SEEMINGLY endless list of chores. He worked every evening and on Saturday, emptying the garden of late vegetables—cabbage, green beans, lima beans, potatoes, carrots—which all had to be chopped, peeled, sliced, or shredded. And there were the bushels of tomatoes to be cooked and put through the tomato press, turning each red-cheeked fleshy tomato into steaming, fragrant juice. John stood in the kitchen all day, or so it seemed, turning the handle of the tomato press at least five thousand rotations, if not ten thousand. All the mutilated vegetables were cooked, the ground beef browned with onion, and then everything was dumped into a Rubbermaid tote, which made Mam fuss a stream of nonsense about plastic and its toxins, compared to a copper kettle that had its own oven in the washhouse. S' Kesselhaus. It was the proper term for the room where laundry was done, derived from the fact that everyone had a brick stove with a round hole on top to fit the cast-iron or copper kettle snugly in its place, and a cast-iron door on hinges where chunks of firewood were shoved through.

Nowadays, there were laundry rooms with linoleum floors and nice cupboards made of finished oak or closets with bifold doors and wringer washers with drains. That was the reason for Mam's fuss. No homemade vegetable soup would taste right, mixed in plastic, but oh well, nothing to be done about it now. Those were the good old days, those *eissa kessla*. John told her it didn't much matter where vegetable soup was mixed, or in what container, it wasn't good back then and it certainly wasn't now.

Mam threw her hands in the air, gasped, and said she had a good notion to clout him across the head with her dishrag. All this work and he stood there telling her it was no good!

He tried to correct this gaffe by telling her the other boys liked it. Mam eyed him with suspicion, then said, no they don't, either, but you know what? Every once in a while a mother needs a break, so eat canned vegetable soup or go hungry.

Wistfully, Mam told John she believed he was the only one that understood just how big her workload was, which made him feel feathery light, as if he could float away, buoyed by her words.

John loved his mother, but most of the time she was too busy or too exhausted to really notice what was going on in his life. His father was quiet, mild mannered, with a workload even bigger than his mother's. There was very little spare time to be found anywhere. If only one brother would stay at home, try to take an interest in farming, but no, one by one, as their sixteenth birthday approached, they worked in construction. Abner and Amos worked for R and S Roofing, Marcus for Hillside Construction, who did mostly rough frame work for apartment complexes, town houses, and single-family homes. Samuel and Allen went to work at B and S Structures, which built storage sheds, garden sheds, garages, and carports. Daniel was helping his father finish up the fieldwork, then he'd be off with the siding crew. They needed a lithe young man to climb scaffolding, and Daniel thrilled to be able to prove his worth.

John swept the extra silage back to the cows' reach with uninspired tugs on the wide, hard-bristled broom. Cows were just so dumb, the way they licked all that silage up with their tongues as long as a yardstick and still managed to push a good portion out of reach, periodically straining to reach it, almost hanging themselves in the process.

Still, he had a deep-seated empathy for these bovine creatures, always hungry, not attractive, plodding through life doing whatever was expected of them, much the same as him.

Make vegetable soup, sweep the feed troughs, assemble the milking machines, feed calves, all thirteen of them . . . by the time that was done, he was hungry enough to drink a bottle of calf starter himself. But he had to wait till the last cow was turned out to pasture, the milkers washed, and the milkhouse hosed down and swept before he could hope to have his evening meal. Mam liked to eat after the milking so that everyone was home, the day was turning cooler, and they could relax as they discussed events of the day. They often ate on the back patio, especially if there was corn on the cob, which made an awful mess.

Tonight there was corn—at least three dozen ears—brought to the patio table steaming hot along with plates of cold butter quarters, salt shakers, mayonnaise, sliced tomatoes, cheese, lettuce, onion rings, ketchup, relish, and mustard.

Dat was taking burgers from the oversized Weber grill, piling the grilled patties high on the platter. "The amount of food we have to make is unbelievable," Mam laughed, shaking her head.

"We'll get married as soon as we can," Abner said in mock apology.

A round of laughter, rippling along the tilted-back chairs.

"Find me a nice girl, Mam," Marcus said.

"She wouldn't take you. Not a nice one."

This from Samuel, resulting in a swift fist on his upper arm. Leaning forward, gripping the sore arm, Marcus squeezed his eyes shut as he moaned pitifully.

"You watch it there. You don't know the power of your own fist."

"Want another one? Huh?" A fist drawn back, a threatening light in his eyes.

"Mam! Make him stop!"

Without missing a beat, she said evenly, "As if I could."

Dat looked over from the grill. "That's enough, boys. Straighten up." He placed the last burger on the platter, set them on the table, and sat down.

Immediately, tilted chairs crashed forward, hands were folded in laps, heads bent, taking their cue for "patties down," the silent prayer that was said before every meal.

Abner was the oldest, of medium height, dark hair, dark eyes, glasses, a pleasant demeanor, and an aura of jaded youth. He was ready to move on, to settle down and start a family of his own.

Amos was tall and skinny with a glint of mischief in his green eyes and a wide face with a pointed chin. Everyone said he looked like his mother.

Marcus had brown, wavy hair, brown eyes, and a hooded look. He was stern-mouthed, with an infrequent smile that lit up his whole face.

Samuel was tall and wide across the chest. He was always happy and carefree, the clown of the family, and movie star handsome. All the best features of both parents had been bestowed on Samuel.

Allen and Daniel looked like twins with their brown eyes, dark hair, and similar height. They were both skinny, coltish, always lifting weights to build muscle, desperate to impress older brothers.

And then there was John.

Mary Stoltzfus lifted her head and unclasped her hands, in awe of these seven young men, all different, and all alike. She had borne and nurtured these young men, and only God knew what each one would prove to be, who would endure unfair trials and who would skip through life unscathed. God had the main control panel, had given them their nature, presented them to Elmer and Mary to guide, to raise, doing the best they could, the job before them phenomenal, but done in gladness if they remembered to depend on *der Herr.*

All this flashed through Mary's thoughts, before she smiled, "Dig in."

Steaming ears of corn were lifted with burning fingertips, rolled across cold better, salted liberally.

"Pass the rolls. Hey, quit with that mustard already."

"Mam, is there more mustard?"

"Pantry," Mam replied through a mouthful of steaming corn. "Samuel, you emptied the mustard. Go."

"You want it. I don't need it," replied Samuel. But then he sighed, pushing back his chair.

They had already gone through nearly two gallons of tea, a mixture of homegrown apple mint, spearmint, curly spearmint, and peppermint.

"Best tea ever, Mam."

"Thanks, Abner. Our pure water helps."

She brought another platter of corn, steam bringing the glistening sweat to her face. It was another sweltering night.

"How many burgers does that make for you?"

"Who, me?" John chewed, swallowed "I'm on my second. Mind your own business."

"Had a letter from my sister Naomi. Rebecca is sure not getting any better. They're taking her to Philadelphia now, to a Lyme specialist. It will cost them thousands of dollars for tests. They don't have it, Elmer."

"Church will help." Another ear of corn rolled across butter.

"I feel so bad for Naomi. She struggles daily, just trying to keep her head above water. It looks hopeless. Hopeless."

"You mean she's still sick? Cousin Rebecca?" Marcus asked.

"You know, Marcus. She doesn't even go with the youth anymore."

"How do they know what's wrong with her?"

"Tests, dummy. They did tests." Daniel answered.

A knife loaded with mayonnaise connected with Daniel's face. General hilarity ensued after that. Even Dat threw back his head and let out a full guffaw, tried to look stern, then gave up and laughed again.

"Our table manners are out of control."

This from Abner, the conservative one, responsible for unruly brothers.

"We're on the patio, not in the kitchen."

"So what?"

Mam wiped her mouth with a napkin, leaned back in her chair and sighed.

"I guess it's true what Daniel said. We relax back here, if it's just all of us together."

"What's for dessert?"

"Schwan's man was here."

Chairs clattered backward. Four boys tried to enter the kitchen door in one shove.

"Ice cream sandwich or Schwan's bar?" A yell from the kitchen.

Dat called out, "Bring both boxes."

Mam enjoyed sitting for another minute. It had been a long day, but what a blessing to have family together on a warm summer evening with good food, health, and happiness.

Dat rested easy, knowing the silos were full up and there were white plastic rows of silage like giant ghostly caterpillars behind the barn. It was a good feeling, knowing they'd have plenty of winter feed. They'd had a bumper crop of corn, which would have to be put in the corncrib. He prayed silently, thanking God for the provision.

School was going from bad to worse.

Anna Beiler was doing the best she could. She had grown up in a home where authority was meted out with hard staccato voices and the children were cowed into respecting father and mother alike. Mercy was rare, retorts or self excuses unheard of, and even the youngest children were expected to obey their parents to the letter. And Anna expected the same of her pupils. Never mind that she was working with kids from twelve families all raising their children with various degrees of love and discipline.

She attacked every problem with the sword of her outraged voice, the children surprised, at first, then confused, after which many of them broke out in nervous tics. Lower graders complained of stomachaches, crying in the morning when mothers shooed them out the door.

John sat at his desk, kept his face lowered to his work, and tried his best to stay out of trouble. But for one reason or another, that was impossible. His best friend, Ivan Beiler, said she seemed to pick on John more than the others—not that she didn't give everyone a hard time.

"John, get the brush and dustpan. Clean up the mud you tracked in. It dries, creates dust."

Bewildered, John stuck one foot into the aisle, then the other. His gray Vans were not muddy. There was only a dusting of it beneath his desk. Leaning forward as far as he could, he inspected the floor beneath other desks. He didn't complain, though, and was actually getting to his feet to carry out her orders when he was stopped with a sound like a thunderclap.

"John Stoltzfus."

He sat down hard, looked intently at his shoelaces.

"Why were you looking below other pupils' desks?"

"I wasn't."

"Yes, you were."

Nothing much to say to that. He guessed he was.

"John, I have caught you in a lie. That warrants a note for your parents. I want it signed, brought back. If you fail to do so, the school board will pay your parents a visit and you may be expelled. Lying is a bad example for the lower graders."

He handed the note to Mam, slouched miserably in a chair, both hands in his pockets, waiting.

"Hmm. What did you lie about, John?"

He told her.

Mam's face was without expression, her mouth like a pinched line in bread dough. Almost, her nostrils flared, her eyes flashed in anger, but she caught the surge of irritation, erased it.

"I'll give this to your father."

And she did. Dat read it twice, looked at John. He repeated his story.

"So you checked your own shoes, checked the other children's spaces, and what was your conclusion?"

John shrugged. "There was more mud, well, dried mud below the lower graders' desks than mine. She picks on me, and I'm a little scared of her. I wasn't really thinking when I told her I wasn't looking for mud. Which I guess I was."

Ashamed, now, he hung his head.

"She expected you to head straight for the dustpan, immediately, without any excuse. I believe that is the way Danny Beiler raised his children. So, we'll sign this, and remember to do better. She's strict, but there's nothing wrong with that."

That was the first incident. By mid-October, John despised his teacher. Ivan was beloved, whereas John did nothing right. Then she started picking on Susan, a seventh-grade girl who walked with a limp, spoke with a lisp, and wore a hair net and barrettes. Her dresses were a little fancy, too.

When John found her crying with abandon, clutching the dreaded note after having been kept in at recess, he ground his teeth in anger. He did not have enough confidence to speak to her while she was crying so heartbreakingly, but he told Ivan about it, and he walked right over and asked her what was wrong, John behind him, hanging back, embarrassed.

Between sobs, the story unfolded.

The teacher had told her that if she couldn't write better than that, she'd flunk seventh grade, and that she had an uncaring, unconcerned attitude.

"I know my handwriting is not the best. It's my hand. Sometimes it's like my . . ." She tapped her knee, ashamed to say it out loud.

She had a bum leg, no one knew why. It was the way everyone had always known Susan.

Wedding season came in November, the community humming with anticipation. The best part for the students was that they had substitute teachers on four different Thursdays. On those days, the students breathed, relaxed. First graders giggled, hands held over wide grins, eyes sparkling with delight. School seemed almost fun.

Henry Zook's Lena was the teacher on the last wedding day. John sat in his desk and listened to the low, husky voice reading the Bible in the morning. He tried hard to keep his eyes on the thumbnail he was picking, but he stole too many glances at the petite, perfect, blond-haired girl standing in back of the teacher's desk.

Her eyes were huge. So blue it took his breath away. Assertive. A good teacher, by all accounts, everyone agreed.

Well, this was something now, wasn't it? There was no hope to win the hand of any girl even close to this . . .

Oh well. He was only fourteen, much too young to be admiring any girl. He bumbled his way through singing class, mostly humming, and felt his face turn fiery red when she asked him to pass out quiz papers. He blushed to the roots of his hair.

After Anna Beiler returned to take up her post, the downward trend continued until a parent-teacher meeting was held on a rainy evening. Nothing good came of it, with Anna saying the problem was a lack of parental discipline at home, children easily skipping over what was expected of them. Children nowadays had too much freedom. How was a well-meaning teacher expected to keep order the way the forefathers did?

Parents squirmed uncomfortably, most of them finding their shoes extremely interesting. A few attempts at challenging her opinions were squelched like the rasp of a closing door, shut off with the same pelting words hurled at her pupils.

When the meeting dispersed, a few low grumbles were heard as men untied heavy neck ropes, backed horses and carriages to a better turnaround position. But mostly the parents renewed their commitment to reprimanding their children and working with the teacher. If parents rebel, what can be expected of the children?

Sent to school with the serious words of his father in his mind, John made a double effort, minded his p's and q's, became even more withdrawn, afraid to raise his hand or voice an opinion.

That is, until little Lydia Ruth was spanked in front of the whole class for missing too many problems in her arithmetic book. A slow learner, having been sent to school a bit before her sixth birthday, she upset the teacher's schedule on most days, unable to comprehend the basics of numbers or letters.

Lydia Ruth was so shy, so tiny, and this assault to her sensitive nerves was more than her frightened body could absorb, so she lost the contents of her stomach all over her new black apron and her new Nike sneakers. The sound of teacher Anna's harsh words as she swabbed viciously at the offending mess was a stab to John's heart.

He scootered home with the full intention of his parents hearing about this, all of it. Something had to be done.

His father listened, nodded. A flush spread across his mother's face. But they both said to wait.

"Why? Why can't you do something?" John pleaded. "You know it's not right. That little girl is doing the best she can."

"John, listen. Sometimes it's best to calm down. Very likely, Lydia Ruth's parents will talk to her, and we'll be minding our own business, which is best."

Lydia Ruth's parents went to the school board, said they would not be sending their child back, they'd enroll her in another school, if it was allowed. Other parents called for Anna's resignation, not only the one incident being the cause, but their own children being subject to unfair treatment.

In mid-December, she was let go, the school board being kind but firm. They hired Henry Zook's Lena, the substitute, which activated a flurry of protests from a few families.

She was too young, they said. Only sixteen! Why, she doesn't look older than her upper-grade pupils. Others said to give her a chance. Henry Zook's girls all taught school. It was in their blood.

After Lena started, new artwork appeared, along with brightly colored name charts, apples in brilliant Crayola colors, the classroom taking on a whole different atmosphere.

John scootered off to school, energized, one leg flying behind him. But a small piece of him felt sorry for Anna Beiler. He pictured her putting her schoolbooks in drawers, fighting what must seem an overwhelming sense of being adrift, her whole identity as a teacher being swept away.

Lena did not allow anyone to speak ill of their former teacher, explaining in detail that God distributed a talent to each person, and perhaps Anna Beiler had not yet found her true gift.

John's admiration of her bordered on worship.

He took to wearing a stocking cap at night, in a desperate attempt to tame his unruly hair. He viewed the flattened mess the first morning, thinking he looked like a drenched cat. The minute he applied a brush, the loose curls sprang back to life, erupting from his head like an unleashed Slinky. He thought of his sisters' hairspray, wishing one of them was still at home.

He searched every drawer in both bathrooms, harboring a hope that his mother would use it, but no, of course not, she hardly had any hair, a fact she bemoaned from time to time, blaming the birth of ten children.

The stocking cap idea was abandoned after a few attempts. He tried wetting the brush, holding the bristles beneath the bathroom spigot, then drawing it through his tangled mass of waves, which only served to give him the distinct appearance of a drowned rat. His eyes were so small, his well-rounded cheeks like two watermelons. And always, those persistent red pimples that resisted the drying effect of the Clearasil.

He wondered if any of his brothers ever went through this form of dissatisfaction about their appearance. But he would never ask, being afraid they'd laugh uproariously at the mere thought of it.

His mother had not raised seven boys without recognizing the signs of adolescence, the accompanying self-hatred. She had pitied each one as they passed through this tender phase, but often found herself unable to help. The boys just became irritated, shrugged off her gentle attempts of buying a product to clear up unsightly blemishes, vitamins for lethargy, and so forth.

John was her baby, and one not endowed with a natural promise of being handsome. Mam felt compassion for her youngest, with that head of hair, the excess weight, coupled with the bad complexion.

She reminded him gently that a bright and friendly spirit had much more to do with a positive image than appearance.

But that only made him feel worse, the way she implied his looks were a lost cause. As if he'd have to make up for his wretched appearance by plastering a knockout smile on his face, which only pushed his watermelon cheeks up to squeeze his small eyes to mere slits and tilted his thick glasses.

Mothers were seriously so bumbling. So well meaning, with exactly the wrong thing coming out of their mouth too much of the time.

That was why he didn't bother saying more than "OK" when she asked him how school was. If he'd tell her each incident that had affected his day, she'd ramble off with some strange story or advice that had nothing to do with the incident itself.

He figured, though, that she couldn't help it, it was just the way mothers were, their head crowded with too many things at once, a workload that pressed on them like a heavy backpack. If she wouldn't plant so many pink petunias all over the place, her workload would be significantly decreased.

CHAPTER 3

THERE WAS NO CHRISTMAS PROGRAM THAT YEAR, LENA HAVING taken over a week before, and Anna Beiler having held a distaste for programs in general. There was no exchange of names, and no presents for the teacher. She didn't feel right, receiving the presents that Anna should have had. Which was true, John thought, his admiration of Lena increasing yet again. But he found a deep-seated yearning to present Anna Beiler with a Christmas present.

He mulled this over for a few days, before deciding he could not accomplish this without his mother's help. So he approached her, shamefaced, afraid she would think him too soft, sentimental.

She had her back turned, chopping cabbage at the sink. When John asked her to accompany him to Rebecca Zook's store because he would like to take a gift to Anna Beiler, the knife stopped, and she held very still.

Uncomfortable, John added, "I don't have to. I just thought . . ."

When Mam turned, her nose was red and she was blinking furiously, her voice quivered and came out garbled with swallowed emotion.

She managed, "Why, John?" and her voice slid to a stop.

"What's wrong with that? I pity her, sort of. I mean, she

was just teaching the way she thought she was supposed to. She didn't know any different."

Mam nodded, her lips trembling.

So on Saturday morning, John hitched up Capper and waited by the sidewalk till his mother bustled out, buttoning her coat, carrying her bonnet. Yes. Yes, indeed, she would accompany him.

They found many beautiful gift items, Rebecca Zook and her three employees harried, too busy the week before Christmas, but friendly, helping each customer as they needed assistance.

John chose a wooden box, with a hinged lid and a bright gold clasp.

"She could keep cards and letters in here."

"Certainly she could. A good idea. I'll ask them to wrap it."

And so John helped his mother tie Capper to the hitching rack at Anna's house, and followed her to the front door.

The house appeared much the same as hundreds of other Amish farmhouses, white, with a washhouse and a porch along the front, a few hedges, a garden with rye sowed, the winter cover crop.

Anna's mother opened the door, greeting them with the traditional, "*Hya. Kommet rye.*" She was gaunt, hard faced, lines all vertical down her face, a permanent scowl. Her father was at the table, thin, spare, piercing eyes, long thin face with a full flowing beard covering his shirtfront.

"Hello, Rachel. How are you?"

"Can't complain."

"We brought a Christmas present for Anna."

"Oh." She moved off, called for Anna, who appeared, suspicious, like a dog with its hackles raised, untrusting.

John stepped forward. "Here. This is for you."

He wanted to say more, wish her a Merry Christmas, thank her for being his teacher, anything to take away that sense of failure she surely must have.

"How nice."

"There's a card." He blinked, self-conscious now, under the crowlike gaze of the father and the mother's cold, calculating stare.

"*Ich sauk denke*," she thanked him.

"*Gyan schöena*."

Anna made no move to open the present or the card. To John's disbelief, the taut face crumbled and silent tears spilled from her eyes. She lifted her gray belted apron, brought out a navy blue men's handkerchief, swabbed at her streaming eyes, her mouth drawn to a thin line as she made an effort to control herself.

"Anna, it's all right," Mam said, very softly.

John felt an unbearable sympathy for Anna. In her thirties, unmarried, living a life tamped down by the severity of her parents' upbringing, surely she would not have chosen this herself.

He cleared his throat.

"You were a good teacher," he mumbled.

"It's nice of you to say that, John, but we both know it isn't true."

She sighed, blew her nose, returned the handkerchief. "I should have been smarter. Known my ways weren't the same as everyone else's. We are all Amish, yes, but we have our differences."

With the parents there, she stopped, respecting her own stringent upbringing. For one reason or another, the blue handkerchief was the most pitiful. How many women used a handkerchief rather than a Kleenex nowadays? The handkerchief was an outspoken symbol of conservatism, a family who clung to the old ways, frugal, nothing frivolous within sight, buying only what was truly necessary. They carried the old virtues like an Olympic torch in the race of life, honoring the belief that nothing was better for the human soul than denial of the flesh, the lust of life, the *ordnung* kept to the letter, come what may.

She stepped forward, placed a large hand on John's shoulder, her voice trembling.

"I will never forget this."

A week later, he received a thank-you note in the mail. It was an apology written in her perfect, cursive hand.

Mam showed it to his father. Dat stared off into space, his face betraying nothing. Finally he said, "You know, most people only need kindness and understanding, don't they? Remember that, John."

Word must have gotten around among the brothers. John was treated with a bit of respect for a while, anyway, so that he had the nerve to ask Samuel, the handsome one, what to do with his untamable hair.

"Your teacher doesn't have anything to do with it, does she?"

John's face flaming, he shook his head from side to side.

Samuel laughed, but it wasn't a mean, teasing sound.

"Tell you what, buddy. Let me go to school, and you can go to work and your hair will be the last thing you have to worry about."

"Ha!"

"I would gladly sit in your desk."

"You can't, so get over it."

"I know. Just kidding."

"No, you're not".

"Not entirely, no."

"This doesn't answer my question."

"Oh, your hair. Other than shaving it all off, I don't know what to tell you. Marcus uses that stuff. Looks like shoe wax."

"That stuff" turned out to be the miracle John badly needed. Worked into his scalp, it tamed the lawless waves and curls, brought them into some semblance of order and changed his appearance to a well-groomed young man in eighth grade. The only problem was using small enough amounts so Marcus wouldn't notice.

This "borrowing" went on for a while, till John heard Marcus bellowing from the bathroom, blaming first Samuel, then Allen, for using his hair stuff. From the bedroom came a stentorian yell, a swift denial. First Samuel, then Allen.

John held very still, turning hot all over, his heart rate galloping. He pulled the covers all the way over his head, as a shield against his own thievery.

"I don't even know what you're talking about."

Another yell from Allen, sifting effectively through the guilt and into John's ears.

"That round black and yellow container of styling cream. It's expensive. You know how much that stuff costs?"

"What do you care? You're the roofer. Making megabucks."

"The next person I catch using this stuff will be given twenty lashes." From another bedroom

"With what? A wet noodle?"

"Hey! Everybody shut up. OK? Let a person get some sleep," came Abner's voice.

John had his own thoughts about Abner. Maybe if he used some of that stuff in the black and yellow container he'd be able to elicit an approval from his long-sought-after Malinda. He went to volleyball games, youth suppers, and hymn singings wearing the same three shirts for months. Blue, lighter blue, or almost blue. No wonder he couldn't get a girl. Plus, his hair was never right, either frizzy, thicker on one side of his head than the other, cut crookedly, or some kind of uncombed pouf in the back. The sneakers he wore to play volleyball would likely have suited his father, black all over, from Walmart, no name brand like Adidas or Nikes. The footwear was important.

Abner didn't care about things like that. Comfortable in his own skin, he was content to let styles come and go, the way they invariably did.

John knew, though, that he was a bit of a loser. He could never have Malinda, he had heard Samuel say. He needed to lower his sights. Emma would take him, but he thought he was much more handsome than some others, and Emma far below his status.

There was nothing wrong with Emma. A bit mousy, perhaps, but an all-around nice, quiet girl, one that would make him a really good wife. That was the snare you could get yourself into real fast, wanting only the best looking, the high steppers, the one everyone else wanted.

Like Lena.

John cringed. He knew he spent too much of each day sitting at his desk, watching her, although he consoled himself with the fact that it wasn't merely her beauty, it was the expertise, the way she moved so efficiently from class to class, teaching all her subjects as if she had been doing it for years.

He was only fourteen, in eighth grade, and he figured it was nothing, an admiration, perhaps even a crush, but never serious.

Until Ivan told him he was planning to marry her someday. It was easily possible, he said. They were only a few years apart in age.

John listened to Ivan's confident portrait of the future, watched the verbal brushstrokes paint a picture suffused with good luck, sprayed with a lacquer of conceit, and said nothing. Best to keep his mouth shut in the face of that steamroller.

And then he noticed small changes. Lena avoided Ivan as much as she could, and instead asked John to light the gas stove, hang up artwork.

As January progressed into February, Valentine's Day hovered. Sure enough, his mother bought the teacher a box of chocolates—Russell-Stover from Walmart, packaged in a pink box with a red ribbon. Plus, three yards of fabric, mint green, from Rebecca Zook's store, wrapped in white foil with pink hearts on it. The worst thing by far was the pink box of candy hearts on top, those fat little hearts that say stupid, lame things like "Cutie" or "My Crush" or "Be Mine."

John agonized over the gift for two days, caught between

being kind to his mother or presenting his teacher with that blatant overdose.

He asked kindly if she didn't think that was too much.

"Why no, John. Of course not. We didn't give her a gift for Christmas, remember? She didn't want any. So sweet of her. Honest, John, I do believe she is an exceptional girl. I dropped a few hints to Samuel. I believe they'd make an awesome couple."

John cringed.

Overweight mothers with thinning hair should never say "awesome." It just didn't fit. They shouldn't say "totally," either. Or the worst of all, Mam had taken to peppering her speech with the word "lame." That was a "lame" bag of insecticide. The Dawn dish detergent that did not produce enough suds was also dubbed "lame."

Mothers didn't get it right, it seemed. They listened to teenage slang like that, tried to incorporate it into their own speech, and it came out way wrong, like a foul ball.

All those thoughts on speech did not make the box of chocolates go away. The present sat on the library table in the living room as big as a cow, and stayed there. John thought of telling his mother how the gift itself was *awesome*, but it would be totally lame to give it to Lena.

But of course, he scootered off to school with the present in the basket, thinking maybe a car would hit him lightly, just enough to scatter the chocolates, candy hearts, and mint green fabric all over the road. He could almost hear his mother's gasp of disapproval at such thoughts.

He had slush all over his backside, the back of his coat peppered with clots of melting snow and water. The present, however, stayed perfectly dry.

He arrived early, hoping that meant fewer pupils would see him carry the present to the teacher's desk.

"Why, John. You're early. Good morning." Lena was wearing a red dress, for Valentine's Day.

"Good morning."

He placed the present on her desk, returned her smile. Polite.

"Thank you."

"You're welcome."

He turned, shucked his coat and straw hat, ran a comb through his hair. *A little bit of styling gel goes a long way*, he thought, guiltily.

More pupils arrived. More presents.

At recess, one of the mothers brought pizza from Benny's, in town, as a surprise for the children. Not just pizza, but Pepsi and Mountain Dew, potato chips, macaroni salad, cupcakes and jigglers. Plenty of everything.

John ate four slices of pepperoni pizza. He was actually contemplating a fifth, but ate another cupcake instead.

Lena had a tower of presents, her pretty face flushed, unable to thank everyone enough. More dress fabric, chocolate candy, tea towels and bath towels, washcloths, even a packet of kitchen sponges, a trio of wooden spoons, all items for her hope chest.

John thought of the mint green dress fabric.

She seemed to think that was the best gift, clearly delighted with the color and texture, her face beaming with pleasure.

Well, wasn't that something then? Perhaps mothers knew a thing or two about Valentine's Day.

By the time school was almost over, John had acquired another few inches in height, his shoe size exceeded a twelve, and he had put on another ten pounds. No amount of styling gel, cream, or spray would ever tame that volcanic thatch on top of his head that most people were fortunate enough to call hair, so he gave up, shampooed and conditioned with whatever the brothers were using at the time—Axe, or Dial, Dove, or Suave, sometimes Pantene. None of it made a difference.

He towered over his classmates and his teacher, his voice a low growl and his feet like rowboats. He was a fearsome ballplayer, of course, his sheer size enabling him to whack the ball far beyond the school's boundaries.

On the day of the picnic, he received his diploma, a framed verse about the future and God and love, which he glanced at hastily, then stuck it back in the box, knowing the tears would form immediately.

With it was a handwritten card, thanking him for his kind heart.

He blinked, then ran out to play ball with the fathers. It was the biggest day of the year, the long awaited ball game between the children and parents.

Hats were thrown aside, black vests flung after them, sleeves rolled up, a few warm-ups by swinging the bat, the softball thrown to loosen the old pitching arm.

Sides were chosen and the cry was flung into the air: "Play ball!"

Lower graders and preschoolers held lollipops, balloons, candy pacifiers and bracelets, all prizes won by games, wheelbarrow races, sack races, everyone participating, everyone allowed a prize.

John was nervous and missed the ball, struck out amid loud moans of disappointment from his peers. He loosened up, driven by determination, then made home runs, hitting the ball as hard as any of the parents. He high-fived his team, his hair gone wild.

Elmer told his sons he believed the youngest son was the best ballplayer yet. Mam grinned, shaking her head.

They were on the back patio again, the first real warm day, with asparagus from the garden, new spring onions and radishes with homemade dinner rolls, fried chicken, and potluck potatoes.

The platters were heaped high, as usual, but it didn't take long for them to empty. The amount of food that disappeared down these boys' gullets was always a source of amazement for Mary.

The other boys didn't take kindly to Dat's comment about John's ball-playing skills.

"The big ox?"

"Never saw a muscle on those arms yet. Where are they? Huh? Let's see what you use to slug that baseball."

Eye contact, a knowing glimmer of "let's get him," and John was hauled out of his chair, carried kicking and squirming down the steps and into the yard, his arms punched and squeezed amid howls of protest.

He gave them a good run for their money, anyway, clawing, punching his way partially out of their grasp.

"You'll quit this in a few years," he told Marcus and Samuel. "I'll pick you up by your pants and throw you over the railing. Both of you at one time, too."

Dat tried to be gruff, authoritative, but there was a glint in his eye, and a wide grin plastered on his face.

They were out of control, these hefty sons. But he loved them all.

There was chocolate cake and canned peaches for dessert, the traditional everyday dessert of busy mothers everywhere.

Mam made a cake almost every day, unless there were whoopie pies or cookies on hand. Shoofly, cherry, raspberry, apple pie. Or the all-time favorite, pumpkin. The record pumpkin pie disappearance was four pies in one sitting. They praised Mam's pumpkin-pie-making skills till her face was flushed with pleasure, and she baked six more the next day.

"Rhubarb pie. French rhubarb pie," Mam called out, carrying the pies, heaped high with buttery crumb topping.

Tongues protruded, icks and yucks following. Mam laughed, winked at Dat.

"Didn't you notice we didn't eat cake?"

"Course we didn't. We have more important things to talk about or notice than what our parents put on their plate," said Abner.

"Oh well. We shall enjoy the fresh pie immensely. You may all help yourselves to a slice," Mam said airily, lifting her chin, closing her eyes as she waved her fork like a baton.

Here was the last of the children passing from eighth grade to vocational class till his fifteenth birthday. What a blessing to be together, celebrating in good health and happiness.

After dessert, Mam said she'd appreciate mulch on the asparagus.

"Manure? Or mushroom mulch?"

"I would use mushroom. We put plenty of manure on in the fall."

This, then, was the reward of being a mother to seven sons. There were always able bodies ready to help out with whatever task was at hand.

Clamoring, shoving, joking, three of them set off for the mushroom soil. Abner and John carried the dishes to the sink, while two more helped Dat with the hay, moving bales to make room for fresh alfalfa.

Mam wiped a tear of gratitude, watched John plunge his arms into sudsy dishwater.

"John, you can hardly reach down to the sink anymore."

"I'm five foot eleven and three fourth."

"No. Come on. Surely not."

"No. Just kidding. I bet I will be six three or four, though."

"Probably. Here. Let water run in this potato dish. It'll have to soak for a while. I left them in too long."

"They were good."

"Oh, I know. Fattening as all get out."

John laughed. Everything was fattening, according to his mother. She lamented the counting of calories every day, but didn't care a whit, once she got hungry. She ate chips straight from the bag, even spread mayonnaise on a slice of bought white bread, piled it with potato chips, and ate it in three bites with a Diet Coke.

Another summer, with its accompanying heat and humidity, the air hanging moist and heavy, draining the good spirits from everyone living in the valley. The river ran sluggish, the color of black tea, river snakes and dragonflies darting between the rocks.

Leaves hung like exhausted rags, listless in the still air. Cows stood up to their bellies in brown ponds, flies swarming in thick black clouds.

A sick deer emerged from the woods in broad daylight, dragging its hindquarters, gaunt, near death.

Dat put it out of its misery, the boy's faces sorrowful. The Game Commission was notified, men in green uniforms with serious faces. Tick paralysis. Hundreds of ticks feasting, engorged on the deer's blood, infecting it with the Lyme bacteria.

Notes were taken and the deer hauled away. Mam panicked.

"I don't know why none of us has ever been bitten. No one has ever pulled a tick off, have you?"

Noncommittal shrugs.

"Tonight I want everyone to examine yourselves. Carefully. This is no laughing matter. You know how your cousin Naomi is suffering. I just heard of another case like hers."

She rambled on and on, the way she always did. John said that it was unnecessary to create that kind of drama. If you found a tick, you pulled it off, and went to see a doctor. As simple as that.

When the last week in August rolled around, John was dressed in a new shirt, his Sunday pants, and his comb in his pocket. He was on his way to vocational class at Benuel Zook's. His wife, Annie, taught the fourteen-year-olds, one half day a week, a total of three hours. Each pupil kept a diary of their workweek, which would be turned in to the state of Pennsylvania, as proof of their education in vocational class.

It was a time of stepping out, these young boys and girls who would not officially be considered teenagers until they were sixteen years of age.

They learned arithmetic, spelling, and German, safety classes, and German hymn singing. The boys kept their diaries up to date and dreamed of which girl they would ask for a date.

CHAPTER 4

WITH COOLING AUTUMN WINDS, MAM FORGOT HER OBSESSION WITH ticks, too busy canning peaches and apples, grape juice and pears, the last of the tomatoes, neck pumpkins peeled and cut.

She worked from five a.m. to bedtime, bustling through the house, her white covering taking on a grayish hue. No time to wash coverings.

She counted over a thousand jars in the cellar. There were two hundred quarts each of peaches, pears, and applesauce, plus spaghetti and pizza sauce, salsa, hot pepper jelly, zucchini relish, fifty quarts of spiced red beets, and hundreds of quarts of dill, bread and butter, banana, and mustard pickles.

The rectangular stainless steel canner bubbled all summer long, or so it seemed to John. He was Mam's helper, turning the handle on the Victorio strainer, turning eight bushels of apples into sauce.

He told Mam he was pretty sure they put a ton of tomatoes through that thing.

"No-o. You think?"

Mam pulled a funny face, her mouth puckered in the way that made John smile.

She was cleaning the kitchen, washing her huge kettles after peeling the neck pumpkin, cutting them in chunks, cooking them, then cold packing the orange mess, for pumpkin pies.

"You like pumpkin pie," she ordered, "so peel, and stop complaining."

Peeling pumpkin was a mean job. The skin was thick, stubborn. It took a steady hand and a strong arm to peel pumpkin, so that job fell to the boys, whoever was available at the moment.

Every one of them gave that pile of pumpkin a wide berth, thinking if they stayed away from the pile on the back patio, they would not be the one collared into peeling.

Inevitably, and usually on a Saturday, with a special breakfast of sausage gravy and biscuits, a mound of fluffy scrambled eggs with white American cheese melted through, grape juice and pancakes with blueberry topping, there was a steep price to pay. Peeling neck pumpkin.

Dat drank coffee with the last of his pancakes, a gleam in his eyes, a grin on his face.

"Frolic today. Enos Beiler's building a dairy barn. Who wants to go? And who wants to help Mam?'

Abner, of course, the chief, said he had a dentist appointment in town. Down came the tilted chairs.

"No, you don't. It's Saturday. You're fabricating a huge *schnitza* to get out of the pumpkins."

"I do have a dentist appointment. Doctor Burns is in on Saturday from nine to twelve."

"I bet."

"You made that up when you saw the pumpkin."

Samuel was going to Harrisburg to the sportsman's show. So was Marcus. Amos was taking Daniel to check out a horse about ten miles away, which would take up most of the forenoon.

So of course, the job fell on Mam and John.

"*Ach, vell, so gehts,*" Mam said, wielding a kitchen knife like an axe, the heavy wooden cutting board taking the "chunk" of her strength.

John resigned himself to the miserable task, but not without telling his mother that he was a real-life Cinderella, except he was a guy.

"Just call me Cinders," he breathed, pressing down on the paring knife, his tongue clenched between his teeth.

"Ach, I know. Poor baby."

She put an arm around his shoulders and squeezed, rubbed his shoulder with affection. John shrugged, drew his eyebrows down to show his manly disapproval of any form of tenderness. But secretly he was pleased.

He went fishing, that afternoon, his mother's gratitude ringing in his ears. He walked through acres of corn fodder, careful to avoid the rough, stumpy remains of the brown cornstalks. A light jacket kept him comfortable, his tackle bag slung across one shoulder, his fishing rod across the other.

He waded through a vacant field, wet and swampy, grasses up to his waist. Good thing he wore his Muck Boots.

Bulrushes were already going to seed, leaves falling everywhere. Brilliant colors of orange, yellow, and red were turning to a dull brown hue.

It all seemed a bit early, but then, there was always the chance of having a long, hard winter, the way his father described from his youth—being snowed in for days, dumping milk from the tank with the milk truck unable to get through.

He pushed his way through heavy grasses, brown milkweed pods, blackberry vines, multiflora roses, those parasitic, prickly growths every farmer fought.

He should put a blade on the Weed Eater, bring it down here to hack a path to the creek, but decided against it immediately. He knew cranky old Mr. Baldwin would never allow it. He barely had permission to catch a few fish.

Reaching the bank of Rock Creek, John was soon situated at his best spot. He had the roots of an old, peeling sycamore tree for a footrest and thick, wide grass for a comfortable seat.

A deep, tea-colored hole was in front of him and the smell of new fallen leaves and skunk cabbage was like a rare cologne. He breathed deeply, closed his eyes, and smiled. Two chocolate whoopie pies and a ripe pear waited in his tackle bag, along with meadow tea and ice in his insulated water bottle. The late October sun warmed his shoulders and his mother's thanks filled his heart. He found himself thinking about the two weddings approaching in November, which he'd been invited to as *hosla*, someone to care for the horses.

Before November the fourteenth, something had to be done about the nipping of Samuel's hair cream. Not a confession, as he had no desire to be beaten up. He knew his limits, and confessing to Samuel was definitely crossing a line.

He had to gather enough nerve to approach Mam, tell her his hair woes. Not that Mam was a hard person to ask for a favor. No, it was just the embarrassment of being caught caring so much about his appearance. Most boys his age didn't seem to care about hair and the state of their skin, or whether they had begun to shave.

He stopped tying a new hook on his line, so deeply was he thinking of his teacher in eighth grade. Lena Zook.

What if she was at the wedding? He simply had to get his hair tamed. He wondered if you could buy hairspray for men.

He hooked a fat worm, purple and squiggly, and stood up and drew back his arm, casting perfectly to the far side of the pool. Then he lowered himself on the bank, watched the dizzy whirl of released maple leaves dropping into the water, and was just ready to open his tackle back for a whoopie pie when the tip of his rod bent, the handle jiggling in his grip. Fish on.

Whoa.

It felt heavy. A nice largemouth, hopefully.

The sun was low in the sky when he walked back through the tangle of grass and weeds, carrying a full stringer of shining bass and bluegill. It was a heavy weight slung across his shoulder, a long walk across uneven fields, but John was powerful, with young muscles that didn't tire easily.

He swung along, hoping to fillet the fish and persuade his mother to fry them tonight. Cleaning fish was one job Mam never attempted. She wrinkled her nose, pronounced them slimy creatures, hated the feeling of scales all over her hands. But she would beat the eggs and ground saltines in a Ziploc bag with the rolling pin, and add the salt and Old Bay seasoning. She would heat her largest frying pans, pour canola oil with a generous hand, dredge the fish in egg and cracker mixture, then drop them in sizzling oil. Put the fried fish on a roll with some tartar sauce and ketchup and it was the best thing in the world. Fresh-caught fish were better than cheeseburgers or probably pizza or French fries.

Plus, he figured tonight Mam would know he deserved it, after peeling all the pumpkin.

"Oh yes," she said. "You go ahead, clean them."

He showed the whole stringer to his father, who raised his eyebrows and said, "My, oh!"

Abner looked out from the forebay, where he was shoeing a horse, and said he was quite the fisherman.

John had planned to clean the fish in the forebay, attaching a hose to the hydrant at the watering trough, but not with Abner shoeing a horse. It wasn't merely the thought of Abner taking up all that space, it was the odor from the trimmed hooves.

"How long till you're done?"

"It'll be a while."

Abner's face was purple, his shirt stained dark with perspiration. A pile of fresh horse manure steamed beneath the horse.

"You stink."

"Thanks."

John stood, watched Abner crouched, holding the horse's foot, the veins in his forehead sticking out, his nose purple. He was alarmingly homely looking. And here he was going around thinking he could have Malinda.

It was well past nine o'clock when his mother served the fish on a paper toweled platter, yawning, saying, my oh, she didn't know what was wrong with her, she could hardly stay awake. Not too many, there, Daniel, John caught them. Two apiece. They were as delicious as John anticipated. Better, if possible.

Mam called over her shoulder as she headed for the shower.

"Church at Benji's tomorrow. No skipping. Elmer, did you remind Samuel and Marcus? Those two weren't in church last time."

Dat peeped over his half-mast glasses, nodded. "I reminded them."

"Good. They get away with whatever they can. Where did Amos go in such a hurry around seven?"

Noncommittal shrugs. Ketchup bottle turned down, tartar sauce squeezed.

"Hey, the tea's all gone," Allen called.

"Drink water, then. I'm tired. It's bedtime."

John rooted around in the spice cupboard till he found an old packet of red Kool-Aid, mixed it with a cup of sugar, added ice, poured some for Allen, and continued his feast.

"What is this stuff?"

Allen lifted the glass, grimaced.

"Kool-Aid."

"Does anyone even drink this stuff anymore?"

"We do," John said, tearing off a sizable portion of his fish sandwich.

"Gross."

"Drink water, like Mam said."

John sat on the hard, wooden bench, dressed in his new white shirt, black Swedish knit trousers and vest, and the hand-me-down black dress shoes. His hair was smoothed, pomaded with the stolen hair cream.

He felt handsome in the crisp white shirt. He sat up straight, listened to the minister's voice, but stole glances in the girls' direction.

Like a flower garden of myriad colors in blues and reds, purples and lavenders, white capes and aprons, black coverings signifying unmarried, the white of the capes and aprons a purity, the meek and benevolent spirit of a young girl.

Girls were so odd, though. They never looked at you in church. That was considered well mannered, he supposed, but it would be nice to know one of them noticed you every once in a while, at least. So starting to like a girl in church was out of the question, which was just as well, being as it was God's holy place.

That's what Mam said, anyway.

Wherever there were two or three people gathered in His name, there God is, she said. So don't sit in church and get all fidgety and irreverent. Sit up and listen, because God is in the room, she said.

John listened to the minister, thought of a great white figure with His whole being stretching from one end of Benji's shop to another, enveloping everyone with a serious holiness and grace. He took notice of two boys on the bench ahead of him, chins upended on palms, elbows on knees, fast asleep. They were probably out last evening.

A baby whimpered, then began to yell without restraint. A harried young woman rose to her feet, her wicker *kaevly* bumping on her arm, a toddler clinging to her skirts.

She was still making her way along rows of seated people when the minister called the congregation to prayer. Everyone turned to kneel, leaving the mother to scuttle red-faced out the door with her crying brood in tow.

John felt a stab of pity for her. The minister could have repeated a phrase, waited till she was out the door. He was ashamed to feel a prick of tears, an indignation at the abrupt

minister. He could hardly bear the thought of Eli sie Linda having to make her way across the gravel drive with two crying
children, knowing she should have waited.

He felt the same stab of tender sympathy when Henry Lapp's
little boy fell backward off the bench, his head hitting the floor
like a chunk of wood. He immediately set up an awful howl after
holding his breath far too long, resulting in a shaken Henry hurrying his bawling son outside, blinking furiously in embarrassment.

He saw his wife hand her baby to one of her friends, leave
quickly out the side door, glowering. He pitied Henry all over
again, having to live with the humiliation of allowing your son
to fall off the bench, plus be chewed out by an irate spouse.

Misery flowed through him like a heavy torrent, unbearably
potent, a scalding drink that seared his throat. He tried to rise
above this too strong emotion, but sank beneath it, tears rising,
pooling, sliding down his cheeks.

Quickly, he lowered his face, sunk his chin to his chest, in
desperation. What was wrong with him? He was distraught,
tired. This numbing pity was too much to be borne.

He just needed more sleep, he guessed.

They were invited to his parents' friends' house for a late supper
of roast beef. A fresh cow had gone down, a hasty butchering
followed.

The children played volleyball, John the tallest, at his best,
spiking the ball, jumping, yelling, his energy boundless.

He knew he was impressing the girls. Barbie, for sure. She
was cute, in a frizzy way. He thought they had one thing in
common: misbehaving hair that had a mind of its own. Her
hair made no sense, either. It was a mousy color of nondescript
brown, and kinky, as if a too-hot sadiron had been dragged
across a nylon handkerchief, creating ripples.

"No fair, John," she wailed, red-faced, exhausted, after
retrieving yet another spiked ball.

"You're tall, and too strong. You don't know your own strength."

"What do you want me to do? Play on my knees?"

She grinned up at him. She was a good sport, and tiny, for a fourteen-year-old. He'd known her all his life. They'd played kick-the-can, prisoner's base, baseball, volleyball. She was good at all of it—tiny, but quick.

Maybe he could marry her and they'd have a pile of children with hair like Brillo pads. Or alfalfa.

"Stop spiking. OK?"

"Come on, Barbie. All of it's fair."

She laughed, bounded off to the corner of the set to send the ball in the air with a mighty wallop from her small fist.

Later they filled their plates and sat together at the children's table, plastic folding tables covered with white tablecloths. John got up to get her a drink, after she said she needed one. She thanked him, smiled at him the way she'd done easily, a hundred times. It seemed to him that her smile contained something more, though, or was it her eyes? They were green as a new leaf.

"You should get rid of those glasses, John."

"Why?"

"Well, they're terribly thick. You must be as blind as a bat, with those lenses. They make your eyes appear only half as big, I bet."

"I never gave it much thought."

"Yeah, well, you should."

"If I take these glasses off, I can't even see your face. It's just a blob."

"Really? Do it."

He obliged by yanking his glasses off his nose.

Eleven-year-old James giggled. "Boy, you look different."

"You should get contacts," Susan said, the pale sister to James.

"No way. I don't think so. I don't care that much about my looks. I will not slide a disc of plastic in my eyes, thank you very much."

"Maybe so. But your glasses are ugly."

"Thanks. I appreciate the compliment."

Barbie laughed again, got up, and went for dessert.

The following morning, John had a dull ache in his shoulder. He winced as he pulled a polo shirt over his head, rubbed the spot with the palm of his hand, and thought no more of it. He fed the calves, shivering in the gray October morning, his teeth chattering.

Perhaps there would be an early, harsh winter. It certainly seemed cold for October. He welcomed the warmth of the cow stable, the steaming hot sinkful of soapy water in the milkhouse, and forgot about the pain in his shoulder.

For breakfast there was chipped-beef gravy and stewed saltine crackers with fried cornmeal mush. Plus fried eggs like miniature suns, melting in his mouth, grape juice, and coffee. The brothers were tired, quarrelsome.

"I have an ulcer in my mouth," Daniel grumbled. "It hurts to eat."

"Your driver's here," Mam called from the sink.

"He can wait. I didn't eat yet."

Dat spoke sternly. "Daniel, go. You don't make a work driver wait, even if it's Monday morning."

Daniel took a few mouthfuls, forced on his work shoes, and stomped out the door.

The rest applied themselves to their breakfast, then sat back, yawning, scratching chests, shoving elbows into ribs.

"Did you ask Cathy last night?"

"Course not."

"Why not?"

"What makes you think I'd ask anyone? Let alone her."

"Well, you found her pretty interesting at the singing table. Either that, or the calendar on the wall behind her head was extremely entertaining."

"Shut up."

"Nobody can ask a girl out before I do. I'm the oldest," Abner said, grinning like a hyena.

Snorts and guffaws sounded all around.

"If we wait on you, we'll all be grizzled old bachelors, thumping our canes at the sisters' children. Nieces and nephews, only."

Mam choked on a swallow of coffee, ran for the sink to deposit a mouthful of the hot liquid, before dissolving into girlish giggles.

"You guys!"

Dat grinned widely, asked his wife if she was all right. Mam shot him a loving look.

A sly expression crossed Abner's face.

"I wish to make an announcement. I have seriously asked a girl for a date next Sunday evening. To your total disbelief, I'm sure, she said yes. Now guess."

Abner sat back in his chair, his thumbs hooked beneath his suspenders, his chest expanded with self approval.

John mentally flipped through the older girls in his group. All of them were unsuitable, somehow. Amid girls' names being dropped like hailstones, he ducked his head and ate his shoofly pie soaked with milk.

"Driver's here. Marcus. Samuel. You know you boys need to get your shoes on before you sit down for breakfast. Now he'll have to wait till you have those big clodhoppers laced up."

"They can leave without us. I know. Martha. Dave Lapp's Martha. Martha Lapp. She works in the office at Hillside."

"Not her. Not Martha."

Come on, Samuel, John thought. Being blessed with good looks was OK but Martha Lapp was at least forty. And single. The kind of girl who would likely marry a widower, or someone much older than Abner.

But John didn't say it. He hardly ever contributed to the conversation when the subject was an important one. Too much age and experience, too much prestige hanging over the kitchen table like a dense fog.

"Just tell us," Dat said quietly.

"Is she from this area?" Mam asked, serious.

"Why sure. I can't believe you can't hit the right one."

John's voice was gruff, quiet. "Ruth. John King's Ruthie."

"You got it!" Abner shouted, shoving his chair back, spying his driver from the kitchen window.

Mom gasped. Dat shook his head.

"Why, of course. John, good for you. Why couldn't we guess her?"

"She's much prettier than you," Allen said, grumpy.

"I'm not supposed to be pretty."

He slammed open the door, burst through it exuberantly, walking cat like in all his victorious procuring of a date with John's Ruthie.

Dat whistled low, the minute he was out of earshot.

"She's shy," Mam mused. "Those girls don't think highly of themselves. But she is . . ." His mother stopped, shook her head.

Amos grinned. "She must have pitied him."

This remark tickled John, for some reason. He threw back his head, roared with laughter, then cut another slice of fragrant shoofly and doused it with milk.

One by one they left to their jobs with drivers, leaving John to help his mother with the dishes. A warm glow suffused the kitchen on this cold morning, Abner's announcement creating an expectant glow of the future.

Mam scraped grease into the trash can, shook her head, muttered to no one in particular. Dat pointed his chin in Mam's direction, silently, his eyes twinkling. John caught on, grinned back. Man-to-man.

Poor Mam. She'd never be able to handle this. As stressed as a moth to the allure of lantern light. They both knew she'd suffered with Abner at his frustration of being unable to win

Malinda, and here he was, on his high horse, asking John King's
Ruthie.

She was nineteen at the most, and neat as a pin. She was a
bit plump, perhaps, but good looking. A sweet girl, by anyone's
standard. Goodness. What if she told him off, had a few dates
and decided he was no Romeo? Well, he wasn't.

Mam's thoughts were churning. Abner certainly didn't
stand out in a crowd. Mr. Mundane. Oh, she had to stop these
thoughts about her own son. Looks weren't everything. She
would pray.

She tried, but her thoughts were scattered by a fresh wave of
anxiety. Abner was not getting any younger. If Ruthie got bored
with him, and moved on, she'd have to suggest Martha Lapp,
maybe. She could do that.

"Mam, you put the orange juice in the pantry."

"Ach, so I did. John, what do you think? You think Ruthie
will regret it, and tell him off? She probably will, *denkscht net*?"

"I have no idea."

He rubbed his shoulder, grimaced. "Ouch."

"What? You have a sore shoulder?"

"From playing volleyball."

His mother didn't hear him, already living in a world with
the rebuffed Abner, comforting his heartache as best she could,
so John let himself out the door and into the milkhouse to finish up washing the milkers, then hitched up the two Belgians to
rake corn fodder.

Back and forth, their heads nodding in time to the placing
of their gigantic hooves, the faithful horses moved across the
field, a cloud of brown dust rolling behind them, the gray sky
like dirty wool, gathering into bunches, churned by blasts of air
from the Arctic.

John shivered in spite of the heavy black sweatshirt he wore.
He wished he'd worn a stocking cap. And he should have taken
Advil for the shoulder. Seemed like every lurch of the cart sent

icy pain through the joint. Not really icy, more like sandpaper grating between the socket and ball.

Lunchtime would be a long way off, being so cold, with the shoulder pain to boot. *Be a man*, he thought. *Toughen up.*

He watched a wedge of geese flying south, heard the thin high honking as they moved along, propelled by muscular wing-beats. He always thought flying geese sounded hysterical, as if they were stuck in a traffic jam and had a plane to catch.

Unbidden, his heart rate accelerated, as if someone had stepped on the gas. His breath came quick and fast.

Stop thinking about the geese. Duh, focus on the rows of corn.

He took a deep breath, then another. Everything will proceed as normal, he assured himself, as he licked his dry, chapped lips.

CHAPTER 5

ON THE MORNING OF NOVEMBER FOURTEENTH, AT THE LONG-AWAITED
community wedding where John was to be *hosla*, there was a cold
north wind accompanied by a gray, penetrating drizzle. He woke
from a thick blanket of sleep, ignored the cloying shoulder pain, did
his chores, ate breakfast amid the clatter of Mam's stainless steel
kettles and roasting pans. She was yanking them from cupboards
and off shelves and inspecting them under her eagle gaze, checking for initials written on the side in Liquid Pearls, a small bottle
of squeeze paint that adhered to any surface. It was a handy way
to mark kettles, bowls, Tupperware, those containers that shifted
among the Amish community bearing cheese spread and peanut
butter spread for church, fruit salad and cake and cornstarch pudding. Having the initials on the side assured a safe return.

There. She thought so. Her sixteen-quart Farberware kettle had "P.K." in lavender paint. Aha. She'd told Priscilla King
she had the wrong kettle at Amos Beiler's wedding in March,
but you couldn't tell that headstrong woman anything. She had
sailed out the door with her chin in the air with her kettles,
obviously. Well, today she would find out she was wrong.

"What, John?"

"My shirt collar is too tight."

"Well, it can't be helped. No time to fix it. Hurry. You have
to be there by seven. Driver's coming at six thirty."

"I can't close this collar. I'll croak."

"No, you won't."

From the stairway. "Mam, I don't have one pair of socks. Sunday ones."

"Wear someone else's."

"You put them in the wrong drawer."

"Mam, have you seen my vest?"

"In your closet. Look. I just washed it."

John opened the first button on his new white shirt and never closed it all day, which was frowned upon by most of the older generation. Well, there was nothing he could do about it.

A group of five young men were on hand to help each team unhitch, the horses led away and stabled, fed and watered. This was their duty, to see that each horse was comfortable. Many guests arrived in fifteen-passenger vans from outlying communities, but they stabled more than fifty horses.

For their efforts, they held special privileges. For one thing, they were allowed to have the mid-forenoon *schtick*, or snack. They piled small plates high with the seasoned chicken filling called "*roasht*," eaten with pepper slaw, a cup of coffee or hot chocolate, and all the wedding cookies or doughnuts they could hold. The relatives and church members of the bridge were all busily engaged with cooking jobs, the making of the *roasht*, the slaw, the mashed potatoes, so they, too, could help themselves to this delicious mid-forenoon snack.

Everyone was in high spirits, jostling, joking, smiling, anticipating the festivities, a day of renewing old acquaintances, making new friends. The air was permeated with good wishes, a wedding being a reason for rejoicing, reminding the old of a sweet love past, the young of their own rosy future.

John stayed in the background, conscious of his open shirt collar. Sure enough, his father caught his eye, pointed to his own closed collar, his eyebrows raised.

"Close your shirt."

"Tight," John mouthed.

A wave of Dat's hand. Whatever.

John closed the button, tried to stretch the collar by yanking, two fingers inserted into the side. No difference.

They were ushered in to take their place on the wooden bench, amid hundreds of people. John was the oldest, and the tallest, by far.

Nothing to do about that, so he kept his eyes averted, sat down as fast as he could, feeling like an elephant.

He couldn't help but be drawn into the ceremony, a visiting bishop speaking plainly about marriage, God's will for a man and wife to live together in harmony.

He didn't make it sound impossible, but rather a joy to give your whole life for someone else, whatever that meant.

When the time came for the young couple to be married, the bishop announced their names and they rose, joined hands, and pronounced their solemn vows.

John wondered just how nervous the bridegroom would actually be. Suddenly he was extremely relieved that he was only fifteen and had no worries about a girlfriend and most certainly not a wife. His life stretched ahead of him in one long sunshiny trail, and he figured he could look forward to his years of being with the youth, that time of *rumschpringa* when weekends would be spent with his buddies.

He had so much fun at the wedding, he forgot about the hair, the thick lenses in his glasses, or the fact that his Sunday trousers were snug.

He ate so much delicious food, watched the "youngie" go to the table, which meant a group of young men were situated in one corner of the shop, the girls in the other, until one by one, the brave young men stepped forward to claim one of the young ladies to accompany him to the long wedding table stretched out along three walls. There, they were served a delicious snack while they sang German wedding hymns from the *"Auskund."*

The *hosla* watched with fascination, secretly nervous for those poor young men, knowing their time would come when this frightening feat would have to be performed by every one of them.

"What if you reached for a girl's hand and she pulled back?" asked Daniel Lapp, the *hosla* next in age to John.

"Like, what if she thinks you're gross?"

Laughter all around.

"They wouldn't ever do that," Mark Glick announced, too loudly.

"Shh. Someone will hear you."

More nervous giggles. John thought some of the girls looked as if they could easily fall down in a faint, their faces the color of chalk.

Poor things. Whoever invented this tradition had no mercy.

The following morning, his throat hurt and his shoulder felt as if it was on fire. In fact, he hurt all over.

Mom put a hand to his forehead, drew back in alarm.

"Why, John, you're so hot. And this is early in the morning." She drew back, searched his face.

"You must have the flu. The wedding was too much for you. You weren't doing things you weren't supposed to, were you? Like smoking cigarettes?"

John was too miserable to answer, so he didn't.

"John? John?"

"Let me alone, Mam. I don't feel well."

"Of course not. Here, I'll just put a sheet on the couch. Bring your pillow down. I'll get quilts. You want Tylenol?"

Why did her questions slam into his head like a baseball bat? He lowered his eyebrows, shook his head, as if to ward off those verbal blows. He didn't know if he wanted Tylenol or not, the decision was too hard to make, like deciding if he wanted to climb a fifty-foot pole or slide off a barn roof.

He rolled on the couch, covered with two quilts. Chills raced across his body, his teeth chattered, his throat was on fire. To move his hands was a monumental task. His shoulder felt as if it was football-sized, and throbbing with fiery jolts of pain.

Of course, the brothers eyed his dark head sticking out of the quilts and pillows, teased and tsk-tsked, saying Baby John couldn't take being *hosla* at a wedding. It was good-natured, without malice, but the teasing voices still scraped and banged into John's world of pain.

After a few days, his symptoms did not dissipate, but kept him in clutches of fever and misery. Mam doused him with every vile concoction she could bring out of storage—bitters and tinctures, pills and drinks—but nothing seemed to touch this stubborn bug.

So it was off to the family doctor in town.

Weak and shaking, alternately chilled and flaming with an inner heat, John sat in the van, wondering if he could stay upright as the driver took the corners at a fast clip. When he slowed at an intersection, he leaned forward so far he had to grab hold of the seat. His hands felt as if there were no ligaments, muscle, or skin covering the skeletal bones, the vinyl seat cover searing the fingers. He lifted his hands to his face, to check if there was the necessary cover on his bones.

Mam turned to see him lift his hands. He lowered them quickly.

Dr. Stephens clucked, looking at his chart.

"Temperature of 104 degrees. Heart rate low."

He prodded and poked, checked his throat, did a strep test, pronounced him sick with a virus, but gave him a bottle of amoxicillin to be sure they'd knock out infection in the throat, even though it showed negative for strep.

He patted John's thigh kindly, told him to get better, he was a tough young man. John nodded through the ever-increasing fog that seemed to be settling over his perception of ordinary conversation.

After a few days the antibiotics made a difference, so Mam said that's what it was, negative test or not, he had strep throat. By now, John was immensely relieved to be better, stronger, able to function at a normal level.

In the middle of Christmas preparations, he did not want to ruin everything for Mam, who loved the hustle of shopping, cookie baking, names exchanged, family get togethers, a time of escalated cheer in the Stoltzfus household.

John felt well enough to keep his aches to himself as he moved from barn to house, helped with chores. Jobs his father asked him to do were accomplished with only a minor bout of weakness.

John's flu forgotten, Mam plowed full steam ahead, into December, sewing Sunday trousers for Abner, who was dating now, going to John King's every weekend, so he needed to look his best. Not that his best was all that good, but she had to do what she could, as far as his appearance.

She mentioned his old black sneakers from Walmart, which set him off. "Nothing wrong with these. What do you mean?"

Mam decided she needed to have a spiritual talk with her oldest son, so sat him down one evening and proceeded to ask if he had prayed about this before he asked Ruthie.

"Well, duh, Mam. Of course. You must think I'm not much."

"No. Oh no, Abner. I just want to make sure you are seeking God's will, and not placing your own ahead of His. I mean, per-haps, uh . . . , you know, God's will for you may not be Ruthie in the end, but rather someone like uh, you know."

She couldn't bring herself to say Martha.

"I mean, Ruthie is, of course, a very nice girl, and I wish you God's blessing, but when, uh . . ., dating begins, there is always a chance it may you know, fall apart, end in heartache. Not that I believe it will. Oh no. I have faith that God's will for you is Ruthie, it's just that, well, I want you to be happy."

She was so ill at ease by now that every word was only serving to sink her farther into the quagmire of speech. She stopped, took a large sip of cold coffee, and choked, spraying it all over her dress front and tabletop.

Abner sighed, his indignation turned to pity.

He watched as she hurried to the sink for a clean dishrag, mopped the front of her dress, then made a few swift circles with the cloth on the table cover.

"Mam, calm down, OK? I know you mean well, but looks aren't everything. I know you think I'm homely. . . ."

Mam lifted a hand. "Never, Abner. That's not true."

Abner ignored this.

"There's much more to dating than appearances."

Mam nodded vigorously, so hard, in fact, that Abner thought perhaps she may have given herself a sizable migraine, after that overdone display of agreement.

"If we are truly for one another, she will come to love me in spite of my physical appearance, and you know that. There's a much deeper level of love, the personality, the attitude, everything."

Abner was telling his mother what she had meant to tell him, but the words had come out wrong. Or something.

Abner laughed, then looked at his mother with kindness.

"I know what you really want to say is Ruthie is too good for me. I'm old, nothing much to look at, and you're afraid it will end badly. You know what she told me last Sunday night? She said I was so easy to be with, so comfortable with who I am, and that was attractive to her. Think about it, Mam. My sneakers have nothing to do with it."

Mam stood up, pushed her chair into place, gathered up the coffee cups, clearly flustered, said, "Oh well," and went to the counter to begin washing dishes as fast as possible.

John observed, overheard, pitied his mother with an almost physical sympathy. The thing was, she meant well. She cared fiercely about her boys, every one of them. She suffered when they suffered, and after all those years of wanting Malinda, his yearning unfulfilled, she assumed this would be no different.

He watched her broad back and capable arms at the kitchen sink, suds up to her elbows, efficiently upending a Princess House pan, reaching under the drainboard for a container of Bar Keepers Friend to begin the rigorous process of keeping her pans gleaming, the pride of her kitchen.

Then she was off to the bulk food store, Abner to the harness shop, leaving John alone on a Saturday with nothing much to occupy his thoughts.

He went to the pantry, found oatmeal cookies. He pinched one between his thumb and forefinger. It was hard as a rock. There was an apple pie that looked as if it had been on the pantry shelf for a week. Some stale pretzels.

He opened the refrigerator door, found a package of cheese. Sniffed. As he thought. Swiss. He replaced it, found a roll of homemade Lebanon bologna, sliced a few thick slices, fried them in butter, placed them on a potato roll with pickles, mustard, and mayonnaise, poured a glass of milk, and squirted a liberal amount of Hershey's syrup into it.

The perfect snack.

Halfway through his sandwich, shooting pain roiled through his stomach. He placed both arms across his front, leaned forward, and squeezed his eyes shut. The pain roared through his intestines. He broke out in a cold sweat, replaced the chocolate syrup, carried the half-eaten snack to the sink and collapsed on the couch.

Eventually, the pains subsided, and he fell asleep. His mother awoke him, coming through the door with plastic bags stretched to the limit with heavy ten-pound bags of brown sugar, flour, oatmeal, confectioners' sugar.

Her trips to the bulk food store meant some serious lifting, hauling all those bags up the porch steps and into the kitchen.

John got up immediately, felt light-headed and dizzy, but the worst of the stomach pains were gone.

He helped carry boxes of Ritz crackers, molasses, honey, olive oil, salt, Jell-O, cornstarch, coconut. There was no end to Mam's stocking up.

The next morning, as he sat up in bed, the bedroom swam crazily, then disappeared altogether, as if a wave had washed everything from his sight. He concentrated, panicked, willed the room back into focus.

His heart raced, a crippling fear of the unknown smacked into his senses, a sensation that he was losing his mind.

For a few minutes, he lay down on his back as his bed seemed to rise and fall, tilt left, then right. He felt nauseous, his breath coming in short, hard gasps, as if his life depended on gathering the next inhale of oxygen.

What is happening? Why am I like this?

He felt a deep sense of shame. His first lucid thought was that he needed to keep this to himself. No one had to know that he was not quite right. He'd beat this by himself, whatever it was. He was a strong, healthy young man, and these puzzling symptoms were nothing he couldn't handle.

He sat up again, but felt as if someone had punched him in the stomach. Taking a deep breath, he steadied himself, swallowed the lump that rose unbidden, blinked back unwanted tears, made his way to the dresser for a pair of clean broadfall trousers.

Opening the door of his closet turned his arm muscles to water. He kept going. He got his shirt off the hanger, poked his arms into the sleeves. His fingers trembled as he closed the buttons. Twice, he tried to attach the tabs of his suspenders to the buttons in the back of his trousers, but each time his arms gave way. Gritting his teeth, grunting to breathe, he accomplished this impossibility. Socks in hand, he went to the bathroom to brush his teeth and wash his face, only to find a white ghost with scraggly brown hair staring back at him from the gold-framed mirror.

Well, he had passed out, so that explained the color. Or lack of it. He made his way down the stairs, unsure what was expected of him. To tell his mother he didn't feel well would bring an avalanche of questions, in which he would be buried. At the moment, it simply did not feel possible to get into his heavy sweatshirt and get himself to the barn.

But he did do it. Weak, cold perspiration beading his forehead, he shivered his way to the calves, hung on to the frame of the vinyl calf hutch with one hand, the bottle with the other. He wished he had a portion of the strength in the calves' butting attempts to get the bottle to release more warm calf starter.

Somehow, by grim determination, he set one foot in front of the other, doggedly doing his expected chores. In the light of the battery lamp hanging in the milkhouse, his face appeared ashen, a thin line of sweat beads on his upper lip, dark circles beneath his wide-open eyes.

His father came in to check the agitator on the tank, turned to notice John's wild-eyed expression, the grim mouth a ghostly slash of endurance.

"You all right, John?"

"Yeah." Nodding.

Dat touched his shoulder, turned him to scrutinize the drawn features.

"You sure? You don't look good."

"I'm all right."

"Guess you are. You did have the flu."

And left him.

John signed with relief. If he could keep his weakness and fear from his parents, he'd be OK. As soon as Mam found anything wrong with him, she'd blabber it all over the neighborhood, people would look on him with pity, and he'd be Elmer's

John, the sick one. *He has some disease, but no one knows what it is*, they would whisper.

I'll soon be sixteen, ready to enter the years of *rumschpringa*. I can't be sick. I won't be. I'll pull myself up.

His appetite suddenly gone, he slid his two fried eggs around on his plate, chopped them up with his fork, pretended to put them in his mouth.

No one noticed. Mam was preoccupied and Dat was hurrying through breakfast to get back to the heifer going through a difficult birth. The boys were in various stages of undress, searching for shoes, suspenders, or both.

John sat on the old navy blue recliner, tipped it back, crossed his legs and closed his eyes. Every bone in his body cried out in protest. A deep sigh, a mental attempt to relax, let the pain go, and he sank down, down into the heavenly folds of the old blue recliner.

"Look at this!"

A low whistle, the recliner caught under the arm, tilted, and John was dumped out on the floor, sprawled across the linoleum like an ungainly rag doll.

"Lazybones."

Daniel and Allen, laughing, already beginning to tease this early in the morning. John gathered himself up, laughing weakly, with hiccups that sounded like sobs, before righting himself and sagging back into the recliner. But he did not tilt it into the reclining position again.

"Dat, you need to find worthwhile employment for this guy," Daniel said, jerking his thumb in John's direction.

"He is gainfully employed," Dat said firmly. "I couldn't run the farm without him, so don't go telling me what to do."

The good-natured Dat was grumpy this morning. Daniel took a long time lacing his shoes, ashamed to look up.

He held his hands to the good heat from the woodstove, before making his way to the washhouse for his outerwear. He called back over his shoulder, "I need you to help pull a calf, John. So get your coat on."

John stayed on the recliner without answering.

"Did you hear him?" Allen asked.

"Course."

But his voice was squeaky, breathless.

Mam turned to look at him, sharply. "Is your sore throat back?"

John shook his head, got to his feet, still wobbling like a year-old child taking his first steps.

Steady as she goes, he thought, his trek across the kitchen a test of stamina and balance.

Mam was gathering laundry, thumping around upstairs, carrying the huge wicker hamper in the hallway, piled high with dirty boys' clothes. Then it was back upstairs for another one.

John stood in the washhouse, watching his strong, ambitious mother bend to stop the drain on the wringer washer, fling the lid open, insert the short hose before turning on the hot water. She whirled around, sorting clothes in rapid-fire motion, lifting men's denim trousers, searching pockets, extracting red men's handkerchiefs, throwing them on a separate pile.

"John?"

Noticing her pale-faced son, she stopped, worry creasing her brown, her eyes kind. "Are you feeling ill? Are you sure your sore throat isn't coming back? I asked you that before this morning, but you never gave me much of an answer. See, if your sore throat isn't better, strep can turn to mono, I think. Or is it rheumatic fever? Anyway, you have to watch it. Eli's Dan's Elsie got mono and was sick for months. Terrible sick. And your father cannot do without you. You look awful, John. Let me fix you vinegar water with honey."

All the more reason to keep his mouth shut, John thought grimly. Honestly, it was like being raked with sandpaper, that onslaught of nonsense. Who in the world was Eli's Dan's Elsie? Who cared if she had mono?

"John, now, I mean it. Don't overdo it today. Better to be safe than sorry. Perhaps our best route would be to take you back to Dr. Stevens."

She yelped, turned to place the hot-water hose into the rinse tubs, reached up to bring down the rectangular box of Tide with Bleach, scattered a cupful across the steaming water before yanking the yellow lever on the air line, resulting in the soft, uneven purring of the air motor sloshing the water by the agitator's back-and-forth movement.

John let himself out into the morning sunlight that felt oppressive, hurt his eyes. He took a few deep breaths before opening the door of the cow stable.

He found his father with his elbows resting on the top rail of the dry cow stall, a worried expression changing the normal good humor.

"I don't know. This has gone on too long. I won't try anything by myself. Think I'll call the vet. She's a first timer, and a good one by the looks of her. I'd hate to lose her."

John nodded, his knees turning all rubbery at the thought of a calf straining to be born. He left, quickly.

"John!" his father called after him. "We're going to clean the horse stables today. You can get started. Dan and Dud need exercise, so get them hitched up a while. You can bring the manure spreader around to the overhang."

"All right."

He almost laughed at the idea of manhandling the heavy harnesses on the backs of those Belgians. Then he leaned on a cow stanchion and cried, wrinkling his face like a baby. From nowhere, a deep-seated despair settled into his chest, attached itself to the walls of his mind, and stayed there.

I can't. I can't. I have to. My mother will go nuts with a round of doctors and tests and crazy cures. I have to keep going. I have to keep all this weakness or whatever it is hidden.

After three attempts, his muscles screaming in protest, he got a five-gallon bucket, upended it, with Herculean effort mounted it with harnesses slung over one arm, stood on his toes and barely, barely slid the whole mass of leather and buckles, snaps and straps across the wide backs of both Belgians.

Panting, shaking, he adjusted the britchment, closed the buckles on the belly band, pulled the harness up over the collar. He sagged against the wall of the forebay, closed his eyes for a moment's rest, before putting on the massive bridles.

Dat pulled on the garage door from the outside, a question in his eyes.

"Wondered where you were."

John didn't answer. He found silence useful sometimes, during his bout of the sore throat virus. His parents could be as suffocating as an airless plastic bag drawn over his head. All those senseless questions that ricocheted around in his head until he couldn't think of a single useful answer. He found no answer handled both of them very well. Eventually, they gave up and left him alone.

The only thing about that was the guilt. He knew better, had always been taught respect, to speak to elders, be polite, friendly, honest, all that good stuff.

He was just so sick. So weak and befuddled, aching with unexplained pain in one muscle, then a knee joint, and back to the ever-aching shoulder.

After the sore throat, it seemed as if a nail was driven into one eyebrow, above his left eye, creating a searing headache that left him gasping with a terrible, dull throbbing ache. He stole ibuprofen, took as many as four at one time.

How are you, John? What's wrong, John?

I don't know. I don't know. I don't know.

CHAPTER 6

BY THE TIME CHRISTMAS ROLLED AROUND, JOHN HAD LEARNED HOW
to deal with the worst of his pain and weakness. He found the
best route to waking up was to stay lying flat on his back, focus
on a spot on the ceiling, and take deep breaths until he felt
steady enough to weave his way to the bathroom. Once there,
he would clutch the edge of the sink until he was stable enough
to perform his morning ritual of teeth brushing, face washing,
and hair combing.

Inevitably there were pounding feet, clattering voices,
pounding on the door.

"Aren't you done yet?"

"What is taking you so long? You don't even shave."

"Get out, John. I'm late."

He learned to set his alarm ten minutes earlier, to give himself time to wake up, feel halfway to normal—what was normal?—before ascending the stairs on shaking knees that felt as
if all his muscles had liquefied, and what remained, the joint
itself, had turned to Jell-O.

Determination was his ally. He found he could perform ordinary tasks on will alone. He dragged his ever increasingly unco-
operative body from one duty to another, his lone objective to
hide it all away.

His sixteenth birthday loomed its gigantic dragon's head, a

fearful spectacle. He had anticipated its arrival for so long, but now he stood on shaky ground, as if an earthquake constantly shivered through his foundation.

To be among the *rumschpringa* was a passage to being older, a status of being among a group of youth whose talents, personality, conduct, and of course, appearance, meant something. It was a time for parents to recognize another young man who had started *rumschpringa*, for girls to come say hello, some shyly, others with boldness. A time of finally owning your own horse and buggy—even if the buggy was secondhand, it was all yours.

To drive his own team into the group of youth was almost more than John could handle. Would he pass inspection? Know where to park?

He knew which horse would be his, had heard Dat speak of it. He was pleased, but kept it to himself.

Crayon was newly acquired from the horse dealer, Mervin Lapp. He was a speedy little brown Standardbred. It was a funny name for a horse, but John thought it was cool. His buggy was upholstered in red, and he already planned to use a red "seddly pad," that heavy, usually colorful pad beneath the piece of leather across the shoulders.

He had a new harness. Made of bio-plastic, it gleamed as if it was wet. He couldn't wait to add the chrome and silver, the white plastic rings.

Crayon was no Friesian or Dutch Harness, with all their flamboyance, their arched necks and prancing legs, their tails held like the mast on a ship. They were magnificent, but John loved speed. He loved to go flying down the road with a small horse tugging constantly, wanting to run, an exuberant little horse that could go for ten or fifteen miles without being seriously winded. Crayon was a horse just like that, Daniel said. He drove him, to break him into the long-distance runs, for John, and couldn't get over the speed, the stamina.

They gave him Equi-lete, the premium horse supplement

with his feed, made certain he had access to plenty of water, top-quality hay.

Surely by the time his birthday came, John would be better. The worst of this stubborn strep throat would be gone.

The girls were coming. That was the thought that drove Mam with single-minded purpose. They were all arriving on Christmas Eve, with the seven grandchildren in tow. Packages were wrapped, set on the old drop-leaf table in the living room, candles and snowmen placed at attractive settings, homemade fudge and caramels, chocolate-covered Ritz crackers and peanut butter, snack mix, trays of cheese and ring bologna, dips and vegetables, crackers and fruit. That was only the afternoon snack.

The Christmas dinner itself consisted of steaming roasters of the ever-present *roasht*, ham sliced in soft, fragrant slices that melted away from the knife, a marvelous kettle of mashed potatoes made with butter and cream cheese.

There were peas and carrots, buttered noodles, pitchers of gravy and coleslaw, applesauce, huge platters of lettuce salad, red beet eggs, seven-day sweet pickles. Desserts were spilling from refrigerators and pantry shelves, but the best one was always kept for last. The pecan pie. Rich with molasses and brown sugar, pecans floating to the top in all their majesty, the crust buttery and flaky.

Christmas Day was always the same. Mostly, you stayed out of Mam's way, moved quickly and immediately if she called on you, ate milky, soaked bread bean soup without complaint, and basically turned into a willing but invisible servant. Her face flamed, her eyes snapped, she mopped her face with her white handkerchief, muttered to herself a lot. She kept lists on the magnetic tablet on the refrigerator, crossed them off with the attached ballpoint pen.

The day before Christmas, John felt a lifting of the enveloping dark cloud of despair and pain. He didn't feel quite as sick and dizzy as normal, in the morning, so he figured his day would be another step up to wellness. He wished his mother a good morning, got through his chores, actually had a good amount of the scrambled eggs and cheese on his plate.

He cleaned the forebay carefully, sweeping the concrete over and over until there wasn't a speck of dust or a wisp of hay. He made sure the watering trough was clean, filled with fresh water, and there was plenty of hay down to feed horses.

Anticipation ran high. Even Dat, the normally relaxed, the good-humored and unruffled one, had a light in his eye, a spring to his step, looking forward to spending time with the sons-in-law, his girls, and beloved grandchildren.

It had been a hard pill for him to swallow, too large, lodged in his throat for too long, hearing the news that a new settlement in Kentucky beckoned to the sons-in-law, the girls all struggling in various stages of *die uf-gevva-heit*. When Mam's eyes had flashed, a verbal discourse followed, told her sons-in-law they were on a wild-goose chase. Why Kentucky? It was hot down there. Too far away. Think of us, think of your wives.

Benuel sie Sara Ann, the second daughter, outspoken and opinionated, heaved the sigh that meant her limit had been reached. It was time her mother gave in, realized her girls' plight, and supported them instead of destroying the delicate web of surrender that was slowly being weaved around them.

"Yes, Benuel, yes," she had spoken to her husband. "I know. You will stay if I refuse." And she had the right to do just that. But she did not want to live with the dark knowledge, like a cloud of flapping crows cawing their way into her conscience, that her husband, the one she had promised—promised, mind you—to love, honor, and obey, was laying aside his pioneering spirit, his dream of farming the land, because of her.

Here was her mother, selfishly thinking only of herself, wrecking the delicate stairs she was climbing to submission.

"Mam, stop. You know this isn't easy. But our husbands want to do this, so stop making it harder. We'll go, and survive. It will be good for us to be apart. You know the old saying."

"Hush. I don't want to hear it."

Mam sobbed into a wad of Kleenex, rushed to the bathroom in a wake of sorrow. The girls shrugged, knowing it was her battle. They had their own private ones to fight by themselves, with God's help.

And so, on Christmas Eve, the reunion was exuberant, having not seen each other in many months.

My, the little ones had grown. Hard to imagine, Sylvia Ann so big, grownup, at four years of age. And little Thomas, cherubic, so hale and hearty, after a wan babyhood, racked by gas and colic. And here was Mary, the sweet one. Her namesake. Clasped to her chest, stroking her back, murmuring, Mam could not hold back the tears.

Mary was so shy, quiet, with large eyes and a timid smile. So skinny. Too thin. Mam's heart ached to think of her darling Mary living in Kentucky, in all that heat and humidity. Chiggers. They had chiggers down there.

Mary was five now and would go to school next fall. She couldn't bear the thought of her shy Mary facing the formidable number of classmates, four looming walls adorned with a stern teacher.

For the thousandth time, she wished they hadn't moved to Kentucky. All the grandchildren were growing, healthy, and by all appearances, happy. Children are resilient, the girls had assured her before leaving. Now is the time to go, if we're going to do it. Yes, yes, it was true. At least the children hadn't suffered. They were too young to know the difference.

She clasped little Andrew in a firm hug, even as he squirmed and reached for his father. Only six months old, he did not know his grandmother, which brought a wave of self-pity, hidden behind a bright smile as she reached for the baby she had not seen. She had not been there after the birth of her youngest daughter's first child, named Laura.

Why Laura? She just couldn't imagine. But nowadays, young people named their children different names, like Katherine and Caitlin, Miranda and Zachariah. Too many Sarahs and Bens, her girls said. Opinions aired easily.

She peered into the baby's face, brushed a palm over all that dark hair, laughed and cooed, held him too lightly. Tears welled.

"He looks like you, Lydia. A lot. Hardly a trace of Alvin."

"Now, if I had a baby picture, you'd have the same look about you. Amazing, isn't it, the way our children are mini versions of us?"

Lydia hoped none of them would inherit her mother's excitable ways, but smiled, pleased to have produced a fine son that moved Mam to tears. Mam had not traveled all those miles to attend her birth, or to help with the housework afterward, having been put in her place by her eldest daughter who told her in a phone conversation that if she was coming to Alvin's she had to be quiet about Kentucky and all its shortcomings or any form of self-pity. Lydia would be weak, in no shape for her lamentations.

Lamentations? Where did Susie come up with that long word straight out of the Old Testament? Seriously, here she was being chastised by her own daughter.

But decided silence was, indeed, golden, and her daughters, bless their hearts, had struggles of their own, living so far away. But she lay at night, her eyes wide open, staring at the nighttime ceiling with Elmer snoring beside her. The ghosts of anxiety wafted in and out of the room, shadowy nothings that whispered dire predictions of a difficult birth, an incompetent midwife, and all the myriad possibilities of things gone wrong for a first-time mother.

Oh, *Himmlischer Vater*, she prayed, over and over, which proved to be the only tool to push the hovering ghosts of fear effectively through the walls of the house.

When the news of the baby Andrew arrived, she proceeded to weep, sitting on the old office chair in the warm phone shanty, the door flung open, allowing the June morning sun to stream through the door, a caress of comfort to Mam's worn-out body, having slept very little all week.

A boy, then, named Andrew. All was well. Lydia was doing fine. Nursing. Yes, they had a wonderful midwife. The best.

And Mary had dried her eyes with the corner of her apron, as a fresh torrent of tears were accompanied by a loud sob, followed by a frantic search for a Kleenex or handkerchief, which she was unable to produce, so she simply honked in the underside of her apron. What no one knew wouldn't hurt anyone.

She sang hysterical songs of praise as she barreled down the rows of the strawberry patch, picking strawberries with lightning speed. She noticed the butterflies and house wrens, the gladiolus and petunias, made enough strawberry jam for the neighborhood, and planned to send a bunch home with the girls, at Christmas.

She handed Baby Andrew to Elmer, and reached for little Kore, the two-year-old, neither shy nor skinny, a robust little chap with a decided stutter and a mind filled to capacity with things other people should know.

"Hey, hey, hey, Mommy."

Always the start of some story punctuated with truths and half lies, fabricating an entertaining version of some event in his short life.

And so Mam raised her eyebrows, drew down her upper lip, goading little Kore into a wild and wonderful tale of his runaway cat.

Kore. Why had they named a child Kore? She was reminded of the story in the Old Testament, the rebellious group who railed against the beloved leader, Moses. A fearful thing, and a grandson named after him. Well, it probably wasn't intentional. But still.

And last, there was Sallie. Misspelled, in Mam's opinion. Should be Sally, as it was in the Dick and Jane reader.

Little Sallie, with wisps of pale blond hair. She was over a year old and still not able to make bobbies, those little buttons of hair wrapped around a bendable cracker twisty. Her too pale eyes didn't focus properly, with one eye wandering. She had always been slow, never crawled like other babies, was almost nine months old before she sat up by herself.

Mam had fussed plenty to Elmer, saying there was, indeed, something wrong with that child. She had urged Susie to take her to a pediatrician, but what else could she do with all these miles between them?

And here she was now, hardly enough hair to cover her scalp, the lazy eye wandering worse than ever, pigeon-toed, clumsy, no speech at all.

Mam felt a stab of fear. Poor child. She couldn't see how she could ever live to lead a normal life. She was such an odd-looking little thing.

"How is my little Sallie Ann, sitting in the sand?" she chortled.

Then, worried, she directed a look at her oldest daughter, Susie.

"How is she doing?"

A toss of the proud head. "Fine. Sallie is fine. Doctor said."

Mam in disbelief. "Really?"

"Of course. You think she's retarded."

Mam winced, followed immediately by swift denial. "No, no. I never said that."

"You didn't have to. I know how you feel. Pediatrician says she's developing in the low . . ." A wave of her hand. "Whatever it's called. Can't think of the word. An eye doctor won't see her at this age. She'll need corrective lenses, perhaps surgery. She's not mentally handicapped, which is the proper term."

"Good. I'm so glad to hear it. So glad you took her to a good baby doctor."

After that, she ignored her own concerns about the child, and the Christmas spirit prevailed.

The sons-in-law were friendly, rife with tales of hard work, good beginnings, price of milk holding steady, a future as brilliant as the sun. They talked of unbelievable soil, a climate made for growing corn with the heat and humidity.

Dat raised his eyebrows, skeptical of hay drying.

The barrage of boys descending, first Abner, sailing on the new relationship with the fair Ruthie, enjoying the girls' questions, their delight in his ability to win her, his attempts at humility thinly disguised.

"About time, you old bachelor."

"Is she coming to the Christmas dinner?"

"Go get her. We want to meet her, see what she's like."

"Is she cute? Do you like her?"

Abner held up a hand.

"She'll be here tomorrow. You know who she is. You haven't lived in Kentucky that long."

"We forget. We don't think about the girls in this area much. We have other, more important things to think about now. We're busy farmers' wives, milking cows, driving the baler, washing milkers."

"I bet."

"We do! Every one of us."

They wore smiles of pride, in spite of the ribbing from Abner. Amos and Samuel greeted their sisters with the direct gaze, the calculating measure of siblings, unspoken questions exchanged in one knowing look.

Susie had to hear about her weight gain. Lynda was wan

and thin. Too thin. This too, was noticed, brought into the open.

"Looks like Susie eats your daily portion of fried mush."

"Hey! Stop it. I had three children. Look at Mam."

"You keep going, you'll pass Mam by about fifty pounds by the time you're her age."

"You're mean. Cruel. Rude."

Laughter lifted the accusation to a softer level, the teasing of well-meaning sisters and brothers raised together in the same house, a large, often unbalanced family, where love and fondness steadied the scales.

The girls eyed Samuel, the good-looking one. My, those haircuts. Almost like an Englisher. Why did Dat let them get away with it? It was a bad example for Allen and Daniel.

They had so much to say. Questions were fired, as if from a cannon, in quick succession. "No girlfriend?" they asked Samuel.

"He wishes," Abner answered. "The teacher, Lena Zook."

Samuel denied it, but he had a flaming face to prove the denial invalid.

Dat took all this in, feeling the gratitude, the love, the pride of having his large brood together, all of them healthy, happy. They were raised with imperfections, and he had not always done his share, the farm taking first priority too often. But here they were. Here they all were, plus the happiness of the acquired sons-in-law, the seven grandchildren like miracles.

Coffee flowed from the Adcraft, the two-gallon thermos, set on the countertop, a tea towel on the floor to catch the drips.

No one needed sleep. There was plenty of cold meadow tea for those who didn't drink coffee.

John was greeted too, but his life was too ordinary to discuss. He was quiet, anyway, never had much to add to the general hubbub.

He played with the grandchildren at a card table in the living room, a DeWalt battery lamp perched on the bureau, the white light illuminating the Candy Land board. Mary and Sylvia Ann were clearly enamored of their tall uncle John. Giggling, picking up the colorful cards, they watched anxiously for the dreaded candy cane that would send them back to the place their little plastic men had started.

Sara Ann was outspoken, never weighing consequences.

"What's wrong with John, Mam? He looks bleached. His face is so white it's almost lime green."

"Oh, the strep throat." Lifted a finger to her lips, rolled her eyes in John's direction.

"Why the secret?"

Mam more emphatic. "Sh. He doesn't like to talk about it."

Sara Ann shrugged her shoulders. John heard every word, thinking this was not what he wanted to be noticed for.

Mam set out trays of cookies, chocolate walnut fudge, a bowl of fruit with a cream cheese dip in the center. There was a tall blue canister of Planter's mixed nuts, one of the cashews, and one of honey roasted peanuts.

Every year, Mam bought these gigantic tins of nuts, and only a few handfuls were ever eaten, so she'd feed them to the birds, who would also largely ignore them, till they lay, bleached and useless in the spring sunlight. But it just wasn't Christmas without the variety of Planter's nuts.

She was making oyster stew, standing at the kitchen range, the smell of browning butter wafting to the kitchen table, a quart of oysters taken from the refrigerator, then another.

"Mmm. Smells wonderful."

"We came the whole way from Kentucky for that oyster stew, Mam."

Benuel, Sara Ann's husband, was full of gallantries, an eagerness to please. But it grated like sandpaper, now. *All the way from Kentucky, all right.*

She gave him a benevolent smile, then turned back to the stove to hide her grimace of endurance.

John finished the third game of Candy Land, then came to the long kitchen table, keeping his eyes averted. How many more of his sisters thought he was the color of a lime?

"John, you look so pale." It was Sara Ann, again.

"I had strep throat, you know." He shrugged, self-conscious now.

"Strep throat doesn't last for months. Mam, did you take this boy for tests lately?"

"No. Not lately."

"He looks awful."

All eyes turned to John as he picked up a glass of meadow tea, turned to go to the living room, back to the card table and the safety of the DeWalt lamp, away from his sisters, their piercing eyes like vultures, sizing him up.

"You should put him on Plexus."

"What's that?"

"It's a nutritional supplement program. Something fairly new."

"Newer than Sisel?"

"What about Relive?"

"No, Plexus is better."

And so forth. The discussion rolled into the living room, swirled around John, tales of magical healing from Epstein-Barr virus, fibromyalgia, Crohn's disease, even cancer of the thyroid, leukemia in children.

"You can talk about that stuff all you want. I guarantee it's all a big money racket." The conversation screeched to a stunned silence, as all eyes turned toward Abner, the stalwart one, the one with the undisputed knowledge.

"Hey, watch what you say. You don't know how soon you might need a good supplement," Susie said, a huge advocate of Plexus herself, religiously swallowing all manner of pills and powders promising instant and long-lasting weight loss. Which, obviously, hadn't done much so far, but she hadn't taken them that long. Not really. Besides, if you paid a hundred dollars a month—more than that—you weren't willing to admit it wasn't a successful endeavor.

"Abner, you know what? Someone who's been healthy their life long shouldn't judge those of us who aren't."

"Nothing wrong with you, by the looks of it."

Susie gave him a look.

"I have adrenal problems. I'm often tired, exhausted by day's end. No get up and go. That sort of thing."

"And Plexus helps?"

"Why, of course."

Mam stirred the oyster stew, tasted with a spoon, added a half teaspoon of salt. She turned to listen to the conversation, watched John's reaction with narrowed eyes, wondering what he was thinking. She knew, with a mother's intuition, that he felt a lot worse than he would ever want anyone to know.

She was suspecting Lyme disease, in spite of her husband's unwillingness to hear her out.

Lyme disease was rampant, especially in Pennsylvania.

Look at the way this boy lived in grassy fields, woods, swampy lowlands. He was always picking ticks from his clothes. He never had a rash or a bull's-eye, though, that infamous circular splotch of red where a tick had been attached.

All around them, people contracted Lyme disease, visited their family doctor, faithfully ingested a ten-day course of antibiotics, and continued their headlong plunge of misery into a deep tunnel of weakness, fear, stiffness, and pain.

Because of the lack of testing and medical support, many of them took the natural route, swallowing handfuls of herbs, drinking glasses of tinctures in dubious amounts. By all accounts, it was a scourge, a plague of Egypt. So much unexplained misery. There was never enough funding for research.

Mam's eyes went back to John, as she absorbed the lively pros and cons of expensive herbal supplements. She'd have to ask John. Perhaps he would welcome an arsenal of pills to help him feel better.

Or perhaps he was merely going through a growth spurt.

CHAPTER 7

JOHN ENJOYED THE SISTERS AND THEIR CHILDREN IMMENSELY, IN spite of his ongoing struggle with debilitating weakness. There was no way to explain the waves of tiredness that surged through his body. It was frightening, and there was no rhyme or reason to the pattern.

The day after Christmas the constant movement, the crying babies and yelling children, the musical toys, and the bang of dishes in the sink grated on his ears with noises seemingly magnified times ten. His head ached, filled to bursting capacity with a cacophony of sounds like a fire engine siren.

He knew his grandparents, Uncle John and Aunt Naomi, Uncle Ben and Aunt Sylvia, would be arriving for the sake of the girls, a sort of second Christmas dinner served. There was nothing on earth he wanted less. He couldn't imagine getting through the day.

His right shoulder was so painful, he sneaked a jar of Unker's from the medicine cabinet in the bathroom downstairs. Unker's was a deep, penetrating pain-relief ointment for arthritis, colds, restless legs, aching joints. That was it. It was just aching joints.

Up to his bedroom, the plastic jar in his pocket, he applied a liberal amount, blinking furiously as the menthol scent ripped through his nostrils. He persisted, waiting for the soothing relief the label promised.

His whole room was permeated with the overpowering scent. He crept to his bedroom door and locked it. None of his brothers needed to stick their nosy heads in the door. Or the children.

He tried to block out noise, the chaos that assaulted his senses. He felt a descending cloud of doom, the urge to get away, find total respite from ordinary life. The motion and swirl of intensified color and sound, the kaleidoscope of bewildering action increasingly immobilized his well-being.

The vague thought that he might die came to live solidly in his mind, and stayed. With it came anxiety so real his heartbeat accelerated until his breath came out in short hard gasps, eliminating the shoulder pain, the weakness.

Suddenly, he was thrown into a galaxy of terror. A heart-stopping panic held him in its grip, took away the ability to harbor a coherent thought.

This was a primal fear beyond anything he had ever experienced, that went on and on. He grasped the covers for protection, his fingers clawing at pillowcases, unable to grasp a solid object. Afloat in his sea of dread, he washed up on towering, heartstopping crests of gigantic waves, to plunge into deep troughs of hopelessness that only death could stop.

He realized that sweat was pouring from every pore of his skin. His palms were wet, his forehead streaming, his shirt that had been slid off his shoulder bunched and wet, the greasy shoulder broken away, a separate appendage that no longer belonged to him.

The room whirled around him in a dizzying spiral, turning clockwise, diagonally, then horizontally, slowed a few degrees, before spilling him into a world of blackened nothingness, a place where, mercifully, there were no thoughts, no sound, and no chaos.

He awoke to the sound of frenzied banging on a hard surface. He struggled to open his eyes, to answer the person who wanted to talk to him, but was held in the clutches of weakness. A key grated in the lock.

His father burst through the door, pale-faced, his eyes wide with alarm.

"John!"

He hurried to the bed, followed by his mother and sisters, their faces ashen.

"Are you all right?"

"What is that smell?

"Here. Mary, Sylvia Ann, no. Susie, take them downstairs."

Children were ushered back out the door.

John turned, lay on his back. His eyes opened. A sickening wave of nausea pulled up the contents of his stomach, hurled the whole sordid mess on the gray rug. He heaved and retched. He felt his mother smooth back his hair, hollering at Lydia to get a bucket with water and Lysol.

Miserably, he finished, lay back, breathing fitfully.

His father knelt by his bed, after the rug had been taken away, the floor cleaned. His eyes were kind, concerned, a magnet that drew John's sobs of misery.

He cried deep sounds of crippling despair, his young shoulders heaving, his body twisting into a fetal position, ashamed of this helpless display of weakness.

"What happened, John? Just tell us what is wrong."

"Why did you have this jar of Unker's?"

His mother's question instilled a deep sense of privacy, a refusal to allow her access to his suffering. The importance of keeping everything to himself overrode everything he had ever been taught about manners, decency.

She didn't need to know. She'd blab all his symptoms to anyone who would listen, and they would pick up the pieces, carry them home under the microscope of their highly esteemed opinions, sending him to Hershey Hospital, or Harrisburg, for the diagnosis of cancer, a round of chemotherapy, and death.

Just when his life was beginning, they'd bring the sentence of death.

So his silence protected him.

The Christmas season ended in dry-mouthed fear, his family whispering in areas of the house that kept their surmising.

"He's so weird. Why won't he say what's wrong?"

"He's very sick."

"You think he's losing his mind? Schizophrenic, maybe?"

Mam was paralyzed with fear. She had no idea what was wrong with John, other than Lyme disease, but didn't think that would render anyone mute.

Everyone tiptoed now, silent, afraid to think of returning to Kentucky, after all this, leaving the family with the specter of the unknown.

John came downstairs, after showering, ate a dish of Froot Loops cereal, sat on the couch and smiled at little Kore—a weak, hesitant smile, but a show of returned normality.

It was Lydia, the youngest sister, who he confided in, speaking quietly, telling her he had an aching shoulder, had gone to rub Unker's on it, but must have passed out.

Lydia did not voice an opinion, asked no questions, merely sat holding her baby, listened without making eye contact.

"I have been weak and tired. Dizzy in the morning. It's . . . sorta hard to do chores. Seems like I get tired easily."

No verdict, no instructions from Lydia. Merely, "Perhaps a doctor could help."

John nodded, but was unconvinced.

The leave-taking was hard for the girls, each one being brave in their own way, blinking back tears that hovered at the surface, hiding it all by settling children in car seats, saying, "There you go, sweetie," handing out pacifiers, bags of pretzels for the toddlers.

The sons-in-law were bright eyed, helpful, eager to return to dearly held farms and animals, hoping the neighbors had had no problem with the milking.

They pitied their wives standing awkwardly as they clung to their mother, eyes bright with swimming tears that finally spilled over.

Benuel wondered if it was too much, if the separation was actually worth the move, then justified it by thinking of Isaac and Rebecca of old. Love between a man and his wife would enable the adhering to one another, to be able to leave family easily. Even nature taught that lesson well.

John stood in the background, his hands in his pockets. Pale-faced, his eyes were dark pools of shame. Lydia looked to see her younger brother standing weakly amid the jostle of strong, healthy siblings in the prime of life. She made her way to him, grasped his shoulders.

"Look at me, John."

He raised his face, the sad, dark eyes a mirror into his tortured soul.

"You're going to be all right. Nothing is going to happen to you that the doctors and your Mam and Dat can't handle. You will be OK. Remember that. God doesn't give us more than He gives us strength to handle. You do know that, don't you, John?"

He dropped his head, nodded.

"I love you, John. You'll get through this."

He squeezed his eyes shut, drew his upper lip down over his lower, his face contorted as he buried it in his large, rumpled red handkerchief.

Pity grasped her in its grip, as she saw her mother fussing over her beloved and highly esteemed daughters, hoping she would remember to take care of John.

In January, she wrote her mother a long letter, after she thought long and hard, talked it over with Alvin, allowed him to read it. With misgiving, she posted it on a wet, cold, Kentucky morning, walking out to the mailbox with a prayer on her lips, hoping her mother would receive the words the way she had written them.

The next planned phone call confirmed her fears. It had not gone down well.

Her mother was terse, tightlipped, asking Lydia what she meant by the letter. Her feelings were hurt. She had enough, dealing with John's illness.

The martyr again, a skill honed well, over the years.

"Mam, I meant well, OK? I'm just so worried about John. He's just so, well, he's not noticed enough, just the way I wrote."

"He is now, with all his sickness."

"Did you have him tested?"

"Not yet, Lydia. He has an appointment the sixteenth of this month."

"Good. I'm so glad. Just don't let the big boys tease him, please, Mam. He tries so hard to be cool. That's why he won't talk to anyone. You'll let me know the results of the Lyme test?"

"Oh, of course I will. You know that."

Lydia sighed. "I just wish I was closer, Mam."

"I know. Oh, I know. But still, we can't complain now. It is what it is. I do take your letter seriously, and I'll try my best to stay calm and stop asking questions. It's just so hard. It goes against my nature so horribly. I have to know things, figure them out, have a solution at my beck and call."

Lydia laughed. Dear Mam. Couldn't stay angry if she wanted to. Bless her heart. Surely there was a special place in Heaven for mothers all over the world.

On a dark night, when there was no moon at all, just before his doctor's appointment in town, John lay in bed, unable to sleep, so tired it seemed as if the floor would open up and swallow his whole bed, and there was no strength to defy this yawning pit of gravity.

He learned to breathe deeply. Inhale. Exhale. Calm, calm. Tonight, it did no good. Sleep simply was not available. His bed was his prison, holding him in chains of misery.

He got up, walked to the bathroom in the dark, opened the faucet halfway, so he wouldn't disturb anyone with the loud gush of water. He took a tepid drink of water from the plastic, communal cup. He went back to his room, but sat on the edge of his bed, his elbows propped on his knees, his head hanging low, too weary to contemplate crawling back into bed.

Was there no one who could help him? No one out there he could turn to during these nightly upheavals, when sleep eluded him like wisps of fog?

Mam would say God, but God wasn't too well known to him, yet. He had heard about God and the Bible and Jesus and the disciples, all of it, in church. He read his Bible occasionally, but mostly, God was still a mystery, not really a friend he could confide in.

What kept him from trying?

Slowly, awkwardly, he slid to his knees and turned, lifted both hands in the position of prayer, and whispered, "God, it's me, John. Help me to best this thing at night. I'm scared. It's awful. Don't let me lose my mind the way some people do. Help me, please."

He was halfway to a standing position when he remembered to say Amen. He collapsed into bed, as powerless as if his limbs were pancake syrup, and lay on his side, pulling up his knees to ward off the pain in both of his legs.

Like a severe toothache, it roared along his muscles, receded, and came creeping back. He thought of the plastic container of Unker's, knew he could never smell that mentholated odor again without being transported straight back to that awful day on second Christmas, when he'd been gripped by a craziness he would never forget.

He groaned in pain, rolled onto his back, and lifted his knees to a V position. He tired to think pleasant thoughts, of times past. Fishing in the Juniata River, the way the water bugs skated across the muddy water in the backwash from the creek. The time Daniel hooked a snapping turtle, landing him on the dock, sending Allen galloping back to the safety of the riverbank. The turtle wasn't very big, for a snapping turtle, but big enough to give them an awful scare.

He must have dozed for a few minutes, but was jerked back awake by his heartbeat going out of control, yet again.

This time, there was no stopping it. Carried along on a wave of sheer panic, he leaped from the bed, paced back and forth across the room, his hands gripping the sides of his head. There were no thoughts, only a yawning chasm of fear in which he would be hurled. Thick fog obliterated all normal thinking. A despair clutched his chest, squeezed the small, rapid breaths until he was gasping.

His heart hammered violently, thumping in his chest, until one thought pierced through the thick fog that rendered his brain incapable.

He was dying. Death would come, take him. He knew with startling clarity that he was not ready. It was too cruel, this sudden dying at a young age.

He began to cry. Helpless sobs of fear and despair racked his weary body. He had to have help. He needed someone, anyone, to stand by him. He was deeply ashamed to let his parents see him in such a state, especially his mother, who would ply him with all manner of inquiries, rambling away on subjects that did not pertain to his symptoms, heaping more confusion and fear on top of everything else.

He had often been alone in his life. He actually preferred the solitary life, the fishing, hunting alone, never with Dat or his brothers. He had never experienced this kind of terrifying separation, however. He barely knew who he was, this sick, exhausted, foggy-brained individual who was obviously not going to survive.

He opened his bedroom door with shaking hands slick with sweat. Stifling sobs, he made his way slowly down the stairs, clutching the smooth wooden railing. He hesitated when he reached the living room.

A fresh wave of panic propelled him to the open door of his parents' bedroom, shivering, shaking and crying.

"Dat."

Instantly, his mother's head shot straight up.

"What? What? Who is it?"

"It's me. John."

She leaped from the bed, grabbed her housecoat from the hook on the door, came to stand beside him. Dat followed, after opening a dresser drawer to extract a clean pair of trousers.

"What's wrong, John?"

His mother's voice was high with her own fear. She grabbed for the battery lamp on the end table, then realized the battery wasn't in it. She'd put it on the charger. Fumbling, she made her way to the kitchen.

His father came to stand beside him, the deep, heart-wrenching sobs from his son like a dagger to his own heart.

"What is it, John? Don't you feel well?"

John shook his head.

Mam clicked on the battery lamp, peered into her son's tortured face. Clearly, there was something creating this poor boy's misery. She had to know, so the questions began, pelting him like a snowball fight with his siblings.

"Are you having a spiritual battle?"

"Do you feel physically sick, or is it mental?"

"Does God seem far away?"

Tell me, John. Tell me what's wrong. Tell us. Tell us. Tell us.

Those two words turned into an endless circle, a bewildering meld of sound that turned into one word that squeezed his brain until the pain above his eyes was white hot. He gripped his head, shook it from side to side, like a wounded animal.

"Mary, stop."

Dat pulled her aside, gently, as she began to cry.

"John, if you don't feel well, why don't you bring your sleeping bag down on the rug here in the living room, and I'll be on the couch?"

John nodded, turned to get the required sleeping bag on the shelf in his closet. He dragged a pillow off his bed, his sobs already subsiding.

Dat would understand. He would not have to know everything. In his own simple way, Dat had an intuition, a knowing of John's need to keep this hideous sickness to himself.

He spread the sleeping bag, arranged the pillow, threw himself down, still crying uncontrollably. Mam hovered, wringing her hands, clearly beside herself, unable to go back to bed.

He watched his father bring his own pillow, find a soft blanket. His white T-shirt and clean denim pants, his pale bare feet, the graying beard and toweled hair, all took on the appearance of a guardian angel, complete with soft, flowing white gown and majestic, celestial wings.

Here was John's help. He had found it. God had heard him, after all. He was not alone, would never have to be separated again. Here was his father, the silent rock he could depend on.

And slowly he slid into a twitching, restless sleep.

There was a strained atmosphere at the breakfast table, with John still in his sleeping bag by the couch. All traces of Dat having spent the night there had been removed.

"'S wrong with the baby?"

A thumb jerked in John's direction.

Mam stood by the stove, dark circles visible behind the lenses of her glasses, stress emanating from her face, the set of her shoulders. She was flipping eggs with the hard motion that meant there was trouble on hand.

"How come he's in his sleeping bag?"

It was a simple question, not unkind, from Abner.

Mam lifted a warning finger to her lips, drew down her eyebrows, and shook her head.

One by one, breakfast eaten, drivers arrived, six of them out the door, casting questioning looks in John's direction. Dat's face was stern, gave nothing away. Mam was like a simmering pot of nerves, so they did not ask any more questions, figured it was bad timing.

The sixteenth of January found John sitting in the waiting room of the family physician, pale, thinner, his chapped lips bitten to shreds, nervously clutching a magazine in front of his face, hiding his weakness from the world.

Of course, it was his mother who accompanied him, sitting in the front seat with the driver, making senseless conversation scattered with lighthearted laughter. She always acted happy in front of drivers.

"John Stoltzfus."

He started, laid down the magazine, looked to his mother, who stood, waiting for him to go first. He had no idea where to go, with all those eyes watching him, so he made a motion for her to go first, an irritated expression on his face.

He found his mother always quieted if he used anger, an expression of resentment, the handy unscalable wall he built around himself like a tall privacy fence. It worked. His mother would gaze at him without the one hundred questions just below the surface, and he was safe.

They sat in complete silence, John examining the charts on the wall, his mother looking rapidly through her checkbook, producing a pen, her brow furrowing as she concentrated.

"Hello there. John?"

He looked up to see a nurse, her body straining against the confines of a too-tight uniform, the buttons pulling the fabric in all directions. Her hair was drawn back into a high ponytail, her round face like a cinnamon roll. She smelled good, like honey-suckle that bloomed in June.

"How are you, John?"

He shrugged, glaring at his mother.

She took in a breath, getting ready to speak, then remembered, closed her mouth.

"I'm . . . I dunno. Weak. Tired."

"All righty, John. We'll get your vitals, let you talk to the doctor, how's that?"

Temperature, blood pressure, height and weight.

He'd lost nineteen pounds. He was almost five foot eleven.

"Cold out there, huh?"

"It is," his mother nodded.

"Could use more snow. I never like to see bare ground in January."

"Oh, me neither. Not good for the crops."

"That's right. You're farmers, then? You too, John?"

He nodded.

"Do you like it?"

Nodded again.

"All right, we'll let you talk to the doctor then. Take care. Bye-bye."

More silence. John sat on the table, the wide roll of white paper beneath him, his mother on a chair, looking heavy and uncomfortable. She had lint on her black sweater. Her shoes were ugly black lace-up leather shoes that would have looked better on Abner. But then, all middle-aged or older Amish women weren't exactly beauties, the way they had all those children. And most of them mixed up food with joy. Or the other way around.

Blessedly, the fog in his head had dissipated, leaving him with a sense of being centered, like coming home after a long journey.

A knock on the door, and Dr. Stevenson entered, shook hands with his mother and then, with him. There were a few kind, professional words of greeting. He looked at his chart, thumbed the tip of his nose, said "Hm."

His hair—what was left of it—was graying, and he had brown inquisitive eyes like a squirrel. He wore a shirt the color of lilacs and pressed gray trousers.

"So, you're not feeling well."

John shook his head.

"Can you tell me about it?"

"Just sort of weak. Tired. My . . . well, everything hurts."

He didn't have to know about the horrifying nights.

"Hm. Sounds like Lyme. You had a tick bite?

John shook his head.

"Never?"

"Not that I know of."

"Well, we'll do a blood test."

He checked John's heart with a stethoscope, listened to his lungs, checked his reflexes, prodded his stomach, shone a light in his ears and down his throat, then paused, turned to Mam.

"You're aware of the cost of the test?"

"No."

"It's expensive."

"We'll do whatever it takes," Mam said, her voice taking on that wobbly quality that John could so easily detect.

"So. We'll go ahead with that. We'll get the lab technician to draw the blood, and you'll be asked to drop the package at the FedEx place. The test is called the Western blot. It goes to Palo Alto, in California, to a place called IGeneX Labs. It's a very good facility. You should have the results in less than two weeks. Now, are there any questions?"

John shook his head, in spite of wanting to know so much more. The more he kept his thoughts and fears to himself, the less his mother could distribute his failings and shortcomings among the community, his brothers, everyone.

Mam, of course, told the doctor about his nighttime upheavals, the crying, everything. Shamefaced, John bent his head, his shoulders hunched, afraid to look at the doctor. Fifteen years old, driven to sleep on the living room floor like an insecure two-year-old.

He listened closely, felt the doctor's eyes on him. As Mam finished with her story—she didn't know the half of it—there was a sigh, a squeak of the chair.

"Not unusual. One of the worst things about chronic Lyme disease is anxiety. We're not sure what causes this, but there are many other neurological symptoms associated with Lyme. It seems to be extremely prevalent in teenaged children. Depression, insomnia, extreme fear . . . it seems to be the pattern. Since John has no idea of having been bitten, no bull's-eye rash, the Lyme bacteria has likely been hiding in his cells for quite some time. It's a nasty little organism called *Borrelia burgdorferi*, causes a bunch of mischief. If you want, I can prescribe an antidepressant like Zoloft, or Xanax. I think in his case you would find it very helpful."

A hand came down on John's knee.

"Good luck, there, buddy. You'll be just fine. I'll call Reba to take you to the lab."

He shook hands with Mam, patted John's shoulder.

He watched the dark maroon-colored blood being drawn from the needle into the vial, imagined his own blood alive with horrible little creatures that would, eventually, cause his demise. How could one doctor and one test do any good if they swarmed and cavorted all through his system, hiding in cells, slowly causing him to become crippled?

He heard the low murmuring of his mother, talking, talking to the doctor, the answers she so desperately sought being murmured back.

CHAPTER 8

THE RESULTS OF THE LYME TEST WERE NEGATIVE.

"Negative?" Mam screeched, then proceeded to blame Doctor Stevenson, the lab in California, the unsuspecting nurse who had drawn the blood.

There was a vein of panic in her voice.

Dat sat on his kitchen chair, unruffled, contemplating this unexpected news, a cup of coffee going from lukewarm to cold. He was surprised at the result of the test, but couldn't see how making a fuss would help John in any way.

So he looked at John, said, "Well, good. No Lyme disease. That means you'll be better real soon. Probably some leftover bug from your strep throat."

John was pale and perspiring, his eyes riveted to his shoes.

Suddenly, he looked up.

"I didn't have strep throat. That test was negative too."

"It was?" Dat raised an eyebrow.

Mam turned from the oven, her face red, holding the tooth-pick she had inserted into the chocolate cake on the rack.

"Yes, it was. But what else could it have been? His tonsils were covered with white splotches. I'm sure it was strep."

"Well, we'll let it go, then, this testing. A thousand dollars down the tube, but at least we know."

John agreed, but felt bad about the money his parents had spent for nothing. He'd work hard, help make up for it.

And for a time, it seemed, life returned to normal.

John experienced a fair amount of hope, doing chores, helping around the farm, cleaning stables until he had to lean on a gate, breathing hard, keeping the weakness at bay, determined, this time, to beat any returning symptoms.

He returned to his bedroom at night, often spending hours lying awake, or falling into a restless half-awake stupor, suspended between sleep and mental alertness. He pushed himself out of bed every morning by a sheer force of will, tried to keep up some semblance of normalcy.

Abner was thinking of marriage by mid-February. John heard him ask his mother how soon he should ask Ruthie if they wanted a November wedding.

"Abner! My word. You haven't been dating very long," she breathed.

"Long enough. A year. Over a year. She's not too young."

Mam stretched her features into her prophetess from the Scriptures face, as John secretly called it. It was the expression she had when she felt calm and good and wise, then set out to liberally douse her sons with the accumulated enlightenment of her years. It was the face of answers, good in her own sight, and one that made John grind his teeth in irritation. She was a good mother, and John knew he loved her very much. It was just that she was so dreadfully full of herself half the time. If she wasn't worrying, or panicking about stupid worthless stuff like bugs on her marigolds, slugs on her cabbage, or if Samuel was ever going to ask Lena Zook for a date, she was philosophizing.

How did she ever consider any of her sons, even the most handsome one, good enough for Lena? She was by far the most beautiful girl John had ever met. Not that beauty ever had anything to do with it, Mam reminded him from time to time, which was another thing she figured she'd better tell her boys, but didn't mean at all.

Ever since he had had Lena Zook for his teacher in eighth grade, he compared every other girl to her, and they all fell woefully short.

It wasn't just the fact that she was beautiful. She may not even be as pretty in the classic sense as many others. It was the aura of sweetness and light, her constant enthusiasm and joy, that drew John from his ongoing battle with darkness, the weakness that kept him bogged down in the sticky mud of depression. Just thinking of her helped him to look ahead to the future, harboring a kind of hope. Not that he could ever have her, of course, but perhaps someday he would find someone who would instill in him that same longing, that same promise.

Her blond hair, combed back so sleekly, like a glistening, satin cloth. The white covering, the V of her neckline, where her cape was pinned to her dress, the many different colors she wore like a field of wildflowers. She pinned her apron high on her waist, perfectly, her small feet encased in all manner of shoes or sneakers, one pair as neat and classy as the one before.

She fascinated John—the lightness with which she moved, playing baseball or volleyball, kickball with the lower grades, an athlete if he ever saw one.

And he could only bumble around the playground on oversized feet and the grace of an ox, squinting from behind his thick lenses, his rabbit teeth exposed every time he'd smiled or laughed. He'd dressed carefully, been picky with the shirts he wore, as if that made any difference.

John gritted his teeth when he heard Mam wondering aloud why Samuel wouldn't ask Lena for a date. She seemed to have already picked her out for a future daughter-in-law.

Well, if he could help it, she'd never find out how he felt about Lena. He couldn't bear to have his feelings analyzed, picked apart, talked about, until not one smidgen of his life was viewed with respect.

In the spring, when March winds had subsided and the rain had soaked the good earth with necessary moisture, John developed a fever, followed by a red rash over his chest and down his arms.

He lay on the couch, warding off his mother's breathless ministrations by his anger, the one thing he could handily use to protect his dignity.

"But John, it can't be the measles. Or mumps. Or chicken pox. You had all your immunizations. The booster before school."

But John . . . but John . . . on and on.

"Which do you prefer, Tylenol or ibuprofen? Let's try aloe vera juice for the rash. Do you mind? What about this?"

She drew a bath for him with water hot enough to cook a chicken. Steam rolled from the bathroom in great, wet clouds, the odor of vinegar overpowering.

"What is in that bath water?"

"Epsom salt, vinegar, and baking soda?"

Why did she put a question to a simple answer? She sounded like she was trying to talk like a teenage girl.

"Mam," John explained patiently, "I'm not getting in that tub of hot water with this high temperature. It can't be good."

"Sure it is. It's a detox. Gets the toxins out. Now listen to me."

John closed the bathroom door, then sat down on the lid of the commode, his elbows on his knees, his head bent, shaking and freezing cold, then so hot the sweat ran down his face. There was no way he was getting into that boiling cauldron. His temperature would soar to 106°, then 107°, and he'd get seizures or something.

He got off his perch on the commode, to riffle the hot water with his hands, to make her think he was actually in it, and after the allotted time she'd told him, he opened the drain to let the water out, returned to the couch, and turned his back.

She was in the garden, so what she didn't know didn't hurt her. When the fever stayed over a period of three days, and no home remedy did anything to bring it down, he was trundled off to Doctor Stevenson's office in town. Again, the same bright conversation with the driver, the same ushering into the room, the same piercing questions.

Yes, he had been better. Yes, he was working.

Good. Good. A bout of the flu. Leftover bug from the winter months. Tylenol for fever. A prescription for the rash.

And with that he was sent home.

With the spring work in the fields, cows having calves, the manure pit full to overflowing, Dat worried, working from dawn to dusk, literally.

John moved from the couch, after his temperature slid back to almost normal, was given light work, but felt the weakness creep back into his arms and legs. He told no one, willed himself forward, the soles of his feet as if on fire with pain. The rash receded, his chest and arms appeared normal.

When the summer sun shone so hot it felt like a heater turned directly on his back, Dat found his son passed out beside the hay rake, the sensible horses obedient to John's single "whoa" before tumbling off the seat, crawling away so sick the world turned sideways.

"John. John . . ."

The words crept like an unwelcome invader into John's consciousness. Slowly, the long, hot grass waving in the bright summer sun made him return to the world he had blissfully escaped. His father was bent over him, his face ruddy, his eyes calm, kind.

No questions, merely a waiting.

John struggled to sit up, willed back the waves of nausea, groaned loudly, before turning his head aside and relieving himself of his half-digested breakfast.

He wiped his mouth, shook his head.

"I don't know, Dat."

"I don't know, either."

"Too hot, I guess."

"Could be."

"You think there's something seriously wrong with me?"

"I doubt it."

Three words etched in gold, outlined in crystal cut diamonds. John hung on to every word, tucked them securely away. If his father thought he would be all right, then he probably would.

"You're a growing boy. You're like a horse in his fourth year. The hard year, my father used to say. Your body is changing, growing fast, using up all the nutrients, likely leaving you with the scraps."

John smiled weakly. "Hm."

The following morning, it happened again.

He sat up in bed, the whole room went vertical, and everything went black. He was brought back by the banging of the bathroom door, heated words from Allen to Daniel, then made his way to his clothes closet, hanging on to the bed frame, the doorknob, anything to support his weight, with legs like quivering jelly.

At the breakfast table, his face was ashen.

Abner was kind, spreading peanut butter on toast, dunking it into his black coffee.

"Only *daudies* eat that slop. Ruthie ever seen you eat that?"

"Look, you eat your eggs, and mind your own business."

"Pass that sausage gravy before you eat it all."

"'S wrong with you, John? You look like a scared rabbit."

Abner stopped chewing, his eyes rested on John's face.

"You still sick?"

"Nah." A shrug of the shoulders.

"You need a dose of horse wormer. Skinny looking."

"He's just losing his baby fat."

Of course, Mam heard everything, came over to the table with another stack of pancakes, piping hot. They disappeared, followed by liberal squirts of the Aunt Jemima syrup that Mam bought by the gallon and put in plastic squeeze bottles.

"You know, someone should take a picture of this. Perfect stack of pancakes. Someone could use it in a magazine as an advertisement for pancake mix."

"I don't use mix, and you know it, Marcus." Mam said from where she stood at the stove. "I make all my pancakes from scratch. Nothing store-bought about them."

She put her hands on her hips saucily, joking with her boys.

"No pancakes, John?"

His mother hovering, questioning. A hand to his forehead.

"You OK?"

"Of course he's OK. All this coddling since Christmas. No wonder he's sick and tired half the time."

Samuel spoke with his mouth full, glared at John. He had no time for weakling younger brothers.

Samuel was impossibly handsome, even at the breakfast table. He had clean-cut features, a youthful vitality, a no-nonsense approach to life, pushing forward to get the job done, but often running dangerously low on patience and compassion. B and S Structures was already looking into his climb up the ladder from foreman to manager.

His father entered the kitchen, giving him a stern reprimand.

"Enough, Samuel. Till we know what's going on with John's health, I'd thank you to keep your opinions to yourself."

"Father has spoken," Marcus said, ducking his head to his pancakes but glancing up to watch Samuel's reddening face with interest.

The day was sultry, humid, the kind of day that taxed man and beast alike. The whole valley lay in an uncomfortable stupor, the sky brassy with heat, the air still and hot, buzzing with blowflies and mean wasps that stung anything within reach. Cows waded into the pond for relief, the flies' torment a ceaseless thing they tried to quell with backward swings of their massive heads, tongues stretching like heavy pink rubber.

Horses hitched to hay wagons and balers had to be rested beneath overhanging branches, fear of overexertion taking first priority for sensible farmers.

They sat beneath the shade of some massive tree, watched a faraway English neighbor barrel along in his latest acquisition, a huge Ford tractor with a baling machine that spewed perfect round bales at regular intervals, which would be gathered up with a skid loader outfitted with forks and loaded on trailers.

Oh well, it was the way of the Amish, clinging to tradition.

Thou shalt not covet thy neighbor's tractor. And they didn't. Better to remain content, at peace with the brethren. You couldn't put a dollar value on that.

Storms in the air, Dat thought to himself. He saw the hairs on his forearms raise, felt the friction on the metal seat. He hoped the humidity would be banished from the valley, driven by a good strong thunderstorm, the kind that brought an inch or two of rain, a clear sunrise, and refreshing winds.

He heard the sound of clinking buckles on harnesses as he drove the rake to the barn. He viewed his fields with satisfaction, eyed the sturdy, deep green stalks of corn, imagined the yellow ears, kernels crowded, dented, deepening to a maize color. He could smell the pungent aroma of the cut stalks and ears, chopped into corn silage, blown into the silo by the power of the PTO shaft.

Nothing like good silage to boost milk production and lift a man's spirits.

He was thankful for the good times. He was grateful for his own good health, the ability to run the farm with help from his wife and John.

John was the one thing that worried him immensely, with a

sick kind of anxiety that bordered on dread. Clearly, there was more going on than anyone cared to admit, but his refusal to see a doctor, in the face of those bouts of losing consciousness, was worrisome.

To force him to go was the answer. Or was it?

Some things in life simply couldn't be spelled out in black and white, so he'd give it another week or two, see if he'd have another stint of passing out.

He just wished the older boys would go easy on him. Good-natured ribbing was one thing, but these accusations of babying him were another. He had a deep-seated hunch about John's anxiety, remembering his own spiritual awakening around the same age John was now.

He'd lived in fear of Jesus returning in the sky, and him a blackened sinner, unable to secure a space in Heaven. He had lived in fear of the devil, thought he might become visible, to him alone, scaring himself witless.

He, too, had lain awake, cried at night, begged God to forgive his sins, all to no avail. At first. Then, slowly, grace filtered through, light and love and acceptance came through the power of Jesus Christ. He was baptized, became an upstanding young member of the church, and never had any reason to doubt this conversion of faith.

The thing that bothered him most, though, was the presence of actual physical symptoms—a fever, a rash, his joint pain, all that crippling exhaustion. No Lyme disease, so what, exactly, was going on?

He found his frustrated wife with two bushels of tomatoes and flies swarming through the house, wash on the line, the kitchen thermometer revealing a mind-boggling ninety-one degrees, coupled by a severe headache.

"You need to drink more water, Mary. I know how much you love tea, but in weather like this, you'll become dehydrated. That's why you have a headache. Where's John?"

When she didn't answer, he knew he'd said the wrong thing. He walked up behind her, put an arm around her shoulders and said, "Sorry, Mary."

She shrugged her shoulders and slid away from him.

"Don't touch me. It's too hot."

"Where's John?"

"I have no idea."

By the time the boys straggled home, one by one, slammed their lunchboxes and gallon Coleman jugs on the counter, went to see if Dat had something for them to do before supper, Mam threw her hands in the air and admitted defeat. Until she had the laundry off the line, lunches and thermoses washed and put away, there would be no energy to make supper in this sweltering kitchen.

She'd serve cold fruit soup for her and Elmer, which was a large bowl with fresh peaches or bananas, blueberries, or whatever fruit you had on hand, liberally sugared, stale bread torn on top, with cold, frothy milk poured over it. They had been raised on *Kaite sup*, but the young generation turned up their noses, pronounced it gross.

Well, tonight, they could eat cornflakes. It was too hot to cook. She felt like a can of melted Crisco. She didn't mind being plump, but these oven-like temperatures made her feel as if she was morbidly obese. She had put on some weight, with John's illness, whatever in the world all was going on with that boy. It just gave her the shivers. He didn't look right out of his eyes. He was sort of wild looking, as if he was frightened. She wondered where he was, hoped Elmer would find him.

Sweat poured off her and soaked the back of her blue dress, the usual apron discarded early in the day. She pulled on the wash line, wheeling the dry articles of clothing in toward her, expertly unclipping the wooden clothespins. A wheel line was a wonder, she thought for the thousandth time. It was a long cable that was wound around a wheel on each end, reaching for hundreds of feet to a sturdy tree, or a heavy metal pole, allowing the single line of elevated clothes to catch even the slightest breeze. She never had to move off the back patio to hang out loads of laundry, or to retrieve it. Wonderful.

"What's for supper?" Daniel and Allen had a one-track mind that revolved around food.

"Cornflakes."

"You're kidding."

"Come on, Ma."

"Don't call me Ma. That's disrespectful."

"Aw, Mom. Mama. Mother, dear mother."

Daniel moved as if to hug her.

She drew back a handful of clothespins and said he'd better not touch her. Then she let fly with the clothespins, Daniel ducking his head, Allen running for cover.

"It's too hot to cook," she shouted, but laughed along, watching the boy's feigned alarm.

"Let's order pizza."

"Now there is a good idea. Everybody chip in, OK? You call, Daniel, and I'll hurry up and get these clothes taken care of."

"I'm on my way, this very day," Daniel sang, in an elaborate crescendo, strumming his imaginary guitar, prancing across the patio and down the steps to the phone.

Mam rolled her eyes at Allen, but her round shoulders shook with laughter. These boys. But love welled up, overflowed.

"Allen, would you please move the sprinkler on that stepstool in the row of lima beans? Thanks."

"At your service, Ma."

"You know there are plenty of clothespins where that first bunch came from?"

"Your arsenal of weapons," Allen said, grinning. "Scary, scary."

The patio table was laden with three large pizzas—one pepperoni, one plain cheese, and one with everything—three boxes of wings, and three twelve-inch ham subs. Everyone reached into their wallet, contributed their share, some happier to oblige than others. They knew that was the only way their father would allow a delivery of pizza. If you want a treat, then help pay for it.

Where was John?

In the middle of all the hubbub, the pizza delivery, the washing up, John had not been found.

"Close the boxes, boys. Did someone call him? Upstairs?" Dat asked, a firm tone creeping into his voice.

"I'll go."

Always Amos, the helpful one, the kindhearted, in a genuine way. He disappeared through the kitchen screen door. Faintly, they heard his calls, then silence as he made his way upstairs.

The rest of the family waited, trying not to imagine ruined pizza with lukewarm toppings and a tough crust or watereddown iced tea.

When Amos did not return, Dat rose to his feet, made his way across the patio like an old man, his face a mask. Mam wiped the perspiration from her streaming forehead, impatient now.

After a while, Amos returned by himself, saying they were supposed to go ahead and eat, they'd be down.

"But is he all right? John, I mean?"

"Yes. He was lying down. The heat is hard for everyone."

Supper began without Dat or John.

Upstairs, John had been lying on his bed in the even warmer bedroom, shades drawn against the midday heat and light that pressed on his exhausted body like a heavy piece of armor. The air he could inhale seemed to evaporate, so he took to inhaling deeply, holding his breath as long as he could before exhaling, resulting in lightheadedness and a fresh new fear of losing consciousness.

This all came out, shamefacedly, his eyes averted as he struggled to keep from crying. He finished with his arms crossed in
front of him, his now thin shoulders held stiffly, the tension in
his young body apparent by the way he was poised, ready to run.

"You're weak," Dat said, asking no questions, expecting no
answers, keeping all conversation to a minimum. For one reason
or another, Dat seemed to understand the importance of this.

"Yeah, I guess I am." Then, "Am I going to die?"

Dat pondered this question, decided to keep it simple. John
was obviously enduring a massive struggle of some sort, and
would likely not absorb a long or complicated lecture.

So he said, "No, you will not die. But it might be a good idea
to tell Dr. Stevenson that you aren't getting better."

"But I am. Some."

"Will you go if Mam makes the appointment?"

"Do I have to?"

"I'm not satisfied with the results of the Lyme test."

They joined the rest of the family, without comment. Dat's
face registered enough seriousness to stop any frivolous questions, and certainly any teasing.

John ate a slice of his favorite pizza, silently, as if he was eating without touch or taste, robotic, his eyes without clear focus.
Mam watched her youngest son, the pizza crust in her mouth
going dry with fear of the unknown.

Dear God, will John lose his mind? Become handicapped?
Mentally ill? She left the table, stood at the kitchen counter seeing nothing.

Dat navigated the patio table surrounded by garrulous boys
who were unaccustomed to restraint, spoke of any problem easily and unselfconsciously, never harbored secrets, and never had
any serious health problems. So he set a light mood, with easy
grace, telling the boys about the two fawns at the edge of the
alfalfa field, the way the clever mother doe thought she'd hidden
them away, in plain sight.

"Hey, you wait till buck season. That daddy is likely Old Grunt."

"You wish! Duh!"

Later, Dat thanked God for sensible young men who picked up on the seriousness of John's situation and turned what could have been a disaster into a table easily accessible with light-heartedness, normalcy, exactly what Dat instinctively recognized John needed.

He saw John break a small grin, even, at the mention of anyone's ability to actually bag the monster whitetail that roamed these Pennsylvania forests.

Dat watched from the corner of his eyes and was gratified to find the spark of recognition.

Later, he had the discussion with his wife, who was steadily sliding down her own steep incline of worry and anxiety. She had been so sure it was Lyme, the diagnosis anticipated, the awaited answer to all the mental issues John was displaying.

A schizophrenic? Their own son, and him on the verge of entering his years of *rumschpringa*. The thought struck a chord of fear, imagining the mental wards, the medication, the label he would have to wear. He would never lead a productive life, shambling through his days confused and disoriented.

Oh, dear God. *Mein Vater im Himmel.*

CHAPTER 9

LENA ZOOK WAS THE THIRD DAUGHTER IN A STRING OF SIX GIRLS, after which a boy had been born to Henry and Elizabeth Zook. They named him Henry Jr. to carry on the father's name. They lived in Lancaster among the thousands of other Amish, below Christiana, until Henry decided farming his fifty acres of expensive ground was a study in futility. He needed more acreage, more cows, and a cheaper mortgage payment, which is what he set out to do. He traveled the Pennsylvania Turnpike to Route 365 and found a presentable, if weathered, set of buildings on 183 acres of good, rich soil that bordered the Juniata River.

His wife, Lena, never demurred from the duties before her. Fiercely loyal, devoted to Henry's happiness, she gamely packed their belongings, bade her family farewell, and rode off to Jefferson County with a light in her eye and an eagerness to her step. She scrubbed and painted, made the old house livable, mowed grass, cut borders, planted shrubs and flowers and a huge garden, scrimped and saved and lived in the warming light of her husband's admiration.

The girls were blessed with their mother's comely face, their father's blue eyes, her graceful stride and sense of adventure. They worked side by side with their parents and became skilled in horse driving, garden planting and harvesting, the milking of cows and the raising of calves.

The Henry Zook farm hummed along and the cows increased in number. The milk check easily paid the mortgage, the cost of living, with a growing nest egg put by. Elizabeth was a contributor, pinching her pennies, wasting nothing, wanting nothing, teaching her girls frugality and the rewards of backbreaking labor.

An acre of sweet bell peppers, then one of tomatoes, followed by squash and cucumber. Before long, the cows were sold, the dairy barn converted to raising steers, and they were running the first successful produce and beef operation in Jefferson County.

The girls worked alongside their parents like young men, shouldering baskets of peppers and tomatoes, driving a six-horse hitch, everyone lithe and tanned and strong. Injected with this work ethic, along with a life of frugality—waste not, want not, a penny saved is a penny earned—the girls were soon followed by a string of eager young men who recognized a virtuous woman when they saw one.

It proved to be the one thing that was the mother's undoing. Every Monday morning, practically, the oldest daughters, Annie and Rebecca, lingered over the breakfast dishes with yet another proposal to be mulled over.

Weren't there any other girls in the community? Elizabeth lifted her hands in exasperation.

Two daughters, and so many boys. It would be the ruination of them. All this lavish attention would swell their egos till they spoiled like grapes on the vine in the hot September sun. No good could come of it, you mark my words, she told her daughters.

Then Lena went off to teach school, turned sixteen, and joined the crowd of youth, her years of *rumschpringa* a vise to her mother's heart. She knew well, among six daughters, Lena was the most kindhearted, the one who was endowed with a natural empathy for the poor, the hurt, the downtrodden.

Every sick calf or injured kitten was nursed back to health under her capable hands, a heart tumbling with tender pity like an overflowing cup. Her brother Henry adored her, following her around wherever she went.

All this came naturally, springing up from the good set of genes on her father's side, Elizabeth reckoned. His sister Sarah had taken care of both his parents with barely any help from the remainder of the family, saying it was a joy to *fersark* them. When any words of praise came up, she brushed it aside like an irksome housefly.

That was the pattern of Lena's life. The empathy came naturally, easily, never planned or done to be held in high esteem by anyone around her.

Schoolteaching proved to be an outlet for all her energy, her enthusiasm, the drive to excel. Kindness wasn't even thought about. She just had a heart for the children, as if God had created that wellspring of love and kindness for the sole purpose of teaching school.

She had only been at the teacher's desk a few days when she noticed John Stoltzfus. Outgrowing any of the school desks, he was painfully ill at ease, conscious of his size and, seemingly, his mop of wavy hair.

His brown eyes contained a certain maturity, an aging beyond his years that was disconcerting. He seemed to view the world around him with a kind of sadness, as if he couldn't quite catch up to the boundless energy of those around him. Defeat, she finally concluded. A certain ownership of having been beaten, left behind.

Lena knew he had six older brothers, knew too the fact that his mother was a hard worker, a no-nonsense kind of person who had no time for gentle pity.

As far as she knew, the Elmer Stoltzfus family was a good one, nothing out of the ordinary, just a normal household that lived according to the *ordnung.*

Or mostly. Samuel and Marcus were on a sizable jaunt of making their mark on the world, stretching the limits as far as they would go.

And that Samuel was a handsome one. Probably the best-looking youth Lena had ever met.

It was nothing new to hear whispers and inane remarks peppered through the girl talk, usually pertaining to Samuel Stoltzfus, or Sam, as he liked to be called. A look or a smile from him would send most of the girls into a whirlwind of blushes and giggles.

Last Sunday evening, he had sidled up to her after the youth had dispersed from the hymn singing, making small talk, and decidedly making her nervous. This was the way it was often done. Talking, caught alone, knowing it would all lead to the question . . .

"Any plans for Saturday night? You want to go out for pizza with Melvin and Arie?"

No, no, and no. But Lena had one huge problem, and that was the immediate kindness that always took first priority. She felt sorry for these young fellows who wanted to enjoy her company. She desperately wanted to please them, say yes, I'll be your girl. I'll love you now and for the rest of my days.

But she knew she was too young, too independent.

Such a short time to enjoy freedom, being an Amish girl.

And so she stuck close to a crowd of girls, trying hard to give no one the assumption she had any longing to be a girlfriend.

Her best friend Barbie, a girl of seventeen, not particularly beautiful but not plain, and one of the sweetest human beings on earth, would have been only too glad to have Samuel draw her away from the crowd.

So why tonight, again, was he circling her? She thought of a wolf, the way they sought out the weakest, the youngest in the herd, then berated herself for such thoughts. Perhaps there was something wrong with her—maybe she was unappreciative, proud. She hoped not. She simply knew she did not want to date anyone, and certainly not this one. His self-assurance was a bit on the arrogant side, just enough so she could tell he was aware of the fact that all the girls would consider themselves extremely fortunate to be asked for a date.

"Lena."

Her heart plummeted, leaving a sick sensation in her stomach. She knew what the outcome would be if he did separate her, ask her out. She detested the polite denial, the disappointment that was always so evident, making her feel heartless, cruel.

No, Lena would say. No. Not for now. Perhaps someday, if it's meant to be in the future. A pathetic Band-Aid, slapped on to assuage the failure to secure her as a girlfriend.

She was only sixteen, and she was ashamed to count the times she had been asked out. There were so many other girls. And guys claimed looks had nothing to do with it.

Lena knew she was gifted with exceptional beauty, but it meant nothing to her. She treated her appearance with nonchalance, passed it off as of no consequence, which was so much a part of her allure.

"Lena."

She pretended not to hear, hoping it would give him a warning signal. Which it certainly did not do.

"Lena. May I talk to you?"

She didn't speak, merely stepped away, a small sigh escaping her lips.

He put a hand on her elbow to steer her in the direction he wanted to go, making her resist the urge to poke it into his side.

Ugh. Here we go again.

But she was slightly surprised at her own reaction to his earnest speech.

In the light from the living room that left a rectangle of yellow against the dark backdrop of the house, his clean-cut features were attractive, coupled with the suave speech he had prepared for weeks.

He made her laugh when he told her how nervous he really

was, and flattered her immensely by saying he knew she could have her pick of any guy she chose to have, and so forth.

She never knew why she said yes. The thrill of actually being the girlfriend of the sought-after Samuel Stoltzfus, making her the envy of everyone? No, Lena just didn't have that kind of competition in her.

She thought it all over carefully on Monday in the produce field, and decided she was simply tired of saying no.

Why not try it?

She had no intention of falling in love, she just took the easy way out this time, decided to see where it led. He was a very nice guy. Nothing was wrong with him, he was just . . . well, so predictable. Just like all the other guys—except she had to admit he was more handsome than the others.

And so Lena bent her back, picked green peppers by the half bushel, listened to the trill of a cardinal in the deep green woods beside her, and shrugged it off. All was right with her world as long as she could work outside on God's green earth, listen to the varied birdcalls, try to match the warbles and whistles to the bird she thought it was, then watch for a flash of blue or red or orange.

Love was likely overrated. Romance was probably mostly fantasy, leading to disappointment. She'd expect less, pray more, allowing God to lead her down the path He chose, trusting Him to show her the way. Her own thoughts and feelings were not always trustworthy, so she appreciated her upbringing, the insertion of God's majesty at a young age, instructions from both parents in the way of truth and light.

She would set off on this dating journey with the wind in her sails, the sun on her face, and God at the helm.

Which was why she often found herself at the Elmer Stoltzfus residence on a Sunday afternoon, being Samuel's girlfriend.

After church, when the parents stayed longer, or went visiting, the teenagers had the run of the place, and often congregated there, to hang out, then get dressed to attend the evening supper and singing.

Usually a large meal was prepared for a group of seventy or eighty youth, with many of the parents in attendance. They played volleyball or baseball in the summer, shuffleboard, table tennis or card games in the winter.

John's sixteenth birthday arrived in a haze of feeble attempts at appearing normal. Energy eluded him again, like a mirage that shimmered on the horizon, just out of reach. A positive Lyme test, this time, had brought sighs of teary-eyed relief, and a round of doxycycline started immediately.

His stomach churned with the awful strength of the hateful antibiotics. Bent over, gripping his stomach with both arms, he groaned aloud in the privacy of his room. After he emptied his stomach he'd feel better for a short period of time.

Mam fussed and stewed, brought probiotics from the health food store, bought tubs of kefir that tasted worse than sour milk.

But it's good for you. Good for you. Good for you.

Over and over the words were ingrained in his cotton-filled head, poked uncomfortably to push aside the fog of his limited deciphering.

She bought an enormous birthday cake at Giant and had it decorated with a leaping bass and a fishing rod. Happy birthday, John. Sixteen green candles, an impossibility presented to him on a sea of nausea-inducing white buttercream frosting, permeated with artificial colors of the leaping fish.

"Happy birthday to you! Happy Birthday to you!"

Blow them out, John! Clap. Clap.

But he could not gather enough oxygen to inhale deeply and blow.

One feeble woosh, the wavering of the tiny yellow flame, before they sprang to life.

"Come on, John. What's wrong with you?" A chorus of teasing. John with a half smile, his dark eyes bright with unshed tears, then the downturned corners of his mouth, before another courageous attempt.

He tried to laugh it off, did laugh it off successfully, then simply let the little neighbor boys take over gleefully, producing powerful jet streams of air from their puckered little mouths, extinguishing the flames of every single candle. He was glad to have the attention off himself.

Lena stood with Samuel on the sidelines, unable to explain the sympathy that welled up like a physical blow to her chest. He was so tall, so huge and dark eyed and woefully shy. Lena wanted to take his arm, steer him away, to a corner, tell him it was OK to have Lyme disease, that weakness wasn't some kind of failure.

She had heard from her handsome boyfriend the results of the blood test and was surprised at his inability to feel empathy.

"Yeah, he's been like this for a long time. Mam babies him so badly, it's no wonder he is the way he is. Doesn't work more than he has to. Stinking lazy. But he's the youngest, you know, so we tiptoe around him."

Then he proceeded to list all the "crap" he was taking.

Lena drew her mouth into a thin line of disapproval and spoke after she counted to ten.

"But would John choose to be weak? He was never lazy in school. I mean, he loved baseball, and was very good. Smart, did all his work on time."

"Could be." Samuel shrugged his shoulders.

John cut his hair, trimmed off the unruly waves, shortened it so much that it changed his appearance drastically. His father reprimanded him sharply, his mother echoed his words, but there was a glint of approval.

My oh, he looked nice. But they'd never say that aloud.

He drove his own horse hitched to the "new" secondhand buggy, and felt a burst of adrenaline, if only for a Sunday afternoon.

His brothers teased him unmercifully on Monday.

"How'd you feel, driving that small brown horse? He looked like a pony, he's that tiny."

"You sat forward, hanging on to the reins as if that little thing was going to get away from you."

"Look out. Here comes Crayon. A brown one."

Laughter like a sandstorm, blowing grit and dust into John's eyes. He blinked furiously to rid himself of the onslaught.

None of them could have known the high cost of driving in that dusty lane in front of a hundred pairs of observant eyes, all turned to him in unabashed curiosity. He had often heard the term "loser," used it himself, but rarely imagined the gut-wrenching fear that sent his heartbeat into a hopping, skipping rhythm, the awareness of being exactly that. A loser.

Why had he even tried?

He sat on the sidelines, his long legs with the newly pressed trousers stretched out in front of him, his weight propped on his hands as he sat on the grass, watching the confusing colors and light of the volleyball game.

He closed his eyes to resist the movement that poked into his weary eyesight. His neck felt as if someone had punched the top of his spine with both fists.

"Nice shirt."

He started, turned his head too quickly. A wall of blackness moved across his vision, so he waited till it cleared.

Again, "Nice shirt, John."

Lena. With Ruthie. His brothers' girlfriends.

"Thanks."

"You enjoying yourself?"

Ruthie peered around Lena.

"Uh . . . yeah. I guess so."

He blinked, looking to the players. John longed to be up against the net, his height a huge advantage, his powerful arms spiking the ball. It was game point.

"First weekends are never fun."

Lena's blue eyes were like tropical waves of turquoise water. He wanted to swim in them. How could anyone have such beautiful tanned skin with that impossible blond hair color?

He turned away.

"How's your Lyme disease?"

He got to his feet, quickly. He reached for the back of a folding chair for support, long enough to gain his footing when the ground tilted to a forty-five-degree angle. He removed himself, put all the distance between him and the question that he could.

He couldn't tell Lena about his sheets soaked in perspiration, the oncoming anxiety that squeezed the breath from his body, the intestines that rumbled with antibiotics and toxins and vitamin C, vitamin D, kelp, aloe vera, a cocktail of vile elixirs.

"Take it, John," his father commanded, though gently. "It's good for you. It will give you energy."

"Nothing will, Dat. This stuff will not give me anything except a stomach roaring with gas and cramps."

"Oh, come on, it's not that bad."

And so he didn't answer Lena, didn't even meet her eyes. He stood awkwardly, grasping the back of the chair, until finally she moved away toward a group of giggling girls.

The fall foliage was exquisite that year. Great clouds of white fluff cavorted playfully on a pristine blue canvas, holding court for the swaths of red, orange, and yellow that covered the hills and ridges of Jefferson County like a brilliant patchwork quilt done in the vibrant colors only God could invent. The air turned crisp and frost cradled the valleys in its icy veil, turning the chrysanthemums even brighter. Pumpkins lolled among decaying vines.

Mam had made fried chicken and mashed potatoes for dinner. Dat was feeling expansive, a fat milk check having arrived in the mail. He was thinking of buying a new baler come spring.

"Who's going to peel neck pumpkins this year?" Mam asked, a twinkle in her eyes.

"John, of course," Samuel said, grinning good-naturedly.

"Yeah. John. He does a great job."

"Johnny peel the pumpkin. Johnny peel the pumpkin."

Marcus laughed along, sending a spray of applesauce and mashed potatoes over Amos's plate.

"Hey, watch it there. Gross."

He got up to rinse his utensils, cleaned his plate with soapy dishwater.

Dessert was fresh pumpkin pie with whipped cream. Mam watched with a light of pride as three whole pies disappeared, a fourth started.

"No one makes pumpkin pie the way you do, Mam."

"Oh, well, now."

She didn't know how to take a compliment, but still glistened with appreciation, her world shining bright as long as she could please the boys and Elmer.

John was looking queasy, Mam noticed suddenly. When he got up to rush to the bathroom, the sounds of retching delivered in nauseating crescendo, eye rolling and sounds of impatience ruined the goodwill that had filled the homey kitchen.

Mam followed immediately, hovered around the bathroom door, pacing, fixing a doily on the walnut desk, waiting till John emerged, when she would pounce on him with her arsenal of questions.

So John stayed in the bathroom.

Dat tried to keep the lighthearted vibe, reveling in blessings and good fortune, but it sputtered and died, like an unfueled engine, when Abner gestured with impatience.

"That boy gets too much crap in his system. He needs to be flushed like a commode. It's no wonder he's sick as a dog."

Tap. Tap. Tap. Mam had her ear to the bathroom door.

"John. John."

No response.

"John, are you all right? John, open the door. John, do you hear me?

Dat growled, a strained version of his previous banter. "Sit down, Mary. Let him alone."

"Elmer, I'm not going to. What if he passed out? He's not answering. He didn't look good at all before he went to the bathroom. John? John?"

"Mary, come here and sit down." Dat's voice was terrible now.

Abner turned his face sharply in Dat's direction. "You don't have to yell at her."

"I wasn't yelling."

"Sure you were."

"He probably just wants us to worry. He's nothing but a big spoiled baby." Samuel got up, left the table, and slammed the washhouse door on his way out.

Mam obeyed her husband's orders and returned to the table, her own stomach roiling with greasy chicken and whipped cream.

Marcus spoke for all of them.

"Samuel's probably right, Mam. He likely overate, that's all. You watch his face the way ship's captains watch the weather monitor. It's becoming an obsession. 'Ooo, John is pale. He needs calcium. John is weak. Give him something else.' It's getting completely out of control."

Mam lowered her face and began to cry, softly, making no sound, discreetly lifting her apron to produce a wad of Kleenex and holding them to her nose.

"Marcus, look what you've done. You made your mother cry. You apologize now," Dat spoke sternly.

"I will, Dat. But I mean what I just said. Everybody needs to calm down about John's health."

He looked over at his mother. "Sorry, Mam."

Daniel got to his feet. "The whole family is being torn apart, one thread at a time. I hate it."

John sat on the lid of the commode, his supper having been flushed away, the stench of his own bowels permeating the small bathroom. He was sweating, his throat raw with vomiting, feeling lower and more miserable than he had ever felt. A year and how many months, with the ever-growing conviction that his intestines crawled with parasites, the spirochetes in his cells slowly eating him alive. He was sure death was imminent.

After everyone left the table, Mam stayed behind, washing dishes. He tiptoed upstairs to the shower, then presented his soiled clothing to her with a face ravaged with anxiety and hands that shook like a palsied old man's.

Chapter 10

Wᴴᴇɴ ᴀʟʟᴇɴ ᴄᴀᴍᴇ ᴅᴏᴡɴ ᴡɪᴛʜ ᴀ ꜱᴛᴏᴍᴀᴄʜ ʙᴜɢ, ᴛʜᴇɴ ᴅᴀɴɪᴇʟ, Mam was relieved. That was all it was, then. John had an intestinal virus, that was all.

He lay in his bed, upstairs, and refused to come down.

Mam carried trays of drinks, the very air around her sizzling with angst. Orange juice. Maalox. Hot peppermint tea. Vinegar and honey water. John turned his back, pulled pillows over his head to smother the staccato sound of her voice.

"You'll become dehydrated, John. You must drink. What hurts? Is it your stomach? Answer me, John. Dat and I can't help you if you refuse to speak to us about it. Tell me, please, John."

All he wanted was quiet. He wanted dark nothingness, where the world disappeared and left him to exist without effort, without trying to hear and understand, without having to pick sentences apart word by word until he knew what they meant.

His stomach was filled with a hard, black pain, a permanent boulder that would not budge. There was a thick wet fog, like soup, a thickened milk soup, like cream of mushroom, in his brain. His thoughts boiled into this paste.

Afternoon turned into night. He drank water from the sink in the upstairs bathroom. The pain in his stomach reached epic proportions, so he wended his way downstairs, woke up his parents, reeling with discomfort.

His mother picked up the questions where she'd left off. Mercifully, Dat shushed her gently, then made his way to the couch. He spread out the sleeping bag, his stomach a rounded paunch as he bent over.

"There you go."

He turned away to spread a clean sheet on the couch beside him. The minute John's head hit the silky smoothness of the clean pillowcase, drowsiness took over and he fell into a deeper, more restful sleep than he'd had for months, secure in the knowledge that nothing would happen to him as long as his father lay beside him.

In the morning, Mam and Dat both agreed it was time to call Doctor Stevenson.

John resisted, but was forced to obey. Reluctantly, he was led into the clinic, accepted the old doctor's diagnosis. A stomach virus may have started it, but to be safe, he'd send him to the lab at the hospital. Sometimes, the doxycycline wreaked havoc with the tender lining of the intestines, and he certainly did not want that. Infection could be the result.

And death, John thought wildly. *This is how I will die.*

As Mam told the van driver they were being sent to the hospital in Rohrersville, John envisioned a chain of events, strung together in one long, sad gray thread. His last breath, his brothers crowded around, crying. He felt the sting of tears, the burning in his nostrils, thinking of the grief, the parting, the ensuing sorrow. A great love for his family swelled in his chest.

When the gray walls of the Rohrersville Hospital loomed out of the October drizzle, John felt a fresh wave of nausea. He said nothing. He laid his head on the back of the seat and tried to will it away.

Everything disappeared into waves of sickness. He had only one clear thought, to make this vehicle stop, to push the button on the electronic sliding door, and to be blessedly sick on the tarmac of the parking lot.

Which was exactly what happened.

Mam gasped, began the string of questions, held out napkins for him to use. There was the strong odor of baby wipes.

He shook his head, looked at the contents beside the van.

"Leave it," Mam said briskly. "Come."

Unbelievably, the pain lightened, softened to an ache. Then there was an emptiness. By the time the overworked lab technician had drawn blood, gave them instructions, he checked out cafeteria signs with interest.

In the van, he felt decidedly better. Lighthearted. Hungry. His thoughts felt clear, razor sharp. He smiled, to test the elasticity of his lips. They were dry, cracked.

The absence of the painful boulder in his stomach gave him fresh hope. Things could always get better, in spite of new and frightening bouts of whatever it was that Lyme disease did to a person.

His health improved over the course of a few days. He felt well enough to play volleyball at the youths' Sunday evening gathering, but was afraid no one would want him, or they had all the players they would need, or that his arms would not be strong enough to deliver a good serve, let alone a wondrous spike. So he sat on the grass, wearing the same neat black trousers and black vest, with a charcoal gray shirt with black stripes.

Another net was being readied. Powerful battery lights were hooked up to buggies. Someone stopped in front of him. He looked up to find a pair of inquisitive eyes, like a chipmunk's, staring down at him, with a smiling pair of lips and very white teeth that were rabbity, like his own.

"You want to play?"

Her chin jutted in the volleyball net's direction.

"Is there room for me?"

"Sure. If we hurry."

He got to his feet, followed the tall, muscular girl clad in an alarming shade of red, like a fire hydrant, or a firetruck.

She stopped till he caught up.

"You don't know me, do you? You're Elmer Stoltzfus's John, right? The youngest."

He nodded.

"I'm Martha. Marty."

Her grip was as solid as a guy's. Calloused, he thought.

"I'm the captain."

"For what?"

"Of the team."

"Oh." Duh. Should have known.

"You any good?"

John shrugged his shoulders. Afraid to answer in the affirmative.

"Well, you're certainly tall enough."

She smiled. He smiled back. Two rabbit people, he thought. Interesting.

She stuck by him, gave him instructions on the pattern of rotation, the setups, the serving. Before an hour was up, he was enjoying himself immensely, pain and fog and Lyme disease forgotten. He couldn't remember the last time he'd had this kind of energy, especially the surges of adrenaline when the ball kept going from one side to the other without being dropped.

Marty was a phenomenal player. She moved at lightning speed, and yelled a lot. In a nice way, though. She encouraged, praised, moved everyone along, her eyes missing nothing, her feet always moving.

As the game progressed, John found himself being drawn to her, in a way he could not explain even to himself. She wasn't beautiful like some girls, like Lena. But she sparkled and glowed, as if there were inner lights that flared up within her. Her eyes popped with delight and those white glistening teeth with a bit of an overbite were the cutest things John had ever seen.

How could an overbite be attractive when he despised his own teeth?

And she talked. She said a lot, which was often humorous. Words tumbled from her mouth in quick succession, so that John could hardly keep up with the flow of her verbal observations.

And then, he fumbled badly.

Close to the net, his heart in his mouth, knowing this was the ultimate moment . . . he drove the ball into the net.

There were wails of disappointment all around.

Marty looked at him, gave him one of her smiles.

"Don't worry about it. Shake it off," she said, quietly.

He nodded, said thanks, but the intense feeling of failure stayed with him.

The following morning, he could barely lift his head from the pillow. His father's calls at five o'clock seemed to be an assault on his hearing, cries that buzzed around his head. When Dat got no response, he climbed the stairs. Finally, John grunted, which seemed to satisfy Dat, and he clattered back down the stairs, leaving John to sort out his foggy existence from his aching arms and legs. His throat was dry, his head felt as if his ears would pop off from the inner pressure, not to mention the intense ache in his neck. He lifted his head, groaned as pain shot across his shoulders and down his spine.

He tried to slide one leg toward the edge of the bed, which caused fiery snakes of pain to shoot up his thighs and into his buttocks. He followed with the other leg, rolled over, and by sheer force of will, he sat up, lowered his head into his hands, and cried.

Defeated, he rolled back into his bed, drew the quilt up over his head to shut out the world.

When his father returned, calling, asking questions, he merely drew the quilt even tighter, burrowed into the safety of his pillow until he went away. It took far too much effort to explain his symptoms. The whole world of pain and confusion was pressing in on him, expelling his breath, until there was nothing to do but find darkness and quiet.

Rest. Even that word confused him.

His mother barged in, full steam ahead, wearing her clothes-pin bag and the odor of laundry detergent and Clorox.

"John, what's wrong? Why aren't you getting up? Dat needs you. You were healthy enough to go *rumschpringa* yesterday, so you can get out of bed. Go help your father. He has too much on his shoulders without you. Come on. Get up now."

"Can we do without the drama first thing in the morning?" said a gravelly voice from one bedroom away.

No answer from Mam as she scuttled her way down the stairs.

"John, get out. Get going." Another yell from another bed. Marcus or Daniel.

John did unravel his aching body from the confines of his twisted quilt, made his way to the bathroom where he did the usual clutch of the vanity top, the cold sweat beading his upper lip as his increased heart rate caused his mouth to dry.

Take a deep breath. Another. You'll be fine. Fine.

Doxycycline with breakfast, vitamins in every shape, size, and color. A probiotic. A detox pill for the colon. Dutifully, he swallowed them all with his breakfast.

Monday brought lowering clouds that scudded across the sky, promising rain and chilly winds, a prelude to shorter days filled with the biting cold.

The fields lay fallow, and torn cornstalks mashed into soiled rows like empty holders, their fruit taken, used up. A gray dust settled over the fields, the garden emptied of its bounty, except for a few scraggly celery stalks and the newly planted tillage radishes.

A great blue heron flapped its oversized wings as it propelled its body through the air, its feet tucked straight back like two broomsticks. The cows milled about in the barnyard, treading the soft dirt into a wet mess with the consistency of glue, their tails swishing the mud and manure around without restraint.

John shoved his hands in his packets and hunched his shoulders against the wind that bit through his black sweatshirt. He had no idea how he would get through the day. The walk to the barn felt like a marathon, the pills wallowing in his stomach. He brought up a few vile tasting belches.

A cat peered around a corner of the horse stall, a sick emaciated old barn cat that should have been put down a long time ago. Patches of hair alternated with bare, wrinkled skin, the head was too large for the rail-thin body, and the long twitching tail had no hair on the end.

John sat on a hay bale, his elbows resting on his upturned knees. Poor cat. He'd be better off dead. He was sick, too old to keep around the barn, unable to hunt mice and chipmunks.

There was no point in letting the sick old cat survive.

"Here, kitty. Come here, old man."

John reached out a hand, was rewarded by the old cat coming to him, the trust glimmering from his tired old eyes. He rubbed up against John's trouser leg, his arched back bony, pitiful.

Quite suddenly, John entertained the thought that the cat was fortunate, old enough to creep behind a bale of straw and pass peacefully away, the way nature intended. He wished he was elderly.

Soon his time to die would come. If the doxycycline wasn't working, and all the vitamins passed through him without a bit of good, what else was left? Lyme disease was a cruel thing.

Crushed by thoughts of defeat, he rubbed his hand across the shockingly apparent ribs on the cat's side. He thought of his .22 shotgun. A small bullet to the head, that was all it would take.

Poor cat.

Dat found him, asleep, between two bales of hay, the cat in his arms. Alarmed, he stood gaping at his teenaged son.

"John?"

There was no answer.

"John?" Louder now.

Startled, John's eyes flew open. He scrambled to his feet, blinking furiously. The cat stayed where he was, lifting his head for a short time before resting it on his paws, like a dog.

"John, is it that bad?" Dat asked kindly.

Disoriented, ashamed, John felt the color creep up into his face.

He shook his head.

"Guess I'm just lazy. You know, not used to *rumschpringa*."

"The truth, John."

His father folded his length onto a bale of hay, patted the one beside him.

"Sit."

John obeyed, unwilling to meet his father's gaze. It was too piercing, too penetrating, far too honest.

"Are we expecting too much of you? Is your Lyme disease actually making you so tired that you can't summon enough energy to stay awake this early in the morning? I do wish you'd talk about your disease more often. Is the doxycycline not working?"

John heard his father's words. He felt the questions like arrows, penetrating his skin, painful, irritating.

"How am I supposed to know?" His voice was curt, with a ragged edge.

"John, listen. This is not only hard for you, but it's hard for all of us. Your mother is slowly turning into a nervous wreck. She doesn't know how to handle this if you won't talk. Communication is everything, especially at a time like this. If you aren't able to do your work, then tell me. I'll hire a *knecht* to help out. If you need to rest this thing out, then tell us. We'll work with you. Do whatever it takes."

Before he could give his father a proper answer, the voices of his six brothers echoed around in his head, taunting, challenging, teasing.

What an unbelievable baby.
Nothing wrong with him, only milking it for all it was worth.
He's lazy, that's all.
Kick him out of bed. He needs to man up.
He's all right on the weekend.

"John, I'm talking to you, and I expect the courtesy of an answer."

"Yeah. All right. Well, I don't know what to say. Just tired I guess."

"Did Dr. Stevenson give you any instructions? Rest, exercise? How are you expected to carry on if you have no strength?"

"I don't know."

John's voice was barely above a whisper, wobbling from his mouth in a little boy's quavering tones.

He lowered his head to his knees. His shoulders shook with the force of his weeping. Wisely, Dat stood by, without comment, allowing the storm to build momentum, before weakening.

"I'm just so tired, Dat. Everything hurts. I sweat at night, and can't sleep."

"Can you sleep if you sleep downstairs?" He didn't add, "with me."

John nodded, miserable with this childish revelation.

"Then, if that's how it is, that's where you'll sleep. We'll get Mam to buy you a larger air mattress next time she goes to Walmart. OK?"

Choking back tears, Dat lay a hand on John's shoulder.

John stood up, but wouldn't meet his father's eyes. He was too ashamed.

"Listen, it's nothing to be ashamed of. You have a disease. I'll have to talk to your brothers."

"What about Mam? Can you ask her to stop asking questions? I don't always have an answer."

Trusting Dat felt like a huge step. He felt a weight roll off his shoulders. His breathing eased, relaxed.

"All right, then. You go on in the house, and wherever you're most comfortable, I want you to stay. If you'd rather be away from the rest of us, then do that. Wherever you can find rest."

John wanted to thank his father, but the words caught on a sob he was unwilling to reveal, so he turned away and walked through the gloom into the house.

Luckily, Mam was at her washing machine, the air-powered device loud enough to hide his footsteps. He laid his shoes behind the recliner and went upstairs, his feet as if they were encased in cement blocks.

That was the morning Aunt Emma and Aunt Sarah came for coffee. They'd heard their sister was under the weather, dealing with her son's Lyme disease. They clattered into the kitchen bearing coffee cake and cinnamon rolls, talkative and caring, bearing their own ideas and hearsays about Lyme.

"All over. It's just all over. Did you hear about the girl in Lancaster County? I think she's a cousin, or second cousin to your Susie's husband, Elam? She has it on her brain. She's so sick and depressed, they're afraid of suicide. Doctor wants to put her on an antidepressant and she, the mother, won't do it. Natural. Completely natural. She won't allow antibiotics, nothing."

Emma bit into a large cinnamon roll, leaning forward so the brown-sugar-encrusted walnuts would not fall on the clean floor.

Emma was older than Sarah by three years, and Mary was the youngest, but each one was well endowed with strong opinions and the courage to fire them into the air at opportune times. Or inopportune times, none of the sisters being very good at gauging which was which.

This subject of Lyme disease had been hashed and rehashed until it was nothing but pulp, mixed with myth, untruths, ill-advised tales that escalated into pure horror stories, Mary thought, tight-lipped.

She allowed her sisters to rattle off mind-numbing statistics, names of herbs and nutritious powders or oils or tinctures that completely cured her husband's cousin.

She drank cup after cup of scalding coffee laced with milk and three teaspoons of sugar, ate two cinnamon rolls out of the middle of the pan to avoid the hard edges. That, and Emma was plenty stingy when it came to making and spreading caramel icing. She'd leave the rolls with syrup and nuts for Sarah—she wanted the ones with icing.

The coffee cake was nothing special, and she told Sarah this, without an ounce of tact.

"Oh, I know. It was in the oven a tad too long. My neighbor came over, with a fall arrangement in a blue mason jar. I never saw anything so ugly in all my life. You know how goldenrod goes to seed? Well, she had that brown stuff mixed with corn leaves. Corn leaves, mind you. Brown as mud, and stiff. I think she had a few mums, purple asters, and what looked like dead weeds. But you know how it goes. I told her it was pretty. She's going for knee surgery. I pity her with that husband of hers. He's so ignorant about a woman having knee surgery. Says it would be cheaper to have her put down. Imagine if someone spoke like that to us."

"Oh, he's nice. He just says that to tease her. I like him a lot. He's the first one to offer help if you need it."

"You don't know my neighbors," Sarah said, prickly now.

"Aren't you talking about the Gutschalls?"

"Well, yes."

"Well, then."

Sarah pursed her lips self-righteously. Emma puckered her own, slurped her coffee with an indecent rattle.

"John doing better?"

"Oh yes. He was at the supper last evening. His Sunday pants have grass stains on them, which tells me he was playing volleyball. He's so tall, I imagine he's good at it. He's in the barn this morning."

"Really? That good! Good for him."

"Yes, it's been quite a siege. I do believe the doxycycline is taking hold, and he feels better again. I mean, if he was playing volleyball last evening, got up and did chores, is working with his father, well, what does that tell you? He's improving, that's what." She spoke triumphantly, with an air of having accomplished what she set out to do.

Emma cut a slice of coffee cake, watched her sister's face with plenty of caution coupled with pessimism. She wondered if John was really out of the woods the way she thought, but said nothing.

They heard footsteps overhead. Water was running in the bathroom.

Sarah pointed a finger to the ceiling.

"One of the boys home sick?"

Bewildered, Mary said, "No."

"Well, someone's up there."

Mary got to her feet, moved rapidly up the stairs. The sisters in the kitchen held very still, straining to hear. When she returned, her face was ashen, her eyes dark pools of motherly concern. She flopped into a chair, her appetite gone, close to tears.

"I guess I was wrong."

She shook her head from side to side, her mouth a slash of iron control.

"The hardest part for me is the fact that he keeps everything inside. He tells me nothing. Nothing at all. He won't answer my questions. I keep telling him all the time how hopeless it is to help him if he won't supply us with answers. It's as if he lives in a cocoon, where he shuts us all out, even his brothers. What is anyone supposed to think? Sometimes I think I just can't face another day of his withdrawal from all of us."

For once, the sisters didn't have an answer. The kitchen became very quiet, the propane gas lamp hissing softly as the dark clouds thickened and churned. Splatters of rain fell against the east kitchen window. The wind picked up, moaning against the edge of the roof, where a piece of loose drip edge began to whir. The clock on the wall chimed ten o'clock, then began its quiet tune of "Amazing Grace."

"It sure is turning into an ugly day," Sarah remarked, the weather seemingly the only subject that was safe ground.

As if this feeble attempt had never been offered, Mary plowed on.

"I often wonder if we should take him to a Lyme specialist. There are doctors in Philadelphia, there's one in Baltimore, Maryland. I heard of a Joe Wenger Mennonite family who had such good results with their daughter. What would you do? I mean, there are so many nutrition programs and natural remedies all over the place, that I'm never quite sure if we're doing enough. Or if we're doing the right thing. I mean, what if we're not doing everything we should be doing?"

"Mary. Mary. Listen. You are not in control. Your son is very sick, perhaps, but that still doesn't eliminate God from your life. You need to look on Him, depend on Him, to show you the way. Your spiritual life is very important at a time like this. Don't you think it's about time to let go and let God? The way the old saying goes."

Mary began to weep softly.

"You just don't know. Our family is being torn apart."

CHAPTER 11

THERE WAS A BIG EVENT PLANNED FOR THANKSGIVING AT THE AMOS Beiler place. Amos Beiler was a man of prestige in the community, a builder of gazebos and garden sheds, chicken coops and storage sheds, all manufactured beneath a huge building with tremendous ceiling space. So when they invited all the youth of Jefferson County, plus cousins and friends from Lancaster, the boys all looked forward to the day of food and indoor volleyball.

Mam grumbled about an event for the youth on Thanksgiving. She didn't like anything going on for any members of her family on that date, simply wanting her own tradition of seeing all her children around her table, the way it should be. The way it had always been.

She didn't like weddings on that date, either. Whoever heard of ruining so many people's holiday, for a wedding?

She had decided that morning to accept the fact that she was no longer considered young, the color of her hair gone mostly from dark brown to grayish brown. Mostly gray, really. She drew the fine-tooth comb through her fading tresses, twisted it into a long rope, and wound it into a tight coil on the back of her head. She pinned a clean white covering on top, turning her head slightly to catch her still youthful profile.

She noticed that her neck looked slack. Well, if she seemed to have an abundance of gray hair it was simply no wonder. She had a lot on her shoulders, with John. And now Samuel was having problems with Lena. He looked extremely crestfallen, nervous sometimes, as if he dreaded a matter that was far above his own understanding. Poor boy. She hoped if Lena wasn't happy with Samuel, she'd end the relationship sooner than later, save him the thought of marriage, at least. Heartbreak. She dreaded the sound of it, but the way Samuel was acting, it was probably inevitable.

And the girls in Kentucky, settled in, seemingly *liking* it down there. They called to leave messages, or on occasion, planned a certain hour to have a real conversation about life, which consisted of listening about babies, birth, farming, and husbands, good or bad. Not that Mam allowed her girls to vent their displeasure on the poor erring husbands. "You married him," she would say. "Don't come whining to me. Are you being nice to him? Cook him a good meal."

Lydia frequently spoke to John, wrote long letters, sent him cards of encouragement, religious poems and verses. John never related any of their conversation to Mam, so she figured she'd give Lydia and John the benefit of the doubt. He needed someone to confide in, so if it was Lydia, then that was all right.

The Coleman queen-sized air mattress had been bought, the pump used to fill it with air, sheets stretched across it, pillows and quilts folded beside it. This was where John spent his nights, the comfort of his father on the couch beside him, knowing it was all right. John never slept well, often staying awake till two or three in the morning, tossing from his aching back to his roiling stomach, and back again. Mam knew how poorly he slept, merely by the sounds from the air mattress, the shuffling rustle, the whomp of plastic, over and over.

He moved constantly, which left Mam sleepless on many nights, too. Dat had a talk with the boys, each one told without preamble, that John suffered more than they knew, anxiety and awful fear kept him from sleeping, and if he ever found out any of them made fun of him, he'd . . . well, he didn't like to make empty threats, but they'd have it coming.

In spite of his best efforts, though, he caught Marcus and Samuel snickering at times, or raising eyebrows.

The usual carefree banter at the supper table was mostly gone, replaced with careful, muted conversation, as stiff and awkward as a pair of stilts. Mam could tell that Marcus and Samuel still thought John was a baby, a spoiled, coddled youngest son who was plain lazy and preyed on his parents' sympathy.

Mam was saddened to hear all this, to see the blatant display of disbelief in John's symptoms. Yeah, sure, there was Lyme disease. That was one thing. But to lie in your room all day? No wonder he didn't have any energy. All those youthful muscles softening like Jell-O.

One night Marcus became emphatic, spoke roughly to Mam. "You should see him play volleyball. In the thick of it with that Marty. Thinks he's so cool."

A note of jealousy?

Mam wiped the Princess House two-burner griddle, flicked her covering strings across her shoulders, then went back to the sewing machine to find a tiny gold safety pin to secure the ends behind her back. They always got in the way.

When she came back, Marcus told her she was trying to avoid what he had to say.

Irritation flickered behind her glasses, like faraway lightning before a thunderstorm. She tied and retied her apron, another sure sign of agitation.

Marcus forged on.

"You didn't say anything, 'cause you don't know what to say. He's lazy. If his Lyme disease was as bad as he says it is, how could he play volleyball? He doesn't look sick. Healthy as a horse on the weekends. Seriously."

Mam drew herself up, glared at her handsome son. If he was still six years old, she'd make him sit until he quit this back talk.

But he wasn't a small boy. He was a grown youth, forming opinions and life views on his own. Here's where it got tricky.

"Marcus, do you honestly believe John chooses to stay in bed? No healthy boy with normal energy levels would choose to ache all over. The volleyball isn't good for him, probably, but Dat and I feel he needs to socialize, keep up appearances of being normal, for his own sake."

She shook a finger at him.

"What is it to you, Marcus? You know nothing about Lyme, so why sit there accusing your father and me?"

"You're babying him."

A few mornings later, the whole thing started over again. Marcus leaned back in his chair, stretched his arms above his head, and yawned. He lifted his shirt and scratched his stomach, then tucked the shirttail back below the belt of his trousers.

"Mam, I need new shirts. Long-sleeved ones for Sunday."

"You mean for Thanksgiving. Big to-do, that day. Why would anyone plan such a thing on a holiday?"

Marcus shrugged. "Nicest shop in Jefferson County."

Mam didn't answer, thinking of John playing volleyball. What if she did have a devious son who was as lazy as he was clever? He would turn out to be a regular thief, or a crooked business dealer. Or worse.

Marcus talked on, waiting for his pancakes and eggs. He was leaving for work earlier, something about finishing a job. Hillside Construction was known as a top-notch builder of houses, the rough framework, so when the pressure was on, it was nothing out of the ordinary to leave at five o'clock in the morning.

"So, are you going shopping before then?"

"Before when?"

"Thanksgiving."

"I can. Give me money. Shirts at Kohl's aren't cheap. Every

time I bring them home from off the clearance rack, every one of you turns his nose in the air. So hand over some cash."

She stretched out a hand, wiggled her fingers.

"Aw, Mam. I only get half my paycheck. You guys get the rest. Surely you can foot the bill for a couple shirts."

Mary stood with her hands on her hips, pancake turner glinting in the yellow lamplight.

"Marcus, do you have any idea what we've spent on John? And now Dat pays for a hired hand."

Marcus spoke with a few curt words.

"Your own fault. I wouldn't cart him off to a doctor."

"Marcus Stoltzfus."

"I mean it. There's nothing wrong with him. You should see him with Marty."

Wisely, Mam remained silent. She could smell jealousy like garlic. He reeked of it. But still.

After Marcus left, she wended her way to the back living room, behind the double doors, and bent down to touch John's shoulder.

"John, are you awake? Do you feel well enough to manage chores with your father this morning? You should be getting some exercise, don't you think? Thanksgiving will soon be here and you'll want to play volleyball, no? Why don't you try getting up at your usual time, John?"

John rolled over, winced. So many questions.

He did make an honest effort. To climb the stairs took every ounce of strength he could muster, hanging on to the railing with both hands, his breath coming in short painful gasps from lungs that felt as if they were underwater.

He knew he shouldn't play volleyball. It took him the rest of the week to regain even a fraction of his adrenaline. He knew the only reason he forced himself to keep going was Marty. Every weekend now, he looked for her brightly clad figure. She always wore brilliant shades of teal blue or lime green, red or purple. Not deep dark plum-colored purple, but a fiery in-your-face color that was like the field of wild columbines by the creek. She was full of energy, color, and movement, everything John longed to possess. She had a natural vitality that came from a happiness within.

Marty wasn't nearly as pretty as Lena, the girl of his dreams since eighth grade, but somehow, Lena faded away. She was Samuel's girl now, and she was always a bit quiet and thoughtful when she was around the house.

Where Marty was a bright and showy tropical flower, Lena was a delicate orchid. Each one held a fascination, but John knew he had no chance with either one, stumbling around in a disease riddled body full of bacteria, a stomach sloshing with vitamins and crazy detox pills, along with that evil doxycycline that would eventually chew a hole in his stomach.

Thanksgiving Day the sun was tucked behind a wall of lowering clouds promising rain and perhaps snow squalls. Mam didn't send the boys with a dessert. Nine chances out of ten they'd forget the fruit or pudding, leaving it to turn mushy or rancid below the buggy seat, accumulating a steady coating of horsehair.

And Cool Whip wasn't cheap.

She put a turkey in the oven, filled to capacity with the usual sausage stuffing, almost cried to think of herself and Elmer alone with the turkey between them.

Well, nothing to do about that. She had thought about inviting aunts and uncles, but they weren't young anymore and had a habit of complaining about the cost of Amish drivers these days, with gas so dear.

It irked her, this flagrant display of bad manners, but she didn't say anything. It wasn't worth causing a family rift.

"Mam, what were you thinking?"

Marcus held the new red shirt out in front of him between his thumb and forefinger like it was a dead animal.

"What?"

"I really do not like this shirt. I look like an elf."

Mam pictured him in a green felt hat and green shoes with pointy toes. She laughed loudly, from deep down.

"It's not funny."

"Oh wear it. Elves are cute."

She laughed again. It felt good, so normal, to kid around with a son who was healthy, who could sleep well and eat well, with an appetite for life.

One by one the boys appeared, having slept in, with various cases presented, shirts too old, too wrinkled, a button popped, trousers too short.

Mam turned a deaf ear. Boys could be worse than the girls ever were. Especially if a girl was in their sights. All except Abner, who lived on a cloud of confidence, wore the same three shirts and black Walmart sneakers and could not have cared less about what the other boys wore or what was in style.

He had no patience for name-brand shoes or jackets or shirts. Why pay that amount for a name written on the clothing? Much more important to sock away his paycheck, make a nice down payment on a substantial home, start up his own business. Besides, style for Amish people was laughable, in his opinion. There weren't a whole lot of options when you were sticking to the *ordnung*.

Mam eyed her oldest son with a critical eye.

"That's an awfully old vest."

Abner gazed down at his black vest, puzzled.

"What do you mean?"

"Turn around. That back is turning purple, it's that old."

"Ah, who cares?"

"Maybe Ruthie does."

"If she breaks up with me because of an old vest, then she doesn't love me very deeply."

Mam raised her eyebrows, dipped her head. She thought

about how she couldn't stand Elmer when he wore the one pair of Sunday pants, the ones that were too short, exposing those horrible argyle socks. But she had married him, of course.

Last, John appeared. His face had turned from pale to an odd shade of green. He sagged into the recliner, turned his head away before anyone could speak to him. Perhaps if he rested a while, the dizziness and nausea would pass.

He had woken up soaked, the bedsheets and his T-shirt wet with perspiration from the dreaded night sweats that plagued him constantly.

The hope of volleyball, and Marty, had gotten him out of bed, but he knew this would be one of the worst days.

Well, he'd lie here a while, see what occurred.

"'S up with you?"

Allen slapped his shoulders, peered into his face. "I thought you always felt OK on the weekends."

No answer.

They all got themselves going and were out the door by lunchtime, eager to join the crowd of youth who would spend the holiday in Amos Beiler's huge shop.

John sat in his buggy, weak and dizzy, longing to wave a hand in front of his face and erase all the symptoms of Lyme disease like a magic wand in the nursery rhymes. He knew with an ever-increasing certainty that he couldn't play today.

A sense of loss crept up, an unwanted specter of a future lying in recliners, incarcerated in a body that would remain in this weakened state.

He was handicapped, at sixteen. He had no idea how to fight it, if the arsenal of medication did nothing. For a while, he had felt better, even with the debilitating stomach cramps. He imagined the doxycycline whapping the Lyme bacteria, one by one, the cells killed effectively.

Then what happened? In all the books he'd read and all the stories he'd heard, it seemed as if not one case of Lyme was the

same as any other. After the Lyme bacteria was zapped by antibiotics, a host of other problems raised their heads. He felt like
a walking cauldron of microscopic bugs that cavorted happily in
his bloodstream, hid in his cells, consumed the herbal vitamins
and minerals his mother so desperately placed before him.

Her latest thing was Body Balance, a liquid supplement
derived from aloe vera and sea vegetables. What in the world
were sea vegetables? He pictured a garden on the sea floor,
wet corn and potatoes and string beans waving in the ocean
currents.

He always drank the four ounces she set before him, shivered, swallowed. It couldn't do any harm, but sure didn't do
much good.

He guided his little horse named Crayon into the short drive
that was already parked full with glistening black and gray buggies. Each was washed and polished, the pride of each young
man's heart. Interiors were upholstered in an array of colors,
dashboards made of glossy wood, cherry, oak, walnut, carved
intricately. Some had speedometers, battery gauges, a small
clock built into the side.

John spied Marty, wearing a brilliant rust-colored dress
and cape, almost orange. She looked like a Baltimore oriole, all
movement and color.

He dreaded telling her. He almost turned Crayon around,
got out of there, home to his room where everything vanished
and quiet surrounded him like a healing balm. His friends clus-
tered around him, helped unhitch, friendly, genuinely glad to
see him.

Ivan searched his face, said nothing.

He told Marty, determined to get it over with.

"I have Lyme disease. I won't be able to play."

She looked at him, her eyes opening wide.

"What do you mean, you have Lyme disease? Bad? I mean,
you seriously have it?"

John nodded, miserably.

"But we need you. Who's going to take your place?"

John shrugged.

"Well, guess it is what it is. I'll ask someone else."

John watched her go, a bright bird that flitted from one group to the next, her objective the same. The game had to be organized, won. Failure wasn't an option.

John lowered himself into a camping chair on the sideline, the sense of failure welling up in him like nausea. He blinked hard to keep the tears from forming.

He felt a light presence, smelled a wonderful scent, like flowers and cedarwood. Strawberries and lemons.

Lena.

She sat on an empty crate beside him.

All around them, young people moved, a sea of colors mixed with the traditional black trousers and vests, the girls' black aprons pinned around their waists.

The shop was enormous, with vaulted ceilings, cement floors, stacks of lumber, half-finished sheds, air hoses, saws, and forklifts. There was the smell of paint and wood, coupled with the metallic odor of nails and screws, air guns and compressed air.

Lena spoke softly. "Hi, John."

He turned to look at his former teacher, his brother's girlfriend. She was wearing a dress the color of a summer sky, a blue so pale it was barely blue at all. With her white blond hair and blue eyes, the effect was almost angelic.

Samuel was a lucky guy.

"Hi."

A small smile.

"You're not feeling well?"

John shook his head, avoided her compassion. He knew without looking that it was there. It always was. Her blue eyes were always kind, soft with caring and sympathy. He supposed it was the way she viewed anything, all God's creatures.

Wounded kittens, dying puppies, whatever hurt or maimed animal or human being crossed the light of kindness.

So, she viewed him the same way. A mewling sick cat, maggots crawling in wet fur, death imminent.

"It must be tough, at your age."

When no answer was forthcoming, she remained quiet, her gaze turned to Marty, organizing the volleyball set, bright, vivacious. Her eyes slid sideways to scan John's face, found a longing that was almost feral in its intensity.

So that was how it was. He wanted to be with her, play his best, prove his worth. She knew his status at home. A loser. Sick in the head. She had heard more than enough from Samuel, had seen firsthand the derision, the eye rolling and snickers.

But they were boys, young men who found it hard to understand the weak, much less have a compassionate heart. Lyme disease was a cruel, misunderstood disease.

She placed a cool hand on John's forearm.

"Don't feel bad, John. Lyme disease always gets better, doesn't it?"

He turned to meet the lights surrounding her, the blue of her eyes so brilliant he could think of nothing else. He felt weak, consumed, drawn into a vortex where nothing existed except the blue of Lena's eyes. Her gaze did not waver, but held his steadily. John blinked, his eyes taking in the golden luster of her face, the plane of her faultless nose and mouth. He blinked, confused with an unnamed emotion that constricted his throat, as if tears were close to the surface, but a wild elation, a rejoicing of his senses held them back.

Her hand was still on his arm.

His answer came in breathless tones.

"Yeah. Well, thanks. It's sort of tough right now. About the time I get my hopes up, I get . . . like this."

He spread his hands helplessly.

Lena shook her head. "Like I said, it must be tough. I can't imagine at your age. And you were so good with Marty."

"Thanks."

Lena nodded. His profile was decidedly attractive. She didn't know what it was that drew her to him. Pity? She wasn't sure. She had always thought him strangely attractive, in spite of his heavy, wavy hair and thick lenses in his eyeglasses. Even in eighth grade, though she would never have admitted it then.

Just then, John tugged at his glasses, blinked his eyes, wiped them with his fingers. Without replacing them, he turned to her.

"If there was only some cure, some antibiotic or treatment."

Lena had never seen his eyes without his glasses. They were not green or yellow or blue, and certainly not brown. Amber. She envisioned a pool in a forest creek, with the sun shining on fallen, golden leaves. His eyes were astonishing, surrounded by the thickest, darkest growth of lashes she'd ever seen. It wasn't the physical beauty that brought the song from her heartstrings, as much as the depth of suffering, the wells of anguish coated poorly with bravery. As if he knew courage was possible, but not within reach.

Oh, John. John. You can beat this horrid disease.

She balled her fists as the intensity flowed down her arms. "John. I'm going to talk to someone I know. A doctor. I clean his home every other week. He's not a Lyme specialist, but he has started taking a deep interest in what goes on with so many people. If your parents would allow it, do you want to see him?"

"Not really. They're all the same."

"You really think that?"

"I do. I read everything about Lyme disease that I can get my hands on. I go to the library. I send for books. I have come to the conclusion that there is no magic bullet. There are many different strains of the virus, besides all the co-infections like Ehrlichia, Babesia, and Bartonella. The Lyme disease bacteria is called *Borrelia burgdorferi*, the main culprit. But, you see, it doesn't matter how much I learn, it won't help a single thing, simply because no one knows exactly what will work best for the chronic Lyme. Likely a tick burrowed its way into my skin when I was a boy, and the virus lay dormant until something set it off. Hormonal changes, another virus that may have weakened my immune system, anything. I'm chronically ill with the disease, which brings a host of unanswerable questions, problems that are simply not able to be solved, without proper research. The CDC is only starting to acknowledge Lyme as a chronic illness."

"What is the CDC?"

"Centers for Disease Control."

"Oh."

"Yeah, I could talk endlessly about different remedies, hundreds of people who have given their testimony about homeopathic cures. Rife machines, so many herbal cure-alls it simply boggles the mind."

Lena let him talk. She sat spellbound, listening, as this quiet boy told her all he knew about his own afflictions.

She saw Samuel push his way through a crowd, his handsome face containing the line between the arch of his perfect brows, a sign of irritation. But he was smiling, if only with his mouth.

"Looking cozy over here," he remarked, hooking his thumbs in the belt of his Sunday pants.

John stared up at his brother, as color suffused his face. Lena could tell he fought an inner battle. She watched as he lowered his face, picked at a thumbnail to hide the array of irritation, helplessness.

"He was telling me about the books he's reading on Lyme disease. I find it fascinating, actually. It's a complex disease, hard to understand."

"I see."

Samuel nodded, the mockery flitting across his face, the challenge to keep his mouth shut met, cast aside.

"Yeah well, that may all be so, but if you're sick in the head your brain can tell you anything and you'll believe it."

John sat, immobile, his head sinking even lower.

Samuel clapped his hands, stretched to his full height.

"Let's find a sunnier subject, old man. No use turning all morose and world-weary, there, old sport."

He clapped a hand on John's shoulder, which felt like a ton of bricks that severed the skin and crushed the bones.

Lena drew back, gasped, as John shot to his feet, white with anger.

"Don't touch me," he ground out, and limped from the shop.

Marty found him hitching up Crayon.

"What do you think you're doing? Going home already?"

"Yeah. I'm not feeling the greatest."

"We missed you at the net. Get better as soon as you can."

Her white uneven teeth flashed in her tanned face, the dimples like parenthesis.

"Yes. I will."

They were watered-down words that meant nothing, and he knew it.

Obviously, Marty was blissfully ignorant of what Lyme really was.

He drove home with all his reserves used up. Depleted. He was a hollow skeleton that clanked in the breeze. He couldn't take this *rumschpringa*. He felt an urgent need to get away from prying eyes, mothers with questions like thrown darts.

But where would he go?

CHAPTER 12

SAMUEL AND LENA SAT SIDE BY SIDE IN HIS SOUPED-UP VERSION OF AN Amish carriage, his fancy horse high-stepping it to match the shining buggy.

He had a Friesian–Dutch Harness mix—the pride and joy of Samuel's life. As they wound their way across the rural roads, through bare woods, along wide-open fields that held nothing but dreary, bedraggled-looking grass, moldy corn stubbles, an occasional rotting round bale that appeared spooky in the light of the waning moon, there was a comfortable silence between them.

They had been dating long enough to no longer need the nervous chatter that accompanied them on their first dates.

Lena was happy with Samuel. He was everything she had always imagined a boyfriend to be. Handsome, eager to please, kind, attentive, she was often afraid she would become spoiled, unappreciative of everything he did for her. He was always willing to go her way, never demanding anything of her that required her to go against her own will.

And, he never touched her. They discussed this at the beginning of their courtship. Lena had strong opinions about any form of bodily contact before marriage, with the courage to tell Samuel her convictions. He had listened, nodded, his face like a stone, which caused her to feel as if she required too much and he'd drop her for someone else who didn't cling to the old ways. But he had respected her in every way.

So Lena was happy, blessed.

Tonight, however, she tried to keep John out of her thoughts. She had been shocked when Samuel aired that awful opinion, making light of John's suffering. There was no doubt in Lena's mind that he had suffered, was going through more pain than anyone had any idea. Lena knew suffering when she saw it.

She mentally shrugged her shoulders, tried to pass off the unkindness as banter among brothers, teasing. Perhaps that kind of talk was normal in the Stoltzfus household with all those boys.

But through the evening spent on the living room couch, Lena was preoccupied, until Samuel asked her what was wrong.

"You seem to be thinking of something else."

"I am, Samuel. I'm sorry. But . . . well, it's just that John is on my mind. He has suffered, is still suffering. Don't you believe Lyme disease is real?"

"No. I don't."

"But . . . It is a medical . . . I mean, blood tests show the bacteria."

"I know. That part I believe, but not the ongoing thing. After a few weeks of antibiotics, he should be OK. All this lying around pitying himself is for the dogs. He's always been coddled. He's the baby."

Lena nodded, hoped to be agreeable.

"I mean, he sleeps in the living room with Dat on the couch. Mam trotted off to Walmart for an air mattress. I mean, come on."

"But surely there's a reason."

"He's spoiled. He's a baby. If he were my own son, he'd be kicked up the stairs and told to go to bed."

There was nothing to say to this. Lena inhaled deeply. She knew when to be quiet and when to change the subject, always tactful and kind, always avoiding confrontation.

John was in the kitchen, making a sandwich, his mother gone for the day, some quilting or other, his father at a horse sale in Ohio.

He toasted bread in the broiler of the gas stove, fried bacon on a burner that was turned too high, splattered grease all over the stovetop. He cut a tomato in thick slices, tore a hunk from a head of iceberg lettuce and proceeded to build a spectacular BLT.

He was in a good frame of mind, having slept well, or at least better than most nights. His mind was refreshed. He felt more alert than he had in months. He was hungry, too.

The smell of frying bacon whetted his appetite, and he swallowed the drool that rose in his mouth, anticipating that first bite.

When had he last looked forward to a sandwich?

Hope rose like a mist, obscuring the days of pain and anguish. Perhaps now the whole load of pills would be proving their worth, finally.

He poured himself a glass of milk, added Hershey's syrup, upending the container and giving it a long squeeze, then stirred. He glanced at the small saucer of pills his mother had set out for him. A pink sticky note was attached to the countertop.

"John, be sure and take these. Love, Mam."

She would never know the difference if he didn't. He could flush them down the commode. Would it be any different today, if he did?

He often wondered if he simply refused, what would happen?

After a few bites of his sandwich, his stomach clenched and the toast became hard to swallow, his throat gone dry. The chocolate milk seemed to curdle, leaving his mouth with a sour taste that turned his stomach even more.

Quickly, he moved to the counter to swallow the required handful of pills, then lay on the recliner, tilting it to the position that was closest to lying down, his gut roiling, his head thick with nausea.

His heart pounded. The thought that these were his final moments on earth pushed its way into his head. Dying. He was dying.

So this is how it felt.

A fog so thick it felt like cotton moved into his brain, obliterating any rational thought of helping himself so he would not die. He tried desperately to push away the thick cotton that kept him from remembering the numbers to summon help, but the effort was too much.

Alone, afraid, his heart pounding in his chest, a half-eaten sandwich and a glass of chocolate milk sitting in a square of weak November sun, the clock chimed the hour of ten o'clock.

A deep moan of despair escaped John's lips. His limbs turned to water, useless. He couldn't lift his hand if he tried, couldn't remember where he was, how he had gotten there, or how he would ever remove himself from this bed, or whatever it was he was lying in.

When Allen and Daniel came home from work, they found their brother in the same position he had been at ten o'clock. They had been warned by their mother to be careful of John's feelings, then received the same stern warning from their father.

Lyme disease was real, it was not an imagined thing. John was doing the best he could. None of them, including himself, had any idea what he suffered at night, the anxiety very common for those who had chronic Lyme.

Dat's words were accepted as authority, pure and potent, at first. Until their own opinions on Lyme disease watered it all down, and they carried their suspicions separately, some having more respect than others.

Daniel and Allen were young, more impressionable than Abner, Amos, Marcus, and Samuel. So when they found John on the recliner, they banged their lunchboxes and Coleman water thermoses on the counter and raised silent eyebrows at one another.

He was pale as a ghost.

Was he dead?

But neither one dared to wake him. They tiptoed past, then tiptoed back. Where was Mam? Why wasn't she along in the kitchen, making supper the way she always did? They were hungry, uneasy with John not waking up when they entered the kitchen. Something wasn't right.

A horse and buggy came clattering in the drive, spraying gravel. Ah, Mam. Now things would return to normal again.

She entered through the washhouse door, untying her bonnet as she charged in, yanked the pin from her shawl, and folded the shawl with hard, jerky movements of her arms. Her wide, pleasant face was pink with cold, her dark eyes popping as she spoke.

"Never in my life saw anyone like Davey sie Lissie. She could well have gotten that quilt out by herself. That would be no hardship to her. But no, my sister Emma says we'll get it done. We'll get it done." She wagged her head in frustration. "There I was, agreeing to her nonsense. We quilted till my fingertips were like hamburger. Every stitch hurt so bad. Plus, I get so tired of Lydia's endless stories about her children and grandchildren. Seriously, does she think the world contains only her and her children? You can only smile, or say that's cute, or amazing, or how talented her girls are for so long, and then you get all washed out. Your mouth puckers when you smile and your cheeks actually hurt and you just want to come home and lay on the recliner with the *Reader's Digest*."

As she spoke, she disappeared through the pantry door, her voice reeling out from behind it.

"Well, it's Campbell's soup tonight. Now where's this bean with bacon? Elmer doesn't mind canned soup if it's bean with bacon. Now, ach, where is it? Don't tell me you boys ate it all. Well, looks like it. Cream of celery it will have to be. And hot dogs. Good thing I bought a few packages of John Martin's cheese dogs. They're the best. Oh, I don't have hot dog rolls. Well, bread it'll have to be. What's wrong with John? John? John?"

She went to the recliner, moving swiftly, bent to touch his shoulder. She shook it gently.

"John?"

John heard his name being called from a great distance. He felt as if he was swimming in oil, thick and greasy, so that his arms and legs had to use every ounce of strength to get through it. After he woke up enough to know he was on the recliner, and it was his mother calling him, slow tears slid down his cheeks, the exhaustion that had used up all his reserves so thick and heavy he could do nothing but cry.

"Are you all right?"

He nodded. His eyes remained closed. It took too much effort to open them. Mam had supper on her mind, so she left him, and for that, he was grateful. To be allowed to rest alone, sound and sight and touch and smell completely relinquished, was all he wanted, or needed.

Winter arrived in the form of rain and ice, slow streams of cold rainwater that formed puddles, the ice surrounding them in thin layers by the morning.

The coal stove in the basement heated the house with help from the heater in the living room, turning the atmosphere cozy and warm, a fortress of comfort against the elements.

Mam stood at the kitchen counter, gazing through the windows with eyes glassy with fatigue. Deep lines furrowed her brow, her mouth puckered with anxiety, vertical creases around her mouth like parentheses. Here it was the first week in December, and she hadn't thought much about Christmas preparations, or anything pertaining to the usual rejoicing of Christ's birth.

She was simply at the end of her rope, as the old saying went. Her strength was ebbing, the mere courage it took to get through the day not always available. She cried slow tears into the swirling water of her wringer washer. She prayed when she stood at the gas range preparing breakfast for her seven boys. She begged God to look down on them with mercy when she packed all those lunchboxes.

Had God forgotten them?

The specter of John haunted her days, kept her wide-eyed at night. She fell asleep in the evening, jerked into wakefulness by the constant sounds from the air mattress in the living room. He wasn't sleeping, yet again.

Fear clenched her insides, roiled her stomach, as pain spread through her chest.

John blew his nose, a rumpled men's handkerchief left beside the air mattress, a testimony to his despair at night.

And still he would not talk to his parents. He fiercely guarded his own anguish, refused a visit to the Lyme specialist in Philadelphia. He seemed to think that if he kept everything away from his family, things would appear normal.

But it was obvious that things were far from normal.

The easy camaraderie they knew so well, the times they lingered at the supper table, the easy banter and unobstructed flow of conversation, the river of her boys' life, the current easy and calming and joyous—all of that had dwindled and nearly disappeared. More and more, time together was spent in uneasiness, covert glances, awkward conversation. Elmer seemed to be aging quickly, his usual sunny demeanor faded, as if a graying mist had successfully overtaken his good humor.

Mary and Elmer were trying their best, but just as waters will toss river stones over and over, back and forth, smoothing and rounding them, so John's health deteriorated the family structure. Unity was blown apart, each of the brothers harboring their own impatience, their lack of empathy. Their faces were encased in stiff, cheery masks of obedience. They could be outwardly nice, the way Dat ordered, without feeling it on the inside.

More and more often, arguments broke out. Mam knew why they fought. It was the underlying frustration, everyone carrying the burden of a crumbling family structure, unable to devise a plan to regain the easy love and closeness they had before John's illness. Borrowed shirts, missing socks, lost wallets—any and all were cause for major eruptions.

Dat and Mam sat wearily, cups of warm cocoa on the table between them. Sleep aids, although neither would admit it.

"Why don't you try and persuade him to go to a chiropractor? The one in town who prescribes natural remedies. You know, Mary. I can't think of his name."

"Elmer, you know as well as I do that it's not going to work. If either one of us is going to take him to a doctor, he'll have to be gagged and bound."

"Are we sure it is Lyme disease?" he asked desperately. "Perhaps he's mentally ill. Do you suppose a psychiatrist would be helpful? A counselor, someone he could talk to about his feelings?" Dat sighed, dropped his face into upturned hands. "It's just simply gone on long enough. Is there no one to help us?"

Watching Elmer start to crumble threw Mam into a panic. That night she didn't sleep at all.

A few days later she gathered the reserves of her usual pluck, marched upstairs, her footfalls sounding hollow on the polished stairway, yanked John's door open, and plopped herself on his bed.

Breathing hard, she lay a hand on his arm where the blue T-shirt stopped and the limp, white arm began.

"John, you have to talk to us. This has gone on long enough. Dat and I simply cannot take another week of this. We want you to see Dr. Stevenson again, do some tests. Or would you rather go to the chiropractor who deals in homeopathic medicine?"

John's answer was rolling away, cocooning himself in the quilt, covering his head, shutting her out.

Mam tried to still her accelerating emotions, the hysteria that rose in her throat. Taking a deep breath, she counted to ten, left the bed, picked up a pair of rumpled trousers, rearranged the cologne and hair products on the wooden tray on his dresser. She looked at herself in the mirror, the mound of impertinence on the bed that contained her son.

Her John. Beloved as he had always been, now turned into this obstinate log. Clamped up like a person she didn't know. A brain gone awry.

She turned.

"Listen, John. Your father and I have to get help for you. This goes on and on, the resting, the refusal to cooperate. We need to do more for this Lyme disease than we have been doing. You need help."

Nothing. Not even a twitch, to show he had heard.

"John? Talk to me, John. We need your obedience to carry out our plan."

When there was no response, Mam realized she stood on the outer edge of a crumbling cliff. She could hear the pebbles loosening from the fragile shelf that contained her sanity, the yawning abyss stretching before her, horrifying in its proximity.

Dear God, she breathed. *Help me.*

She turned, fled down the stairs, away from the unnatural silence that was her son. Shaking and crying, she began to gather a clean rag, a bucket of soapy water, the smell of Mr. Clean and Windex a balm to her unstable mind. Here was normalcy— scouring and cleaning, attacking soap scum in the bathtub, wiping mirrors and windows, sloshing the toilet brush in the bowl as if the very ferocity of her movements would banish the Lyme bacteria from her son's body.

She knelt by the bathtub with hands uplifted, moaning and crying in supplication, prostrating herself for the thousandth time before the throne of grace.

Christmas was a strange, subdued affair.

John looked worse than ever. The sisters from Kentucky were alarmed. Mary and Elmer were a shadow of themselves.

Lydia sat on the couch with Andrew, eighteen months old, the joy of her existence, and tried to imagine what her mother must be enduring. The suffering and exhaustion was oppressive—she sensed it as soon as she came through the door.

It was time for a family conference, and she would initiate it. Everyone needed help whether they admitted to it or not.

But here was Ruthie and now Samuel's friend, Lena.

Lydia hardly knew what to make of that. This Lena. She was a rare flower, a tropical orchid. As sweet and kind as she was beautiful.

Life wasn't fair. Appearance dominated. Of all these brothers, Samuel was the handsome, arrogant one.

Lydia sensed that something was amiss, between the two. He was too sure of himself, and she was like a trailing vine. Compliant. Kind. And she kept her eyes on John much of the time.

The family conference did not go well. They waited for Abner and Samuel's return from taking their girls to their respective homes, which made it close to midnight before everyone was assembled, in various stages of exhaustion and overeating. Coffee flowed, but mostly, the men just wanted to get to bed. John excused himself, refused to participate.

Susie and Sara Ann thought Lydia was being manipulative. Who did she think she was, being the youngest and all?

She forged ahead.

"Something needs to be done with John."

Silence.

"None of you seem to realize how bad he's gotten . . . and how it's weighing you all down. This thing has gone on long enough. He looks awful. Why isn't he getting help?"

Mam began weeping, sniffling into a wad of Kleenex. Dat cast a sympathetic glance in his wife's direction, cleared his throat, steeled himself against his own breakdown of emotions. He was the head of the house—he should be able to remedy his son's suffering.

"He won't go. He refuses to see a doctor. Hides everything away from us. Fiercely protects his own thoughts and feelings." Dat said quietly.

"I already know that. I talk to him on the phone."

Mam nodded. "I'm glad. He needs to talk to someone."

"He is obviously a victim of chronic Lyme. He is the type who experiences intense and debilitating anxiety. He told me about a month ago that he's convinced he's dying, slowly."

A snort from Samuel.

Lydia glared at her brother. "I thank you for keeping your ridicule to yourself."

"Hey, get real, everybody. You'll never get to the end of this till you all figure out he's a spoiled brat, and can't have what he wants, so he's sucking up everybody's pity. It's disgusting. He needs a kick in the butt and to be sent to work. There's nothing wrong with him."

"Yeah. Sam's right. You should see him on the weekend. Normal. As happy as a lark. Laughing, watching the girls. He likes Marty and she doesn't like him, so go figure."

Mam saw her husband's nostrils flare, turn white, and braced herself for the thunderous outburst that was sure to follow.

"Samuel. Marcus. Leave the room. You are wrong in your opinion and are showing no mercy toward your brother, who is obviously racked with a disease that affects his nervous system. Until you read up on Lyme disease, try to understand, you have no right to those uncensored opinions. Go to your rooms."

There were baleful glances, but they didn't leave before muttering, "But . . . we're the ones with him on the weekend."

Allen interjected softly, "He doesn't play volleyball, Samuel. Mostly he sits around."

Daniel nodded, agreeing quietly.

After Marcus and Samuel obeyed their father and left, Lydia tried to calm the tension by saying their response to John's weakness was probably normal.

When Abner spoke, Lydia was appalled at first, then outraged. He believed in Lyme disease, believed John was a victim of the chronic illness. But his parents did nothing right, according to his surefire plan.

Lydia couldn't look at either one of her parents, bowed down with the months of John's refusal to cooperate with any plan they presented. This blame was heartless, a flagrant display of the eldest son's self-righteous position.

If anyone should be sent to their room, Abner should. She bit her tongue to keep from lashing out.

Then Amos, the quiet, sensible one, spoke.

"I think John is sick. If it is all in his head, what's the medical term for that? Anyway, if it is, he's still sick. I think he should go live in Kentucky with Alvin and Lydia for a while. He should get away from Mam and Dat. Obviously, he harbors a deep need for privacy, looks on his parents as destroyers of something very important."

Mam stood up and left the table. No one was taking John away from her. No one understood him the way Dat did. No one would see to his medication. No, he was her son. Hers and Dat's.

Amos tried again, more gently this time. "Mam, it would be for the best, maybe. I know you mean well, but I honestly feel you're stifling him. It's like he's sipping on small amounts of oxygen in order to breathe, when he needs great, deep lungfuls of air to even begin to feel better."

"I won't allow it."

At that, everyone busied themselves with coffee—pouring fresh cups or dumping cold forgotten cups. Children were carried to bed. Susie began to fill the sink with hot water to wash the empty cups.

Later Dat got out the prayer book and they all knelt around the table as he spoke the soothing German words written by the sacred forefathers, the prayer so appropriate for the times when family members were ill.

Lydia was ready to do battle. After Mam's display of clutching ownership of her son, Dat's noncommittal shrug of indecision, and the boys' attitudes, she saw the whole picture with laser sharp insight.

No wonder John rolled himself into a quilted cocoon and refused to talk. And there was a very real tornado on the horizon in the form of the beautiful Lena, Samuel's girlfriend.

CHAPTER 13

In the morning, everyone left John and Lydia alone. Mam had no intention of allowing his move to Kentucky, but figured she might be able to glean a bit of information through Lydia.

She brought him a portion of the breakfast casserole—hash browned potatoes on the bottom, eggs, sausage, cheese, bacon and crushed corn flakes on top.

"Here you go, John. A dieter's dream."

He smiled faintly with his mouth, but nothing changed in those haunted, weary eyes.

She cut a square for herself, filled a glass with cold orange juice, poured a mug of black coffee. Children played around them—scooting trucks, galloping horses, a game of whack-a-mole among the older ones.

Softly, Lydia started in.

"You should get new contacts. Those lenses do nothing for your eyes."

There was no indication that he'd heard.

"You always had gorgeous eyes."

She detected a spark of interest. "Gorgeous?"

"Well, nice eyes. Handsome eyes."

He cracked a small smile.

He took a sip of orange juice. When he didn't offer any form of conversation, she sipped her coffee, ate her portion of the casserole.

"Did you hear about our new venture? Or should I say projected stupidity?"

He watched her, but had no response.

"We're thinking of raising dogs. Puppies."

"A kennel?"

"If the loan goes through."

"How many?"

"Puppies? Or kennels?"

"Hmm."

"You should come help us."

"Me? I'm no good to anyone."

"Sure you are."

"No, you don't understand. I have days when I can't do anything. Climbing the stairs is like hauling myself up a cliff."

"You never did that. How do you know?"

"Well, you know."

Lydia asked no questions, never mentioned his health, always played down his version. Like training a colt on a long lead, she allowed him to choose the pace.

Before anything could be accomplished, Mam and the sisters returned, the sons-in-law come back from helping Dat with chores, and general chaos resumed.

John returned to his room, where he stayed the remainder of the day. He was not present when the large van arrived to take them home to Kentucky. The goodbye hugs were stiff, handshakes completed without eye contact. *This family is falling apart*, Mam thought, but she had no regrets about not allowing John to leave.

She was glad to see the girls return to Kentucky, though she would never admit it. No one was taking John. She was the one who saw to all his needs. Lydia had no idea.

Lydia sat on the second seat of the van, little Andrew strapped into his car seat between her and Alvin. She reached over and smoothed her husband's collar, then slipped a hand through his straight dark hair.

"Well, Alvin, I never thought I'd see the day when I'm glad to return to Kentucky. That was a harrowing experience."

Alvin nodded. "It's tough, chronic Lyme."

"I would love to have John."

Alvin nodded. "Absolutely, he needs to get out of that house."

The first few hundred miles, the conversation was centered on John and the situation with his brothers, the parents too occupied in their single-minded purpose of protecting their son from every form of adversity. They were blind to John's ongoing battle with severe depression.

"It is amazing what a whopper of a mess Lyme disease can make," Lydia concluded. "But I am not finished. I have only just begun to fight."

"Famous last words."

"You watch."

Back on the farm, Mam set her house in order, Dat helping her put away folding chairs, carrying benches to the basement, immensely relieved to be alone, their authority intact.

To have John removed would be to concede defeat. They were strong, stalwart Amish people, hardworking, used to facing trials, plowing through whatever God chose to send their way, a song on their lips, heartache and disappointment hid away. Everything was all right, and would always be. They had managed before, and they would manage again.

The girls had pooled their money and bought a musical clock for Mam. It was an expensive affair, but well worth it, the soft tones of a harmonica playing gospel music wafting through her kitchen now, the song "Eagle Wings" making her nose burn. She succumbed to tears of emotion, overcome now with a great and abiding gratitude for her family.

Yes, yes, we will wait upon the Lord. We will rise up with the wings of an eagle.

She mopped the floor, washed the remainder of the dishes, then sat down at the kitchen table with the Nature's Warehouse catalogue and sent for another new herbal remedy she felt would do John good.

His appointment with Doctor Stevenson came up the first week in January. John grudgingly agreed to go, which surprised and delighted Mam.

His heart rate was low, his iron low, and he had a vitamin D deficiency, which was common among Lyme patients. When John was taken for more lab work, the doctor had a hurried conversation with Mam and listened to her account of his reclusive behavior, his unwillingness to talk.

Without a doubt, he was depressed, which was very common, as well. He prescribed a good antidepressant and an anti-anxiety medication, which he felt was all John needed to be able to resume his usual work.

But John asked questions, read about antidepressants, and refused them, leaving Mam with no choice but to store them in the back of the cupboard and hope for the best. Dat tried to get him to change his mind, to no avail.

The snows of January kept John in the house, his mind foggy, never quite able to decipher what he read or what people meant when they talked to him. The ever-present exhaustion clung to his limbs, the night sweats and joint pain a steady rhythm of the passing days. He was making progress with the anxiety, however.

Or was it the fact that he slept beside his father, the air mattress a place of comfort, the snoring presence of him on the couch the anchor that kept him from the life-sucking whirlpool of fear? He still lay awake at night, raw with the fear of the unknown, but had learned deep breathing exercises did help to calm him, especially the crazy heart palpitations.

His weekends lurched by in abysmal sequence, one as tiresome as the other. He watched his brother Marcus circle around Marty, sizing up his prey, take over his spot on the volleyball team, husky, muscular, making spectacular leaps to spike the ball over the net.

Marcus and Marty began dating in March, just when there was a hint of spring in the air and every young man's heart had turned to thoughts of love.

Samuel and Lena were going strong, and Abner asked Ruthie to marry him and walked around with the silent reverence of the newly engaged.

Then, as if Mam didn't have enough drama already, Amos started to hang out with Naomi Miller, a plump, bright-eyed girl who came to Jefferson County to work for her cousin and his family.

The teasing was astronomical, of course, and for a while that spring, it seemed as if the family was back on solid ground. John helped his mother plant seeds in the newly tilled garden, tried sleeping upstairs again, and did, for a while.

He gained a bit of weight in April, and fed calves on his good days. Then the phone call came from Lydia. She wanted to talk to John. Mam told him grudgingly that his sister would be calling at seven.

John sat in the phone shed, jumping when it rang before the allotted time.

"Hey, John."

"Hey, Lydia."

"Good. You came to the phone on time. You ready to help with the dogs?"

"You're not serious, are you?"

"We sure are. We need someone."

"But, I can't work. Who would do my pills?"

"John, you are an adult. You will take care of your own pills."

"I can't. You have no idea how many I take."

"Can you read? Can you count?"

"Of course. Duh."

There was a moment of silence. Then he asked, "What about Mam?"

"She'll let you."

The telephone receiver slid in his hand as he broke out in a sweat. How could he attempt such an undertaking? To leave everything dear and familiar and safe, in the weakened state he was in, would take superhuman effort on his part. Then there was the monumental effort of persuading his parents.

How could he learn about raising dogs when his brain wasn't functioning properly? What if his thoughts got scrambled and he messed up, even hurt the dogs? It was too overwhelming.

Obviously no one realized the extent of his weakness. He had thought Lydia understood him, but apparently not.

He replaced the receiver, walked slowly back to the house, climbed the steps up to the porch, and sat on a wooden rocker. Immediately, his mother's face appeared at the kitchen window.

"What did she want?"

"She wants me to move down there and help in the kennel."

"What? I thought we told her clearly that we didn't approve. How dare she go against our wishes?" She was shrieking, like fingernails on a blackboard.

John shook his head, pushed past his frantic mother, and climbed the stairs to his room, where he flopped on the bed and allowed weak tears to seep into his pillow.

He talked to Lena on the porch swing that Sunday evening. Samuel was in the shower, and John was dressed to go to the supper for the youth. He had to pick up Ivan, whose horse had thrown a shoe.

"What should I do?"

Lena picked at a thread on the underside of her sleeve.

He could see only the top of her light blond head, the contour of her tanned cheek. Dressed in the color of a deep pine forest, her eyes looked turquoise.

Suddenly, she straightened, looked into his eyes.

"John, you shouldn't be asking me that question. First, you figure it out on your own. Do you want to go? And if you want to, then you should persuade your parents to let you do that. You need to be the one to decide."

"But, I don't know if I can."

"Can what?"

"I mean, do it. Do the work."

"Because of your Lyme?"

"Yes."

"Only you can answer that."

Confused, John lowered his eyes. It wasn't up to him to decide how strong he felt. Was it? He had to wait until the exhaustion went away, till his joints stopped hurting and all the weakness and brain fog cleared. Which could take years.

"What if I go, and can't do my job?"

"You'll never know if you don't try."

"What about my parents?"

"You'll never know if you don't try."

Her voice was mischievous now. He caught her blue gaze, laughed. She reached out to slap his arm, playfully, but he caught her hand. She tried to pull it away, at first, then found the depth of his wounded heart and soul in the amber of his eyes. There would never be a clear understanding and certainly no words for what passed between them. It was closer than a kiss or an embrace. Her touch was like warm honey, liquid gold that could not be named.

"John, I . . ."

She drew her hand from his.

John swallowed, shaken to the core. All the loss in his young

life disappeared, and all he knew was that he had found something so precious it was sacred.

He didn't dare look at her. Then he didn't dare not look.

She was looking at him with a wide-eyed expression, then
slanted her eyes away, downward, her hands clasped on her
black apron.

They smelled Samuel's cologne, heard his energetic whistling
before he burst through the screen door with his handsome tan
face and floppy blond streaked hair.

"Hey, did you wear my green shirt?"

John's voice breathless, shaken. "Why would I?"

"Why would you do half the stuff you do? With you, you
can never be sure."

John blushed, always aware of the loser he was.

Lena smiled. "You look nice in that one, Sam."

"Yeah, but I wanted to match your dress. You sure you
haven't seen it?"

"Nope."

After that encounter on the swing, John's whole world turned
upside down and inside out, like a piece of machinery that flew
apart in every direction. He felt as if he needed to search the
earth for pieces of it, anything he could use to explain what had
occurred. He knew Lena was no flirt. She was far too kind to
lead another person into believing she had an interest in him if
she did not. He reasoned that it may have been that dangerous
trap of infatuation, lust. He could hear his mother's words in
his head, *"Don't be drawn to carnal pleasure by the wiles of the
devil."*

But he knew on some deep level that this was no ordinary
attraction. He had discovered something important. And he
had been discovered as well.

That didn't make sense, either. Perhaps it was just good old
Lyme disease, messing with his brain, scrambling his emotions.

But her words stuck with him, clung to his back like the pro-verbial monkey. *You won't know if you don't try.*

Trying was the onslaught of despair. Failure was such an active part of his life that he had come to accept it. It was much easier to fail than to try. He had no heart for Mam's tearful excesses, or his father's wounded pride. But why would he want to move away from Lena? Oh, there was Samuel. *Oh, right.*

And so his thoughts spun out of control, came back to be centered, examined in a new light, then relinquished.

He caught his father alone in the milkhouse, surrounded by the warm steam from the deep stainless steel tubs of hot soapy water he was using to wash milkers. Dat washing milkers was so unfair. A sadness welled up in John, an empathy for his over-worked father, trying to keep the farm afloat with almost no help from his boys.

He should not be the one washing milkers. Susie or Sara Ann or Lydia had always done it. Or Mam.

Dat looked up, wiped a cheek with two soapy fingers, leav-ing a smudge across his glasses. He turned to wipe his hands on a towel and removed his glasses to look at John. His eyes were encased in wrinkles, as if someone had permanently drawn fine lines around them with a black ink pen. He looked worn down, his enthusiasm dulled.

"What brings you out here, John?"

He crossed his arms, leaned against the double tubs, placed one foot over the other.

"Oh, nothing. I mean, well, yes, something. Not much."

John swallowed self-consciously and ran a finger across the smooth, cold side of the bulk tank, leaving a wet trail.

"I just . . . Lydia wants me to come help them with the dogs."

"She does?"

"Yeah. She called."

"So what do you think?"

"Well, it's not what I think. It's what you and Mam decide."

Dat chuckled. "You heard your mother."

John caught his eye, nodded. Blinked. "I don't know. Could I leave her?"

Dat said sure he could. He never thought he'd rebel against his wife's wishes, but that is exactly what he was doing. He'd finally come to the conclusion that it was largely up to John to figure himself out if he refused to cooperate with his parents' efforts to help him.

"Perhaps the best thing for you would be to get away from everything, try something totally new. I don't know . . ."

His voice trailed off.

John stood by the bulk tank and watched the confusion in his father's face until his own thoughts started to cycle downward. He would die, likely, at a young age, but there was nothing he could do to change that. He would go when his time was up.

He couldn't tell his parents that, though. They'd think he was crazy, take him to a facility for the mentally ill.

But the thing was, after all the exhaustion, all the mental suffering, all the excruciating pain in his joints, what was so horrible about dying?

If you understood grace and God and Jesus Christ, then he only needed to believe that He died on the cross. It was a gift. Nothing he had to pay for, or earn. That was another thing he couldn't tell his family, that the whole plan of salvation from beginning to end was very clear, coming to him one night, like a whisper. A soft and infinitely precious knowledge of Christ's love for his poor, suffering soul.

He wanted to keep it in his heart, sacred, hidden away, forever. If anyone saw a change in him, then that would be praise to God, and not to him.

Dat nodded. Their eyes met, each one knowing they were old souls, well-versed in the way of suffering, of hitting brick walls and dead ends and cul-de-sacs wide enough to let them turn around, change an opinion.

"So, you think you will go, then?"

"Probably. If it's not too difficult for Mam."

"We'll see. Let's go eat supper."

They walked into the house, side by side.

Of course, Mam immediately listed all the reasons it was a terrible idea, why no one else could care for him the way he needed. There were the pills, first off, followed by detox baths, gluten-free food, limited sugar intake, footbaths, and on and on.

She called Lydia and left a message, telling her to be in the phone shanty at seven, then proceeded to chastise her erring daughter up one side and down the other until Lydia drummed the tips of her fingers on the plastic folding table and hummed as loud as she could to shut out her mother's voice. That resulted in a shriek of "What is wrong with this phone line? Don't they have a decent phone service in the hills of Kentucky?"

But in the end, Mam calmed down. Tears dribbled down her face and dripped off the end of her wobbly chin, and she told Lydia it was just so hard to see him go, as sick as he was.

And Lydia said that she understood. "But Alvin and I think it could really help him. And we think with his kind and gentle nature he'll do great with the dogs."

Mam thought but did not say, "That upstart Alvin knows zero, zilch, nix about Lyme disease so how can he know what is good for John and what isn't?" They parted on a friendly note, then, as mothers and daughters generally do, even laughed about the humming phone line.

Absence makes the heart grow fonder, they reasoned for the thousandth time, each one returning to her workload with a lighter heart, if not a spring in her step.

John thought his mother was remarkable, though, in the end. She gave up, accepted the fact that he was going to live with Alvin and Lydia, and set about sewing new denim pants, going to Walmart for new underwear and a few shirts. She stocked up on his pills, wrote detailed instructions for their usage, went over everything every day.

She ran back and forth to the phone shanty, making arrangements, calling drivers and Amtrak and Lydia. She called Susie and Sara Ann and told them both to keep an eye on the situation, that Lydia could be bossy and a tad flighty, so if they saw any indication of John's unhappiness they were to call straight away, and not put it off, either.

John said goodbye to his friends, with a wistful feeling he hadn't thought possible. Marty hugged him lightly, glanced his way flirtatiously, as if she wanted him to remember her. John knew it was only to add him to the string of addle-brained admirers she already had, but she was a sweet girl. She'd given him a boost of confidence when he needed it most.

His brothers were awkward, clumsy in their goodbye wishes, suddenly unsure if John would be all right, half apologizing for their lack of understanding. Samuel gave him a fifty-dollar bill, told him to stay well, awkward as a bumbling first grader.

He didn't say goodbye to Lena. She stayed away from Samuel's home, was not present at the youths' gathering, either the supper or the hymn singing. John searched for her bright head among the milling crowd, but finally realized she simply wasn't there.

Which was for the best. He had no right to feel anything for his brother's girlfriend. That was sure.

Chapter 14

A WARM SPRING RAIN FELL FROM BUNCHED GRAY CLOUDS ON THE day of his departure, the windshield wipers swishing back and forth in hypnotic rhythm, the tires on the wet highway hissing beneath the fast-moving minivan on Route 695, on their way to Altoona to catch the 11:45 Amtrak.

The driver was chugging coffee from a stainless steel cup with a black lid, having been out till two o'clock in the morning. "Them Amish kids," he muttered. "Wouldn't be so bad if they were ready to go when I get there. I waited thirty-five minutes for Lee Beiler's boy to leave his girlfriend's house, which made me late to pick up the girls at Abner King's. So then I had to listen to their yakking. Ah, it's tough, hauling these kids late at night. Chewing gum stuck to the carpet. Half-empty soda cans. Always stop at Sheetz to load up on snacks and junk. Why can't they date in their own county, I'd like to know?"

The cell phone rang, a startling outburst of sound that caused the driver to scrabble wildly in his right T-shirt pocket. The van lurched to the left as he switched hands on the steering wheel, but kept up his speed of 70 mph, the tires hissing, sending up a steady spray of water from the slick tarmac.

"Hello," he answered, much too loudly.

An eighteen-wheeler loomed, sending a heavy mist across the windshield. The driver flipped the turn signals, pulled into the left lane, zoomed past the tractor trailer, a concrete barrier on the opposite side, talking into the phone pressed to his ear.

"Is that right? Yeah? Well, I'll have to check my book, but I think next Wednesday is free. What time? You said nine? Oh, eight thirty. Is that the appointment or the time you want me to pick you up? Okey dokey. Righto. See you then, Henry. No problem."

The cell phone was dropped back into the pocket, the memo book held to the steering wheel, a pen procured to jot down the time.

John breathed a sigh of relief when the memo book was replaced, the traffic thinned, and the concrete barrier came to an end. To be wedged between a large truck and a wall of concrete, moving so fast in a steady downpour, made John break out in a cold sweat. He found himself breathing hard, a tic beginning in his right eye. He grasped one hand with the other to still the tremor that began, slightly at first, then more powerfully until he had to clench his jaw to keep his teeth from clacking.

He breathed deeply, then again. He glanced at his mother, seated beside him, unaware of anything amiss, calmly watching the gray, soaked countryside move past the window. His father sat in the front seat, his straw hat laid beside him, his seat belt fastened, relaxed, smiling.

John breathed in, held the breath deeply, then let it out, feeling his stomach contract, loosen.

They had decided to accompany him, afraid a bout of brain fog would impede his journey to Kentucky. Lydia had had a few words with Mam on the subject but had relented, voicing her frustrations to the supportive Alvin, as always.

"He'll never be free of her."

Alvin calmed his wife by reminding her that she was, after all, accepting the fact that he was leaving, so what were a few more days?

The Amtrak station and the ride to Kentucky were spent in a tiresome battle to overcome the threat of the unknown, the cloying sense of impending disaster.

He arrived in the Amtrak station in Kentucky. Stepping outside, he felt a sweltering sun, humidity that brought rivulets of sweat dripping down the sides of his face. Shaken by the fresh onslaught of fear, John stood white-faced, his hands hanging loosely, his mouth partly open, a blank, dark stare from behind his thick lenses striking a response close to revulsion when Lydia faced him. She shook his hand, smiled warmly, but thought he appeared mentally impaired, otherworldly. She had a moment of apprehension, but refused to show it.

Her parents were oblivious to John's appearance, greeted Lydia effusively, if a bit falsely, Lydia thought.

"You're looking well, Mam."

"Well, yes, of course. It's always good to get away. We had a relaxing trip. Enjoyable. I think John enjoyed it as well. Right, John?"

John nodded, dutifully.

His eyes. Lydia felt the panic rising. His eyes were like a wild person's. Why was he so frightened? They were like dark pools of misery, flecked with hopelessness.

Lydia blinked, swallowed her tears of tender sympathy. She wanted to take him in her arms, rock him to sleep the way she rocked Andrew, put him to rest, a deep, long sleep till years passed and the dreaded bacteria that lurked in the deepest, tiniest cells were completely eradicated.

What if he was more than they could manage? Was he already so far gone, losing his mental powers so rapidly, that he would turn into an invalid, drooling on a wheelchair? For the first time, Lydia felt her own inadequacy, her lack of knowledge.

Should they ask him to return with his parents?

The air-conditioning in another minivan was heavenly. John sank into the back seat, folded his long legs into some semblance of comfort, and fell into a deep sleep, lulled by the hum of tires on macadam. Dry macadam. A thin, middle-aged woman drove along the highway, alert, quiet, while Mam and Lydia's voices rose and fell, a cadence that soothed and relaxed.

He was awakened when the van pulled off the interstate. He watched the small towns, forests, hills, corn and barley fields, thinking how much the state of Kentucky seemed like Jefferson County.

They entered a fairly large town, with warehouses and glass-fronted office buildings, brick factories and apartment complexes.

Harrodsburg, he supposed.

They drove into a winding country road with spectacular views from lofty heights. Great rolling hills were dotted with horses. White board fences and immaculate pastures surrounded horse barns, fancy stables with white pillared mansions. These homes spoke of racehorses, money, expertise, men born and bred into the racing industry, their lives taken up with the production of fine horseflesh.

When they arrived, John spied the new building immediately. He noticed the gray siding, trimmed in white, a porch along the front, nestled between the implement shed and the horse barn. The gravel driveway had been elongated to reach the kennel, tall ceramic pots containing a cascade of purple flowers spilling over the sides like a lace collar.

Wow. Leave it to Lydia.

The house was a small two-story with old yellow aluminum siding, rusty white shutters, and no porch. There was no word that described this odd little dwelling better than ugly. It lacked any real charm, no matter which angle you came from or how hard you tried to find something pleasant about it.

The old wood-sided barn had been red at one time, but had been scoured by the sun and wind for decades, so it appeared to be pink, a scaly, peeling shade of grayish pink. A new hip-roofed dairy barn had been built to the front, sided in gray, like the new kennel, which only served to make the original barn appear even more decrepit.

The corn was heavy and dark green in color, planted uniformly, and the alfalfa had already been cut. Fat, sleek cows grazed in a lush, low pasture, so there was an aura of hard work and dedication about the place.

It was just like Lydia to choose to build a kennel rather than do cosmetic work on that house. She was a manager, a forthright realist with a sharp mind. She planned every move with eyes toward the future, pinched her pennies, and fell only a hair short of being the leader, drawing Alvin along on waves of her own planning.

The Kentucky folks agreed that she wore the pants, if they never spoke it. Alvin was a workaholic, going, going from before the crack of dawn to sundown, always willing to lend a hand, lay down the reins of his own team of horses to help his neighbor, leaving his ambitious wife clucking her tongue.

But the yard was immaculate, flowering bushes trimmed, trees pruned, old shrubs cut into neat oblong shapes, yews and boxwood and juniper holding court along three sides of the faded yellow structure.

The garden was a rectangular plot, edged to perfection, a profusion of well-fertilized vegetables growing in neat rows.

Mam walked along the perimeters, commenting on pea stalks already gone, chicken wire on wooden stakes rolled up and stored in the rafters of the garden shed, lime applied to freshly tilled soil, and lima beans planted twelve inches apart.

Lydia told her there were seventy-two pints of peas in the freezer.

"My oh, Lydia. When did you do them all?" She harbored a fierce pride in her youngest daughter. She was the one who handed down the gardening knowledge, who taught her daughters when to plant, when to harvest, how to can and freeze, giving timely advice to daughters grateful to receive and apply their mother's gardening wisdom.

"Will you do another planting of red beets?"

"I have more than enough. I did thirty-some quart. Alvin loves red beet eggs."

Mam smiled. Yes, she had taught Lydia all of this.

They entered the house from the back, stepped up on a small platform made from treated lumber, no railing, no backs on the steps. Mam spoke before she thought, searing her daughter's feelings.

"Alvin could have built a decent patio."

Lydia pretended she hadn't heard, which was the easiest way out of fumbled explanations or announcements that would clash with her mother's own.

Her mother did not need to know how much the kennel cost, Lydia being the one who wheedled her husband into its existence.

The patio could wait.

The interior of the house was dim and cool, clean, with the homey feeling of an old house, like a trusted friend. The linoleum had scuff marks, holes, and tears, but was waxed to a high sheen. There were a few old kitchen cupboards painted white, and white walls with gray wainscot. In one corner stood a beautiful oak hutch, and in the center of the kitchen were a matching table and chairs. A floral arrangement on the table took Mam's breath away.

It was Lydia's turn to smirk.

"It's easy, Mam. That's daylilies, fern, echinacea, bee balm, vinca." Her voice was lofty.

Mam grimaced, laughed. "Now you're *grosfeelich*."

The small living room was dark, with shades drawn against the heat, painted floorboards, rugs scattered, a heavy gray sofa and chairs. The cherry dropleaf table held another, similar arrangement of flowers.

"My oh, Lydia."

The whole inside of the house was adorable, new furniture mixed with old doors and walls painted white, an opening stairway with a striped runner going up the middle, Mam tsking about how to get that carpet clean.

"It's called a battery-operated sweeper, Mam."

A snort. "Whatever."

She could hardly keep up with the conveniences of the younger generation. Twelve-volt batteries hooked to inverters produced brilliant LED lighting, set blenders to mashing berries and bananas into cold smoothies, or sent mixers whirring, whipping cake batter to perfection without using arm muscles that should rightly be brought into play.

The young generations didn't value sadirons and kerosene lamps properly. But she guessed time marched on and waited for no one, especially the ones who clung to the old ways, like her, who would eventually turn into an eccentric old lady with seventeen cats in the house.

John's room was on top of the stairs to the right, above the kitchen. It was low ceilinged, with wide floorboards painted white, a sleigh bed and oak dresser with an oval mirror hung above it. A patchwork quilt was tucked beneath fat goose down pillows on the bed and a decorative throw pillow that said "Happy" on it.

An old recliner was in one corner, the arms worn, a loosely woven throw slung across the back, a low stand and a battery lamp beside it. He had his own closet and two windows, one on either wall, for a summer breeze at night.

Lydia didn't mean to, but she hovered inches away, like an anxious cat. Was it OK? Would he be comfortable? The bathroom was just across the hall, all right? Sorry, we have to use it, too. Only bathroom in the house. John reminded her he was used to sharing with six brothers.

"The recliner is there whenever you need to rest. There's a fan, on hot days. Let us know if you need help, when you feel bad, mentally or physically. Here's a Bible, for when you need a spiritual boost, too. Are you a Bible reader?"

John shrugged, felt his face color.

Lydia nodded. "I know, when you're young . . ."

Her voice drifted off.

Supper that night was a lighthearted affair, both of his parents happily prattling on in an easy manner, away from responsibilities, reveling in the appreciation of their children's farm, their hard work ethic, secretly taking a portion of the honor for themselves.

John ate the meatloaf, the creamy scalloped potatoes, added a generous dollop of homemade ketchup, and helped himself to a heaping spoonful of peas. Delicious.

"You blanched these peas just right, Lydia. I can tell you didn't let the water boil. You only leave them in till they change color, you know."

Lydia chewed, swallowed, said, "They're not blanched."

Confused, Mam poked the tines of her fork into the peas. "But . . ."

"You just pick them, don't wash them at all, pour them into a gallon ziplock bag and put them in the freezer. When you need peas, you shake out the amount you need and put the bag back in the freezer."

"But you said you got seventy-two pints."

"Divided into gallon bags."

"Ach. How can it be? Who told you about this?"

"Everybody does it now. Well, except for a few grandmothers like you who find it too hard to change."

Andrew slapped the tray of his high chair with his plastic spoon, sending cooked peas bouncing over the side. He bent over, looked at the peas rolling and sat back up, his eyes wide, his mouth in a perfect O. He lifted his face, his eyes closed as he laughed.

Lydia caught his hand as he prepared to send more peas over the edge of his tray.

"Nay, nay."

He watched his mother's face for the degree of seriousness, tried again, but was stopped by Alvin's hand this time. He looked to his mother, who shook her head and said, "Nay, Andrew. Nay, nay."

Mam was proud to see them working together to teach the little boy the meaning of no. She approved of so much—in fact, of everything she saw. Her spirits soared in gratitude. What could be more uplifting than seeing that your children walked in the way of truth, respected the teaching of their youth, honored their father and mother? This was what they had strived for, she and Elmer, and here was the fruit of their labors.

The grand tour of the kennel took place after chores. John had already been inside, with Alvin, but they'd only taken a few steps before the dogs set up such a clamoring and howling that Alvin said they'd return at feeding time.

John felt intimidated by the state-of-the-art dog kennel. It was a long building with battery lighting, white walls, sloped cement flooring, new metal caging with large, airy pens. It was clean and compassionate, built around the dogs' comfort.

Alvin fed each dog their ration of dry dog food, then allowed everyone entrance to the main walkway.

A German shepherd with distinctive black markings lay panting in a corner, unable or unwilling to eat. Her stomach was distended, her teats engorged, her gentle brown eyes seeking John's, as if she was begging for relief. John looked at her, felt the sharp pang of sympathy, the accompanying lump in his throat, and whispered, "It's OK, poor dog. You'll get through this. I'll help you."

Thump, thump went the long, plumed tail.

Alvin joined him, said quietly, "She's due any day."

John nodded, too shy to say more. The truth was, he knew nothing about dogs. They had never had one on the farm, due to his mother's aversion to them. Even now, she stood just inside the door with a distasteful expression on her face. The only thing he knew about them was the fact that they barked when someone arrived, some of them were good for herding animals, and occasionally, they could take a chunk out of a leg.

There were miniature schnauzers, gray and white with black noses and cheeks, black hairs on their ears, and large, curious eyes. They were friendly little chaps, dancing and leaping against the wire mesh of their enclosure. He felt the same pang of pity, wanted to open the gate and let them run. Run and run and run.

Well, this was simply not going to cut it, all this pity and wanting to release the animals. He was here to work, to help Alvin and Lydia be successful in raising puppies that would be sold as pets.

There were so many different breeds. The Alaskan malamutes were just beautiful creatures, every one. The puppies took his breath away. He had never seen anything so cute.

Suddenly, he experienced an intense longing to show these puppies to Lena. He had hardly thought of her since they'd started their trip, but now he wished she were here.

What would she say? She loved every living creature.

There were boxers and Scottish terriers, poodles and Samoyeds. There was a section for the mastiffs and the Newfoundlands, the biggest dogs that took a bit more care and expertise, a fact that Alvin said made him nervous. They were expensive dogs, requiring experienced help at a birthing. Lydia looked forward to the challenge, he said. He hoped John would be like his sister.

"We have a lot of money tied up in this kennel. Sometimes it scares me a little, what all could go wrong. We've got some stiff payments to make, so I'm counting on you, John."

He clapped a hand on his shoulder, looked up to give him a comradely grin. John felt his heartbeat quicken, his knees turn to Jell-O, the strength draining from his shoulders. His fingers went numb.

Looking around, he remembered to nod, let Alvin know he had heard, before folding his tall frame onto a stack of bagged dog food. He almost slid off and collapsed in a destitute heap on the floor.

It was too much. The responsibility flattened his strength, smashed his resolve, left it tinkling like shards of broken glass. Why, oh why, couldn't he be normal like other people? Why had he even come to Kentucky?

They should have told him beforehand how much was actually expected of him. He knew nothing, and half the time he didn't even have the strength to drag his weakened body out of bed in the morning.

He sat on the bags of dog food, listened to Alvin explain each breed to his father, felt his strength ebb away like the tide in the ocean, going out, out, out, leaving a pile of sand and hermit crabs and dead jellyfish, a stinking mishmash of dead sea creatures that represented yet another failure.

He went to bed early, then cried wretchedly, unable to stop the sobs of a grown boy. In the morning, he stayed in bed till his mother became frantic and banged on the door.

When he didn't answer, she went back downstairs and had a long and whispered conversation with Lydia, sparing nothing.

Lydia drew her mouth in a straight line, told her mother they'd take a day at a time, and see what occurred. Lydia brushed her off like a pesky housefly, which only served to infuriate Mam.

John would get up when he was ready, Lydia said. Alvin knew he wasn't healthy and had already hired a neighbor boy to help around the farm.

Lydia was perceptive, had seen John fade in the kennel, after Alvin's challenge or pep talk, or whatever you wanted to call it.

Well, he'd meant well, so no use getting irked at her husband. He didn't know John, didn't understand the disease. If this was a setback, then so be it.

That's what the recliner was for.

The parents visited Elam and Susie, Benuel and Sara Ann and the grandchildren, then set off for the Amtrak station.

At the station, Dat looked deeply into John's eyes, shook his hand, and said, "This will be a good experience, John. You'll learn from it. I just have a good feeling about you and Lydia."

John dipped his head as quick tears sprang to his eyes.

"Thanks, Dat. I'll do my best."

Mam was a flurry of anxious reminders. "Don't forget the Nature's Way pills, and Body Balance, and the detox—it's all upstairs in the bathroom cupboard. And don't forget vitamin D. Take extra. Bye, John. Take care. Lydia has our phone number. Bye!"

And she disappeared, his father's hand on her elbow, steering her through the knot of travelers boarding the train.

He tried to sort through his feelings on the return trip to the farm. Lonesome? Bereft? Not really. Just empty, drained. So tired. So physically weary. He'd have to tell Lydia that Alvin couldn't depend on him. He wasn't feeling strong at all.

Since there was no porch on the house, Alvin and Lydia produced comfortable lawn chairs and pulled them up to a fire ring made of large, chunky fieldstone. The chairs were the old type, metal with a frame bent into a C, a fan-shaped back painted bright yellow. If you sat on them, you sank back and bounced up and down like a rocking chair, but better.

Alvin threw a few pieces of wood on cardboard and newspaper, held a propane torch to it till he was rewarded with a crackle, then sat back, rested his elbows on the arms of his chair, his fingers woven on his stomach, and began to talk.

He talked constantly, a flow of words coming from his

mouth. He shared simple stories or opinions or his views on life, or people, methods of farming, how he felt when he met Lydia, how his brother made so much money being on a roof all day.

He often laughed uproariously at his own jokes, slapping his knees and howling, almost falling off his chair.

The firewood crackled and burned. Night would soon close in around them, but it was a friendly night. The darkness was soft with the heady scent of hollyhocks and delphinium, the roses along the west side of the house. Fireflies lent their ineffectual lights to the velvety dark, pigeons cooed their warbling wishes to each other. Bats wheeled in the last light of the day and owls rumbled their throaty calls.

This would be the first of many evenings spent by the fire. Sometimes they made s'mores with graham crackers, marshmallows, peanut butter, and chocolate bars. Other times, they simply drank lemonade.

John came to look forward to darkness, the time he had dreaded most since becoming ill. After the campfire and a hot shower in the clawfoot tub, he fell asleep, more often than not, tired, clean inside and out, the sound of Alvin's voice like a warming cup of hot chocolate.

And never once did any one of them mention Lyme disease or the state of his well-being.

CHAPTER 15

THE HOT SUMMER DAYS TURNED INTO A RELUCTANT AUTUMN WITH crisp, foggy mornings and searing afternoons, when the sun refused to relinquish its heat, as if the morning coolness would threaten its domain over the land.

Hot days reached into October. John's feet ached constantly as he slogged through each day, doing whatever Alvin expected of him, without interest, as if he got through each hour by his determination alone.

From her kitchen window, Lydia watched him walk to the dog kennel, shuffling his feet like a man nearing the end of his days. His head was bowed, his shoulders stooped. Part of her wanted to shake him, knock him around, put some sense into his head, tell him to look around, notice his surroundings, be thankful, think of someone else other than himself.

He showed no interest in making friends, never even tried to join the youth group in spite of the invitations Lydia knew were proffered.

Mam's phone calls were unwelcome thrusts into her already busy life, shoving all resolve into uncomfortable twinges of regret for what she did or did not do. No, John was not doing well. No, he showed no interest in the dogs, ever. Yes, he did his chores. At first he'd done better, for a while.

Mam's latest suggestion had been to ask John to come home.

"Home to what, Mam?" Lydia asked, painfully aware of all her resolve that had fallen short.

"Well, us. His brothers. His normal life."

Lydia kept it together for all of thirty seconds before she let loose a volley of pent-up fear and frustration, resulting in her mother telling her goodbye before gently replacing the receiver.

Later, in the cool dusk, she sat on the chair by the fire pit and cried silent swallowed tears in the half-light, listening to John's brave attempts at joining Alvin's conversation.

Undone by her mother's phone call, afraid of the looming appearance of her own failure, she contemplated the question she never thought she would ask.

The following day, the Alaskan Malamute had a litter of six healthy puppies. John did spend some time under Alvin's supervision cleaning her cage, making sure the puppies were nursing sufficiently.

The kennel was immaculate, fans whirring to keep the temperature at a reasonable sixty-five degrees. The dogs lay in corners, relaxed, comfortable, or when they felt energetic, they had access to the dog run, a long fenced-in area where they would receive fresh air and sunshine.

John made a final round before checking the clock on the wall, then headed to the house for lunch. He had been fighting nausea all morning, finally guessing his sour stomach was due to that latest bottle of whatever concoction was in that vile-smelling tincture.

His head down, his thumbs hooked loosely in his pockets, he was shuffling across the driveway when the sound of an automobile horn tore through his reverie.

He jumped, looked around, wild-eyed.

A small gray car pulled to a halt. The door was flung open, slammed shut, and a tall, slim, black teenager about his own age stood with one hand on the hood of his car, one leg crossing the other at the knee, toes propped on the ground, one elbow jutting out to the side. He wore a gold-colored sweatshirt and some odd-looking pants, cropped below the knee, with long white socks pulled mid calf, encased in purple high-top sneakers with gold laces.

He nodded, grinned, said softly, "Hey, ma man."

His face was all merriment and eagerness. His skin glowed with a deep bronze shine, like an old copper penny.

John nodded, said hello, softly, his throat riddled with phlegm. He had hardly spoken a word all day, so his voice was rusty. Embarrassed, he cleared his throat, then cleared it again.

"'S'wrong with da voice, man?"

John grinned sheepishly, shrugged his shoulders.

The white teeth appeared in a blinding grin, a second and he had loosened his nonchalant stance and hopped on the hood of the car. John winced as his backside slammed against the gray metal. Immediately both purple-clad feet were stuck straight in the air for leverage, his arms bunched at his sides, a roll from his back and he cleared the hood of the car, landing expertly on his feet with a practiced move he must have done hundreds of times.

He slapped his fists together, bounced on the fronts of both feet, laughed out loud.

"Name's Dewan. Dewan Reynolds. Live a few miles down the road from here. Came to see Mister Alvin Beiler."

"I'm John. John Stoltzfus. Lydia's brother from Pennsylvania."

A hand whipped out to meet John's faltering one, gripped his fingers like metal tongs.

"Glad to meet you, John."

John, being unused to formal introduction, mumbled some reply that made no sense. Something between "pleased to meet you" and "me, too," which came out "pleased me, too." Or something like that. His face flamed. He felt the heat in his neck.

"Yeah, John buddy. We friends. Buddies. Brothers. Bros."

A long dark hand snaked out, clapped his shoulder and stayed there.

"So, call me Dewan."

John grinned a sickly grin, like curdled milk, shivery and unsure. What was he supposed to do with this fireball of words and energy? Were Amish boys his age allowed to hang out with someone as polished and worldly as Dewan?

Before he could gather his thoughts one way or another, Dewan began his life's story, complete with his knuckle cracking and arm swinging, which was fine with John. At least the hawkish grip on his shoulder was gone.

He was born in Detroit, Michigan, to a sixteen-year-old mother. Never knew his father. His mother raised him and his two siblings, with the help of an aunt, who kept the children for free while she worked the night shift at Walmart and took cleaning jobs during the day.

Boyfriends came and went, some of them nice, some of them not so nice, but all of them were temporary, none of them a permanent father.

When the aunt died, they moved to Dexter Falls to be with another aunt, his mother's sister Neva. They lived in a trailer park, went to school with mostly white kids. His mother got a good job as a worker at the Dart Corporation, worked her way up to floor manager, and brought home a decent wage, which enabled them to purchase the house on Circle Drive.

"She still works there. Don't have no man. Says she don't need one. But she goes out sometimes. I finished school this year. *Grad*-uated! Yeah!"

John watched Dewan clap once and pump a fist in the air, feeling a slow rise start in his chest, a deep and abiding bubble of pure mirth. He had never experienced anyone quite like this, someone so effusive, so . . . free.

"Yep, I do have that diploma. The world can know, Dewan Reynolds has succeeded. A force to be reckoned with. Here I come, folks. I gonna study to be a veter-*inar*-ian!"

John couldn't stop smiling, reflecting Dewan's own confident grin.

"My mom, she say go ahead. You can do it, baby. She know how smart I am. Yeah."

John watched Dewan's face, took in the glow from the smooth, dark skin, the cropped curly, kinky black hair. He was one of the most handsome men John had ever seen. His eyes snapped and sparked with vivacity, an endless flow of good humor.

Now Dewan brought his swinging arms down to the front, then back again, only to slap the palms together once more. He looked at the barn, then back to the house, a question in his eyes.

"Think Mr. Alvin could use some help? See, I need to work with the animals. See if I do have a knack for my *chosen* profession. See, he don't have to pay me much. I already got a job at Wendy's in town. I flip them burgers."

He demonstrated with both hands, face lifted to the sky. John half expected to see burgers falling from the clouds, as intent as Dewan's eyes were.

"Not too bad, that job at Wendy's. I'm saving. See this car? Seven hundred, man. Seven hundred. Paid cash. No car payment. See, you can't hand out all that money that goes to interest. Drowns you before you can even start swimming. Sure it does."

John nodded, feeling like a dead fish—bland and dull and lifeless. He was afraid of his own shadow, flecked with the spittle of Lyme disease. He had no future, no choice, no nothing. No horse and buggy, no friends, stuck in the middle of Kentucky.

"So what's up with you, ma man? You look a bit peaked. You're about the color of brand-new notebook paper."

John felt a flush of anger.

"Don't worry about it," he mumbled.

"Yeah, don't mean to take you off but you are *white*. I know I'm black, but you are the whitest white I've ever seen."

Fortunately, at that moment, Alvin appeared at the kennel door, a puppy in his hand. He stopped, took in the gray car, the two boys, then walked toward them, the puppy nestled in both hands, a smile on his face.

"Yo," said Dewan.

"Hello."

"Name's Dewan Reynolds. How you doin'?"

"I'm well, thank you. Yourself?"

"Awesome, man. I doin' awesome. What you got there? That a German shepherd?"

Dewan reached out to touch the puppy, which had just opened its eyes at three weeks, the coat of hair now clearly containing black and brown markings. Alvin dumped the puppy in the long black hands, and a friendship was born.

Dewan sat down in the middle of the gravel drive, cupping the tiny dog against his gold sweatshirt, cooing and whispering, his head bent over the helpless animal in his hand. He forgot Alvin and John and simply held the puppy in wonder.

Finally, he lifted his face, his brown eyes full of feeling, and asked if there were more where this one came from.

Dewan was strangely silent during the tour of the kennel. John became uneasy, fearing he would find the dogs' life in pens unendurable, worthy of a visit from the animal rights activists. Alvin kept up his usual stream of words, proudly showing Dewan the various dog breeds and describing in detail the careful construction of the kennel.

Dewan nodded sometimes, but mostly had very little to say.

When they were through, Dewan shook hands gravely, said he'd be in touch, got into his car calmly, and drove slowly away.

Alvin raised an eyebrow.

John shook his head.

By the first week in November, the days turned cooler, the sun's heat giving way to a lukewarm, winterish cast that was far more comfortable.

The forests surrounding the farm, the rows of trees along the fences turned into fiery colors of red, orange, and gold. The hemlock and shortleaf pine provided a cooling backdrop of green and dark brown, scattered among the brilliant display that created a wild array of light and pattern.

There were strands of healthy Virginia pine, white pine, and red cedar that provided a pungent scent, a sharp, earthy fragrance unmatched by any other scent John had ever experienced. He love to walk among these trees, breathing deeply. He stumbled upon a huge area of wild rhododendrons and plum bushes, their waxy leaves a new discovery for him.

Ferns completed the woodland forest like a multicolored, waving rug, providing hiding places for chipmunks, deer mice, and gray squirrels.

John walked to these restful places in the evening to get away from the barking dogs and Alvin's constant verbal onslaught, trying to sort through his exhaustion, the crippling brain fog.

There was so much pressure. The kennel was filling up with litters of puppies that would be ready to sell for Christmas. Alvin had his hopes pinned on astronomical prices for the off-spring of the more expensive breeds, relying on the incoming cash flow to pay off the line of credit he had acquired to purchase the mothers. These included the mastiffs, those immense creatures that required constant vigil while birthing the litter of ten to fifteen offspring; the Norwegian elkhound, an expensive risk; the Old English sheepdog, and the Newfoundland. The care of these dogs' coats required hours of brushing, a task that fell to John. He brushed the thick, dense coats with a special brush, grooming the gentle mothers endlessly, never once feeling any real affection for any of them. He swept the aisles with a stiff broom and hosed down the crates, his arms like floppy half-filled balloons.

Alvin and Lydia got very little sleep, surviving on a few hours a night for weeks on end. They were snappish and short tempered, both of them, so John retreated to a world of his own, cutting both of them out. He moved among the dogs, did only what Alvin required of him, and retreated to the woods at day's end, finally admitting that he hated this place. Homesickness followed on the wings of that self-discovery, a deep, abiding sense of wanting his father, his brothers, his own horse and buggy, the youths' company on the weekends.

The despair and exhaustion overtook him again, and he took to his bed, refusing to get up many mornings. He lay on his back, staring at the ceiling, wishing he could disappear off the face of the earth.

There was no reason to go on living. He couldn't keep up. The frenetic pace surrounding this farm, the intense pressure to keep every puppy alive and well, the befuddling array of shots and wormer and antibiotics and Oxytocin, when to call the veterinarian, when to feed special rations, records on the wall like a jumble of Japanese writing . . .

Lydia stopped caring about his medication, let pills and medicines, tinctures and capsules run empty. Their little boy, Andrew, was carted around like a sack of feed, on a backpack, in a stroller, on a wagon with red rails inserted into the sides. Sometimes he wailed from his crib in the morning when Lydia was still out at the kennel, and John would stumble down the stairway, through the messy kitchen and into the bedroom. He'd lift the pajama-clad little boy out and onto his lap on the recliner, his heart racing, pumping the quick thrusts of blood into his head until he thought his head had to be like a helium-filled balloon.

It was on a morning like this that John sat at the kitchen table, a dish of Froot Loops set before him, feeding Andrew the colorful orbs soaked in milk, last night's supper dishes staring at him from the countertop, unwashed piles of laundry sorted on the kitchen floor.

He knew he should wash the dishes and start the laundry, but the task was too monumental. He wanted out of here, away from the demands that accosted him everywhere he turned.

Why didn't Lydia come get her neglected little guy? He was heavy, the arm John looped around his middle numb, without strength. He stopped feeding him the Froot Loops and set him on the floor, which resulted in a high thin wail, a clinging to John's pants leg.

That was the sight that met Lydia's eyes when she slammed through the door, her hair disheveled, her eyes red and bleary from lack of sleep.

She hung up her sweater and black head scarf, shot him an impatient look, and hurried across the kitchen to pick up her son, crooning assurances.

She changed his diaper, dressed him in a clean shirt and little-boy trousers, then sighed, before opening her mouth to release a shower of words.

"You could have picked him up, John. Is that too much to ask?" The words shot from tight lips.

"My arm was tired," John mumbled, shamefaced.

"Your arm was tired, John. Really? My whole body is numb with fatigue. You lay in your bed pitying yourself, counting all your symptoms, storing them away to bring each one out when it suits. Trotting out your stupid excuses behind the blazing neon sign that says "Lyme disease." I'm sick of it, John. We've done everything we know what to do, and you're no better than you were a year ago. Don't you think of anyone but yourself?"

She was crying now, deep, hysterical, gulping sobs, her face red, her eyes scrunched up like a child's, her mouth wobbling uncontrollably.

"You don't even try, John. How can a body gain strength just lying around like a wet dishrag?"

She honked into Kleenex she had grabbed from the box on the stand by the couch. She set Andrew into his high chair, gave him a graham cracker, filled his sippy cup with apple juice, and plunked it into the holder.

John blinked, hung his head.

"I know I'm tired myself, probably about at the end of my rope. We lost two of the elkhounds last night. We need your help, John. We can't do this by ourselves. I figured, surely, after the heat of the summer, you would gain some strength, perk up, show some interest. Instead, it's the same old same old. Just lying around."

John looked at her dully. Her words were like flapping pigeons, flying just above his reach. If he chose, he could pluck one and examine it, but it took too much effort, so he let them go. He just wanted out. He wanted to go home to the kindness and benevolence of his mother and the understanding of his father, to see Lena occasionally, to be in her presence. He had failed Alvin and Lydia, same as he failed everyone and everything before.

"I want to go home," he mumbled, blinking furiously.

Lydia turned from the sink, where she had been throwing greasy casserole dishes and dripping drinking glasses onto the countertop with frightening force.

"You do? Well, you're not going. You promised to help us out and you're going to see it through. We can't manage without you, the way we have been. Get upstairs and get dressed. Get out of those loathsome old sweatpants and that filthy T-shirt, get a shower and brush your teeth. Stop obsessing over every little twinge you feel through your muscles. Everybody has aches and pains."

She stopped, her eyes boring into his.

"Git. Go."

"But . . . Lydia."

"But what?"

Her fists on her hips, her eyes wide, she planted herself above him.

"I have Lyme disease."

"So what? Maybe I do, too. Who knows? Lyme disease or not, you have to make an effort. Ask God to help you. We all have to call on a higher strength than our own at times. Go."

And John went, deeply humiliated, blinking back tears of frustration and helpless rage. He returned to the kitchen to find Alvin sitting at the table, eating five fried eggs, a mound of stewed saltine crackers and sausage gravy, a glass of home-canned grape juice and a steaming cup of black coffee.

Alvin grinned up at John, who was now showered and dressed.

"You're looking good."

John couldn't think of a reply, still stinging from his sister's harsh words.

They heard the crunch of tires on gravel, a car door slamming.

The knock was deafening. Not one or two, but five or six. Alvin rose from his chair, opened the door, and welcomed Dewan Reynolds into the kitchen, warm and inviting with the smell of breakfast.

"Hey, ma man Alvin!"

"Good morning. Good to see you."

"Yeah. Yeah!" Dewan shook Alvin's hand with exuberance. "What we got here? Little man?"

He walked over to Andrew in the high chair, bent low to address him in soft tones. Lydia watched, expecting her son to yell hysterically at the stranger, but was amazed to see a broad smile crease his little face, then the corner of a soggy graham cracker extended to the visitor.

When Dewan took it in his mouth, Andrew raised his face and laughed, his eyes crinkled with delight.

"Yeah, little man. You like Dewan, don't you?"

Andrew raised an arm, extended a hand, and wiggled his fingers for more graham crackers, which Lydia produced, and Andrew promptly fed to Dewan.

Alvin shook his head. "Never saw anything like it."

"Babies? They love me. All babies. Dewan their man."

He laughed, swung his arms to bring his left fist into the palm of his right hand.

"Sit down, Dewan."

"Thanks. Thanks, man. 'Preciate it."

"So what brings you?

"Well, I went home a few weeks ago, and thought about my *chosen* profession, the whole veterinary bit. Seems as if I got some growing up to do. Pity them dogs in them cages."

John thought, *Aha, I knew it.* Dewan was a secret animal rights person who would try and shut down Alvin and Lydia's kennel. He watched Dewan with narrowed eyes.

"But . . ." Here, Dewan lifted his eyes to the ceiling, gave a low whistle. Did the man always have to be so demonstrative?

"The way I look at it, the suffering of animals ain't goin' nowhere. I mean, there will always be kennels, horses penned up, cows in stanchions, and one old black boy ain't changin' any of that. I gotta grow up, learn things, do what I can to help sick and dying animals. I love them all."

"Just call me James Herriot. Yeah. Read all his books. I'm no white British guy, but you bet I got it in me. Now, I'm asking if you'll allow me to become an assistant. Don't need top dollar. Just let me observe, get some hands-on experience, get to know the process. A'right?"

He watched Alvin's face for a reaction.

Alvin looked at Lydia, who had her back turned, washing dishes. She dried her hands on a dish towel, nodded her head, smiled. "Yes, of course we can use you. We're in over our heads right now. We'd be glad to have you on board."

Alvin nodded.

"We have John, but he doesn't always feel good, with his disease."

"Oh yeah, that. . . . What is it?" Dewan put a hand to his forehead.

"Lyme disease."

"Oooh, nasty little bug, those ticks. People die, right?"

"Not if it's treated."

"Antibiotics, huh?"

"A chronic case like John's takes more than that."

Lydia waved an arm in the direction of John's pill bottles on a tray.

"What? He take all that?"

Dewan whistled, bent to read labels, shook his head.

"You take all this stuff every day, brotha? Every single day you swallow a pill out of every bottle?"

"I try to," John mumbled, desperately embarrassed now.

"That's good. It's all good. God bless you, ma man. You gonna need it swallowing all them. Whew!"

He clapped a hand to his forehead, rolled his eyes, and grinned at John.

CHAPTER 16

Lydia hung laundry on the line, allowing herself a moment of watching the stiff November breeze fan out the bedsheets and pillowcases, flap the colorful bath towels like billowing kites in an untrustworthy wind.

She sighed, weary to the bone.

All this energetic planning, jumping feetfirst into both ventures—the kennel and then John—and here she was, fighting off defeat without armor. The fat was in the fire now. She'd had her say, and figured John and her mother would never forgive her.

Would they?

Had she only made matters worse? She took a deep, cleansing breath, and then another. Her eyelids drooped. No use trying to figure things out when she had only slept a few hours for so many nights she couldn't remember what a good night's sleep felt like. She turned, took up the clothes basket, and went back into the tiny lean-to they called a washhouse.

Someday, she'd have a decent laundry room, but for now, this would have to do. She put Andrew down for a nap, then collapsed on the recliner for a short rest before starting lunch.

Dewan Reynolds began working that Friday, arriving in a cloud of gravel. He wore a red sweatshirt with a black Nike

symbol on the chest and a pair of jeans tucked into sensible
Muck Boots.

He tapped John's arm with the back of four fingers.

"How's it going, dude?"

John was fighting an intense emotional battle of his own
and found Dewan's energy suddenly grating, so he acted as if
he hadn't heard.

Alvin walked over, and told Dewan to follow him, he'd get
him started. John glanced back over his shoulder, glared at both
of them. He wanted out, worse than ever. He wanted to get on
that train and go home to his family, to kindness and understanding. At home, if he felt ill, he could rest. If he had a bad
day, feeling depressed or overwhelmed, he could rest, too. That
Lydia had turned into a mean old shrew, unable to handle her
own life and taking her own frustration out on him.

She didn't understand Lyme disease. You had to rest. If you
pushed yourself past reasonable limits, you only suffered the
following day.

Homesickness welled up in him. At home there were decent,
well planned meals, a clean bedroom, plenty of books to read,
the complete trust that if he chose to lie in bed with a good
book, it was fully and generously accepted.

Not here. Not after Lydia's tirade.

This morning, she had stood at his door, yelled his name,
and kept on yelling till he answered, then told him to get up or
they were not going to pay his wages anymore. "You have to get
up," she'd said.

He did get up, slammed the bathroom door as hard as he
could, then put the lid of the commode down, sat on it, and cried.

She was a cruel slave driver. And now he'd have that happy
Dewan to put up with. He was amusing on that first day, but
since then was nothing but annoying.

He sat in the office, at Alvin's desk, to upgrade a few records
for the Welsh corgis. Queen Mary, the caramel-colored mother

with a litter of only four, needed to be put on higher protein, more fat.

Every dog had a name, every puppy in each litter had to be named for the registration. Naming the puppies with Lydia was one of the few things John slightly enjoyed.

They would hold them up to see the expressions on their faces, then consult the book of names for babies, joking about choosing "Goliath" for the smallest dog or "Rosebud" for a mastiff, who would quickly grow to be enormous like her mother.

But John refused to help with the naming now. Not until she came to see how unreasonable her expectations for him were. He had Lyme disease. Wasn't that enough to elicit at least small amounts of empathy? She had judged him without mercy. Now he planned on making her regret that error.

The telephone on the desk rang.

John was so startled he almost forgot to answer, but caught it on the fifth ring.

"Hello, Kentucky Kennel. How may I help you?"

"John? Is that you?"

"May I ask who is speaking?"

"Lena. Lena Zook."

For a moment, it seemed as if the floor would open and the desk chair containing him would plunge through. He could not think of a single thing to say.

"Are you there, John?"

"Yes. Yes, I'm here."

"I wanted to speak to you anyway, so it's a good thing you picked up the phone. How are you?"

"All right."

"Improving?"

"I don't know. Some, maybe."

There was a brief silence.

Then, "Do you think you could arrange for a driver to pick me up in Dexter Falls next Thursday? The twenty-seventh?"

Stupidly, he stuttered. "N . . . n . . . next Thursday? Why?"

"My cousin has a child near there who needs a tutor. She's a special ed student, and she's having seizures, so the regular special-needs teacher won't take her anymore. I promised to spend the winter with her."

John felt like his brain was swimming in thick, green pea soup. Finally, he mumbled, "You're coming here."

"Yes, for the winter."

"What about Samuel?"

For a long moment, there was no answer. Then, in a very small voice, she said, "It's a long story. Will you schedule a driver?"

"Yes. Do you want me to come with him?"

"If you wish."

If he wished. He definitely wished.

They said goodbye and he replaced the receiver with hands that shook like aspen leaves. He tilted the office chair and stared off into space, his mind racing around the sentence, "It's a long story."

The remainder of the day he bounced between his usual exhaustion and lack of interest to shots of adrenaline that coursed through his limbs.

He left Dewan in the kennel, went to clean the horse stable, thinking he'd be better by himself, the way his head was spinning.

He found Dewan at lunchtime, opening a brown paper lunch sack, peering into the bag, then retrieving the largest sandwich John had ever seen. He laid the sandwich aside and produced a white napkin, which he spread on his lap, carefully smoothing out the rumpled corners. Then he brought out a bag of potato chips and an apple, smooth and round and yellow.

"Dude, you're staring?" The gentle sentences Dewan uttered always ended in a lilting question, as if the listener had the right to question the statement he had just made.

It spoke of his nature, John supposed, for he was a polite, reasonable young man who knew what he wanted, gave no one reason to doubt he would obtain his goal, but was somehow completely humble at the same time.

"That's a big sandwich," John observed.

"That's my mama. Yeah! My auntie mama. I love this woman."

He unwrapped the sandwich from the layers of waxed paper and nodded his head as he lifted the corner of the top slice of bread.

"Ham. Lettuce. Mustard. Hot sauce. Cheese. Mayo. Onion. Fried onion. Mm-mm."

He raised the sandwich to his mouth, expertly shoved a portion into it, and closed his eyes and chewed, uttering small bursts of sound from his throat.

"The best sandwich ever. *Yeah!*"

He yelled so loud, a few of the dogs began to bark. Puppies yipped their high-voiced chorus.

John watched him take another bite. For the first time in a week, he felt hungry. He wanted a sandwich just like that. With potato chips.

"You hungry?"

"I'll go to the house."

"No need, bro. Got another one jus' like it."

He bent his head, rummaged in the paper sack, and came up with another very large sandwich. Immediately, John's mouth watered. The sense of being hungry was like coming home. *Honestly*, he thought, *now where did that come from?* Lyme disease was, indeed, extremely weird. He was devastated a few days ago, adrift in a crumbling raft of homesickness, lying in bed, not caring whether he lived or died. And now, suddenly, he could hardly wait to bite into that sandwich.

He relished every bite. Mustard squeezed between slices of ham. Mayonnaise squirted out between lettuce and fried onion, dropped onto his pants leg and lay there in unnoticed white blobs. He ate ravenously, nodding his head to everything Dewan was saying, but caring only about the next bite.

They were in Alvin's office, a square allotment of space, with painted walls and dusty linoleum floor, metal filing cabinets, wooden shelves containing large volumes of books pertaining to canine health, breeds, dog foods, and everything Alvin could possibly need to know. There were calendars with dogs, of course, extra chairs, a rumpled rug by the door, windows that were so speckled with fly dirt you could barely see out.

Dewan told him he had a girlfriend, a Hispanic girl from out beyond Rohrersville. He stood up, began slapping both back pockets, produced a worn, leather wallet and extracted a faded picture of a round-faced, dark-haired girl who smiled into the camera.

"Only picture I got. Alvin makes me leave my phone in that drawer." He poked a long, thin finger in the direction of a filing cabinet, then looked at John.

"You don't have one?"

"No. I did for a while, but my dad doesn't like it. I'm out of the loop way down here in Kentucky. I want to go home."

He knew it wasn't the truth, even as he said it. It had been, though, till the phone call from Lena.

"You need a phone. Don't matter where you are, you text and call. Send pictures, do whatever. Yeah, man, I be like . . ." He mimicked with his thumbs, then lifted his head in time to his words. "Yo, Mama, where you at?" Or, "Hey, baby!"

"My girlfriend? Her name is Dawnita. She is the most beautiful, the most sweetest girl on the face of the whole earth. I'm one fortunate brotha."

With that, he pushed against the desk, propelling the office chair backward until it crashed back against the metal desk. He hung his head across the back of the chair, pumped a fist to the ceiling, and let out a howl that reverberated through the small office.

John smiled awkwardly. To the Amish, it was considered ill-mannered to show excessive emotion of any kind. Even praying was done in secret, or read from an old German prayer book. He'd never been around—or even imagined—so much spontaneity, such grandiose gestures.

"She work at Chipotle. You know, that burrito place. Best. Thing. Ever."

"What is it?"

"Restaurant. You know, eating place. Don't tell me you ain't allowed going there? No cell phone, no electricity, no television, no nothing. Sheesh!"

John smiled again. Wished he had another sandwich.

"You got a girlfriend?"

"No."

"Just no? That all you got to say? Never did? You telling me you're not allowed to date, either?"

John couldn't help laughing. It was a strange feeling, and it sounded even stranger. Instantly, he felt self-conscious, ashamed of the rusty, clacking sound of his dumb laugh.

Dewan's brown eyes stayed on his face.

"Why you wear them thick glasses, man? No wonder you got Lyme disease. I'd have a disease, too, if I was behind those thick lenses."

John smiled. His hands went to his glasses, lifted them at the temple. He took them off his face, pulled out his shirttail and wiped them.

"You got nice eyes." A casual observation, not meant to flatter.

"Thanks."

"Tell you what. You get yourself an appointment. I'll take you to get them little round contacts."

He mimicked inserting a contact lens, lifting his upper lid, then burst out with an infectious sound of pure enjoyment.

They went back to work when Alvin returned. Dewan helped him wean a few litters and give injections amid the chorus of usual barking and high-pitched whining. John stayed at Alvin's desk, working on records.

Maybe he should get contacts? With Lena's arrival and all . . .

He felt a decided flutter in his stomach. How could God have chosen a more perfect time for Lena to arrive? He would have gone home, there was absolutely no doubt in his mind. He had hated it here, and still did, in some ways. He avoided his sister, determined that she would be the first one to apologize for treating him so callously.

He decided not to tell anyone about Lena's arrival, least of all Lydia.

He tumbled wearily into bed late that night, wondering how he could ever summon enough strength to climb out in the morning. His shoulder ached as if the inflammation was, indeed, flammable. He lay on his side, which sent searing pain down his right shoulder blade, then switched to his stomach and turned his head to the right, which didn't work well at all. He sighed, rolled onto his back, crossed his hands across his chest, and closed his eyes.

Lena was coming to Kentucky.

Who would be teaching her own school, back in Jefferson County? She must be a gifted special-needs teacher to be summoned to Kentucky. Was it merely a coincidence, or fate, or the hand of God, leading them together? Would she remember the touch, that day on the porch swing?

Over and over, he wondered what she meant by saying it was a long story. If Lena and Samuel had broken their relationship, wouldn't he be one of the first to know? Surely Mam would have mentioned it to Lydia on one of their phone calls.

He'd place his trust in God, which was the substance of his faith. God didn't always work things out the way everyone thought He would. Or should. If Lena was to be a part of his life, that was all right. If not, that was all right, too.

Or so he tried to convince himself. Really, he wanted Lena to share his life, which was asking too much, he knew. Riddled with anxiety and every other mischief of Lyme disease, how could he ever think he was good enough?

He wasn't good enough, that was the thing. And yet he hoped, tossing and turning his weary body far into the night, hearing Alvin leave the house to check on mothers and puppies, then returning.

He pictured Lena's bright face, the light in her eyes, her white blond hair, the graceful contour of her neck. She was the loveliest girl he had ever seen, or imagined. He thought of Dewan's explosion of feeling, the freewheeling office chair, the honesty. How frankly he knew he was *the* most fortunate dude. John smiled. He felt an expansion, a bubble in the region of his chest. He rolled over to muffle the sound of his laugh, that unused cackle that sounded so stupid to his own ears. He laughed again. His shoulders shook. Tears squeezed from beneath his scrunched-up eyes.

He gasped for breath. He was still laughing. He could only describe the feeling as delicious, like a square of warm blueberry cobbler with homemade ice cream.

The laughter turned to soft chuckles, and then slowly he drifted off to sleep.

Customers began rolling into Alvin and Lydia's dog kennel around the last week in November. It wasn't a good time for John to ask Alvin if he could have the afternoon of the twenty-seventh off.

Lydia was often busy showing puppies, talking to customers who wanted to know every detail about the shots the puppies had, the wormer, the proper registration. Sometimes it took a whole afternoon with one customer, leaving Alvin and Dewan to keep the work going, or talk to more customers themselves. When John finally did ask, Alvin agreed quickly, too distracted by another customer pulling up to ask questions.

John made an appointment at the local eye doctor, and Dewan took him, threading his way through traffic like a seasoned taxicab driver, music pounding out of the speakers in the back, reverberating along the walls of the car, rattling the windows, pulsing through the seats.

He had been warned against exactly this type of music, these spoken lyrics called rap. John tried to extricate himself from the pounding beat, the words that assaulted his ears, but he didn't have enough nerve to ask Dewan to lower the volume.

So he rode through town, Dewan thumping the steering wheel, propelling his head forward and back in time to the beat.

He was relieved to get to the optometrist's office, glad to hear the doctor say his contacts could be picked up in three working days.

Quickly, he counted. Yes, he would be wearing them to pick up Lena.

Contacts proved to be difficult, especially putting them in every morning, but by the time the Thursday of Lena's arrival came, he was fairly comfortable going around without his thick glasses.

He asked Lydia to get a driver for him. She didn't ask questions, simply nodded and called a local, older gentleman who made some extra cash taking short trips to town, hauling Amish.

So Lydia did not know Lena was arriving, which suited John well. For one thing, she'd jump to conclusions, especially about the contacts, which he would not be able to deny. For another, dozens of questions would follow, which he would be unable to answer. It was best to keep everything to himself.

He slept very little the night before she was to arrive. He dozed fitfully, dreamed he was late to pick her up and she turned around and went back home. His heart hammered in his chest. He broke out in a cold sweat and sat up slowly, waiting for the weakness to pass before making his way to the bathroom. He caught a glimpse of his pale face in the mirror, a sheen of sweat on his upper lip.

Would Lyme disease always be with him? Would he never bounce out of bed with no thought of his health? The road ahead seemed endless, a quagmire of defeat, ravines and mountains of fear and doubt.

He'd thought perhaps the thrill of Lena's arrival would fortify his strength, make him forget how weak he actually was. And here he was, pale and sweating, peering bleary-eyed at his watery, unguarded reflection.

He began berating himself. How could he hope to have a chance? His brother Samuel was a fine specimen of young manhood, strong, smart, climbing up the ladder at B and S Structures. Here he was, groaning though his days, naming puppies, sitting at Alvin's desk half the time, no friends . . . except for Dewan, he supposed.

In the morning, he showered and combed his hair, grateful that Lydia had cut it. She had trimmed off the worst of those upturned curls, resulting in a headful of manageable waves. With that and the use of men's styling gel, he had to admit the situation had vastly improved. He flipped through the row of colorful shirts, finally settling on an almost white shirt with a narrow beige stripe.

He'd be wearing a coat, so the shirt wasn't important.

Lydia raised an eyebrow when he entered the kitchen.

"You shouldn't have any trouble with flies," she remarked wryly, sniffing his scent.

John grinned, nodded.

"What gives?"

"Going to town."

"Dressed like that? Come on. What's up?"

Andrew yelled, beat his spoon on the tray of his high chair, chirped like a little bird, then threw his yogurt container on the floor. He watched his mother's face for the expected disapproval before bending sideways to assess the damage.

"Andrew!"

He looked at John, blinked, then opened his mouth in an oblong O.

John smiled, ruffled the little boy's hair.

Lydia went to the sink, swiped a dishrag from the counter, bent to wipe spilled yogurt.

"This doesn't answer my question."

"All right. I'm picking someone up in Dexter Falls. At the Amtrak station."

"Someone? Who?"

There was no use trying to hide it now.

"Lena Zook."

"What?"

Lydia plopped into a kitchen chair, still holding the rag that contained blobs of yogurt.

"Why not? What's wrong with that?"

"But why is she coming here? I thought she was a school-teacher. Who's teaching her school?

"Her cousin has a special-needs child that she'll be tutoring. Teaching."

"Who's her cousin?"

"I have no idea."

"Why did she call you? Why not me or Alvin?"

"I was doing bookwork. So I spoke to her."

"Ah, John."

"What's that supposed to mean?"

Lydia shook her head, sagged against the edge of the table. She could see nothing but trouble descending in the form of one very pretty girl who belonged to the far superior Samuel.

Dear God in Heaven, I come before Thee in supplication. Without realizing she was praying, she felt quick tears behind her eyelids.

Turning, she rose.

"How many eggs?"

John shook his head. "I'll eat cereal."

"There's bacon. I'm mixing pancake batter."

"Cereal's fine."

He poured his favorite, Cinnamon Life, added milk and sugar, brought it to the table, began to eat.

"Your pills. Did you have your protein shake?"

Dutifully, he shook out the natural vitamins and supplements, mixed the protein powder in water, shook it, gulped it down, then returned to his cereal.

"Think that stuff helps?"

"I imagine it does."

"John, promise me something. You know Lena is a very attractive girl, a perfect match for Samuel. Promise me you will not fall for her and add more heartbreak to your life. I'm so afraid for you. Somewhere, when your health is better, God has a girl picked out for you. Please wait on God to show you the way."

John stopped eating, looked at his sister, shrugged.

"You think I don't know all that?"

"Of course you do, John. But romance is serious business. Young people get married so often for all the wrong reasons. They place appearances and self will ahead of patience and seeking God's will. It's a small wonder we have so many marriage problems in this day and age. We're all spoiled. Too many material goods, too much prosperity, and selfishness thrives."

"Boy, you're a prophet of doom and gloom."

"I'm serious. The only reason I talk to you about this subject is because I care so much. You're in a weakened condition, which leaves you open to so many more emotional missteps. I just want you to be very careful."

He had been careful, hadn't he? If he was to blame for what happened on the porch swing, well, so be it. He had been nothing but careful since then. He'd moved to Kentucky, for goodness' sake, removing any chance of meddling in Samuel and Lena's relationship. Why God had sent Lena down after him he didn't know, but it hadn't been his doing. Surely there was nothing wrong with meeting her at the train station and making sure she got settled safely.

CHAPTER 17

ANTICIPATION COURSED THROUGH HIS VEINS, IN SPITE OF HIS SISTER'S serious words. The small car couldn't contain his eagerness, so he found himself pushing against the floor of the vehicle with the soles of his shoes.

The gray November landscape rolled past, a blur of stark trees, small ranch houses, single storied, with garages, two vehicles parked in the driveway. Occasionally, there was a larger, two-story house, but mostly, the countryside was dotted with small, affordable homes.

The driver's name was Clyde. Clyde Johnston, he'd said. Retired from the state. Worked on the roads all his life, driving big equipment.

And then, mercifully, he fell silent until they entered town, saying they were early, did he want to do anything else first?

John couldn't think of a single thing to do. He'd gag on coffee, his nerves already as taut as a guitar string. So he said no, they'd sit in the parking lot to wait. Clyde seemed to find that satisfactory and found a spot to park the car, turned off the motor, and adjusted the back of his seat.

"Might as well go in. Trains are often early or late."

John went, having no clue which door to enter, where the passengers would get off the train, or exactly what time it was.

A stiff wind tugged at the collar of his coat, as he bent to close the door of the car.

He appreciated his height, able to see over the milling crowd, the constant movement of vehicles, a whirl of light, color, and sound.

He found the gates, with neon, blinking lights, numbers, an information booth, service desks. He realized he knew nothing about Lena's exact arrival time, or which train she would be on.

"Excuse me." It was a harried mother tugging crying children, their faces smeared with tears that ran into chocolate.

Quickly, he stepped aside, mumbled an apology, felt as big as an ox. He was afraid to sit down for fear of missing her. He found a spot with a good view of the departure and arrival doors and hoped for the best.

He'd never done this before, so how could he know? He heard his mother's voice in his head, "John, John, not here. She'll never see you here. Come this way."

No, she would not think this suitable, but she wasn't here. He was on his own, and had chosen this point to watch the crowd. He'd do his best.

He leaned against the wall, crossed one leg over the other, and lifted his coat to insert his hands in his pockets. He hoped he appeared nonchalant, at ease, a man of the world.

All around him, humanity flowed like a colorful stream. Small, thin women wearing tight jeans and cropped sweaters, obese women in brilliant colors, elderly ladies with bewildered expressions, carrying leather purses in fearful grips. Black women with dozens of thin braids swinging below their waists.

He watched an older black man, as black as night, gathering his wife and children into long and tender hugs, tears streaming. So much love and feeling, with no apparent shame. John could not imagine hugging his own mother and father like that.

It wasn't the Amish way, and John accepted that. But still he felt an emptiness, a need to be cherished, embraced.

John swallowed and wiped his hands on the leg of his black trousers. He was sweating and he didn't want to shake Lena's hand with a clammy palm. How could she have come by herself? Was it safe for a young woman to travel alone? Samuel should have accompanied her.

The soles of his feet ached. He shifted position, eyed the benches longingly. A wide, middle-aged woman caught his gaze, slid her enormous purse over to make room for him. She smiled, mouthed, "Sit."

John smiled back, shook his head.

The clock on the wall was enormous, black and white. 10:30. That was the time she'd given him. His pulse raced. His mouth went dry. A clanging, a rush of movement, the building taking on a buzzing, a reverberation.

His eyes turned to the arrival gate. He waited, standing tall now, no longer slouched against the wall. He knew Lena was not tall, reaching only to his shoulder. She would be immersed in the roiling, moving stream of people.

But she was easy to spot in the crowd. Her pale blond hair and white covering, the small, lovely face with huge blue eyes scanning the crowd. She was carrying a fairly large piece of luggage, drawing it along by the handle. She looked at ease, certainly not frightened, searching faces around her for signs of him.

She looked straight into his eyes, then looked away and kept walking.

What? Bewildered, frustrated, John hurried after her.

"Lena?"

She moved on, seemingly without hearing him. He repeated her name. She stopped, turned. Uncertainty moved across her lovely features, then a glad light came into her blue eyes, a wide smile revealed her pearly white teeth.

"John!" she gasped.

Speechless, he extended his hand to shake hers. She bent to set the large wheeled suitcase on its edge, shrugged off the smaller piece of luggage, and extended both hands. John caught them in both of his, held them.

"I didn't know you. I looked straight at you. Where are your glasses? What happened to your hair?"

Her face was flushed now, her eyes large and blue and bewildered.

She tugged her hands away, so he could do nothing but let them go.

John smiled, laughed aloud, pointed to his eyes.

"Contacts."

"You've lost weight. You're even taller."

Flushed even more, embarrassed now, she fell silent, her eyes never leaving his.

What is it that goes on between eyes that lets you know it's all right, expected, to take someone into your arms? John couldn't name the quick rush of emotion, he only knew he had to hold her. And he did. He moved toward her slowly, his arms soft and so careful, until her arms crept about his waist and held him, and he crushed her to himself.

He half noticed the appreciative glances from passersby. For a moment, he heard his mother's voice. *John, don't. Aren't you ashamed of yourself? You're Amish.* Shick dich.

"Lena, I . . ."

She buried her face in his black woolen coat, would not relinquish her hold. When she did, her eyes were limpid, wet pools of emotion, that rocked John's world. Everyone disappeared from his sight, and there was only the sweet, flushed face and the blue of her eyes. A midsummer sky. A bluebird's wing. A forget-me-not.

"John, I apologize. I . . . wasn't prepared. You'll think me bold."

"No. Oh no, Lena. I'm just so happy that you're . . . well, you know, glad to see me."

"I am."

"Let me carry the luggage," he offered. "Is there anything you need to do? Pay? Leave tickets or anything?"

She laughed, a soft, tinkling sound. "You're obviously not a seasoned traveler, either. First train ride, shooting off into the unknown. Totally clueless."

They made their way to the station exit, out onto the city streets, across to the parking lot, the raw November air whipping leaves and pieces of paper, dust, and dry grasses around them. Cars moved out of the parking spaces, trunks popped open like huge mouths, swallowing luggage and boxes, plastic totes containing travel items.

He felt no pain in his shoulder as he slung the strap across it. His strides were quick and strong, his hand clenched around the handle of the enormous, wheeled piece of luggage. The cold air was invigorating, lifting his morale, his entire outlook on life. He did not understand it, but accepted the feeling of well-being, if only for a minute.

They found Clyde sound asleep, his seat in a reclining position, his cap pulled low over his eyes, his mouth open.

John hesitated, not wanting to scare him out of a deep slumber. He tapped on the window, softly.

Immediately, he jerked awake, looked around, then unlocked the door, adjusting his seat, arranging himself before putting both hands to the steering wheel. John asked him to open the trunk and was rewarded with a button being pressed, the lid of the trunk opening. They arranged the luggage, then John opened the back door for her, before sitting beside the driver in the front seat. For a moment he wished Clyde was a taxi driver in the true sense, allowing him to sit beside Lena, ignoring the driver. But that would not be polite.

Clyde yawned, asked where to.

John looked back at Lena.

"I have the address here."

She rummaged in her purse, produced a slip of paper.

"Gideon Lapp. 134 Stonewall Drive. Akron."

"Gideon Lapp."

Clyde put a finger to his chin. "Don't know a Gideon Lapp."

"Do you have a GPS?"

"Sure."

"I'll give you the address again."

"Are you hungry, Lena?" John interrupted.

"Actually, I'm starved. I was too tight to buy breakfast on the train. An egg sandwich for five dollars? I think not."

They moved out into traffic. John told Clyde to pick a good diner, then asked Lena if she was in a hurry to get to her cousin's house. No, her cousin had no idea what time she'd arrive, so they hadn't made arrangements about lunch.

Clyde pulled into an old-fashioned diner, complete with a glossy silver exterior, a row of windows along the front, strips of neon lights at roof level along the entire length of the restaurant.

"The Comet" blinked on and off on a diagonal sign that rotated on top of the roof.

"Best hamburger and fries around," Clyde said gruffly, as he steered the car into a space close to the door. John offered him a ten-dollar bill to pay for his lunch, and pushed it on him when he declined.

"Thanks, appreciate it," he said, slapping John's arm, before hurrying into his favorite barstool to take advantage of his free lunch and lighthearted banter with Edna, the buxom woman behind the counter, coiffed hair stuck into a massive hairnet, red cheeks, and a quick wit.

John felt shy, suddenly. Samuel would know exactly what to order, when to pay, how to joke with the waitress. John would always feel ill at ease—he'd always be the bumbling, oversized boy, topped with a wild array of unruly hair, eyes peering out from behind thick lenses.

He could hear his brothers' taunts ringing in his ears. *Lazy. All in your head. Get over it already. Lazy. Lazy. Lazy.*

And now here he was, with the most beautiful girl in the world, who belonged to his brother Samuel.

But she made it so easy. She was excited about being in Kentucky, talkative. She glanced at the menu, then said she'd order whatever he was having.

His confidence building again, he ordered two waters with lemon, please. Two cheeseburgers with everything, fries, and two chocolate milkshakes.

Lena gave him the full benefit of her smile, and his spirits soared even farther. He'd done the right thing. For once in his life, he had not done anything stupid at an important moment.

She said the child she would be teaching was an autistic child, and she would also be asked to include a five-year-old Down syndrome child after a few months. She looked forward to the challenge. She had read books on autism, spoke to parents of autistic children. Gideon Lapp was married to her cousin Barbara and they had four children, all boys, and Mark was the oldest.

John listened, watched her face, the expressions crossing and recrossing the excitement at her new venture, the daunting possibility of failure quickly replaced with an air of bravado. It was the most endearing display of emotion John had ever witnessed, so in spite of his resolve to stay out of any gray area that involved falling in love, he felt the magnetic power of her eyes, found himself with bated breath, waiting for the next laugh, the next smile that produced a loveliness of expression beyond words.

He floundered like a hooked fish, with Samuel at the other end of the line. She ate with enthusiasm, ketchup clinging to the side of her mouth. John wanted to reach out and wipe it away, but restrained himself. She ate French fries two at a time, smothered in more ketchup. She slurped her milkshake without a thought of being delicate about it.

John ate half his burger and forgot most of his fries, he was so occupied listening to her.

He had to know about Samuel, but could not think of a casual, roundabout way of asking.

"Aren't you feeling well, John? You aren't finishing your lunch," she asked.

"I'm fine."

The silence that followed was uncomfortable, punctuated by the clink of silverware, bursts of laughter, the hum of machines, traffic moving on the highway.

John struggled for dominance over the fear of failure, the sure knowledge that he was the Lyme-ridden younger brother who mistook any affection for a love that was completely conjured by wild imagination.

He couldn't begin to hope, or harbor a longing for this sweet, unspoiled young woman, superior to him in every way, even in years. The real reason for the hug at the Amtrak station was consolation, a pure empathy that sprang from her caring heart. She lumped him in with the autistic children, the boy with Down syndrome.

When Clyde finished his lunch, he walked over to their table and said he was going to the can. He told them to take their time, but John knew it was the beginning of the end of this time together.

He opened his mouth, closed it again. Asked if she wanted dessert.

Coward hides behind stupid question, he thought, wincing.

And suddenly, he had to know.

"What happened between you and Samuel?"

Startled, her eyes flew to his face.

"Nothing. Yet. I mean . . . well, like I said, nothing."

"But you said it's a long story."

Her eyes turned away from his, slid to the left, watched the traffic in the gray light, moving colorlessly on the gray road.

She sighed. She picked up her napkin, folding it in half, ignoring the grease and ketchup stains, and folded it again.

"Samuel asked me to marry him next year. It would be a long engagement that would have to remain a secret till spring. It's what I've always wanted, for him to ask me to marry him. But when it happened, it was . . . colorless. It wasn't what I expected. I had always imagined I would be overjoyed, but I couldn't bring myself to give him the answer he planned on. I am hanging from a cliff, John. A yes is too much, and a no is letting go, falling into an abyss of uncertainty. I don't know if I can do all the hard work that goes with a yes. Do I have the strength to pull myself up till I reach the top of the cliff, and will it be all right when I get there? Marriage is hard, John. Dating is often hard. It's so . . . so different from what I imagined. Samuel is handsome, talented, the perfect boyfriend. Every girl in the Amish settlement would take him in a heartbeat. The thing is, I don't understand myself and my lack of feeling. Am I simply unappreciative? Am I dating Samuel because every other girl wants him and I'm the winner? Human nature is competitive, and I am no exception."

The waitress arrived with the bill, wished them a good day, before gathering plates and cups.

"We should go," she said, in a small voice.

"This time away will be good, Lena," John said, his voice gruff with the tears that sprang too quickly. He blamed his weakened condition.

She lifted pained blue eyes. He looked into the blue of her gaze, and felt his resolve slip away. He reached for her hand, held it, traced the veins on the back with his thumb.

What passed between them was a replica of what they had experienced on the porch swing that memorable evening. It was the sure feeling of having been found, of finding an unnameable substance that was beyond themselves.

"Don't be in a hurry to give Samuel an answer, OK?"

Lena nodded, lowered her eyes, as teardrops slid unhampered down the perfect contour of her cheek. John reached out and wiped them away, his eyes holding her startled gaze.

"Lena, I would never ask you to do anything that doesn't bring you happiness. If Samuel is the one for you, then I'll accept it." He was surprised at his own candor.

Bewildered, she asked why he said that.

"I know I'm only the little brother. But I care very much about your happiness. Surely you know that."

She shook her head as more tears coursed down her cheeks.

He had to strain to hear.

"I had no idea."

"I don't mean to complicate things even more."

She swallowed, fought for control of her emotions. He watched her throat constrict as she struggled. Then she shook her head from side to side, slightly at first, then more decided.

"You're not."

"You guys need coffee? Dessert?"

The brash voice jangled through the mist of feeling, dispersing the moment. They both glanced up, assured her they were finished, left a tip, and rose to their feet. John paid the bill, stood aside to let her go first, placed a hand on her waist, the rough fabric of the coat like spun gold.

She did not look at him as he helped her into the back of the car.

It turned out Gid Lapps lived approximately fourteen miles to the south, into the Kentucky hill region, the home tucked into the shadow of a long, sawtoothed ride, flanked by deep stands of white pine and hemlock. The house was built of faux logs, the roof made of expensive cedar shingles. There were large windows facing east and porches and decks built on all four sides. The yard sloped down to a tumbling creek, the driveway winding up along the south side of the slope.

There was a shop and barn combination off to the right, the driveway turning into a Y with stacks of lumber and pallets of what appeared to be slabs of rock set in precise rows. John could only guess at Gideon's occupation.

The house was impressive, but the landscaping was even more so, with huge rounded flowerbeds planted full with all kinds of shrubs and perennials.

Ferns spilled from moss baskets suspended from porch beams, with caladium and coleus tucked into clay pots strewn all over the wide porch floors.

"Oh my goodness," said Lena, softly.

"Wow!" John whistled.

"Don't look much like an Amish home in my opinion," Clyde chortled. "At any rate, here you are, young lady. Looks like you'll have a pleasant place to stay."

The door was flying open. Barbie was fairly flying across the porch and down the stone steps to throw her arms around the awaited cousin.

"Lena! Oh my word! So good to see you. As beautiful as ever. Come on in. My, it's freezing out here. My ferns and coleus are living on luck and plenty of water. Come in. Come in."

Noticing John, she asked who the young man was.

"My boyfriend's brother, John. John, Barbara."

John shook her hand, complimented the home, said it was nice to meet her.

"Yes. Yes. We worked hard, but do appreciate it every day. I love it here."

"Good. It is lovely."

Lena looked at him, asked when the youth would be getting together for a supper or hymn singing.

John blushed darkly, deeply ashamed to tell Lena he did not join the *rumschpringa*.

Barbie looked from one to the other, bewildered. Clearly, Lena became agitated at the announcement, while the young man blushed to the roots of his hair. So who was whose boyfriend? Whatever.

They parted with a few mumbled words about Alvin and Lydia's phone number.

Lena found the opulent home disconcerting, to say the least. She had been raised with strict rules pertaining to frugality. The home should be threadbare, she'd been taught, without a display of worldly goods. Hard work in the produce fields had always been her life, without payment of any kind, until she reached the age of sixteen, and then it was only twenty dollars a week.

By now she was considered an adult, her own boss, allowed to keep her wages, and still she spent little and saved most of it.

The teaching of her parents stayed with her, and she felt guilty spending on anything she wanted, so she didn't. But Barbie would not need to know this.

She walked into a beautiful, airy kitchen, built in the latest style with a pot rack above a massive island surrounded by barstools.

The propane gas refrigerator was the only Amish thing about the kitchen. Photographs of the children were held in place on the refrigerator by magnets. They were thin, brown-haired children with brown eyes and prominent teeth, resembling their mother, except for the oldest, whose face contained a vacant expression, with bewildered, empty eyes.

Lena was taken on a tour of the remainder of the house, into a cavernous living room and tasteful playroom, a massive master bedroom done in soothing tones of gray and beige. The open stairway led to the upstairs, smaller than Lena had imagined, but as serviceable and pleasant as she could have hoped. The children's rooms were adjacent to her own, with a large, well-lit bathroom that had a skylight in the ceiling. Her room was furnished with a four-poster bed, a chest of drawers, and a long low dresser with a mirror, all in cherry. The bed was made perfectly in a rose-colored quilt, with an array of gray accent pillows and shams. Candles burned in their glass containers and silk flowers draped tastefully from cut glass vases.

Lena's eyes grew wide at the candle-scented room, the beauty of the furniture, the soft rug beneath her feet.

CHAPTER 18

JOHN RETURNED TO WORK, HIS MIND AND BODY SPENT. IMAGES OF having been put through a gigantic wringer washer flashed through his head. He'd been spun mercilessly into the hot waters of an old love brought to life, wrung through the rollers of knowing his love still belonged to Samuel, and likely always would.

Didn't most girls experience a case of indecision? Cold feet?

Well, at least he'd had the courage to ask, then stated his intentions. Well, not really, but he'd let her know how he felt. And she hadn't seemed upset about that.

Dewan waltzed into the office, unzipped his windbreaker, hung it on a hook, catwalked over to the desk, and clapped him on the shoulder.

"Ow!" John yelled, leaning sideways.

"You wanna know something? Of all the cream puffs I ever met, you are the creamiest. Where's your mojo?"

"My what? I don't know what that word means."

"Mad today, are we?"

"Go away."

"Happy to, ma man."

"I'm not your man."

"You sure ain't. You ain't nobody's man. You out there, dude. All. By. Yourself. Yeah!"

He banged through the door, and John heard him remove the cleaning tools. Good. Let him clean the cages. His shoulders ached, his head was spinning as if he'd stuffed it full of cotton candy, and his stomach felt sour, with a churning in his lower intestines. At home, his mother would have pried until he relayed every symptom, and then would have brought a collection of herbal remedies to his side. Here, he had learned to battle through the anxiety, calming himself by his own deep breathing technique, living with joint pain and stomach ache, night sweats and nausea.

He learned to wait out the weakness. On mornings when it was the worst, he'd go back to bed. Lydia could pound and yell all she wanted, but there were days when he was simply not getting out of bed. Sometimes he had to rest, close himself off from the rest of the world, especially with the customers that arrived by the carload, taking Alvin and Lydia both to cater to their unreasonable demands. Not all of them. Most folks were fair, understanding, polite, but all in all, John still found them exhausting.

The puppies sold. One by one, the folks from as far away as Lexington came to buy the expensive purebreds. Prices ranged from a thousand dollars to as high as three thousand. Every day, the people rolled in the gravel drive in SUVs, low sports cars in brilliant hues, leaving with puppies in pet carriers.

After that, buggy rides to church with Lydia and Alvin were different. There was lighthearted banter, easy subjects, a good conscience, having paid a whopping amount on the loan they'd taken out for the kennel. Lydia refused any of the money for home improvements, saying no, her house was just fine, they didn't need a porch till that kennel was paid for. Alvin told Lydia on the way to church that he felt like the man in Proverbs who praised his wife for selling her wares in the marketplace.

"I am blessed to be married to a virtuous woman. You know, if it hadn't been for you, I'd never dared build a kennel."

Lydia pooh-poohed that idea, saying modestly they were in it together. But Alvin kept saying what a lucky man he was, that the day he married her was the best day of his life.

"Not every wife would be content to live in that house, Lydia."

John thought of Gideon and Barbie. To each his own, he thought. He didn't know the cousins of Lena's, so who was he to think less of one couple than the other?

He found himself longing for a relationship of his own, but only with Lena. No one else could ever take her place. So strongly did he think of her, so sure was his love. If Samuel was the one she would choose, then he'd stay single. There were worse things.

As if reading his mind, Lydia turned to him. "You never said much about Lena. Did you find her cousin's house from the station in Dexter Falls?"

"Yeah." No other information was offered.

"What's their name again?"

"Gideon and Barbara Lapp."

Alvin turned his head. "Is he the guy who makes those mini cabins on skids?"

"I don't know."

"There's a guy, hasn't been in Kentucky too long, I think his name is Lapp, began making these rustic looking little cabins, sets them up on customer's location, landscapes and everything. They say he's making money like crazy."

"Money, money, money. It's this generation's idol." Lydia's voice became low, modulated to a holy tone. "We are approaching the house of the Lord and all we talk about is how much money we are making, or how much someone else is. Talk about temptation coming in a sneaky way. We're losing out spiritually, Alvin."

He nodded soberly, in total agreement.

A hush pervaded the interior of the buggy, driving up to the forebay of the old white barn, lined with men wearing wide-brimmed black hats, black suit coats, and trousers with white shirts barely visible beneath long beards.

Alvin passed the barn, drove up to the house, pulled the one rein to the right to give Lydia easier access to the ground. She exited neatly, holding Andrew in one arm, then turned to rummage below the seat for the bag containing four loaves of homemade bread. The young women generously offered to make bread, or soft cheese, or peanut butter spread, for the lunch that would be served after services.

John helped Alvin unhitch, then went to stand with the unmarried young men assembled in a group just inside the shop door. John had never bothered trying to make friends in Kentucky, always too sick to care. He spoke when someone addressed him, but certainly didn't go out of his way to be friendly, so most boys let him alone.

He heard snatches of who would be going where, Christmas festivities, but didn't bother asking details. Of course he wanted to go, now that Lena was in Kentucky, but if she wanted to see him, she'd have to call.

He'd have to practice patience, that was sure.

The congregation was seated in the large basement, the older men removing their hats when the young men filed in. They shook hands with the ministers before being seated. The number of a page was spoken from a young man in the back row. Black German songbooks were opened, until the right page was found in the *Ausbund*, then a strong voice led them all into the proper cadence of the old, lilting plainsong.

John felt his eyes fill with tears, touched by the beauty of a hundred voices raised in German praise. It was good to be here, good to know he belonged to a group of Christian people who still, after all these years, wanted what was right and good for them and their children. It was good to see eye to eye with like-minded brethren, although hardly ever in perfection.

Acceptance and forbearance often smoothed the rough spots, the difference of each man's conscience.

Someday, if the Lord willed it, he would regain his health, take instruction class to learn how to live a Godly life, and become a member of the Amish church.

He dared not think of Lena by his side.

Vaguely, his gaze wandered down the row of single girls, dressed in a colorful array of dresses, with white capes and aprons pinned to them, neat and starched in their Sunday best.

A few dark-haired, dark-eyed girls were attractive. He noticed a slim blond girl who dimly resembled Lena, but no. Not one of them could even begin to stir his interest.

Perhaps someday, though, when Lena married his brother, Samuel, he'd have to consider a girl such as these. He sighed, then berated himself.

His mind wandered to Lena constantly. He only heard a fraction of the sermon. When his lower back began to ache, he sat up straighter, reached back to massage the aching muscles, grimaced, then leaned forward, his chin cupped in his hands.

What, if anything, would ever stop this roving pain that moved from his right shoulder to his elbows, then his knees, even the joints of his toes?

He was young, stunted by Lyme disease, and now, clenched in the grip of a hopeless and despairing love.

He had fallen hard, flat on his face, helpless as a newborn puppy, at the mercy of God. Wasn't it God who gave true love to young men's hearts?

Of course it was.

But he couldn't justify his own feelings for his brother's girlfriend, coming before God in the house of the Lord, even if it was held in the basement of a large white farmhouse.

The indecision, the self-denial, proved to create a vortex of stress into which he tumbled headlong. He took to his bed, refused his sister's frustrated calls, quivered in the grip of a numbing weakness and the knowledge that he must die.

Over and over, he recorded the palpitations of his heart, imagined it fermented with inflammation, soon to gasp its last pump of blood. Sick and perspiring, he clutched his pillow with clawed hands, begging God for mercy for his sinning soul.

There was no excuse for loving Lena.

Lyme disease is a marathon, not a sprint, the old doctor had stated. Hormonal diseases crop up like a fungus, and must be addressed. Detoxifying the body is very important. But who could know?

Lydia and Alvin were beside themselves.

Lydia took to the phone, spoke to her mother. Her pride would not allow as much as a tremor in her words as she related the story of John taking to his bed.

"Lydia!" A note of hysteria. "That is why I didn't want him to go. These breakdowns come and go. If it was up to me, he'd be seeing a doctor ASAP. But there are no Lyme doctors in Kentucky, probably."

There she went, assuming they lived in hillbilly country.

Lydia said icily, "How would I know? We have no reason to find out, neither of us having contracted the disease."

"True, Lydia, true. Well, I can always prescribe the detox bath. It's a cup of vinegar, a cup . . . "

"I know the recipe. John does, too."

"Well, then. See that he does it. Give him the Emergen-C drink while he's in there. That should clear up some of the brain fog."

Lydia took a deep breath. "Mother, I don't know if he has brain fog. I don't know anything. He won't talk. He just rolls himself in his quilt and shuts me out. It's as if he has this need to turn himself into a cocoon. There is something so wrong in the way he acts. As if his suffering has to reach out and pull me in, too."

"Lydia, I know exactly what you're talking about. Absolutely. And yes, it is weird, the way he does that. But have you ever read a book on Lyme disease victims? It affects the central nervous system, and they often become so weary in their head, their nerves, whatever, they can't take the ordinary ebb and flow of life. Did anything unusual occur in the last week? Anything that could have affected him deeply?" Mam asked.

That was when it hit Lydia.

"Oh my, yes. Just now I thought of it. Lena came to Kentucky on the train."

There was a sharp intake of breath, followed by a cutting shriek.

"Lena? Abner's Lena? Samuel's girl?"

"Who else?"

"But Samuel didn't say anything."

"Did you ask?"

"Why would I? I didn't know she was going to Kentucky."

"Mam, let me tell you something. There is something going on between John and Lena, don't you know that? It's like his heart is in his eyes when he talks about her."

"But there's no way. No possible way. Samuel is older, a real manager where he works, he's so handsome and confident . . . just everything John isn't. John is pathetic, with those hair and glasses. He's sick, Lydia. How could Lena even compare the two? He has no right, Lydia, no right to even think of his brother's girlfriend."

"Mam, calm down. I think it's probably just a crush. She was his teacher, remember?"

"Yes, yes I do."

She told her mother why Lena had come to Kentucky.

"But why didn't Samuel say anything? Why didn't I know?"

There was a trace of hysteria creeping back into her voice.

"Whatever the reason, her coming may have triggered John's relapse."

"Oh my. It means there are definite feelings there. Now what? Well, one thing sure. You'll be coming home for Christmas, and I'll have a long talk with John. I'll let him know how wrong it is to have . . . well, to allow himself to have an attraction to his brother's girl. I'll straighten it out."

Famous last words, Lydia thought.

Dewan Reynolds was invaluable to Alvin and Lydia. He was a fast learner and his spirited ways were a boon to the puppy sales. He was meticulous in all his work and had genuine affection for the dogs housed in cages, making sure they had access to the dog run every day.

With John out of commission again, Dewan was at the kennel from early in the morning till late at night. Alvin was often busy in the dairy barn, even if Lydia tried to do most of the chores and most of the milking. The harvest was finished for the year, which was a good thing, with the kennel taking up so much of their time. The situation with John was beyond frustrating.

Lydia looked forward to the van ride to Pennsylvania to relax, get away from all the hard work and responsibility, if only for a few days.

Alvin was considering selling the dairy cows, but Lydia stayed adamant. No, there was a debt load there, too. The cows were necessary.

A litter of Labradoodles had arrived. Six of them. At a few weeks old, they were the cutest thing anyone had ever seen, their doleful brown eyes like liquid gems, the curly hair already apparent, the mild manners from the Labrador retriever bred into them.

Dewan sat cross-legged on the cement aisle, the cage door open, holding the black one to his face, rubbing a hand over the back, between the ears.

"This one's the cutest. Man. John needs to see this. Lydia, you mind if I go upstairs, show this little guy to him?"

"Go ahead. See if you can help him."

Dewan got to his feet, cradling the puppy in both palms, against his chest. He took the steps two at a time, knocked on the closed bedroom door, listened, then knocked again. When there was no response, he put his mouth to the door, and yelled as only Dewan could yell.

Still, there was nothing.

So he opened the door and went in. The shades were drawn, so he blinked a few times until his eyesight adjusted to the dim light. He frowned at the heaps of clothing strewn across the floor, the opened drawers sagging from the dresser, T-shirts hanging from the sides, an empty glass on the nightstand, a wrapper containing a few Ritz crackers, stale pretzels that appeared to have been there for at least a week. It smelled of stale bedsheets, unbrushed teeth, perspiration.

"John, it's Dewan."

He bent, cradling the puppy in one hand, pulling back the quilt from the greasy, unwashed hair with a forefinger.

This was gross. This was not John.

"You depressed, brotha?"

The soft lilting voice, the question that always gave the listener the benefit of the doubt.

"Hey there, ma man. You gotta see this little guy."

No response.

Dewan leaned over, pulled the quilt back even farther.

"You dead in there, or what?"

He was rewarded by a convulsive shrug, the quilt drawn up even farther. Dewan stood back, pursed his lips, held his head to a side, then drew himself up to his full height.

"Ah-right. I get it. You don't want no help. Well then, you lay in that moldy bed and go right on pitying yourself for as long as you want. I don't understand your disease, but I understand good manners. You headed downhill fast if you keep this up. I'm leaving the puppy, so you get your wobbly backside outa bed and help the little guy when he whines. I'm going back to work, Mr. Lyme Disease."

He placed the puppy on the floor and left, closing the door behind him but waiting on the other side to listen.

Silence.

Then a snuffling, the sound of a soft body being moved, inch by inch.

John pulled the quilt up to ward off any sound that infiltrated his world. A lot of nerve Dewan had leaving the helpless puppy. Or had he? Perhaps he hadn't even left him, and it was all a trick, a devious plan to get him out from beneath the quilt. Well, sorry. Dewan had no idea what it was like to be a victim of this cruel disease. None. So no stupid little puppy was going to be the bait to draw him out, either.

He heard a soft whine. Then another.

What had Dewan just called him? Mr. Lyme Disease. That was just cruel. Mean and heartless. He shrugged the covers up over his head and wrapped it even tighter to shut out any whining.

Another pitiful whine found its way through the quilt. John turned aside, put a pillow over his head, willed the puppy away.

Now the whining became louder, a shrill, high-pitched sound of desperation, which turned into a full-blown cacophony of sound.

John shrugged off the quilt to press the pillow tighter to his ears. This trick wasn't going to work.

When the high-pitched whining turned into short, mournful puppy sobs, John threw the pillow off his head, turned his head, and opened one eye.

At first, he thought it was one of Andrew's stuffed animals. Then the mouth opened, a tiny pink tongue emerged, and a heartbreaking sound reached his ears.

John lifted his head from the pillow, opened both eyes. He had never seen a cuter puppy, that was sure.

"Come here, little castaway. Come on."

He spoke gruffly, barely above a whisper, his voice unused for so long.

"Come on, come here."

The journey to the bed was too long, so the puppy flattened himself on the floor and let out a series of yelps.

"All right, all right."

John rolled out of bed, crawled over to the shivering black puppy, and scooped him up. He sat on the edge of the bed, holding him against his white T-shirt, against the beating of his heart, without thinking if it was pounding out a regular rhythm or not. The puppy was cold, shivering, and likely very hungry as well. He should be allowed to have his mother's milk. What was wrong with that Dewan? He should know better. The puppy could take sick, and those Labradoodles were valuable.

"All right, little castaway. We'll get you warm."

He bundled him into the quilt against his chest and stroked the curly-haired back until he quieted. But he knew he couldn't keep him here very long, he'd get too hungry.

John felt a warm glow of accomplishment, having soothed the crying animal so soon. The puppy had been helpless, taken from his mother and siblings, placed on the cold hard floor of his bedroom.

Perhaps they were both castaways. Thrown out into a strange world without comfort, cast away from the society they knew.

John swallowed, the lump that rose in his chest another sign of weakness. All this puppy had ever known was the warmth and comfort of his mother's milk, the heat from her body, the comfort of lying in a pile with five brothers and sisters. Then Dewan's hands had lifted him away to a barren, cold bedroom floor that filled him with new sensations of fear and loneliness.

The puppy slept.

John's thoughts continued to unfurl, creating the slim shadow of a path through the thicket of Lyme disease. He couldn't help the fact that he was its victim. He couldn't help it if he was crippled by the onslaught of frightful encounters, circumstances that roared into his life like raging lions.

Neither could he help himself from the fear of death, or losing Lena, or the fact that his heart was deteriorating beneath the skin of his chest.

It was hard to face life. Stress stripped away the strength to fight anything. So he did what worked best, which was to rest, hide away from the clashing words and pounding questions.

One excuse after another.

Now where did that thought come from? He wasn't excusing himself for any of his actions. It was a necessity, a means of survival.

Eventually, he would have to return to the comfort of his family, like the sleeping puppy. He would need to be strong enough to meet inquiring eyes, to answer questions, to make decisions, and yes, to deal with Lena.

His heart dipped to his stomach at the thought.

And he knew the decision would have to be made. He had to face up to it. He should tell her that it was a mistake to come to Kentucky, that she should go back to Samuel. Perhaps he was standing in the way of her happiness and was only a blip, a notch in an otherwise smooth surface. Maybe she was trapped wondering if he would make the better husband, when all along he wasn't fit to even survive.

He was only a joke, a temptation, before she gave herself up to the will of God.

He cried, then, quietly, swallowing his sobs in a manly way, the tears leaving tracks down his cheeks and disappearing into the soft, curled hairs on the puppy's head. With the surrender came release, peace like the full power of the sun after the storm's fury has been dissipated. He felt a small amount of strength in his arms, an interest in his surroundings, and knew in a quiet, whispered way that God had been here, in this room, had shown him the way, perhaps dimly, but it was there.

Give her up. She is not yours. She belongs to your brother.

He sat up. The puppy whimpered.

"All right, little fellow. You lie down here till I brush my teeth, OK?"

Brushing them proved to be a hurried affair, with the awful cries that came from his bed, the puppy feeling the full pangs of his hunger. He raked a comb through his unruly hair and yanked a shirt off the hanger and shrugged into it, then scooped up the howling bundle and made his way shakily down the stairs.

Tucked beneath his coat, John kept the puppy warm till he reached the heat of the kennel. He found Dewan cleaning the aisle, whistling, thumping his broom in time to the endless beat in his head.

"Hey, hey! The lost has been found!"

"Shut it, Dewan."

"Oh, come on, dude. Spread a little cheer out here, yeah! That's cool. Rhyme, rhyme. Spread a little bit of cheer out here. Get it?"

John couldn't stop the smile that slid across his face. He laughed outright as he stooped to return the puppy to the fold, watched as his mother nuzzled him and then began the serious chore of licking him clean.

CHAPTER 19

With two sick cows and three expectant Newfoundland mothers, the Christmas trip to Pennsylvania began looking very bleak. Lydia said there was no way she was going. Alvin looked pale and stressed. Andrew came down with a sore throat coupled with a barking cough and a fever of 102°.

John said they should go and he would stay. He was feeling better again, and between him and Dewan, they had everything under control.

The truth was, Lena was going along, back to her family for Christmas, and John knew everything would be better if he stayed. Yes, he had a plan now, a fresh resolve, felt he knew the will of God, so why put it in jeopardy?

If he saw her again now, he might lose his resolve.

Alvin said no. Lydia shook her head in agreement. But John refused to go. So when the van left, Alvin, Lydia, and Andrew were packed into the third seat, waving goodbye after voicing their appreciation with more than a little apprehension.

And so began the three days that tested John's stamina unlike anything he'd ever known. Still reeling from the time he'd spent away from his duties, away from all human interaction, he was forced to deal with an overworked, underrested veterinarian, resulting in the loss of a cow.

Then one Newfoundland had her puppies during the night,

and had already suffocated two of them by lying on top of them, her huge, loose body never suspecting the little lumps were her own offspring. She was a first-time mother, and this was not unusual, but John felt it was all his fault. He should not have fallen asleep so soon or so soundly. If he'd been there sooner, the puppies may have survived. Just like if he'd called the vet sooner, the cow might have lived.

Dewan shored up his faltering courage, saying that cow woulda died anyhow, the infection in her intestines beyond help, which John knew was true.

But still.

They ate Chinese takeout and Kentucky Fried Chicken, cereal for breakfast, and bags of potato chips and onion rings, washed down with copious amounts of Pepsi or Mountain Dew. John made fried-egg sandwiches, watched Dewan pour hot sauce and squirt mustard all over the eggs, then tried it for himself. He ate the whole sandwich and ran to the bathroom all day, much to Dewan's knee-slapping glee.

"You weak," he chortled. "You weak as a kitten. Can't take no hot sauce, no mustard."

John glared at him, reminded him of the fact that he had Lyme disease. "You know what? When anything goes wrong in your life, you hide behind that disease of yours," Dewan said, draining the last of his Pepsi before crushing the can.

John shrugged.

"You have no idea. It's complicated. I could explain Lyme disease all day to you and I still wouldn't be finished."

Dewan wiped his hands on his jeans, ridding himself of grease from the barbeque chips he was eating, and shook his head.

"I don't wanna hear it. You need to stop thinkin' about it. Maybe that Lyme bug's gone and all that's left is in your head."

John knew it was useless to try and correct him, so he got to his feet and went to the dairy barn.

Back in Pennsylvania, Mam was occupied mostly keeping the frayed edges of her once solidly woven family tapestry from unraveling completely.

With John absent, everyone felt free to speak their mind, which was a constant crossfire of opinions, speculation, and half-truths. Dat's face was strained, his mouth a taut line of disapproval. But he knew youth was impetuous and selfish, and he would only add to the chaos to voice a series of reprimands and disapproval.

How had they come apart so fast?

A year ago, he had started to sense the lack of unity, but now, there was no patching up these wretched ravines that snaked through a once solid ground.

Lydia was the main speaker.

Wasn't she always?

Dat leaned back in his chair, crossed his arms, switched the toothpick in his mouth from left to right, felt his stomach rumble, laden with turkey and ham, filling and mashed potatoes, and listened.

She described in full detail how his latest episode had been the worst. How he'd stayed rolled in a quilt, refusing to talk, shutting them all out. How do you deal with something like that?

Lena sat beside Samuel, her red dress the color of the poinsettia on the countertop, her face ashen, the blue eyes underlined in dark shadows.

Samuel was leaning back, in a matching red shirt, an arm draped possessively over the back of her chair, his blond hair like a regal lion.

"You were sure you could handle it, Lydia." There was a slight sneer.

"Don't be unkind, Samuel."

"I'm not unkind. John's just up to his old tricks. He drove Mam crazy, now he's working on Lydia. He knows he can, so he does. He doesn't feel the best, so he's taking it out on everyone else."

Marcus nodded, in total agreement. Marty was beside him in her outlandish silver dress, her face a study in restraint. She had a soft spot for John. He was cute.

Lena lifted her coffee cup. Wise Abner saw the tremor, the too-white face, the slightly dilated nostrils, the blue eyes gone dark. Samuel better watch it.

Fueled by his brother's agreement, Samuel went on.

"I believe John has been sick in the past. But now? He's not sick. I've said it before, he's crazy in the head."

His sister Susan jumped to John's defense. After that, it was a volley of retorts, a few arguing for John's side, most against him.

"Does he do any work at all?"

The father had spoken, hushing the clamor of voices.

"Yes, of course. When he feels good. I have to yell at him and tell him to get out of bed, get going. Nobody is ever going to get better lying around day in and day out."

"But Lyme patients need rest. Lots of it. That's why it's so hard. People around them do not understand. They assume they're lazy, unmotivated." Mam took up for John.

"They are lazy," said Samuel.

And then Dat spoke, his voice well modulated, even, his words without rancor.

"This discussion has gone on long enough. No one knows what is truly going on in John's body but God Himself. John doesn't even know, neither do his doctors or anyone else. So how can we?

"I believe Lyme is a disease of many different faces. Symptoms vary from person to person, as do cures. Some of it may be in his head, after these years, but that, too, is part of the disease. I think I've spoken these same words before, so all I can do is repeat them. Don't judge John harshly. Don't make assumptions or look down on him. He is struggling with issues that are very real to him, whether or not a doctor could diagnose them at this point. Lyme takes time to heal. So give him time. He'll be all right. We're not concerned about ourselves, but perhaps we should be. We must be losing out spiritually or we wouldn't have all this bickering. Remember the easy feeling of wanting to be together? Always accepting, looking up to each other? And here we are."

Samuel was ready with a retort, barely acknowledging his father's words. "Here we are, what? There's nothing wrong with *us*, it's him."

"You know things aren't the same," Marcus said, angrily.

"Enough," said Dat. "Time for dishes, then presents."

Mam got up, bustled to the sink, began pounding dishes on the countertop. The girls rolled their eyes but got up to help, bent to wipe the children's faces, chucked them under sticky chins, kissed greasy little cheeks.

But Christmas was not the same. John not being present was a testimony unto itself. He obviously didn't feel much of the old magnetic pull of home, that was sure. Sara Ann hissed to Susie in the pantry that this had all been a valuable lesson for Lydia, brought her down a notch or two.

Samuel gave Lena her gift later, after the family had dispersed to finish tidying the kitchen, put the little ones to bed. It was a wooden, ornately carved chest containing a twelve-place setting of silverware. It was Oneida, the handles heavy, the knives bigger than the everyday knives Lena was used to. The forks had long, beautiful tines, the spoons were sculpted into lean, graceful contours. The chest was lined with blue velvet. It was the perfect pre-engagement gift.

Instead of the surge of love she should have experienced, she was riddled with indecision, an agony of doubt. The silverware chest was beyond anything he had ever given her, a beautiful token of his love. The cutlery was meant to grace the wedding table, the esteemed and honored *eck*, the table with her own carefully chosen tablecloths, her own china and stemware, the wedding cakes and fancy dishes laden with delicacies.

Samuel was handsome, successful, perfect. She imagined the wedding, flanked by members of the bridal party, every whim catered to, the awaited grand finale of the years of *rumschpringa*. It was every young Amish girl's dream.

But after that . . .

The days stretched on in her mind, a never-fading ribbon of trying, doing her best, performing a job, impressing friends and family with her abilities. They would see her as the perfect housewife, and soon, mother to the cutest babies.

The whole thing brought on an indescribable fatigue.

But she smiled. She bent her head over the beautiful chest, lifted a spoon, stroked the velvet, and said all the right things. When he drew her close and kissed her, she responded appropriately, smiling into his blue eyes and hoping the light in her eyes matched the fervor in his.

Then, the dreaded question fell like an axe from the ceiling.

"Lena, do you have an answer for me?"

She laid her head against his chest to hide her eyes. The kindness of her nature could not bring herself to say no, the future she knew would be hers would not allow a yes. Caught between two worlds, she was as afraid of one as she was of the other.

She caught her breath. He drew her closer.

"I love you, Lena. You know that, don't you?"

"Yes."

"I don't believe you have ever told me you loved me."

"Oh. I . . ."

The tension dissolved into sobs, soft, despairing cries that stemmed from her total lack of understanding what was going on in her heart.

Samuel released her so suddenly she almost fell.

"What is wrong, Lena? Why are you crying at a moment like this?"

His face had gone pale.

She sank back against the couch cushions, bent her head to hide her shame and confusion. He did not try and comfort her, but merely watched her with narrowed eyes and quickening breath.

Finally, she got up to draw a handful of Kleenex from the box on the lampstand, pressed them to her nose, and blew so delicately Samuel couldn't be sure she had even blown her nose.

"Samuel, I can't give you an answer because I don't know what to tell you. I'm . . . not sure. Perhaps it's just me. I think I need counseling, someone to help me understand matters of the heart."

When there was no answer, she searched his face. Cold, hard, his jaw set in a firm line, he turned away from her.

"There's someone else."

"No, no. Samuel, no."

"I don't believe you. Why did you go to Kentucky?"

"I told you."

"It's John, isn't it? Big pitiful baby John, preying on your sympathies."

"No, Samuel. It is not John. I'm merely having some indecision. It's normal for every girl to have second thoughts occasionally, isn't it?"

"I don't know. I'm not a girl."

A spark of anger flared, was extinguished. Lena took a steadying breath, laid a slim hand on Samuel's arm.

"May I have till spring to give you an answer? May I be in Kentucky while I sort out my feelings?"

He shouted, then, empty accusations hurled across the few feet that separated them.

"I'm sure John will gladly help you decide."

"John has nothing to do with this. Why are you dragging him into it?"

"Look at me and say that."

She could not. Kindness and honesty were her best virtues, and the test Samuel threw in her face was too much to withstand. She bowed her head, the wad of Kleenex pressed to her face as fresh sobs shook her slender frame.

Samuel got to his feet, grabbed the silverware chest, and glared at her bent form.

"Have it your way, but you will regret your decision. You will live to be a bitter old woman, saddled with an invalid. You have only sympathy for John. You're mistaking pity for love."

But then he paused, seemed to grasp the severity of his words. On his knees now, the silverware chest beside him, his hands grasped her shoulders.

"Lena, I love you. I want you to be my wife. Consider your choice, what I have to offer. Financial security, a healthy body, everything. You don't want John, you pity him."

She nodded, raised her eyes to his, swollen and red rimmed.

"You may be right."

He drew her against him, sat with her on the couch, and promised her his whole life, if only she would say yes. They parted with the understanding of a letter written at the end of January, a simple yes or no, neither of which she was capable of.

The van returned to Kentucky, filled with the lively discussions of three married sisters and their spouses, children fussing, singing, whining when they were thirsty or hungry, Lena largely forgotten.

In Virginia, it began to snow, fat, lazy flakes that kept the windshield wipers slapping back and forth, creating a wide arc of visibility only slightly better than above or below its reach.

"Getting slippery," the driver commented.

"Why don't we find a rest area or restaurant? Take a break," Alvin suggested.

Lena declined to join them, saying she wasn't hungry, then lay back on her pillows and disappeared from view, which brought some speculation among the sisters. She looked like a ghost at the Christmas dinner. Didn't look very happy, especially given she hadn't seen Samuel since before Thanksgiving.

Barbie was overjoyed to have Lena back.

Naomi was hopping up and down, her mouth open, though there were no words, no sound from the display of pleasure. Lena got down on her knees and opened her arms, but Naomi turned away, her thumb in her mouth, her eyes frightened.

She knew Naomi didn't often like to be held, but it was a disappointment, anyway. "Naomi, look what I brought you," she said, getting up to rummage in the large tote she had brought from home. She found the deck of "Go Fish" cards.

The cards became Naomi's constant companion. She ate her meals with them, slept with them, shuffled them continuously. Mark and Josh teased her by taking them away, which upset her so badly that she became violent, throwing dangerous objects across the room.

So Lena was thrown headlong into her challenging duties and was introduced to the Down syndrome child named Eli Ebersol, his parents living only half a mile down the road. He was walked to the schoolroom at Gideon Lapp's every day, and walked back home, bundled into many layers of warm clothing.

Her days were busy, all day, every day, working with building blocks, flash cards, trying new kinds of play therapy she had read about. They took long walks when nothing else seemed to work, strolling among bare trees and old brown leaves.

Snow was infrequent, soft, mushy, layers that never lasted very long.

At night, in the privacy of her room, she thought about Samuel and John and the differences between them.

John had written her a letter just before she left for the Christmas break, saying he wished her a wonderful holiday with Samuel and that he hoped he hadn't caused any confusion that would upset their relationship or cause her any stress. He would love to be friends with her if she was comfortable with that, and she should let him know if she needed anything while in Kentucky. She hadn't responded. What could she say? But she held on to the realization that John had put her happiness above his own. Samuel had elevated himself above John, practically shouting at her that he was the better choice for a spouse. Shouldn't that tell her something?

But John was younger, and yes, he had Lyme disease. Perhaps he would never recover, would only get worse. Would he expect her to be his constant nurse? Would she be willing to do that?

How he ever got Gid Lapp's telephone number was beyond her, but Barbie stuck her head into the room and said some guy wanted to talk to her.

Her heart fell. Surely it was Samuel, perhaps wanting an answer sooner than they'd agreed.

"How are you, Lena?"

It didn't sound quite like Samuel's voice.

"This is John."

"Oh! Hi, John."

"I thought I'd call, see if you'd like to come shopping with me some Saturday evening. There's a huge mall about thirty miles from here. I need some stuff. Shirts. Shoes."

"Of course I'll go. It sounds like fun. Who else is going?"

"No one. I got Clyde to go. I could ask Dewan to join us?"

"Who is Dewan?"

"Someone I work with."

"Oh. Well, he would probably be all right."

"Clyde's OK, too."

She laughed, the sound different to her own ears. When had she laughed like that?

She dressed carefully, wearing a sky blue dress with a black apron and soft cable knit cardigan, also in black, a gift from her mother.

It was very serviceable, very married-woman type of clothing, but Lena preferred it over the heavy woolen coat.

Barbie eyed her with approval, shook her head wryly, said she could wear feed sacks and be the most gorgeous girl at the mall. Lena's cheeks flushed at the effusive compliment, but she hid her pleased expression.

"Who's this John?"

"You met him."

"Did I?"

"Yes, my boyfriend's brother. Just a friend."

She hid her expression after that statement, too.

The unexpected rush of pleasure at seeing him again was clearly not something she had expected. It was a homecoming, only better—a light in a window, in the middle of a dark forest.

How could she explain what she felt? Baffled, she became quiet, sitting alone in the back seat, without hearing Clyde and John's conversation. There was no valid reason for this unexpected joy, unless it was just sympathy, pity, or leftover admiration from his school years. She had always admired John, she knew, even as an eighth-grade student, mostly for his kindness, his unselfish attitude.

As the car wound its way along narrow country roads before turning onto a wider highway, flat and smooth, Lena was still lost in thought.

But once they got to the mall, her mind eased. She simply accepted the joy of walking beside his tall form, looking into his astonishing eyes, listening to his quiet voice—just being there, in the aura of humility that surrounded him.

His attitude about the world and the people who lived in it was filled to capacity with a generosity of spirit that far surpassed her own. It occurred to her that to honor and obey him would not be a strenuous task. He didn't even seem very sick. Perhaps he was really recovering this time.

John looked down at her as they walked past the dizzying

array of stores, promising slashed prices, money saved. How
could you save money by spending it?

"You're quiet tonight, Lena."

"Am I? Sorry about the dull company I'm turning out to be."

"Do you have a lot on your mind, maybe?"

"I guess you could say that."

"How is your work? Being with the children all day must be
tiring."

"Oh, no. No. It's not the children."

She wanted to tell him that it was *him*. If she was honest
with herself, she wanted him to hold her again, the way he had
at the train station. But this was her boyfriend's brother, not to
mention the fact that they were in a very public place again. And
what if that letter he had sent her meant he really did want her
to be with Samuel, that perhaps he had met someone else?

They stopped for supper. The restaurant was dimly lit, with
muted sounds, booths that left them alone, a private corner that
suited them both perfectly. John was young, but had an air of
maturity that spoke of a much older man. She fumbled her silverware, found herself folding and refolding the napkin, taking
anxious little sips of water, excusing herself to go to the ladies'
room, where she sat and had a very tiny nervous breakdown
before returning to the booth, hoping her eyes would give nothing away.

"You were crying."

"No. Well, just a little."

"Do you want to talk about it?"

"Not now."

He let it go, spoke to the waiter, ordered food for both of
them, telling her the crabcakes were delicious here. Lena had
never eaten crabcakes, and certainly didn't know what a Caesar
salad was. But she found the food delicious and ate every morsel
with the same abandon she had eaten the cheeseburger that day,
which John found endearing.

But no. This was Samuel's girl. He had picked up hints from Lydia that Lena hadn't looked well over Christmas and he was worried she had never received his letter and was suffering because of him, somehow. He became sure he had written the wrong address, his mind foggy as it often was. He needed to clear the air, be sure she didn't make a big mistake because of his blunders.

He wiped his mouth, leaned back, and looked at her. Like an appraisal, she thought, but kinder. When his gaze did not waver, she became uncomfortable, then looked at him with a question in her eyes.

"I asked you to go with me tonight to tell you it bothers me a lot, the fact that I made it known to you how I feel. I have no right, Lena. You are Samuel's girlfriend, and I want you to say yes, to marry him. You are the perfect couple. I don't know what I was thinking, saying the things I did. I'm sorry."

Lena was busy straightening her knife and fork, her eyes downcast. Her lips trembled very slightly. The lighting was too dim to decipher the true extent of her feelings, but he heard her say softly, "I got your letter."

"You did?" he said, surprised and a little embarrassed. So he was just repeating himself.

There was silence, and he thought perhaps his letter hadn't been strong enough, clear enough for her to see where he stood.

"I'm sick, Lena. I have Lyme disease. I have to wait till I'm healthy to even think about a girl. It could be years till I'm completely better. Plus, I'm going home. I miss my friends, my family."

Now Lena could not hide her dismay.

"Home?" she whispered.

"Yes. I am nothing but a burden to Alvin and Lydia, unable to pull my share. I have no interest in the dogs. Their workload is overwhelming, and with Dewan, it's just . . ."

"Who is this Dewan?"

"He's helping at the kennel. He has so much energy, such a positive outlook, he's a great worker. He . . . makes it hard for me, saying Lyme disease is all in my head."

When Lena said nothing, he panicked.

Her, too? Did she feel his weak spells were all in his head, like some mentally ill person who heard voices? Or worse, that he didn't have Lyme disease, was only an overgrown, paranoid hypochondriac? How could you explain any of these symptoms if not the Lyme bacteria wreaking all that chaos in an otherwise healthy body?

"Lena."

She looked up. Her blue eyes were blank, devoid of feeling.

"Do you believe I have Lyme disease?"

"I do. Although to be sure, you would need to do another test. Which is possible. I think Lyme patients have impaired nervous systems, weak cognitive abilities, simply an overall sense of fatigue, which, yes, can alter the brain."

"That's a nice way of saying it's all in my head."

She didn't respond, and John wished he hadn't come. Why hadn't she at least written him a short note to let him know she received the letter?

Finally, after a silence laced with tension, Lena spoke, quietly, placing one word to the next, like carefully strung beads.

"John, you have to stop running away from other people's opinions. You left home to get away from your brothers, and now you're running away from Lydia and Alvin and Dewan."

"That's not true," he mumbled, but he couldn't look in her eyes.

CHAPTER 20

In Kentucky, spring arrived long before John noticed the running water, the softening of the chilly air, the odor of dead, wet grass being awakened by the kiss of the sun. Creeks ran full, rushed purposefully toward larger tributaries, emptied into rivers that carried nutrient-rich waters into the sea.

Gentle rain pattered on the roof of the dairy barn, the gutters holding the runoff that gushed across the gravel drive. The cows stood huddled in the barnyard, contentedly chewing their cud, rain running down the patches of black and white, the split hooves set solidly in the ever-increasing quagmire of mud and water.

If you stood still and listened, you could hear the short, high yaps of puppies trying out their ability to bark. Occasionally, a mother would answer in a series of high whines or yelps, shooting through the music of the rain in an uneven cacophony, short bursts that shattered the sound of pattering raindrops.

Alvin Beiler opened the door of the cow stable, raised his face to the sky, picked his straw hat off his head by the front brim, and scratched his head. More rain. Well, that would settle the urge to hitch up the Belgians and get an early start on the field-work. He replaced his hat, scraped the sides of his Muck Boots on the cast-iron blade cemented on the stoop of the entrance to the dairy barn. He'd go have a cup of coffee with Lydia. She'd said something about baking whoopie pies.

The sound of singing rose above the rain and the dogs.

It was Dewan. Alvin shook his head, a smile crinkling the lines around his eyes. That guy was truly the happiest, most vocal human being he had ever encountered. He had endless energy, endless good humor. He had no family to speak of, except the aunt who raised him. How many children would be so accepting of their fate, harboring no malice, no self-pity? Alvin had realized early on that Dewan was an exception, had lucked out having him in his employ. A godsend, that's what he was. He was so glad his wife had encouraged him to give him a chance.

He headed for the house, hunching his shoulders against the rain, suddenly eager to be in the presence of his talkative wife.

The kitchen smelled of sugar and chocolate. He found her emptying a cookie sheet of perfectly formed, soft round chocolate cookies, flopping them neatly on a layer of newspaper, where two dozen more were laid out in rows to cool.

Little Andrew was on the floor, the homemade wooden barn beside him, animals from the plastic white container scattered around it.

The kitchen was warm, too warm, evidently, with a window open, the sill speckled with raindrops. Alvin went to close it, his movements arrested by a shrill, "Don't you close that, Alvin."

He hesitated, looked at her flaming cheeks, shrugged, and left it open.

"Whoopie pies done? Is there coffee?"

"Icing isn't mixed."

From the floor came a series of whinnies, followed by a clopping sound, the hard plastic of the horses' feet being thumped along by Andrew's chubby hands.

Alvin got down on the floor and helped him arrange the cows in their stalls.

"Nay. Nay, Dat!" Andrew yelled. The brown cow did not belong in that stall. The one beside it.

"Alvin, you can mix the icing. That takes some arm muscle," Lydia said, dumping cups of 10x sugar over piles of Crisco.

Dutifully, he got to his feet, his strong young arms whipping the icing into the creaminess Lydia wanted. He spread a thick layer on a warm cookie, pressed another one on top, lifted the lid of the Lifetime coffeemaker, then flipped the burner on.

"Mmm. The best whoopie pies ever."

"Thank you, kind sir."

Lydia smiled, pleased to hear the compliment though she knew it was coming, its sweet meaning as effective as always.

"You're a great cook, Lydia."

"Alvin, I'm baking, not cooking."

"Well, I can't say you're a great bake."

They laughed together. "Try baker. Or the classy version, pastry chef."

"Whoopie pies aren't pastries."

"Whatever."

They smiled. Alvin sipped his coffee, finished his whoopie pie, reached for the knife to put icing on another.

More whinnying sounds from the floor.

The rain fell steadily, dripped off the pine branches by the open window, splattered against the north windowpanes, slid down to the sill and across the layers of yellow siding. The propane gas lamp hissed softly. A piece of wood fell in the woodstove by the dining room door, rattling the door latch on the front.

Alvin hoped the roof wouldn't leak after he patched the flashing around the chimney. Brown water stains marked the old pink and white floral wallpaper upstairs in the spare bedroom, where moisture had seeped down from the attic floor.

It was to be expected, living in an old house, one that had been in a state of disrepair when they bought the place.

"You need to take a couple of these out to Dewan."

"I will."

But he stayed sitting in contented silence, soaking up the warmth and coziness of the kitchen.

"John called," Lydia said.

"This morning?"

She nodded, expertly slapping a thick wad of icing on a soft chocolate cookie, placing another on top. She took up the yellow box of Saran wrap, the cheaper version from Aldi's, pulled a square of clear plastic wrap, tore it off in a deft downward movement, clapping it on top of the whoopie pie and wrapping it in another quick motion.

"How's he doing?"

"All right, I guess. He doesn't say much. He asked about the dogs, Dewan. But I always get the feeling there's a lot more he'd like to say, but can't. He's holding back, I can tell, the way he drags out the conversation, then abruptly hangs up without further ado."

"When's he coming back?"

"He's not. You know he never cared two hoots about the dogs or the cows. He had absolutely no interest in this work. And I felt so sure he would love the kennel."

Alvin nodded. "He's young. He'll find his vocation."

"Will he? Or will he always be the baby with Lyme disease? Oh, I guarantee you, Alvin, since he's back home Mam is stuffing him with every pill imaginable. The latest craze is some pill that has five different herbs in it. I forget what all she said. Supposed to detox at a cellular level. Some medical doctor spent forty years perfecting this miracle capsule."

"Your mother is gullible."

"I know."

But she herself hadn't been much better, she thought, so sure living with them would cure him in no time.

Early spring in Pennsylvania brought the usual bitter March winds, the crocuses pushing through last year's mulch, bravely answering the call of the sun's light and warmth, bursting into colors of purple, lavender, yellow, or white, only to be covered with six inches of heavy wet snow that didn't last more than a few days. Tulips showed their brilliant display to be blown into a confused disarray by tremendous gusts of March winds that tore the delicate petals into limp, hanging strips.

Mary Stoltzfus watched as the wind tore at the long line suspended between the house and the barn, the towels flapping in a frenzied dance orchestrated by gusts of up to thirty-five miles an hour.

She shouldn't have pegged them on the wheel line like that, but sometimes on Monday, with every hamper brimming with wet towels and Friday's work denims, she had to get them into the hot soapy water in the wringer washer and out on the line. It was vital to her well-being.

There was something to be said for the sorting of clothes, the smell of powdered Tide with bleach for that first load of whites, the undulating purr of the air-powered motor, the satisfying job of feeding the wet clothes through the wringer into the hot rinse water turned blue with a cap full of Downy fabric softener.

It was grounding, stabilizing.

To see John limping whitefaced through the washhouse, his eyes blank and dark, living in his own world of misery, was not getting easier.

Although now Samuel eclipsed her fears for John.

Samuel stomped around the place in an ill-concealed fury, slamming doors, refusing orders, just being a pain far above anything John had ever been.

And she knew why.

Lena still had not given him an answer.

Well, at least Abner was happily married. The wedding had gone well, Ruthie's mother Anna a good manager, a husband willing to manage alongside her, the sermon touching, as she knew it would be, preached by the home bishop, a gifted minister filled with much godly knowledge.

Abner had appeared surprisingly immaculate, his *multza* wide across the shoulders, his black bowtie straight across the white collar of his wedding shirt.

Even his trousers were exactly the right length, his shoes polished to a high sheen. Not exactly handsome, perhaps, but a presentable young man, who would prove to be a fine husband for the winsome Ruthie.

Here was her firstborn son, flying from the nest to make one of his own. She shed a few discreet tears into her lace-edged handkerchief, but couldn't help the gleeful thought: *One down, six to go.*

Ah yes, it had been a nice wedding and the visiting afterward a joy. Tradition required each guest to have the honor of a visit from the couple, a rite that took up most of the winter following the wedding.

Mary had enjoyed this all, pink-cheeked with good food and lots of honor and attention. And now Amos. So fortunate.

Well, one by one they'd leave, and likely it would all happen too fast. In the blink of an eye, she'd be sitting with Elmer in the hollow-sounding house. Empty nesters.

Ah, but the tiny amount of laundry on her tired back.

The cooking reduced to quart-size saucepots.

Then she felt ashamed, having such selfish thoughts. *My oh.*

Well, if things went on like this much longer, she'd have to stand up to Samuel, no matter how much she dreaded it. She had had it with his foul moods. One thing that boy would have to know was any girl with that kind of indecision was just that, seriously undecided, which all added up to the fact that she wasn't sure if she wanted him or not. Which, she should know.

Oh, she knew. Mothers usually did. John had been very wise, displaying a maturity far beyond his age to leave Kentucky and Lena. It was the best thing he could have done.

A car pulled up and a middle-aged English man came to the door, struggling with his flapping coat.

Mary opened the door, stepped aside to welcome him in.

"Good morning, ma'am."

"Good morning."

"Windy out there. Whew."

"It certainly is."

Of medium height, wearing thick glasses, he would certainly not stand out in a crowd, an ordinary working-class man who would never turn heads.

But there was something about him. A light in his eye. A spring in his step. Mary watched him closely, with a keen, measuring eye.

He told her he was in the vicinity, looking for Lyme disease victims. He had a story to tell, if she had time to listen.

She did. Of course she did.

She pulled out a chair, offered coffee. Tea? A drink of cold grape juice? She wanted to call Elmer in.

He had been a very sick man, for years. Pain and inflammation had settled in his heart. He'd had terrible joint pain and numbness. He had his funeral arranged, with the doctors giving him up to eighteen months to live.

Mary leaned forward, listened intently.

He had been taking up to fifty pills a day. His wife introduced him to the pill called "Protandim." LifeVantage products.

The washhouse door opened, and Elmer appeared. There was a round of introductions, and he was seated, rapt, as the man spoke, repeating his story for his benefit.

Sick, discouraged, at the end of his rope with chronic Lyme disease, he'd waved her away. No. No more pills. Just let me die, to be rid of this pain. His wife begged until he gave in. What was one more pill? OK. All right. And he swallowed it with all the others.

Inexplicably, he began to feel better. In three months, he was back to work, sleeping at night, pain free.

It was a short story, to the point, well spoken, giving God the honor. No gimmick, one pill a day at a cost of forty-five dollars a month. It was all natural, as safe as eating a salad.

He left, leaving two bottles and God's blessing.

Elmer was unimpressed, but Mam was grasping tightly to the handle of wild hope that rose within her for the thousandth time. Maybe. Just maybe this time John could lead a normal life. Become better.

Could it be?

They ate lunch together that day. Elmer, John, and her, the boys off to their jobs. She made potato and onion soup, thickened with cheddar cheese and hard-boiled eggs. They had celery sticks and baby carrots with ranch dressing. For dessert there was butterscotch pie left over from the weekend.

They talked about cows, the weather, the local news.

John seemed to be vaguely aware of everything—the hot soup, the conversation. He twirled a carrot in dressing, but didn't actually eat anything. His face was gaunt, gray.

They mentioned the pills, received the reaction they expected—a dull look, minimal comprehension, a shrug of the shoulders.

"Whatever."

"But did you hear, John? The man was in a bad way. Dying, really. So why wouldn't you at least give it your best shot?" Dat asked.

"I said, I'll take them. I just won't get my hopes up."

"We'll try it, then. The way he said, these pills are good for high blood pressure, headaches, other natural calamities," Mam added.

"Calamities? You mean maladies." John corrected his mother.

They laughed. Mam forgot what a nice smile John had. It seemed as if he was finally growing into his features, or his hair was controllable, or something. He was not overweight, by any means. He was average weight, considering his height. He really was one nice-looking young man, if you didn't notice the unhealthy pallor of his face. But so quiet. He never voiced an opinion when his brothers were present, merely sat back and kept his thoughts to himself.

Supper that evening was as tense as always.

Dat wisely omitted the mentioning of Protandim pills. Marcus was still puffed up from his weekend of winning at volleyball, the gregarious Marty at his side. Actually, the only sour grape was Samuel, who had taken to being more outspoken than ever. Mam recognized this as the shoring up of a battered ego, and did her best to receive his opinions in the light of a mother's love.

John was mostly quiet, but sometimes surprised everyone by gently agreeing with Samuel. Such humility, given how Samuel continued to take jabs at John whenever he could, calling him lazy, a coward, a quitter.

Almost, Mary grasped something that was just out of her reach. Would the time come that she would be thankful for this dreaded disease? Surely, it had given John unusual wisdom and humility, even as it brought waves of depression and what sometimes seemed like self-pity, even to Mam.

God moved in mysterious ways to perform wonders, and who was she to resist?

"Potatoes."

"Potatoes." Louder.

"Somebody hand the dish of potatoes to Allen, please."

"Ew. Scalloped. Why don't we ever have mashed?"

"Allen, stop it. You eat what is set before you and you're thankful." Dat spoke, displeasure all over his face.

"Pass the meatloaf."

"Hurry up with that ketchup. Dump it all out, why don't you? Now there's none left. Go get more."

"Marcus, go down cellar and get it yourself."

Samuel watched his brother go, then spooned some ketchup onto John's plate.

"I don't want it."

"Eat it."

So rather than get into the fray, John spooned the ketchup onto his meatloaf, which did not go unnoticed by Marcus.

"Ketchup vacuums. Every one of you."

"John isn't. He has Lyme, remember?"

Eyes to the parents' faces, followed by silence. John chose not to answer. He could take it. Lena had about hit the nail on the head, saying he couldn't run from folks, brothers, coworkers, whatever, that disapproved of him for being weak, tired, unable to function the way he had. Dewan had been OK, he just voiced his opinions the same as he did everything else. John missed him, actually.

Now they were discussing the farm.

"Seven boys and not one farmer. Sometimes I can't believe my hard luck. None of you enjoy it. Not one," Dat was saying, in a mock mournful tone.

Heads shook.

"You work like a maniac, Dat. If you'd count the hours in a day, you'd be making about five dollars an hour, the way milk prices are going."

"Aha! You forget. My farm is worth a lot of money. Besides, who can measure the satisfaction of sitting on a plow, watching the sun, the clouds, and the birds, the smell of the wet, freshly tilled soil? You guys don't know what you're missing."

John thought, *I do.* But he didn't say it.

He had never wanted to leave the farm. He had always helped, learned by milking, feeding, driving horse-drawn equipment. He knew when to plant and when to harvest. He knew oncoming weather by cloud formations and wind directions. He could treat a calf with runny scours, knew when to call the vet for a down cow. He harbored dreams of produce fields, and most shameful of all, fields of flowers, to cut and sell. He thought of Lena, her upbringing, but cut himself off from imagining her by his side. She was too perfect, he woefully unworthy.

The meal ended with chocolate cake and canned peaches, Mam's old staple. A chocolate cake could be whipped up in ten minutes, and canned peaches were always in the basement. The boys loved it, so why not?

That night, John dried the dishes for her, without saying anything.

She asked him what his thoughts on the new pills were.

"I probably feel the same way he did. I don't even want to try them. Like, getting my hopes up is risky business."

"But you sleep better. Remember, you used to sleep on the living room floor with Dat. So you are doing some better."

"Yeah, I guess. Anxiety is something you have to overcome, even if it can take a few years. Probably some of the medication helped."

"Do you ever feel stronger?"

"Sometimes. But I always slide back. It's worse when I don't sleep."

"You're not sleeping?"

"Not always."

"Well, we'll try the Protandim, see how it goes."

John laid his tea towel aside and went to his room. He lay on his back, stared at the ceiling, his arms crossed on the back of his head, and thought about Lena. This was the middle of March. She'd told him she'd give Samuel an answer by end of January. Evidently, she hadn't done it yet, according to his moods. Or perhaps she had, and the answer was not what he had hoped.

He had done the right thing, leaving her and coming home, away from the temptation, when she still belonged to Samuel, in spite of her protests.

Or was it only the kindness of her heart?

He couldn't know, having broken all contact with her.

Being with the youth on the weekends, especially with Ivan, had been like therapy. It made him realize this was not the end of everything. There were good times, fun, excitement, other girls to be around, to get to know. There was Sylvia—tall, willowy, vivacious Sylvia, whose aura of energy and high spirits were like a cold drink of water to a thirsty person. Like Dewan, she drew you from the depth of your own thoughts, the discomfort that dragged down your own optimism. Then there was Susan—small, round, dark-haired Susan who was so shy, she hardly ever spoke a word, but was so easy to talk to, one on one. He could imagine himself seated in a buggy, easily leading the conversation, feeling like a real man, capable of entertaining this quiet girl.

But the winning of a girl's hand had to be turned over to God. He was the Master, the director of the orchestra of love. John knew that God is love, a deeper, more mysterious love than the initial thrill of first sight, first touch. What, then, had it been, with Lena on the swing, the discovery of hands touching, the homecoming of his heart?

Or was it merely the desire for a young man for the body of a beautiful girl? How did one know the difference? Was there a difference?

He had often touched Marty, even linked her arm in his, threw an arm around her shoulders, high-fived after a game of volleyball. Nothing had ever come close to the touch on the swing with Lena. He sighed. Well, apparently she wasn't Samuel's girl, either.

Samuel was a walking thundercloud. Still, John couldn't blame him, knowing how hard it was to wait for the unknown, unsure of the outcome, wanting a happy ending so badly it destroyed your peace.

No more. He'd given her up.

He fell asleep thinking about how she ate the cheeseburger, the glow of the sun on the finely turned cheek, the satin of her blond hair, the hours that ticked by like seconds every time he was in her beautiful presence.

CHAPTER 21

KENTUCKY IN SPRING WAS THE CLOSEST ONE COULD GET TO HEAVEN here on earth, Lena thought, as she walked down the winding road with Naomi's hand held firmly in her own.

Overhead, the branches of a maple tree were loaded with buds, a yellow green, the color of the daffodils before they burst into the beauty of their ruffled yellow display. The sky was a deep cornflower blue, with clouds that resembled little cotton balls stuck to the blue at random, the air heady with purple violets and primroses, wild bluebells and early calendula.

Drab brown hills turned into patchwork quilts, squares of dark tilled soil, mixed with the deep green of new alfalfa. Tractors moved steadily along the edge like overgrown red ladybugs, changing the squares as they drew the plow.

Lena was amazed at the view, the ever-changing scenery that fell below her as far as her eyes could see. She never tired of her and Naomi's daily walk, the air mild and filled with the scent of all the new growth.

A chipmunk skittered across the road, an impossibly swift streak of brown, black marks across the back, a tiny bottlebrush for a tail.

"Chipmunk, Naomi. That was a chipmunk."

She stopped, bent her knees to be on eye level, tried to make eye contact. But it was not possible today, which was often the case.

"Did you see, Naomi? That was a frightened little chipmunk."

She kept up the usual chatter, her face bright, but inside, another drop of despair fell into the unstable pool that was steadily widening.

What part of autism was not simply cruel? Why couldn't the doctors unlock the secret to the troubled mind of a child who had simply retreated from the normalcy of everyday life? So many unanswered questions, such a freefall into her own sense of failure.

She was in awe of her cousin Barbie. She was always patient, mostly hopeful, even on the worst days. Truly there had never been a better mother or caregiver for a special-needs child.

The bedwetting had begun since Lena's stay, which carried a blame all its own. Thinking she'd been too hard on the child, she had apologized to Barbie, which was met with a wave of her hand, a refusal to accept anything so ridiculous.

As far as Lena could tell, she was making no progress at all. She may have even worsened the situation. She knew she had to get away, if only for the summer. She felt she needed to educate herself better, in the ways of autism, the nuances and quirks of being a caregiver.

But she knew, too, that that reason for looking forward to summer was only secondary. She wanted to be home with her family, to see the ridges and hills of Jefferson County, where life was simple, predictable meals were on the table on time, food that had been home-canned, frozen, pickled, preserved in the way her grandmother had taught Lena's mother. The plentiful roasts of beef, the ground meat, bacon, loins of pork, even the chickens were butchered by her parents with the help of her siblings.

Here at the Lapps, provisions came in a dizzying array of colorful boxes and bags, snacks, and foreign-sounding dips and processed meat and cheese.

Lena had learned what salsa was, and the corn tortilla chips you scooped it up with. Guacamole was a dip made from avocados, another new food she had read about but never tasted. Grocery buying was done every week, the bags bulging with all kinds of interesting food that was made into yet another new dish Barbie had found in a cookbook or magazine.

She admired her friends in so many different ways, but this buying of expensive groceries was not one of them. But then, perhaps there was an endless stream of plenty, an overflow of cash, and a few hundred dollars here or there made no difference. Besides, it was none of her business, so she ate the food, the rich desserts and spicy casseroles, and said nothing.

Naomi stopped, pointed.

Alarmed, Lena looked in the direction of the pointed finger.

A flash of brown, the white flag, the underside of a deer's tail, and it was gone.

A deer! Lena exclaimed, "Good girl."

Where a normal child would have shown delight, hand clapping or a shout, Naomi merely stood expressionless.

Lena got down on her knees again. "You saw a deer, Naomi. The deer ran away before we could really see it. Did you see it run away?"

A flicker of recognition, an intake of breath, and almost Naomi spoke. Instead, she lifted a hand and laid her palm on the side of Lena's face, the touch as light as air, but a gesture that lifted Lena from her sense of failure to the first rung up the ladder of accomplishment.

The small gesture made the weeks of patience worthwhile, and they returned to the house with renewed energy. It was only late at night that Lena wrestled with the decision that still loomed before her, an ever-widening gulf of doubt and misgiving. She found only small solace in prayer.

She blamed herself for being so confused, for not being able to tell right from wrong. She should not have gone on so long, allowing a relationship to continue when her heart was no longer in it, and now she was enmeshed in the bewildering situation of how or when to extricate herself from Samuel. It was cruel, hurtful.

She came to realize it was much like removing a festering splinter. The initial pain of having it removed would free her to live the life she wanted.

Was it OK to do that? Did God approve of choosing one young man over another, after dating for so long? Was it only self-will and infatuation with John?

Would one man be a better husband than another, or was it simply a mix of each one having faults and talents, good qualities and bad ones, so that it didn't matter which one she chose? Would John even still have her?

There were questions everywhere she turned, a ring of unanswered questions. She felt like a struggling animal caught in a sucking quagmire of quicksand, her flailing only making it worse.

Sleep came slowly, uneasily. She popped awake at the slightest creak, the anguish of her heart rushing back, before sleep could overtake her again.

Taught to be obedient and to hold the act of sacrifice in high esteem, it was uncomfortable to think about what *she* wanted, and when she tried to think about what was *right*, everything went murky.

She should say yes. Live her life with Samuel. It would be hard work, but wouldn't the sacrifice bring its own reward? God would bless her infinitely with a lasting peace, looking on the smoke of her offering as he had looked on Abel in the Old Testament story. God would supply the love after she gave up her own will. Samuel was an example of fine, young manhood, and had invested so much time in their relationship.

Samuel would be the kind of person who would lead the singing in church, be voted on the school board, on financial committees who were appointed to help poor souls who had plunged into debt far beyond their means. She knew him so well—the confidence, the whip-smart ability to make choices.

And how he looked down on others from his self-appointed perch on his pedestal.

Dear God, I can't do it. I can't follow him all the days of my life, grinding my teeth in frustration, subject to that attitude.

Somehow, somewhere, she had to find the strength.

To be at home on the farm was an elixir all its own, a spring tonic that cleansed the soul, brought the tumultuous boiling thoughts to a blessed calm. Everything was simple, orderly, done predictably by the season.

The time of planting was here now. Her father had applied the lime and fertilizer, the tillage radishes plowed under, the spike-toothed harrow working the loamy soil to a perfect crumbly, moist texture.

She walked the gardens, observing the rows of peas, close beside each other, a space in the middle. They were double rows, so the pea vines could climb up the chicken wire attached to wooden stakes. Spring onion sets dropped with precision, then covered, the hoe raking the thick soil over them. Radish and red beet seeds were sprinkled in shallow rows, so tiny you couldn't drop them like peas. If they came out of the ground too thick, her mother would thin them, carefully pulling up the tiny new growth and leave them to wither, knowing if they were planted too heavily, it would affect the size of the beets and radishes.

New lettuce plants were set out, cabbage and broccoli and cauliflower. As always, it was windy, the air carrying that early biting chill, a sweater being a necessity, a scarf tied over the head.

Lena was nervous, her movements fast, her speech tumbling from her mouth in quick succession. She had agreed to meet Samuel.

He would be arriving at the usual time on Saturday evening. Seven o'clock. That too, should have been simple, a normalcy that was both grounding and calming, an anticipation of meeting her beloved. The realization that he was not her beloved, that she was not betrothed, slowly emerged through the shroud of her indecision. To come home to her old surroundings, the homey goodness of her frugal life, the love of family, the rock of her own well-being was a blessing she could never take for granted. After she told Samuel her answer, there would be this, a time of renewal, of sameness, dwarfing the astronomical fear of the future.

The fear itself was not sent from God. A large part of it was the stinging reality of what the community around her would say. What would they think of her, breaking up with a fine young man like Samuel after everyone expected her to be grateful to find such an excellent match, and from a family held in higher regard than her own?

For her father was not one to be held in high esteem. He was a quiet man who never sang "fore," had no way with words, drove an old horse hitched to a tired-looking carriage, his Sunday suit worn to an often-washed shade of purple. The buildings on the farm, like his Sunday suit, bordered on shabby, the peeling paint on the wooden fence a testimony to the reluctance to buy the expensive five-gallon buckets of white paint.

No one knew, though, the amount of money that drew a steady interest from the local bank in Dexter Falls.

Lena was ready at seven, dressed in navy blue. She couldn't bring herself to dress in a light or bright color, given the somber situation.

It wasn't a mourning, but it may as well have been.

When she walked out to help him unhitch, she was struck by his beauty, the only word that could describe a young man of his golden good looks.

His blue eyes lit up at the sight of her, a smile widened his perfect mouth, revealing the flash of white.

"Lena!"

She stepped up to him, extended a hand for a polite handshake.

Bewildered, he took her hand.

"No hug?"

She laughed. "Someone might see."

"You're right. It's still early."

"Not that we ever did much of that, remember?"

Their conversation remained light, informative, with all that had gone on in their lives the past six months. Most of the talking was done by Samuel, his work at B and S Structures always foremost on his mind. He'd been promoted to floor manager, and now, had taken on the duty of ordering materials, even some of the scheduling, setting up appointments to deliver sheds and dog kennels.

Having done without a good night's sleep for so long, Lena found herself stifling yawns, which she suspected was partly due to nerves. She did manage to tell him about her cousin Barbie's gorgeous home and lifestyle, the complexities of autism, which brought lowered brows from Samuel.

"If they have all that money, how come they don't hire a professional? Did they pay you anything?"

"Oh yes, of course. I thought they were actually very generous."

"To the tune of what?"

Irritation welled up. It was, really, no business of his. But it would be rude not to answer.

"Two hundred dollars a week."

"Peanuts. You're crazy."

Lena took a deep, steadying breath.

They picked at the snack Lena had prepared and packed in a basket—chocolate chip bars, cups of coffee, popcorn with ranch dressing mix. How many times had she done this? How often had she sat at the kitchen table with him, watching him enjoy what she had prepared, then moved to the couch in the living room? She felt a wave of nostalgia.

They had had their good times.

The hour was late when Samuel finally cleared his throat after a long silence, and was able to ask if she had an answer for him.

"I do, Samuel."

She steadied herself again, with an indrawn breath, light as a butterfly.

"I have been away for a reason, Samuel. I have had time to think, and for that, I am grateful. My answer is no."

The silence that followed was punctuated by the loud ticking of the clock, the dropping of a chunk of wood in the old kitchen stove.

Finally, Samuel asked why, his voice shaking, his mouth tense.

"I am in love with your brother, John."

"But you can't be!" he burst out. "You're crazy."

"That's the second time you told me that this evening, so I suppose it must be true."

"Don't get smart with me, Lena."

She chose not to answer.

"Can you give me an explanation? A valid one that starts to make sense?"

"No. Not really. All I know for sure is that I have always had something for John. Even when I was his teacher."

"That's just sick."

"No, it isn't. I was sixteen and he was fourteen."

"It's still sick."

"I'm sorry if you think so."

"Well, I think so."

Again, there was nothing to say to this.

"Does he love you?"

"I don't know."

"Of course you know. You've been together in Kentucky all winter."

"No, Samuel, we haven't. We were together once after he picked me up at the train station. He asked me to go shopping and told me he was returning to Pennsylvania, that it wasn't right for him to harbor thoughts of me when I was your girl."

"You're still my girl."

"No, Samuel. I am not."

"You just said you won't marry me. You didn't say we were breaking up."

"I mean that, though. I told you why."

Lena would think back on this as one of the hardest moments of her life, sitting beside Samuel as he lowered his head in his hands and cried, his body shaking like a leaf in a strong gale.

"I just don't understand. I love you so much. I'd give my life for you, do anything you asked of me."

Lena remained quiet, but knew Samuel didn't have any idea what it meant to give his life for her or anyone else. His entire life revolved around himself, his abilities and talents, his thoughts, and above all, his opinions so easily launched, no matter who was in the audience or whether it mattered how it affected them.

She had not been wrong about the hard work life would require of her. When she remained still, he reached into his pocket for a handkerchief, blew his nose, shook his head as he pocketed it.

"How can you be so hardhearted? It's like your heart is made of stone. I always thought kindness was one of your best qualities. Apparently, I was wrong."

"Samuel, please."

"How can you do this to me?"

"I don't know."

Then came a stream of entreaties. He promised to change whatever it was she didn't like about him. Didn't she know how unhealthy John was? He drew a vivid picture of his mental instability, sleeping in the living room on an air mattress. What would she do if he suffered a relapse? She couldn't expect to be financially well off, if she chose John, the way he became weak and exhausted at unexpected times.

"I don't expect you to think about these things," he finished, as if he was doing her a favor by pointing out all the things she couldn't possibly have thought of herself.

As the night wore on, everything became crystal clear. As far as she could see, the sunshine before her revealed a trail illuminated by the courage of her choice. No, no, and no, Samuel. No. I am not crazy. Neither am I incompetent. God has given me healthy thoughts, the wisdom to know right from wrong. The only thing I needed was the courage to speak up.

Where Samuel robbed her of her sense of well-being, John supplied it. Where Samuel tore her self-esteem down, John lifted it up.

The difference was almost palpable, something she could reach out and touch. She must never again allow a shred of doubt or fear to cloud her decision.

Finally, he hitched up his horse, stood beside his carriage, begging yet again. He reached out to draw her close, bent to kiss her lips, but she turned her face and he kissed her cheek like a child. She was calm, relieved, as limp as a rag doll, her strength drained away.

As she watched the lights from the buggy move slowly out the driveway, she whispered, "Goodbye, Samuel. Thank you for allowing me to see and understand what love is."

There were no tears for her. Only a sea as calm and still as glass. Love was not even close to what Samuel had for her. She was only an acquisition, another step up the social ladder, the girl everyone else wanted. She did berate herself for that thought, but knew it was true.

She felt pity, then, a deep stab of empathy for how hard this must be for him. To face this humiliation among his peers, his brothers eventually knowing about John, the youngest, the heavy, pimply, nearsighted one with Lyme disease.

She knelt by her bed and prayed for John. He would have his own race set before him, living with Samuel.

She lay in her bed, and for the first time in her life, allowed the love in her heart to grow, to develop into a strong emotion that created a wellspring of yearning, an anticipation of the future, hand in hand with the man who possessed all the qualities she longed for—kindness, a spirit awash in humility, gentleness, meekness. She couldn't help but imagine the fruits of the spirit like a basket containing glistening red apples, magical, God-given ethereal ones.

Samuel approached John on the patio the following week.

"So you accomplished what you set out to do, huh?"

Bewildered, John stopped, turned.

"What?"

"You know what."

"I have no idea what you're talking about."

"Oh, don't give me that."

"I don't."

"Does Lena ring a bell in that cloudy, Lyme-infested head?" Samuel asked, his blue eyes darkened with pain and anger.

John could not hold Samuel's irate gaze. His eyes fell to the tips of his shoes as a painful blush crept across his features, darkening even the throat at the base of his collar.

"I see you turn as red as a beet. You're no better than King David in the Bible, stealing Uriah's wife."

With that dire portent, Samuel stalked off the porch, his golden head gleaming in the orange glow of the sun.

And so began the fiercest battle of John's precarious hold on normal life, his immune system weakened, his emotions tattered by Lyme disease. His appetite waned to the point where Mam spoke to Dat about John being anorexic. He paced the bedroom floor at night, Mam lying in bed, each footfall above her increasing the pounding of her heart.

He developed migraines so bad he took to his bed, spoke to no one, shut out his family, refused to attend any of the youths' functions.

His heart palpitations raced out of control, until he was taken to the emergency room at the Good Spirit Hospital in Dexter Falls. There he was given antianxiety medication, told he was experiencing panic attacks. His tests showed normal, they said. A slight vitamin D deficiency, but for a person with Lyme disease, that was fairly normal.

"You're good to go, young man. You've come a long way if you were as sick as your parents say. You'll be fine."

John gulped back the emotion he could only describe as an all-encompassing relief. Perhaps he would not die. All the old fears had come roaring back after Samuel had hurled that accusation. He knew too well what had happened to King David in the Old Testament, the chastisement and lost blessing from God.

The worst of his anxiety was the fear of being capable of providing for Lena, if and when God would eventually bless their union. To know he had done wrong, taking Lena from his own brother, was a sin, just as Samuel stated.

But he had not done that.

Or had he?

He prayed for forgiveness, felt the power of the Spirit, then. He humbled himself even more, telling his Lord and Savior he would stay away from Lena until Samuel found love again, and if she didn't wait, then it was meant to be.

And he followed his promises.

He helped his father on the farm whenever he was able, which was most days now. His father encouraged him to get out of bed in the morning, even if he felt weak and sweaty. It was something to overcome, by the grace of God.

John did his best. The anxiety medicine helped control his sleeplessness, so with a week of good night's rest, he was in the fields by eight o'clock, having done his early morning feeding and eaten breakfast.

Samuel kept his distance, ignored him. None of his brothers mentioned any of this, not Samuel's breakup or John's hospital visit. They merely passed him by, made small talk, and shrugged their shoulders.

By himself, John soaked up the sun, shirtless, knowing the best source of vitamin D was the heat of the summer sun. He ate beef liver and onions, Mam's spinach salad from the garden, and slowly returned to his former self.

The brothers eyed this tall, thin, tanned version of John with new respect. Older now, his shoulders and arms filled out, and he was nothing like the fat younger brother who had peered out from behind thick lenses.

When he began lifting weights in the basement, he did it in secret, until Allen and Daniel came down to play a game of Ping-Pong and caught him soaked in perspiration. So began a friendly competition.

The basement rang with their shouts, egging each other on. From the kitchen stove, tears of gratitude welled up in Mam's eyes.

Was he really getting better?

Was there hope, this time? What had changed?

Oh, she knew by the look on Samuel's face that Lena had not promised to marry him, but found out via Daniel that they broke up altogether.

How the mighty has fallen, she thought. But she never put two and two together. In her eyes, John was not eligible to be dating. It was his health. He could never provide for a wife. And Elmer was so tight with his wages. His pay was only half what other people paid workers.

She talked to Samuel, hovered over him like a kindly drone,

annoying him in the process. She said exactly the wrong thing at the wrong time, all while congratulating herself for having helped Samuel accept life without Lena in his future.

"There are so many other girls, Samuel. Levi Lapp's Susan. Now there's a winner if I ever saw one. They say she's an excellent quilter for a young girl. Over at Ez Miller's, they had a tan and black Bargello quilt in frame, they said she quilted rings around everyone else."

Samuel pictured himself being quilted, like a web being spun around his body by a spider named Susan Lapp.

"Or that new girl. What's her name? Sylvia or Suzanna. She's a real looker, that one."

Samuel cringed at her old-fashioned way of talking. "Looker." Who said that anymore?

"But you know, Samuel, you must pray for a partner. Evidently Lena was not the one for you. God just hasn't revealed it till now. So you must be brave and keep praying. In time, His will is made known. It always is."

"Oh, and I wanted to mention another girl. Fannie Esh. She might be a bit older than you, but with her dark hair and eyes, you'd make a specular couple."

Samuel groaned aloud. She always said "spectacular" like that. Speck-u-ler.

"Mam, I'm not ready yet, OK? So no suggestions, please. I appreciate your concern, though."

He gave her a surprisingly kind look.

Now when did Samuel ever voice appreciation? Mam wondered.

CHAPTER 22

AND SO ONE SUNDAY IN THE MIDDLE OF JUNE WHEN THE TRADI-tional peach-colored roses bloomed in profusion all over the white wooden trellis, the air heavy and sweet with the sound of bumblebees hovering greedily over the nectar from the purple clematis, John dressed to go to the youths' supper at Isaac Beiler's.

He blinked at his reflection in the mirror, thanking the sun for all the vitamins, feeling only the beginning of a renewed sense of vigor.

Tanned, slim, his hair as decent as he could expect, he shaved his face with the new triple-edged razor, the new shaving cream, and aftershave lotion, chose a light beige shirt and the traditional black trousers and vest.

He had gotten new trousers, since none of his old ones fit.

Crayon was eager to step out, brushed and combed, his coat glistening like an old copper penny, tugging impatiently at the reins, wanting to run faster than John would allow. They traveled over the one-lane bridge at Jack's Crossing, along the narrow country road that bordered the ridge to the north of Jake Stoltzfus's, the wind in his face, the sun at his back.

It was a rare evening in June. It was only natural, then, that his thoughts turned lightly to thoughts of love, of Lena, the one who had always represented his heart's longing.

What would her reaction be when she caught sight of him? He had no idea if she would be there. Perhaps she, too, despaired of social life after Samuel. He knew only that it was time to rejoin the *rumschpringa*, that he had conquered nearly all of his real or imagined symptoms.

Were they imagined? He wasn't sure. He only knew that tonight he felt better than he had for years.

So far, anyway.

He drove up to the barn, met his friend Ivan, along with a few other boys he knew well, threw the reins across the protruding headlight, and hopped out.

"Hey, John! What do you know? He's back!"

Ivan was childishly excited to see his old friend back in the circle. John grinned.

"Boy, you are one good-looking dude!" Ivan said, followed by a piercing whistle.

"Hey, cut that out."

And so the evening began on an easy note, John falling into the pool of camaraderie, events unfolding as if they'd never left off.

Marty and Marcus played volleyball, Marty like a brilliant peacock in her dress of iridescent teal blue, bare feet, covering strings flying.

John smiled to himself, thought of Mam's compressed mouth at the sight of that color.

He could watch her play volleyball all night. She was a study in efficiency, making every one of her flying moments count. Marcus was a perfect match, spiking, setting up, a fierce server. Was it just John's imagination or did his shirts tend to become more and more colorful?

Like birds of paradise, those two.

And then he saw her, walking down the slope from the white one-story house. He could never remember what color she wore that day, if she wore shoes, if she was smiling, if she was with another girl. He only knew that it was Lena. Across the length of space between them, their eyes met, and the world went away. Only Lena existed.

"John. Hey. Back to earth, you."

Ivan struck an elbow into his ribs to get his attention.

It was when he was in line to fill his plate at the long row of tables that she came up to him, softly said hello, told him quietly to come eat with her.

He nodded, but his hands shook when he lifted a wobbling square of meatloaf onto his plate.

No one would think it unusual. They had often eaten together.

He was, after all, still the little brother.

They were seated at the far end of the large, well-lit shop, leaving room for others to join them. But quickly, before their privacy was disturbed, they found each other's eyes, their gazes locked and held.

"John, I . . ."

"I know. I know."

"But you . . ."

"Is it over?"

"Samuel?"

He waited. There was no need for further words. Her eyes told him everything he had wanted to know.

Marty bounced up, knocked over Lena's glass of water, shrieked, and apologized, and the moment was over.

"Hey, John. Boy are you looking good or what? Wow! What happened to you? You're, like, all grown up or whatever."

Lena smiled at John, freely, gladly.

"I mean, seriously. You rid of the Lyme or what? Shoo!"

Lena laughed outright.

"Marcus will hear you."

Marty laughed. "He won't mind. He knows he's a keeper for me."

The evening passed happily, coasted along on stardust for John. When darkness fell, the stars winked at him, the quarter moon smiled alone for him. She appeared at his side, after the last hymn had been sung, and he never asked if he could take her home. She simply helped him hitch up, climbed into the buggy, and they talked the whole time it took Crayon to trot nine miles to her house.

They hid the buggy in the forebay, left Crayon hitched to it, and closed the garage door. Her family could not know John brought her home. It was too soon.

In the half-light from the neighboring pole light, they sat on the buggy seat and talked, saying everything they had wanted to say for so long, but couldn't.

"I'm going back to Kentucky in August," she stated.

His heart sank. He hadn't expected this.

"You're serious?"

"I am, John. I feel it's my duty. I can't let Gid and Barbie down. They need someone."

John nodded. "That's true. Well, it's up to you. Whatever you decide. I am going to ask you, though, when we can start to date. You know, see each other on a regular basis. If you want to spend a year in Kentucky, that's fine. I'll wait."

"Oh my, John. That is so kind of you. You won't be going?"

"No. I see no reason to return to my sister. They have good dependable help with Dewan, who bonded with the dogs more than I ever could. And my father needs me."

She sighed. "Oh, John."

There was a space of silence, a restful acceptance of being there, seated beside each other, with no one to interfere. They both contemplated their good fortune, the blessing of living in a culture that allowed each individual to follow their heart, in spite of having gone through the years of sickness and indecision.

Samuel approached him on Monday evening, as John knew he would.

"You took her home," he stated, his blue eyes boring into John's.

"Only as a friend, Samuel. As a favor."

"Expect me to believe that?"

"You can believe what you want."

John was shocked when Samuel lowered himself onto a patio chair, put his head in his hands and groaned, a sound so filled with loss and hopelessness, it wrenched his heart. His own brother, his flesh-and-blood sibling, enduring so much suffering because of him.

John stood, shifting his weight from one foot to the other, pity rising like a slow winter sun, but pity nonetheless.

"I'm sorry."

From the depth of Samuel's cupped hands came a muffled, "You should be."

He lifted his face, tearstained, his eyes dull with anguish, and begged John to let her go, for his sake.

"Do you think for one minute the Lord can bless your union if you took her away from me? Like I told you, it's no different than King David taking Bathsheba, you mark my words. Nothing good will come of it. What am I expected to do? How am I supposed to carry on with my life, knowing I'll have to live the rest of my days seeing you two together? It's not right."

John lowered himself into an opposite chair, across the table.

"You think there was ever such a messy affair in the history of the Amish?" John asked wryly.

Samuel shrugged his shoulders.

"Well, if it makes you feel any better, she's going back to Kentucky."

"And you're not?"

"No."

Hope flickered across Samuel's tired face. John knew he hadn't even started to give up the desperate hold on Lena. His own will, his pride, all that had ever mattered to Samuel, was torn out of his grasp by one beautiful, sweet, kind, unselfish girl named Lena.

"So you'll let her go?"

"I will. I'll talk to her."

"You'll try and persuade her to come back to me, right?"

"That is her choice. Not mine."

"But if you told her you don't want her, start dating another girl, she'd change her mind. She did love me, in spite of what you think."

John stood up, pushed back his chair, and looked steadily at Samuel.

"All right. I'll tell her we won't be in contact, but I can't tell her I don't want her. That would be a lie."

That brought another outburst from Samuel, hurled accusations, bitter words like flailing, pecking blackbirds. John felt as if he needed to lift his arms to his face, duck his head to ward off the verbal blows. He felt the numbing weakness in his chest travel down his arms, the core of his body turned to jelly, his legs tingled with weakness. He broke out in a sweat, his eye flickered, the familiar maddening tic in his right eye.

He turned, left the patio, stumbled blindly up the stairs, and fell across his bed.

Mam had watched her sons' encounter on the back porch, which had filled her with dread. Dire premonitions swirled around her, the end of her peace for days to come. How would something like this ever be patched up? Mam threw a mug into the rinse water, heard the snap of the handle breaking, and began to cry.

This was just the limit. After all this time with John's illness, the days of worry and prayer, the indecision, making choices and wondering if it was the best thing to have chosen, and now this. Life simply wasn't fair.

She enjoyed a moment's reprieve as she gave herself over to a big helping of self-pity, fat tears sliding down her plump, pink cheeks.

And now here it was June. The time of heat would soon be upon them, the ninety-five-degree afternoons when work stared at her from every direction and she had all these big boys to feed and clothe and wash for. It was all too much.

John had simply taken Samuel's girlfriend. Now what was she supposed to do? She hardly knew Lena. What was all the fuss about? She was pretty enough as that went, but she sure didn't come from much. That Henry Zook was so tight his pennies screeched from pinching them. His wife was no different.

She'd heard they socked their money away, never went on vacation, and lived out of those produce fields of theirs.

Having spent the day sewing trousers for her six boys, she had a crimp in her neck, a sore lower back, and eyes weary with focusing on dark fabric, pedaling that treadle. There were weeds in the garden and no one to help her with them. She blew her nose in the paper towel she'd used to wipe the window on the door, recoiled as the strong ammonia smell of Windex hit her.

Probably Lena wouldn't even buy Windex. She'd make her own homemade window cleaner. Well, if Samuel got her he'd have to change his ways.

Frugality was a virtue, to be sure, though.

It didn't surprise her a bit, actually, Lena picking John. The difference in those two boys was vast. She liked to think John took after her side of the family. Well, her, anyway. But she knew some of his obedience, his sweet nature, came from her Elmer. He was a good man.

Oh, that Samuel was Elmer's brother Yoni. Absolutely no doubt. Good looking, suave, could have had anyone. Anyone. He picked the flashiest girl and they had their share of marriage problems. That Betty was a piece of work. Didn't she go and bid up the grandfather's clock at the family auction to over six thousand dollars? They didn't even have it.

She lifted her coffee mug, drained the last bit, grimaced, spat out the annoying coffee grounds, and thought for the thousandth time she would have to start using coffee filters. Those Lifetime drip coffee makers were just the ticket, but some grounds always escaped the tiny holes in the bottom.

She wiped the counter furiously, felt her hips jiggling from the vigorous motion. That was another thing that depressed her. Her weight. Eli sie Emma went on Plexus, some new herbal supplement that was supposed to cure everything, plus take weight off in the bargain.

Well, she'd mow lawn till bedtime, for the exercise. She leaned into the handle, putting her weight into the reel mower as she plowed through the thick, late spring grass. She must start mowing this section more often. Her breath came in hard puffs, her face felt as if it was on fire. Purple, probably. Her knees felt wobbly, but she charged on. Nothing was better for the heart.

"Hey, Mam."

From behind her, she heard John calling. She finished the row, started back, threw the handle of the mower down, wiped her face with the hem of her apron.

"Let me."

"Ach, John. I need the exercise."

"I'll do it."

He reached for the mower handle.

"You sure you feel well tonight?"

"Well enough. Good, actually. I am pretty good. Don't baby me."

He grinned. Mam grinned back. "I'm good at that, right?" Then, because she couldn't help it, "John, what are you going to do about Lena? I saw you and Samuel on the back porch and it just makes me weak."

John lowered his gaze, kicked at the reel with the toe of his shoe. When he lifted his face, his eyes were so full of misery, it was like a physical blow to Mam.

"I don't know."

"It's a hard situation, John. I'm afraid it will get the best of you."

"I'm all right. I haven't been dating her. It's Samuel I'm worried about. He hasn't even started to give her up."

He told her, then, that Lena was going to Kentucky for the fall and winter, to help her cousin with their special-needs child.

Mam nodded. "Lydia says you're not going back."

"No. They have dependable help with that Dewan Reynolds."

John laughed, a sound Mam so seldom heard. She watched his face, sharply.

"The happiest person I ever met."

Mam smiled. "So, what about Lena?"

"I told you, I don't know. Samuel wants me to tell her I am no longer interested, but it's not the truth."

Mam shook her head.

"I suppose the best plan is to wait, right? If she goes to Kentucky, and Samuel and I stay here, then we'll leave it to God. I will not contact her, or try not to, and perhaps Samuel will move on. What do you think?"

Mam nodded. "The best plan, I would say. But a sacrifice."

"She's worth it. It's nothing compared to seven years."

Mam looked up, puzzled.

"You know, the story of Jacob and Rachel."

Understanding dawned on Mam's flushed face. She smiled, nodded.

"Poor Jacob of the Old Testament. Do you think there is one young man nowadays who would work for someone for seven years to win his bride? Then he was cheated by Laban, given Leah instead of Rachel."

John grinned. "Poor guy. I don't know if I'd do that or not. Fourteen years he worked, and he said the time was short. So you see, I can do this. Aren't these old stories written for an example for us?"

"Why sure they are."

"I thought so."

And with that, John moved off, pushing the reel mower.

Incredible, thought Mam. Here was John, the silent Lyme disease victim, the mute, tormented young man that pierced her through with sorrow and anxiety, mowing grass, holding a conversation with her.

Spiritually, she prostrated herself by the throne of grace, weeping with a grateful heart.

Thank you, thank you.

She thought about how five years ago she never would have thought to say thank you for her son mowing grass. Was this disease a call of awakening? A chastening of the Lord for the entire family?

Ah, but the wrecking ball of the Lord had wrecked the once-sturdy family structure. Or had it? Were the hearts only learning now what love was? The kind of love that was not conditional?

What had appeared on the outside as harsh trials and sorrows had actually been teaching all of them what love really was. Patience, forbearance, sympathy, tolerance for one another. Life would always present you with people who did not act the way you thought they should, causing you to lower your brows in disapproval, voice an opinion, feel superior in and justified by your own judgment.

Ah, but we can do better.

She envisioned all the boys as rust-colored pottery, soaking wet, spinning on the wheel that formed a vessel for the Master's use. Abner, an experienced roofer, a light of happiness to those around him, a wonderful match for Ruthie. Amos so mature, already coming into his own.

All of them, actually. All of them. A great love enveloped her. A gratitude lifted her from the everyday cares and worries of the day. Blessed. She was blessed.

After mowing the lawn, John started up the Weed eater, turned it upside down, and began edging the borders of Mam's flower beds.

He went to bed with a pounding headache and no reason not to believe his Lyme symptoms were coming back the minute he overexerted himself.

A long hot shower did nothing to relieve the pain, so he went to the kitchen for ibuprofen.

His mother was on the recliner, a book on her lap, her hands folded, sleeping so soundly she never heard him enter the kitchen.

Her pale blue housecoat with the buttons down the front sagged open at the throat, revealing the pale line where her dress covered her neck and shoulders, the deep tan where it didn't. John felt a tender pity for his tired mother. She looked so vulnerable, so helpless in her deep sleep, when in life, she was so smart, so in charge, always talking, always capable.

He smiled at his father who sat on the other side of the room, reading.

"You hurting?" he asked, peering over the top of his glasses.

"Nothing much. Headache."

Dat nodded. "Too much lawn mowing."

"I have to toughen up, Dat."

That night, his dreams kept waking him up and his heart pounded as the familiar tremor overtook him. He rolled onto his back, opened his eyes, and prayed, took deep, cleansing breaths that he counted—in, out, one, two—keeping his concentration centered on calming his mind and body.

He had learned this was effective most of the time now. He no longer felt as if he was slipping away into a chasm of no return. He strongly believed the anxiety was due to the Lyme disease, but he alone could battle it by learning methods of relaxation, which pretty much eliminated his nights of terror, the dread of sleeping alone, the fear that rose like weird shadows on the wall.

And God heard his prayers, that was another thing.

Battling on, through days of fear and weakness, he had come to feel God, a Higher Being, a strength when he was weakest, an unexplained assurance that all would be well. He depended on this faith to help him up the ladder of the deep valley of Lyme. He had fallen so low, the cavity of his pain and fatigue so deep, that death seemed like a mercy.

But he was getting better, one joint pain, one panic attack at a time.

Morning brought a dense brain fog, a head that felt as hollow and empty as a helium balloon. The spot between his shoulder blades felt as if someone had taken a baseball bat to him. But he got out of bed, brushed his teeth, dressed, and went downstairs to start his day.

One day at a time. Teeth clenched in determination, muscles screaming, he took a hot detox bath with Epsom salt, vinegar, and baking soda, then drank a glass of water with a raspberry-flavored Emergen-C packet dissolved in it, and made his way out to the barn to help with the morning feeding.

His sister Lydia called a couple hours later. He found himself getting emotional, missing her a lot. They talked of everyday mundane subjects, Dewan, the dogs, the crops not getting in on time. She said she wished he was there.

Then, "Barbie says Lena's coming for another year. What's up with that? I mean, did she ever . . ."

A long pause.

"What?"

"Well, isn't anything happening between you two?"

"I wish."

"Well."

"No, Lydia, it's Samuel. He's not taking this well. We talked, Lena and I. We're going to wait for a year, hoping Samuel will be able to move on. I can't do this to him. He's my own brother."

"Oh, come on, John. He'll get over it."

But she knew kindhearted John would stick to his word.

Lydia told Susie and Sara Ann the next time they had sisters' day, which brought on two sets of eyes that bulged in disbelief, hands flung in the air followed by sharply expelled breaths of disapproval.

Whoever heard of such a big baby? Samuel needed to buck up and move on.

Seriously, these things happened all the time. Lena didn't want Samuel, it was that simple. He needed to get over himself.

They fed on each other's lack of sympathy, one as disdainful as the other. Then they all went home and worried they'd been too harsh. Each wrote Samuel encouraging letters of sisterly love.

It was one thing to be seated around a table agreeing with everyone else, and quite another to come home and picture your brother's handsome face, the gleaming blond hair, bent in pain and misery.

CHAPTER 23

It was August and a new family had moved in from Lancaster County. The girl's name was Emily, and the youth were gathered for her eighteenth birthday, an unusual event, as birthday parties were normally reserved for the sixteen-year-olds, as an introduction to the world of *rumschpringa*.

Mam had given out all the information any of the boys would need. The new folks were named Joe and Mary Beiler. From Intercourse, down the 340 off Leacock Rd. He was a farrier by trade, but was opening a harness and tack shop, would fix carriages, something the community badly needed.

Emily was the oldest, and she had a sister turning sixteen in the fall. Looking pointedly at Samuel, she hoped Allen and Daniel would look nice, behave in a manner that would encourage girls to become interested.

The sun slid behind the wooded ridge, brought an end to its pulsing heat, twilight a welcome reprieve from the day's high temperatures.

John drove Crayon, allowing him to find his own pace, thinking of Lena, knowing this was his last chance to see her before she left for Kentucky.

Every supper with the youth, every hymn singing had been a form of torture, watching her from a distance. Samuel was usually beside her at the volleyball net, Lena smiling, laughing with him, and John could not know if she had a change of heart, or if this was only her way to soothe his battered ego.

Not once did she allow herself any form of communication with John—no eye contact, nothing.

John was amazed to see a palatial home situated on a long, low rise, surrounded by woods, a picturesque setting, a costly home that only the more fortunate could have acquired. A large shop was being built, a wagon lined with horses, carriages pushed into decent rows.

When there was not enough space for horses in a barn, a borrowed flatbed wagon served the purpose, scattered with blocks of hay, horses tied to each side. John found a spot for Crayon, spoke to different acquaintances, and found Ivan seated at a picnic table.

All the guys feigned disinterest, but were subtly looking for the new girl, taking in the views of the grand brick and vinyl siding home, the large windows and many different angles of roof and walls, the well-kept lawn and costly shrubbery.

Here was no ordinary Amish farmer, indeed.

Emily made an appearance, with Lena, walking together, deep in conversation. John's heart swelled, knowing Lena's kindness, thinking about Emily being introduced to a new group of youth, displaced from her friends. Of course, Lena would do everything in her power to make the evening easier for her.

Emily was dressed in a brilliant shade of pink, setting off her dark skin and black hair. She looked like a tropical hibiscus flower. John could not help staring a few moments too long. Her smile was stunning. She was of medium height, perfectly formed with a grace about her that caught every young man's attention.

Lena paled beside her, but not in a bad way. Lena was delicate, like a white flower with her blond hair, the aura of light that surrounded her. And John knew where his heart, his whole life, belonged.

Hesitantly, Emily joined the next game of volleyball, with Lena's urging. John smiled, knew it would take Samuel less than an hour to take up the space beside her, which is exactly what happened.

Blond, blue-eyed, his skin tanned to a copper color from his days on a roof, his pale blue shirt magnifying the blue in his eyes, Samuel was Jefferson County's golden boy, for sure. When he placed himself beside Emily and spoke to her with the confidence of one acquainted with his own ability to be a charmer, Emily responded the way dozens of girls had always done, and would continue to do.

When darkness fell, two lights were set up, powerful battery-powered bulbs that lit up the entire field. There was a call to come to the house for refreshment. Emily was situated by the birthday cake and there were swells of singing, a blush of color in her cheeks, before she bent to blow out the eighteen candles.

There was a tremendous amount of food. Huge piles of wraps, dips, sandwiches, trays of cut vegetables and fruit, cheese, and some squares and wedges of meat paste concoctions John had no idea how to eat. All of it was delicious. He went back for seconds and found Samuel with a lopsided grin on his face.

Samuel mouthed, "Wow."

John caught his eye and noticed the old sparkle. Samuel was up on his pedestal, rediscovering his sense of well-being. He had been introduced to the tropical brilliance of Emily and found he still possessed the power to charm. He could outshine every other guy present. John could be set back in his place, as second, third, even fourth.

John caught the sense of Samuel having regained his leadership, and sank back into his own comfortable niche, one that, hopefully, he would no longer want to share. But he shook his head, thinking how shallow love could be. A few short months ago, Samuel had been immersed in hopeless longing, begging John to let Lena go.

It wasn't over yet, however. This Emily may prove to be elusive, so he would not get his hopes up just yet. No matter how he longed to be with Lena, he had made a promise with his brother and meant to keep it.

Loyal, kind, his thoughts never strayed to judgment of Samuel, only saw clearly what was unraveling before his eyes.

When John was hitching up his horse, she came like a wraith of mist, softly, speaking in a voice only above a whisper.

"I would like to be taken home."

John said, in a tone that matched hers, "Get in."

The night was as mellow and soft as warmed milk, the dew hanging heavily on verdant grass, the sky a deep indigo punctured by the many stars that winked above them. The light from the headlights pierced the night, the horse with the gleaming black harness flapping in rhythm to his trotting hooves, the sound of steel buggy wheels on soft macadam, the spray of occasional gravel, creating a sense of peace, of purpose.

"John."

She placed a hand on his arm.

"This is to say goodbye. I can't go to Kentucky without knowing how you feel. It's hard for me to do this. Knowing we made a promise to one another. To Samuel."

When he didn't answer, she drew in a sharp breath, then burst out, "But you saw, John. Surely you saw what was happening."

"I did, Lena."

"Does that make it all right for us to be together this last time before I go?"

John's answer was to shift the reins and draw her hand into his free one, clasping it as if he would never release it. United by the touch, words escaped them, leaving only the sound of the horse drawn buggy traveling through the night.

"I don't want to go," she whispered, finally.

They were at her house, Crayon slick with sweat, breathing hard, standing still at the yard gate, content to rest. John looped the reins over the headlight, got out of the buggy before helping her out, on his side, away from the house, away from parents who would peer through the darkness, curious to see who had brought their daughter home.

She stood close, her face lifted.

He reached through the door to snap off the lights, turned and sighed.

"This isn't easy, Lena."

"My resolve to spend the winter in Kentucky is weakening by the moment," she said, in answer to his honesty. "Samuel was completely taken with her. Emily. You saw."

"He seemed to be, yes. But how can we be sure it wasn't to make you jealous?"

Lena laughed, a low, sad sound.

"It's his nature. Why I won't marry him."

"You mean . . . ?"

"No, not that he would prove unfaithful, just the sense of knowing he is capable of attraction, the overblown sense of his own ability to master anything and anyone, when I struggle with my own lack of confidence. Our marriage would have been constant emotional work."

"You speak in the past tense."

"It is in the past. After tonight, especially. But let's not talk about Samuel."

"About us, then?"

"Yes."

John took a deep breath to steady himself, then spoke with more courage than he knew he possessed.

"Lena, for me, there is only you. I have never felt about anyone the way I feel about you. I suppose I'm the kind of guy who only falls once, and falls hard. When you dated Samuel, I thought perhaps I could become interested in Marty, but it didn't seem right. But I guess I'm so afraid of doing something wrong that I can hardly begin dating, with Samuel hovering on the edge of my conscience. And you know, it's the disease I have. You might be committing to a whining, worthless good-for-nothing that cannot provide a decent living for you. I guess after Lyme disease, my doubts and fears are so deeply imbedded, after being disappointed for so long, that I can hardly grow wings of hope and soar the way a young person should."

She answered quickly. "That is why I need to return to Kentucky. I am aware of Lyme, and all you've been through. Your improvement shows, though, and in another nine or ten months, won't it be even better? Tell me the truth, John."

"There are no guarantees, with Lyme disease. But I would think so. My times of relapsing are far less, the symptoms less severe. And I'm learning to work through many of them."

They stood, uncertain, ill at ease, each one longing for the comfort of each other's touch. John's thoughts raced, wondering what was proper. A handshake? A hug? He had never held her close enough. He thought wildly of kissing her, though he had never kissed a girl in his life and had no idea how it was done. The courage he summoned seeped away like water through a sieve. He couldn't do it.

But Lena remembered the magic on the porch swing, couldn't face the long winter in Kentucky without the reassurance of the same sprinkling of stardust.

She took two steps toward him. Her arms went to his shoulders. His arms closed around her waist as naturally as the rustle of the breeze through a field of grain. He drew her closer, his heart beating a furious rhythm.

He whispered, "Goodbye, Lena."

She lifted her face, whispered, "Not yet."

Their faces inches apart, uncertain. Being this close was enough for one moment.

She was on tiptoes. He bent his head. Then drew back, his courage evaporated.

"John," she whispered, a note of pleading like a song.

Their lips met, as light as the smallest moth settling on a delicate flower. The sense of having been found was multiplied, sent all rational thought spinning into the warm night, as he pressed his lips to hers, held her even closer. He knew only the sweetness and softness of her.

When they broke apart, he was in awe of what God had created. He could only sip at the nectar of what He had planned for a man and a woman, but that one taste was more than enough to give his life, any sacrifice this love would require of him, the year in Kentucky a mere blip on the screen of his future.

She clung to him, her breath on his chest, the scent of laundry soap and his cologne, the sweetness of the hollyhocks by the yard gate. She desperately wanted to stay there, to experience another kiss, but knew the time for sacrifice had come.

"Lena, I know it's too soon, but let me tell you this one thing. I love you. I will always love you, give you my life."

She stepped back. Her hands fell away, hung at her sides, aching with emptiness.

"I love you, too, John. You are the reason I could not marry Samuel."

His limbs weighed a ton when he tried to step into the buggy. With a groan, he crushed her to him one last time. This time he kissed her with all the manly knowledge of this aching goodbye, before he could give her up.

"Goodbye, Lena."

"Goodbye."

"I'll write. We'll see how things go with Samuel."

He picked up the reins and she reached to clasp his hand, his arm, and said again, "I love you."

The sound of buggy wheels wrenched at her heart. John hated every inch that expanded between them, but knew it was for the best. Every flap of the harness was a song, every clop of the horse's hooves a line of poetry. He was in awe of his undeserved blessing.

Far more than fortune or fate, this was a love designed and finished by the God of love, the One who made manifest every twist and turn of fate. Who wrote the plot for billions of humans.

He felt puzzled, watching the brilliant beams of light, accompanied by a profusion of orange ones bearing down on him, seemingly too far to the right. He heard a roar that gained momentum by the second. Involuntarily, he slowed Crayon, drew back on the reins, then hauled back on the right one, suddenly aware of the monster truck that bore down on him, much too far to the right, his lane.

Crayon responded immediately, jumped nimbly into the shallow ditch by the side of the road as John cried out, knowing impact was inevitable.

Elmer and Mary Stoltzfus were asleep in the back bedroom on the ground floor of the farmhouse, having fallen into a deep sleep after an evening spent at her sister Rachel's house eating too much of her good cooking.

Mary sat up, grabbed Elmer's arm.

"Dat. Wake up. Someone's here."

Elmer heaved himself out of bed, fumbled with the buttons on his trousers, felt light-headed and disoriented at the blinking lights, the blue revolving one. He saw two officers, badges and belt buckles gleaming.

Every parent's nightmare.

To be taken to the scene of the accident clouded over by a puzzling fog of unreality was one thing, but to see the overturned truck, the dead horse, the buggy in haphazard pieces, the flares, the lights, the ambulance and medical vehicles, was almost beyond human comprehension.

Mary cried out, covered her mouth with both hands. Tears crowded the scene into a spinning vortex of orange, blue, and white lights for both of them. The officers formed a path through the crowd.

Mary threw herself on the still form of her son on the stretcher, but was immediately drawn away. Elmer had enough presence of mind to note the fact that John's face was not covered.

He lived.

But he lay still as death. There was blood everywhere. His hair. The luxuriant brown waves plastered to his skull, his face with how many lacerations?

He heard the throbbing of a helicopter.

Daniel and Allen were there, Marcus with a sobbing Marty on his arm.

Where was Samuel?

The helicopter settled in the alfalfa field like a gigantic furious wasp, whipping the air around it, tufts of alfalfa flying like nighttime creatures.

Oh, the reality. The cruel, stark fact of what had occurred under the starry skies on a hot summer evening.

Side by side, the parents stood, whitefaced, weeping, but drawing on the reserves of quiet stoicism so characteristic of the Amish. God had allowed this, therefore a bowing to His all-encompassing will was in order.

They rode to Pittsburgh with their driver. Mam was in the second seat, Daniel beside her, wringing her soaked men's handkerchief, trying to stop the tears, get ahold of herself.

The boys were whitefaced, sober, without questions yet.

They arrived at the hospital without fanfare.

How small and insignificant, this band of parents and sons.

Elmer spoke at the desk.

The brilliance of the lights made them wince. The unbelievably cavernous lobby, the mystifying array of hallways and elevators, the unsmiling faces that hurried by, each one intent on a certain duty, carrying on the work they had been trained for, with years of schooling.

John was in surgery on the seventh floor.

Seven. A good number, Mam thought quickly. Not thirteen. Then she berated herself for allowing myths and old wives' tales to penetrate her thoughts.

They were told where to go, which elevator.

In the elevator, there was a weird bluish light that cast dark shadows like half-moons beneath eyes, turned a pale blue lavender. Ghostly. Mam was glad to step out, leave the boxy interior of the elevator, glad to get away from light that turned everyone malarial.

They found their way to the waiting room, at the nurse's station, a half wall filled with plants dividing them. A row of windows with slatted blinds half drawn allowed them to see the city spread out below, rectangles and squares of white and yellow lights like big square fireflies. They could see round street lamps, traffic lights suspended above them, vehicles crawling along with bright headlights, small orange taillights.

The air-conditioning blew strong. Accustomed to August's heat and humidity, they crossed their arms, rubbed calloused palms across short sleeves and bare skin.

Mam sat beside Dat, her pink face the color of cream, lines tugging at bleary eyes crisscrossed with red veins from lack of sleep and weeping.

Dat leaned forward, the brim of his straw hat clenched in his calloused farmer's fingers, looking out of place in the sleek, modern waiting room.

He looked down at his old-fashioned high-topped black leather Sunday shoes, tied tightly to above his ankle, scuffs around the toes.

Marcus spoke. "How long do you think it'll go?"

Dat shook his head. "We have no idea the extent of his injuries."

Daniel, his mouth twisted to keep from crying, asked if he was expected to survive, or would he die in the hospital?

"We have no way of knowing, Daniel," Dat said with so much gentleness even Marcus sniffed and blinked.

An elderly couple sat with hands clenched. A youth in torn jeans was joined by an obese girl wearing shorts that did nothing to hide her figure. Politely, the boys averted their eyes, but did look when Dat wasn't noticing.

Mam sat still, grappling to come to terms with the accident.

Why John? After all they'd come through. And now, if he did survive, how would he recover with that Lyme bacteria hiding in his cells?

For the first time in his life, Mam felt a fleeting anger, a clenched fist shaken at his fate. The poor, poor boy. Enough was enough.

She said as much to Dat in quick whispers, which was met with a wagging of his head.

"No, Mary, don't do that. God never lays more on us than He gives us strength to bear up under. Those thoughts are from the *deifel*."

She felt ashamed, but did not lower her mental fist immediately.

The driver was drunk, intoxicated. He had a blood alcohol level that had officers shaking heads.

He'd rolled his truck twice, but was unharmed. Yes, he was wearing a seat belt. No passengers. When he roared around the curve in the road he failed to negotiate the turn properly, hit the left side of the horse and buggy.

How was that fair, Mam wondered? She hoped he was at least bumped around. Where would forgiveness ever begin or end if John passed away at his young age, after finally seeming to recover from the Lyme?

She couldn't begin to imagine the spiritual warfare of her heart. Dat asked for coffee at the nurse's station. He was handed large Styrofoam cups with small plastic containers of cream, red stirrers, and small white napkins.

"If you need more, let us know. We have two pots going all night," the nurse informed them.

Mam was grateful for the strong coffee, but found it difficult to swallow, so she held the cup, staring at the odd picture on the opposite wall, like wide brushstrokes going in every direction with no sense or purpose.

She lost her ability to breathe, her heart plummeting, when a tall thin man dressed in loose clothing and what appeared to be a plastic shower cap on his head beckoned them to follow him.

Like sheep to the slaughter, Mam thought, expecting the worst, steeling herself for it. What was the worst? Dead? Paralyzed from the neck down? The waist? Losing a limb? Or worse. She felt herself hyperventilating, the blackness, the raspy puffs of breath.

Give me strength.

They followed him into a private room.

He thrust out a long hand with tapered fingers like velvet, shook hands all around, introduced himself as Doctor Bluntheim, the surgeon on call.

"I'm assuming you are John Stoltzfus's family. Sit down. Now, John has been in a car accident, I gather."

The parents nodded, their faces almost unrecognizable with foreboding.

"Well, he has been on the table for close to four hours. His injuries are extensive, but given his age and his state of health, he should be mended in three months."

Dat and Mam exhaled. Color returned to their faces. They fixed their gazes on the doctor's face with childish eagerness, eyes too bright with unshed tears, mouths wobbly with relief.

"His most serious injury is his left knee. The leg that was on the side that was hit, apparently. His kneecap was completely torn off, the . . ."

And here he used medical terms, naming ligaments and muscles, small bones and large ones which meant nothing to any of

them, although they nodded in recognition to his highly edu-
cated description.

A broken pelvis. Mutilated knee. Internal bleeding. Damaged
liver. Mam's terror mounted.

"He . . . he has Lyme disease. How will that affect his
healing?"

The thick eyebrows were raised. "We'll have to wait and
see. The severity and extent of his Lyme will definitely be a
factor, but I see nothing life threatening. I'll need a list of his
medications."

"Yes." Mam nodded.

"So, we're looking at the highest level of care in the ICU. No
visitors. It is extremely important. We'll take a day at a time."

"May we see him at all?"

The doctor raised a finger, got to his feet. "I'll be back."

He never did return, but sent an assistant, a short, dark man
who gave them instructions, brought a nurse bearing gowns,
masks, and booties to slip over their shoes, and led them to
another waiting room, where they sat like puffy green mum-
mies. The boys tried to keep straight faces, but finally gave up
and laughed aloud, pointing fingers at each other.

Dat smiled, as if he couldn't help himself. Mam frowned,
restored order. Relief or not, the situation was grave. No use
sitting here grinning like idiots.

Where was Samuel? Where had he been so late at night when
all the other boys were home in bed? He should be here with the
rest of them.

Finally they were led to a long, narrow corridor, then turned
left through heavy doors that opened by a round appendage on
the wall. They came to a large white-walled room filled with
wheeled beds, computerized monitors, blinking screens, lights,
beeps, buzzes, and clicks.

John was against the far wall, completely unrecognizable.

His face was bruised and swollen, his head shaved on one

side, a row of stitches like a zipper above his torn ear. He was attached to so many machines, had tubes in his nose, had his left leg in a cast from his thigh to his toes. His eyes were closed, only a line of lashes peeping from the swelling on his eyelids.

"He doesn't know you're here. He's still heavily sedated, but you may touch him, talk to him. Go ahead."

The dark, swarthy man stepped back, crossed his arms.

Dat went first, stroked the only visible part of John, the top of his right hand. His lips trembled and he bowed his head, then stepped back and dug in his pocket for his Sunday handkerchief and brought it out, neatly folded and ironed. Mam moved as if in a dream, said "John," then bit her lip and burst into deep, hysterical sobs. Dat hurried to her side, a hand on her shoulder, and led her away.

The brothers stared at shoe tops or the ceiling, drew eyebrows down, but in the end, wiped tears and walked away. It was too hard to talk around the lump of emotion in their throats.

Arrangements were made. They'd all go home now, but Dat and Mam would return and stay till he was out of the ICU. Chores and milking went to Abner and Amos. Ruthie and Sylvia would help.

On the way home they stopped for breakfast at an all-night diner, sat, and bowed their heads over their food with real thanksgiving. They drank coffee and talked about life and John and Lyme disease and God.

Through the coming months, the little diner and the conversation with the boys, the hot coffee and stacks of pancakes remained a beacon of faith and hope and love for Mam.

CHAPTER 24

WHEN LENA HEARD OF JOHN'S ACCIDENT MONDAY MORNING, SHE dropped into a chair with an expulsion of breath that drained the color from her face.

She wrestled with an odd assortment of emotion—disbelief, panic, guilt, and an overwhelming sense of foreboding. Taught in the ways of obedience, her first thought was the fact that she had asked him to take her home. If she would have stayed with Samuel, this horrendous accident may not have occurred.

All my fault. A sign. A sign from God. An omen.

Her parents could not comfort her. Shaken, filled with self-doubt, knowing she could not see him was almost more than she could bear.

She knelt by her bed, not knowing what words to pray. As each evening passed, an inner conviction was planted, took root and grew. She would stay true to what her heart told her. Crippled, deformed, paralyzed, or suffering bouts of Lyme disease his entire life, John was her love, and if marrying him meant caring for an invalid, then so be it.

If the accident was an act of God, then it was a test for her.

Samuel hadn't arrived back home on the farm until after everyone had left to go to Pittsburgh. He read the note on the table. He was duly shocked, but figured John would probably be all right. His thoughts were filled with a dark-haired beauty dressed in pink. He'd go visit John tomorrow evening. Someone had to do the milking.

In the ICU John drifted between pain and a numbed sleep that took him away from everything.

He was conscious, some of the time, felt the nurse's white presence, hands on IV lines, tubes, and blinking lights. But he had no clear understanding why he was there or what had happened.

He dreamed grotesque accounts of gigantic ticks crawling over his skin, imbedded, swollen with his own blood. He tried to cry out, knew no one would hear. He felt trapped, held in a painful vise on his left leg.

His parents hovered, called nurses. They went to the hallway and cried out for help, forgetting they could just press the button.

On the sixth day he was mostly alert and spoke through cracked, bleeding lips. His throat was so dry that his voice was barely above a raspy whisper. His eyes were almost swollen shut, discolored, unrecognizable, except for the sliver of amber and the tears that leaked out from the sides.

Rejuvenated, stung into action, Mam leaned over his bed, rubbed his shoulder, wept quietly, asked questions, and in general, became a mother who only increased her intense hovering, her insatiable curiosity, until Dat gently pulled her away. "Give him time, give him time."

He was moved from the ICU to a room on the fifth floor, and the brothers flocked into his room like colorful birds, dressed in black Sunday trousers and an array of blue, yellow, or red shirts. Self-conscious, ill at ease, they didn't know what to say, this being their first time in the hospital.

What was a good bedside manner? What were the proper words?

An array of friends began to arrive every evening, but Lena was never among them. John knew and understood. She was preparing to leave for Kentucky.

He had no memory of the accident, strangely forgetting the moments before, when the truck bore down on him. But he did remember the night with Lena, standing by the buggy. It was the thought that sustained him in the worst of his pain and discomfort.

She did come to say goodbye, one afternoon when he was home again, lying on the recliner in the living room, a bedside table to the right, the shades drawn against the hot afternoon sun, a battery-operated fan sending a cooling breeze over his aching, battered body.

Mam hovered with the fly swatter and tried to stay in the background, but heard every word they exchanged. So she was going to Kentucky. Hmm. Well, wasn't that something.

She knew nothing of Samuel's infatuation with the dark-haired Emily, so she remained in the same helpless, hand-fluttering stage she had been.

She didn't see much going on here, between her John and the fair-haired Lena, so who knew?

Who knew the ways of the heart?

She went out to the washhouse for the fly spray and missed the handholding, the intense longing in each other's eyes, the swift kiss Lena planted on his mouth, the anguish of their goodbyes.

John's healing was slow, punctuated with many doctor visits, therapy, and a fog of pain and stiffness. The left leg was the worst, with pins and screws to hold the fragmented bone, but by Thanksgiving he was walking with a special boot, the scars on his face barely visible.

Mam applied vitamin E oil, squeezed from capsules, her breath garlicky against John's face. She fed him bone and tissue capsules, some natural, herbal remedy that left a dry taste in his mouth, replete with constant burping.

"You'll heal faster," she assured him, bringing yet another glass of water and another handful of pills.

He was getting around on his own, pale-faced with pain and fatigue, when the eagerly awaited vanload of relatives pulled in on the evening before Thanksgiving.

Frost had covered every remaining vegetable in the garden, freezing the color and vitality from grass and weeds, turning the petunias and dahlias to a drooping slimy mass of ruined vegetation. Mam grumbled to herself as she heaved masses of dead flowers onto the garden cart, knowing she should have extricated these voluminous plants before the frost. But what was she to do, with John's care, all the canning and freezing at the summer's end?

John had helped, with the rake, hoeing flaccid dandelions from the bare flowerbeds, raking the mulch, cutting borders with the new, light, battery-operated Weed eater that purred like a kitten.

Samuel was a bright presence now, a bouncing, talkative young man who offered help in the garden, mowed grass without complaint.

So there were always blessings.

The bills had arrived from Pittsburgh General, which left Elmer and Mary Stoltzfus reeling helplessly in the face of the astronomical fees.

They waited for a visit from the deacon, Eli King, who appeared at the door one drizzly, fogbound evening, a cheerful smile and a face that beamed with kindness and mercy.

"Things happen," he said gently. "We're here to help one another."

So the following Sunday, when the bishop announced special council, they walked out, a show of humility, while the remainder of the church conferred among themselves. And all agreed.

With the discount, the bill was still over one hundred thousand. Elmer had pledged the amount of ten thousand. They could pay that much. The deacon would see to it now. He would write letters to deacons of other Amish communities until the remaining ninety thousand was paid in full.

The bishop spoke with tears in his voice.

"A blessing we have, this gift of alms. In time of need, no one needs to suffer unduly." He then reminded the congregation to keep on striving for what was right and good, to embrace the old ways handed down by the forefathers, a precious heritage never to be taken for granted.

And a great weight was lifted from Elmer's shoulders. A savings account depleted was a small thing, never to be regretted. They still had John, and after all he'd been through, God must have a purpose for his life on earth.

So when the vanload of siblings rolled in, more than one of them wiped tears, turned away with a discreet handkerchief to their noses.

John stood, his hands in his pockets, his shoulders hunched, thin, pale, but without the former eyes blackened with fear and brain fog. His eyes were alert, showing his gratitude and good humor, the gladness he felt wringing Alvin's hand as he greeted him warmly.

Lydia gave up all restraint and cried and hugged and said far too much, not caring whether he liked it or not.

"I missed you so much, John. Then the awful accident, and we had to wait till now. Almost unbearable. You look awful. A ghost of yourself. Like a shadow. Are you sure you're going to be OK? What is that thing on your foot?"

John grinned, thinking she was another Mam. DNA copied to perfection. Sara Ann and Susie were all over him, children staring wide-eyed.

Far into the night, the family sat around the elongated kitchen table, cups of steaming coffee and mint tea, sugar and cream, whoopie pies and Swiss roll bars, Chex mix and pop-corn, children reaching across parents' laps to make faces, steal whoopie pies.

Mothers were too engrossed in conversation to notice how late it was getting until a child howled in unwarranted anger. "All right, all right. Time for a bath. He's tired."

Mam was pushing back her chair, saying, "Here, I'll go with you. Battery lamp on the shelf, Susie. I'll get the towels and washcloths."

Sara Ann followed, a howling whoopie-pie-smeared Kore in tow, headed for the bathtub, where the three of them spoke as fast as they could, in low tones, the door closed securely against John and Samuel.

"Isn't it something, Mam? How Samuel has given up? Oh, and he just gets better looking. He's so happy, I could cry." Susie wailed, sniffed.

Mam snorted, as she bent to get clean washcloths, yanked open a door in the bathroom cupboard for towels.

Little boys splashed like fish in the sudsy water.

"His happiness is not, let me assure you, not from giving up his will. It has nothing to do with Lena or John. His happiness comes in the form of one fancy, worldly girl named Emily."

Gasping, Susie straightened from her hunch over the side of the tub.

"Not English? Mam!"

"No, she's not English. But . . . well, just wait till you see her."

Questions sprang from Sara Ann's normally serene face.

"They just moved in, from Lancaster. Joe and Mary Beiler. Remember S' Dans Amosa Joes?"

Waved her hand in dismissal.

"No, you wouldn't remember. You were little girls. Anyway, their daughter Emily is, well, picture perfect. Wild, even. So fancy you have no idea. She . . . well, she's coming tomorrow.

Samuel insisted. They had their, I don't know, second or third date last weekend. He is smitten. Forgot all about Lena, evidently. Oh, I just can't see any good come of it."

"Why didn't you tell us?" Sara Ann shrieked.

"Shh," Susie warned.

"But, Mam, surely you can tell us one good thing about her. I love her name. You can't judge a book by its cover."

Mam crossed her arms, drew up her shoulder.

"You can't?"

And the girls knew exactly what their mother meant.

She watched them stuff resistant little limbs into pajamas, draw a comb through wet locks, amid varied sounds of outrage, howls of exhausted little bodies that had traveled all the way from Kentucky, and wondered how she ever raised ten babies.

But then she sat on the recliner, rocking, one baby in each arm, kissed the tops of damp little heads, breathed in the smell of Dial soap and Downy fabric softener, and remembered very well why she had had ten children. She could not have known back then how grown children tramped all over your heart, wearing sturdy boots. Some of them hobnailed. It was so important to pray they find the right partner, for God to place a shield around them, protect them from lust and infatuation, wrong choices, high pedestals.

Or were there wrong choices?

God was in control. He led them together, didn't he? He allowed the marriage to take place, so there you go. Well, He allowed accidents, too. And death.

Just wait till the girls met Emily.

She drank cup after cup of coffee, then lay awake, wide-eyed, rigid with worry and consternation. Finally, she fell into a fitful sleep and dreamt senseless dreams she only half remembered and didn't care about at all.

She wore her new brown dress, for fall, and Thanksgiving. It was a nice fabric, with just the right weight to it. A bit of a pucker in the weave. She hoped the girls wouldn't think her too fancy herself. She knew she'd bought that dress and sewed it with Emily in mind. Well, she couldn't wear her old brown "peach skin" one either. No use being as frumpy as she could when a new girlfriend appeared for Thanksgiving dinner.

"Nice dress, Ma."

"Don't call me Ma."

The girls laughed, raised their eyebrows and rolled their eyes. Now who was fancy?

John felt good.

He had so much to look forward to, so much to live for. The lively banter around the kitchen table had been an elixir, a boost to his mind and spirit. The months ahead seemed like only a short time, and then Lena would return. Nothing could hold them back now, with Samuel so completely taken by Emily. He showered, dressed in a sage green denim shirt, his black denim trousers, strapped on the cumbersome boot on the injured foot, slipped a warm brown sock on the opposite foot, and went to join the group around the kitchen table again.

Little Sallie barreled toward him, collided into his knees and wrapped her arms around his legs. Dressed in her pajamas, her blond hair like a dust mop, she was the most winsome of them all. John bent to lift her up, hobbled over to the table, and slid onto the bench beside Daniel.

"Oatmeal or cereal?" Mam called.

John wrinkled his nose. "Coffee."

So much to say, so much to listen to. John had not felt such a lifting of his spirits in years. He had no idea what the injuries he'd sustained in the accident had done to his Lyme disease, but he did know his body could heal itself, same as everyone else, so he must not be too bad.

Perhaps the impact had knocked all the Lyme right out of him. Who knew? He knew one thing for sure. The anxiety that had been the worst of all the Lyme symptoms had not returned after the crash.

Perhaps he'd been so close to death that nothing mattered, eliminating the dread and anxiety, the constant foreboding of being terminally ill.

He would grasp a newfound hold on life, on the good contained in a world that had almost been torn from the thin, unhappy grasp he'd had on it.

It seemed to him he'd been only a fourth of the person he could be. He'd been so weak, tired, aching, pain buzzing in his joints like miniature chain saws, ears rasping and pounding with pressure, until he thought he would surely lose his mind, listening to the high insistent ringing.

He'd been swallowing thousands of pills over the years, soaking in detox baths and pitying himself, growing old and bitter long before his time.

Was it really over?

The fear of the symptoms' return made him break out in a cold sweat, until he made himself stop thinking about it. Thoughts were often difficult to control, but it could be done, with God's help. Absolutely.

Forge ahead. Keep your eyes on the goal. Ask God for His help. You'll get there.

No one told him Lena would be there. No one as much as threw a hint that she had traveled with his siblings, all the way from Kentucky.

He was lying on his back, his knees upraised, Sallie combing his hair with Dat's large, orange comb, Andrew straddling his stomach, yelling, "Come on, Giddup. Go. Go," with Kore building a runway for his jet from a pile of colorful Legos.

He heard a commotion in the kitchen, turned his head to see what was going on, to find a vision in a black wool coat standing shyly by the counter, the girls chattering like magpies.

Lena!

He sat up, dumping Andrew into the pile of Legos, which set up yells of disbelief from Kore, shrieks of outrage from Andrew, and a stiff scolding from Sallie, who wielded her comb and ordered him to lie back down this minute.

She turned her head. Their eyes met. He felt the heat in his face. He struggled to his feet, amid more yells from his niece.

"Hey! Sallie, stop that," from Sara Ann.

He hobbled over, took her hand. Blond hair, white covering, blue eyes and porcelain skin melded with the black wool of her coat as a mist formed in his eyes.

He remembered watching eyes, stepped back with decorum, said, "Hello, Lena."

"Hello, John."

The girls were making all sorts of strange grimaces, blinks, clearing their throats. They said later they had never encountered anything so sweet in their entire lives. You could feel it. The love. It gave them chills. They rubbed their palms up their forearms and blinked madly to keep the tears and the wobbly chins at bay.

They sat side by side on the sofa in the living room. They had eyes only for each other, talking in low, muted voices. The children crowded around like curious chipmunks, eyes bright with interest, but too shy to speak.

Samuel brought Emily.

Together, they stepped into the warmth of the kitchen, laughing, red-cheeked, cold after the long buggy ride. The girls hung back, suddenly bashful, eyeing the burnt orange hue of her dress. No cape. Short sleeves.

Short sleeves?

What? For Thanksgiving dinner with the boyfriend's family? Boy, Mam wasn't kidding. Her shoes. *Oh my word*, thought Susie. They looked like crocheted baby booties. Well. And her hair combed like that? And that was a tiny covering by anyone's standards. Well, best to stop staring, gather themselves together, and make introductions to the best of their astounded ability.

Samuel took over, suave, confident, making the girls feel like babbling pre-schoolers.

"Emily," (he pronounced it Um-i-lee, and Lydia felt like gagging). "This is Susie. The oldest. Married to Elam over there."

In that tone of voice, Susie thought she may as well have married a badger.

But she managed to smile, step up, and shake a limp hand.

Sara Ann and Lydia used up all their hidden reserve and brought forth bright smiles and polite words. "Hello. Good to meet you. I've heard about you."

Emily smiled, shook hands, said all the right things, clung to Samuel's arm like a parasitic ivy, but spoke kindly to the children, greeted Mam with a flash of recognition, a wider smile than the one reserved for the girls.

Mam's voice rose a few octaves, along with her eyebrows, putting her in a state of anxious benevolence the girls called "Emily Alert."

"It's good to see you again, Emily. I hope you can make yourself at home with all these."

She waved a hand.

"I heard your mother is making coverings now. That's so necessary in the community here. Maybe she can help me with my pattern. I have such a time with the pleats. Does she make yours?"

"Yes, she does."

Lydia thought, *She does, does she?* Probably wouldn't fit the six-year-old. She bent to pick up a toy, redeeming her bad thoughts.

Well, she was here. She was definitely here. Samuel was flying up there with the jet streams on a cold November sky. Emily seemed enamored of her blond Samuel, and, as they both knew, they made a striking couple. One any mother would be proud of. As Mam clearly was.

They were going upstairs to Samuel's room to play Rook with John and Lena, Lydia informed the women bustling around in the kitchen.

Mam nodded, deflated, the beginning of a turkey wattle on her neck, her ears a fiery red from nerves and tension and steaming kettles. Lydia felt a stab of pity and went to lay an arm across her strong, wide back, tucking the drawstring up under her covering.

"It'll be all right, Mam. She's very pretty. I think they make a nice couple."

Mam patted Lydia's hand.

"Thanks. I need to hear that, *gel?*"

"She'll be all right. She was raised this way."

Mam was lifted from her clutch of tension, her courage bolstered by the daughter's kind gesture, and served the remarkable dinner with aplomb, her eyes snapping as she sailed from stove to table with her entourage of girls in tow, children underfoot, Legos schpritzing out from shoe heels, children's books kicked out of the way, shooting looks at Dat.

Help me out here. Don't sit there like a stump.

The four youngie were clattering down the stairs. John was hobbling, his face alight. Lena was wearing a deep burgundy color, with a neatly pinned cape and black apron wrapped high on her slender waist. Her hair was like platinum gold.

Emily was a striking, dark figure, the color of a sun-kissed pumpkin, her black eyes flashing with gaiety and delight. The men's eyes watched her, then turned politely to the care of children.

They bowed their heads. Thirty-four people were seated at the extended kitchen table that held twelve leaves, plus the plastic Lifetime tables with folding chairs and benches.

John sat beside Lena, his heart too full to pray without tears. He bit his lip, endured the burning of his nose, and felt a gratitude so deep and wide he could never grasp it all. To have Lena here was beyond anything he had ever expected, or deserved. To be healed from his injuries, to be seated here at all, was so much more than he deserved.

His sound mind, the anxiety and crippling fear a receding shadow, was another reason for gratitude. The realization that he may always have bouts of pain or fatigue, but that he was so much better than he could have hoped to be, even a year ago, was amazing.

A song found its way into his mind and heart.

"Father, I adore Thee, Lay my life before Thee, How I love Thee."

When everyone raised their heads, eyes met, and smiles sprang from thankful hearts. Samuel turned to look at Emily, who in turn, looked at him, exchanging glances of glad recognition. If not yet love, they certainly had an attraction that would lead to it, even if it was the kind of love that required trials to deepen it, secure it, nail it down against battering winds of life.

John had endured a giant's share of life's winds of adversity, but couldn't know how many more God had planned. He turned to find Lena looking at him and smiled, returning the adoration in her eyes.

"Mashed potatoes!"

Sylvia Ann was hungry, meant business.

When everyone laughed, she looked around, pinpointed the person closest to the serving dish piled high with buttery white potatoes, and said, "Emily, pass those potatoes, please."

Emily, clearly delighted to be singled out, complied immediately. Which warmed Mam's heart. Perhaps there was more between the pages of this book than what met the eye. Samuel beamed.

Was it too much to expect happiness and good things? Did one go strolling down the meandering path of life without peering anxiously around jutting boulders? Didn't one need to expect blows in the form of Lyme disease and car accidents and daughters marching off to Kentucky with new husbands carrying the proud banner of pioneerism?

No. You picked up each day with both hands and held it. You appreciated all the good, even if you had to sift around in a messy pile of ill feelings and regretted words to find it.

This day I choose to be thankful, Mam thought. *This day I will love Emily, be thankful for her, in spite of not being what I expected or wanted for my golden Samuel.*

And here was John. *Ach John. My John.*

She ate turkey and gravy, stuffing and mashed potatoes prodigiously, along with pumpkin pie and cornstarch pudding. Afterward she washed dishes and went for a long walk with the three girls in the biting November wind, the bare branches of the trees whipping and creaking in the woods beside them, their skirts billowing out in autumnal hues, glimpses of white knees that rose out of black stockings like mushrooms.

Mam yanked at her skirt and marched back home, flopping red-faced into the recliner and falling asleep with her mouth open, Andrew on her lap.

CHAPTER 25

He was with Lena again at Christmas, when Alvin and Lydia hosted the whole family for a crowded Christmas dinner in the old yellow house.

The farm brought back memories, but mostly, a sense of remembered anxiety, the unsettling knowledge that he had been sick with Lyme disease, weary, drained, struggling to rise above the turmoil in his head. By measuring those days with the way he felt now, he knew he'd come a long way.

He gave the one pill, Protandim, a lot of the credit, although who knew? He'd take what he could get. Wellness for him was likely not the same level as a person who had never had Lyme, but to be able to work, to function at an acceptable level in everyday life, was something he'd gladly live with.

A good night's sleep, normal rambling thoughts about anything and everything, just being, without fear of losing your mind or worse, were all things he had never thought to be thankful for till now.

When his joints ached at the end of the day, he could accept that, too. They might do that for the rest of his life. Sometimes they'd ache, and other times they'd be fine. That was Lyme disease.

The doctor had said it would always lurk somewhere, although he could enjoy good health. He had been right. A fresh appreciation for the medical field, together with alternative remedies, anyone who devoted their time and energy to help the victims of this disease, brought emotion to his throat, a lump he quickly swallowed, blinking to avoid his brothers' scrutiny.

They wouldn't understand. They had not gone through the valley of fear and suffering. And that was all right.

Was that, then, how mercy for other people came about? After you went through your own suffering, sucked into a whirlpool of Lyme disease, did you become sympathetic? John guessed that was the way of it, human nature being what it was.

He felt a surge of joy.

He punched Samuel's arm with all his strength, resulting in a yowl of pain and outrage. John swung back, escalating their playful scuffle.

Dewan Reynolds stood back, his eyes wide, a shocked expression on his dark face. He held out an arm, pointed, then made a silent, flying leap, wrapping his arms around John in a hug like a giant squid.

John struggled to breathe, then laughed. His brothers gawked, clearly amused at the easy flow, the eager spontaneity.

He gripped John's shoulders, said, "You look bad, man. Bad."

"Yeah, well, you know I was in an accident."

"I heard. You gave Alvin and Lydia a scare. I mean, they, like, flipped out."

"I'm all right now."

"Yeah? Hated to see you go, John. You shoulda stayed. Dogs multiplying like rabbits. I got a *raise*!"

They spent the forenoon in the kennel, inspecting dogs, learning what Dewan did, which seemed to be manage the entire line of dogs and puppies, cleaning, just everything. Samuel commented on the fact that Alvin had really lucked out, finding someone like Dewan.

He knew every dog, and they knew him. Puppies clambered over each other to reach him, and he greeted each one by his own nickname, creating his own special bond with every animal in the kennel, large and small.

John watched with something akin to envy, knowing he had been a flop, never coming up to the standards Alvin and Lydia had hoped for.

Well, he'd tried. Perhaps he could make it up to them somehow, eventually.

John still had plenty of trouble with that left knee, but he was alive, with a promise of love in the sweetest, most unselfish girl he could ever hope to meet.

He caught her eye at the dinner table, smiled. She smiled back. They bundled up in coats and scarves, walked for miles and miles in the biting wind, unaware of distance, time, or what the family would say.

A few long months and they could be together.

The brown hills fell away like an enormous pan of apple dumplings, the forests and fence rows of black tree limbs like burnt sugar.

Gravel crunched under their shoes, tired, passing dusty weeds hanging from their dry roots, dying for winter, knowing they'd be resurrected in spring.

Blue jays screamed from oak trees, scattering the nervous little wrens and nuthatches that gorged themselves on goldenrod seeds.

Chipmunks and squirrels watched bright-eyed from perches in branches by the side of the road, going unnoticed by the young couple.

They spoke of autism, of Down syndrome and special-needs children, how God blessed folks with the ability and ambition to become wealthy, and what the future held for them.

"I don't know what kind of farmer I'll turn out to be," John said quietly. "I just know nothing else interests me. I couldn't keep up with Abner and Amos, roofing. My legs would never take that kind of torture."

He stopped, looked at her with all the soft humility he felt.

"I hope you realize, Lena, you might be saddled with a husband who turns out to be worthless. I mean, what if the Lyme comes back and I'm flat on my back, yet again?"

"It won't. And besides, who says I'll marry you?"

Embarrassed, color swept across John's face.

"I'm sorry. I have a habit of thinking out loud."

"Oh, John."

She grabbed his arm, stopped him, and stepped into his arms, wrapping her own securely around his waist.

"You are the sweetest guy, the most humble person I know. Don't apologize for saying that. It was like fine music, those words."

John looked down at Lena, his beloved friend who had encouraged him over the roughest times, the thought of her always like a beacon, a light of hope.

"Thank you."

The kiss they shared held a new reverence, a new appreciation, a dedication of their love for the future.

They walked hand in hand, a silence between them like a golden web, binding two hearts with the knowledge of their belonging.

Was love, then, always like this? The joy of your existence, the anticipation of what was to come? A marriage of two souls blessed by God, living in a perfect world?

John knew better. Having lived in a world of pain and disease, watching his family hide their angst, bite their tongues to avoid more disagreement and ill feelings, he knew they, Lena and he, would have their moments, their days, when things went awry and tempers flared.

He smiled, squeezed her hand.

She looked up at him.

"What?"

"Oh, nothing." Still smiling.

"You're thinking about something."

"I'm just happy."

Satisfied with his answer, she left well enough alone, spoke of missing her family at Christmas, although the holidays meant much less to them than many other families.

"My parents are extremely frugal people, as you've seen. So Christmas at our house holds very little in the way of presents or elaborate, expensive foods. It's just . . . well, different. And I worry, afraid of what you'll think."

"That has nothing to do with it."

"Oh, but it will, I'm afraid. My father has a bad attitude about the festivities of any holiday. He talks harshly, actually condemns the Amish church for allowing the shopping and gift giving most families enjoy. I see the longing in my mother's eyes but she would never let on. We get German books for our gift, and nothing else. So, you see, we'll have things like that to take into consideration."

"Of course we will. But we'll cross that bridge as soon as we get to it, right?"

She smiled. "Of course."

They returned to the old yellow house packed with family, children underfoot like slippery rugs. Everyone turned to see them step inside, faces red from the cold, by all appearances, a healthy, happy couple flushed with the joy of living.

Mam's eyes filled with tears. Dat's mouth shook, a slight tremor that wobbled his graying beard. Their eyes met.

We've come this far, together. We made it. Things weren't perfect, we argued, had our share of ill feelings, too many unnecessary expenses, but we did it.

Lydia peered over the steam that rose from the pan of *roasht* she was taking from the oven, thought John must have bumped his brain around real good in that accident, felt a bit miffed that she couldn't claim any honor for his well-being.

There you were. Went to all that trouble, did what she could, and nothing ever amounted to a hill of beans. He lay in his bed and carried his anxiety and weakness around like a flag for everyone to examine, didn't even try to bond with the dogs the way Dewan did.

It irked her. He went home and got into an accident that could have killed him, and here he was, as healthy as a horse, for Pete's sake.

She stirred the *roasht* with the force of her frustration, flipped a sizable portion onto the cracked linoleum, snorted, and scooped it up with her hands, shaking them to avoid the heat, her shoulders hunched as she scuttled to the wastecan. She tripped over little Benuel, who set up a fierce howling, his mouth wide, his eyes mere slits in his round, red face.

"Oops, sorry. Ach my, Benuel. You poor thing. Here, come here."

She bent to pick him up, thought what a homely, clumsy child he was, blessed with his father's florid face. How Sara Ann could stand to live with that man and his controlling ways was beyond her. But she just smiled and apologized when Sara Ann came bustling over, said it was all right, it was all right, she should have watched him, and met her sister's eyes and knew the spark of irritation meant she was in agreement with that.

John reached out for little Benuel, smiled at Sara Ann as he did so, then sat on the couch, the large child with the homely features settled in the crook of his arm. He produced a white handkerchief, wiped the tears gently, then produced a keychain, which he dangled and Benuel grabbed, the beginning of his good humor returning.

Lydia saw.

She also saw the look of reverence from Lena, who clearly adored John. In sickness and in health, she would be there for him. Chills washed over her. Seriously, she was becoming soft in the head.

Who was to understand the way of the Lord? Who could see the entire picture of life, a jigsaw puzzle of pieces put together by the Father's hand, glossed over and hung on the wall?

She went back to the Christmas dinner preparations, nudged Susie away from the steaming kettle of potatoes, saying, "My turn."

"I just started."

"Let me."

Always the same, this potato-smashing ritual at holiday dinners. It was a huge sixteen-quart kettle of soft, boiling potatoes, into which would go salt, butter, milk, and cream cheese. Steam came in hot waves as the women took turns hunched over the kettle, stomping around in the huge kettle with the too small potato mashers, arguing about saving the water the potatoes had been cooked in, when to add the butter, what was the best time to add milk, how much salt.

Mam stepped away, leaving her daughters to argue.

She pictured herself as she'd been throughout John's illness, trying to make sense of one perplexing path after another. Sometimes she'd had her husband's support, but often, she'd felt so alone.

Ah well.

Perhaps it had been unnecessary, but she'd done the best she could. John was so much better, and with Lena now. A gift. A gift.

Seated around the Christmas table, Elmer Stoltzfus sat at his son-in-law's right and bowed his head to give thanks for the food, for the gift of the dear Son who was born this day, and for his family.

He lifted his head and surveyed the line of sons, misty-eyed.

Each one would find a partner, a life companion, one who pledged her love and dedication, for the remainder of their lives. A miracle. Another gift.

He smiled his inner appreciation, passed the steaming bowls

and platters, listened to the talk that fell like rain, easily, naturally. Talk that nurtured, drew together, strengthened bonds of
family, informative, easy to listen to.

Realized this, too, was a gift from above, from the Father of
light. One it had never occurred to him, not once, as a thing he
should be thankful for.

All those supper tables, when John was absent, or sat silent
and sick, always producing stilted, unnatural sentences, eye
rolling, looks of contempt. Mam scurrying like a nervous cat,
aching to patch things up, keep the peace, just for this one meal.

And here they were, with girlfriends like bright, happy
poinsettias.

The parting was even more difficult than John had imagined. He
knew it was only till May, but five month seemed like five years.

Lena clung to him.

"Oh, John. I know this sounds stupid, but I already miss you
and you haven't even gone yet."

He drew her closer, closed his eyes as he laid his cheek on
top of her bright, blond head, crushing her white head covering
effectively.

"I love you so much, Lena. If I live to be a hundred, I'll still
love you as much as I love you now."

"I would hope our love would increase," she said, coyly.

John laughed. "They say it does."

"They're probably right."

And John knew a bright vision for his future, the love of
a girl like Lena, an undeserved gift, given to him by the same
God who had plucked him from good health and set him in a
dark valley of Lyme disease, finished him off with a near fatal
accident, before presenting him with Lena, free and willing to
spend the remainder of his life with him, sending Emily to heal
Samuel's broken heart.

He saw himself working in the fields, his beard graying, Lena with a thickening waistline, wrinkles on the sides of her eyes, children picking the tomatoes and peppers and eggplants, in various stages of growth. He imagined a fat little boy with riotous waves of brown hair and a petite, beautiful girl with a headful of hair like spun gold.

And five months seemed like a falling star. A streak of flashing light in a dark sky, and she would be at home in Jefferson County, where he would drive his horse and buggy to her parents' home every weekend until the day they became as one, bound by a love that had been intensified by the trials of the disease, the hard choices she had encountered. Each one proved its worth, purifying their souls by the fire produced by the Master's hand.

THE END

GLOSSARY

Ach, vell, so gehts—Oh well, so it goes

Auskund—hymn book

Ausry—the English, outsiders

Chvischtot—relatives

Daudies—grandfathers

Deifel—devil

Denkscht net?—You think not?

Der Herr—the Lord

Dick-keppich—thickheaded

Die uf-gevva-heit—giving up one's own will

Eck—the table where the bride and groom sit at their wedding

Eissa kessla—iron kettles

Fersark—see to their needs

Gehorsam—obedient

Gel?—right?

Grosfeelich—proud

Gyan schöena—You're welcome

Himmlischer Vater—Heavenly Father

Hya. Kommet rye.—Hi. Come in.

Ich sauk denke.—I say thanks.

Kaevly—basket

Kaite sup—fruit soup

Knecht—hired boy

Mein Vater im Himmel—My Father in heaven

Multza—coat
Ordnung—rules
Pucka—pimples
Rumschpringa—a time of courtship, in which Amish teenagers
    participate in organized social events
Schnitza—lie
Schtick—snack
Shick dich.—Behave yourself.
Verboten—forbidden